Praise for the novels of Deanna Raybourn

"Raybourn's first-class storytelling is evident…
Readers will quickly find themselves embarking on an
unforgettable journey that fans both old and new are sure to savor."
—*Library Journal* on *City of Jasmine*

"With a strong and unique voice, Deanna Raybourn
creates unforgettable characters in a richly detailed world.
This is storytelling at its most compelling."
—Nora Roberts, #1 *New York Times* bestselling author

"Raybourn skillfully balances humor and earnest, deadly drama,
creating well-drawn characters and a rich setting."
—*Publishers Weekly* on *Dark Road to Darjeeling*

"A great choice for mystery, historical fiction and/or romance readers."
—*Library Journal* on *Silent on the Moor*

"Raybourn…delightfully evokes the language, tension
and sweeping grandeur of 19th-century gothic novels."
—*Publishers Weekly* on *The Dead Travel Fast*

"Raybourn expertly evokes late-nineteenth-century colonial India
in this rollicking good read, distinguished by its delightful lady detective
and her colorful family."
—*Booklist* on *Dark Road to Darjeeling*

"[A] perfectly executed debut… Deft historical detailing
[and] sparkling first-person narration."
—*Publishers Weekly* on *Silent in the Grave,* starred review

"A sassy heroine and a masterful, secretive hero. Fans of
romantic mystery could ask no more—except the promised sequel."
—*Kirkus Reviews* on *Silent in the Grave*

Also by Deanna Raybourn

Historical Fiction

City of Jasmine
*Whisper of Jasmine**
A Spear of Summer Grass
*Far in the Wilds**

The Lady Julia Grey series

Silent in the Grave
Silent in the Sanctuary
Silent on the Moor
The Dead Travel Fast
Dark Road to Darjeeling
The Dark Enquiry
*Silent Night**
*Midsummer Night**
*Twelfth Night**

And watch for *Bonfire Night**, available soon from Harlequin MIRA!

*Digital Novellas

NIGHT
of a
THOUSAND
STARS

DEANNA RAYBOURN

HARLEQUIN® MIRA®

Recycling programs
for this product may
not exist in your area.

ISBN-13: 978-0-7783-1775-3

Night of a Thousand Stars

Printed in U.S.A.

First printing: October 2014
10 9 8 7 6 5 4 3 2 1

NIGHT
of a
THOUSAND
STARS

For Caitlin—
another beautiful girl from an eccentric family making her way in the world.

They would have reached the nursery in time had it not been that the little stars were watching them. Once again the stars blew the window open, and that smallest star of all called out:

"*Cave,* Peter!"

Then Peter knew that there was not a moment to lose.

"Come," he cried imperiously, and soared out at once into the night, followed by John and Michael and Wendy.

Mr. and Mrs. Darling and Nana rushed into the nursery but it was too late. The birds were flown.

—*Peter and Wendy,* J. M. Barrie

ONE

March 1920

"I say, if you're running away from your wedding, you're going about it quite wrong."

I paused with my leg out the window, satin wedding gown hitched up above my knees. A layer of tulle floated over my face, obscuring my view. I shoved it aside to find a tall, bespectacled young man standing behind me. His expression was serious, but there was an unmistakable gleam in his eyes that was distinctly at odds with his clerical garb.

"Oh! Are you the curate? I know you can't be the vicar. I met him last night at the rehearsal and he's simply ancient. Looks like Methuselah's godfather. You're awfully young to be a priest, aren't you?" I asked, narrowing my eyes at him.

"But I'm wearing a dog collar. I must be," he protested. "And as I said, if you're running away, you've gone about it quite stupidly."

"I have not," I returned hotly. "I managed to elude both my

mother and my future mother-in-law, and if you think that was easy, I'd like to sell you a bridge in Brooklyn."

"Brooklyn? Where on earth is that?"

I rolled my eyes heavenward. "New York. Where I live."

"You can't be American. You speak properly."

"My parents are English and I was educated here—oh, criminy, I don't have time for this!" I pushed my head out the window, but to my intense irritation, he pulled me back, his large hands gently crushing the puffed sleeves of my gown.

"You haven't thought this through, have you? You can get out the window easily enough, but what then? You can't exactly hop on the Underground dressed like that. And have you money for a cab?"

"I—" I snapped my mouth shut, thinking furiously. "No, I haven't. I thought I'd just get away first and worry about the rest of it later."

"As I said, not a very good plan. Where are you bound, anyway?"

I said nothing. My escape plan was not so much a plan as a desperate flight from the church as soon as I heard the organist warming up the Mendelssohn. I was beginning to see the flaw in that thinking thanks to the helpful curate. "Surely you don't intend to go back to the hotel?" he went on. "All your friends and relations will go there straight away when they realise you've gone missing. And since your stepfather is Reginald Hammond—"

I brandished my bouquet at him, flowers snapping on their slender stems. "Don't finish that sentence, I beg you. I know exactly what will happen if the newspapers get hold of the story. Fine. I need a place to lie low, and I have one, I think, but I will need a ride." I stared him down. "Do you have a motorcar?"

He looked startled. "Well, yes, but—"

"Excellent. You can drive me."

"See here, Miss Hammond, I don't usually make a habit of helping runaway brides to abscond. After all, from what I hear Mr. Madderley is a perfectly nice fellow. You might be making a frightful mistake, and how would it look to the bishop if I aided and abetted—"

"Never mind!" I said irritably. I poked my head through the window again, and this time when he retrieved me he was almost smiling, although a slim line of worry still threaded between his brows.

"All right then, I surrender. Where are you going?"

I pointed in the direction I thought might be west. "To Devon."

He raised his brows skyward. "You don't ask for much, do you?"

"I'll go on my own then," I told him, setting my chin firmly. Exactly how, I had no idea, but I could always think of that later.

He seemed to be wrestling with something, but a sound at the door decided him. "Time to get on. My motorcar is parked just in the next street. I'll drive you to Devon."

I gave him what I hoped was a dazzling smile. "Oh, you are a lamb, the absolute bee's knees!"

"No, I'm not. But we won't quarrel about that now. I locked the door behind me but someone's rattling the knob, and I give them about two minutes before they find the key. Out you go, Miss Hammond."

Without a further word, he shoved me lightly through the window and I landed in the shrubbery. I smothered a few choice words as I bounced out of his way. He vaulted over the windowsill and landed on his feet—quite athletically for a clergyman.

"That was completely uncalled-for—" I began, furiously plucking leaves out of the veil.

He grabbed my hand and I stopped talking, as surprised by the gesture as by the warmth of his hand.

"Come along, Miss Hammond. I think I hear your mother," he said.

I gave a little shriek and began to run. At the last moment, I remembered the bouquet—a heavy, spidery affair of lilies and ivy that I detested. I flung it behind us, laughing as I ran.

"I shouldn't have laughed," I said mournfully. We were in the motorcar—a chic little affair painted a startling shade of bright blue—and the curate was weaving his way nimbly through the London traffic. He seemed to be listening with only half an ear.

"What was that?"

"I said I shouldn't have laughed. I mean, I feel relieved, *enormously* so, if I'm honest, but then there's Gerald. One does feel badly about Gerald."

"Why? Will you break his heart?"

"What an absurd question," I said, shoving aside the veil so I could look the curate fully in the face. "And what a rude one." I lapsed into near-silence, muttering to myself as I unpicked the pins that held the veil in place. "I don't know," I said after a while. "I mean, Gerald is so guarded, so *English*, it's impossible to tell. He might be gutted. But he might not. He's just such a practical fellow—do you understand? Sometimes I had the feeling he had simply ticked me off a list."

"A list?" The curate dodged the little motorcar around an idling lorry, causing a cart driver to abuse him loudly. He waved a vague apology and motored on. For a curate, he drove with considerable flair.

"Yes. You know—the list of things all proper English gentlemen are expected to do. Go to school, meet a suitable girl, get married, father an heir and a spare, shoot things, die quietly."

"Sounds rather grim when you put it like that."

"It is grim, literally so in Gerald's case. He has a shooting lodge in Norfolk called Grimfield. It's the most appalling house I've ever seen, like something out of a Brontë novel. I half expected to find a mad wife locked up in the attic or Heathcliff abusing someone in the stables."

"Did you?"

"No, thank heavens. Nothing but furniture in the attic and horses in the stables. Rather disappointingly prosaic, as it happens. But the point is, men like Gerald have their lives already laid out for them in a tidy little pattern. And I'm, well, I'm simply not tidy." I glanced at the interior of the motorcar. Books and discarded wellies fought for space with a spare overcoat and crumpled bits of greaseproof paper—the remains of many sandwich suppers, it seemed. "You're untidy too, I'm glad to see. I always think a little disorder means a creative mind. And I have dreams of my own, you know." I paused then hurried on, hoping he wouldn't think to ask what those dreams might be. I couldn't explain them to him; I didn't even understand them myself. "I realised with Gerald, my life would always take second place. I would be his wife, and eventually Viscountess Madderley, and then I would die. In the meantime I would open fêtes and have his children and perhaps hold a memorable dinner party or two, but what else? Nothing. I would have walked into that church today as Penelope Hammond and walked out as the Honourable Mrs. Gerald Madderley, and no one would have remembered me except as a footnote in the chronicles of the Madderley family."

"Quite the existential crisis," he said lightly. I nodded.

"Precisely. I'm very glad you understand these things." I

looked around again. "I don't suppose you have a cigarette lying about anywhere? I'd very much like one."

He gestured towards the glovebox and I helped myself. As soon as I opened it, an avalanche of business cards, tickets, receipts and even a prayer book fell out. I waved a slip of paper at him. "You haven't paid your garage bill," I told him. "Second notice."

He smiled and pocketed the paper. "Slipped my mind. I'll take care of it tomorrow."

I shovelled the rest of the detritus back into the glovebox, and he produced a packet of matches. I pulled out a cigarette and settled back then gave a little shriek of dismay. "Heavens, where are my manners? I forgot to ask if you wanted one."

He shook his head. "I don't indulge."

I cocked my head. "But you keep them around?"

"One never knows when they'll be in demand," he said. "How long have you had the habit?"

"Oh, I don't. It just seems the sort of thing a runaway bride ought to do. I'll be notorious now, you know."

I gave the unlit cigarette a sniff. "Heavens, that's foul. I think I shall have to find a different vice." I dropped the cigarette back into the packet.

He smiled but said nothing and we lapsed into a comfortable silence.

I studied him—from the unlined, rather noble brow to the shabby, oversized suit of clothes with the shiny knees and the unpolished shoes. There was something improbable about him, as if in looking at him one could add two and two and never make four. There was an occasional, just occasional, flash from his dark eyes that put me in mind of a buccaneer. He was broad-shouldered and athletic, but the spectacles and occupation hinted he was bookish.

There were other contradictions as well, I observed. Being

a curate clearly didn't pay well, but the car was mint. Perhaps he came from family money, I surmised. Or perhaps he had a secret gambling habit. I gave him a piercing look. "You don't smoke. Do you have other vices? Secret sins? I adore secrets."

Another fellow might have taken offence but he merely laughed. "None worth talking about. Besides, we were discussing you. Tell me," he said, smoothly negotiating a round-about and shooting the motorcar out onto the road towards Devon, "what prompted this examination of your feelings? It couldn't be just the thought of marrying him. You've had months to accustom yourself to the notion of being the future Viscountess Madderley. Why bolt now?"

I hesitated, feeling my cheeks grow warm. "Well, I might as well tell you. You are a priest, after all. It would be nice to talk about it, and since you're bound by the confessional, it would be perfectly safe to tell you because if you ever tell anyone you'll be damned forever."

His lips twitched as if he were suppressing a smile. "That isn't exactly how it works, you know."

I flapped a hand. "Close enough. I always had doubts about Gerald, if I'm honest. Ever since he asked me to dance at the Crichlows' Christmas ball during the little season. He was just so staid, as if someone had washed *him* in starch rather than his clothes. But there were flashes of something more. Wit or kindness or gentleness, I suppose. Things I thought I could bring out in him." I darted a glance at the curate. "I see now how impossibly stupid that was. You can't change a man. Not unless he wants changing, and what man wants chang-ing? The closer the wedding got, the more nervous I became and I couldn't imagine why I wasn't entirely over the moon about marrying Gerald. And then my aunt sent me a book that made everything so clear."

"What book?"

"Mrs. Stopes' book, *Married Love*."

"Oh, God." He swerved and neatly corrected, but not before I gave him a searching look.

"I've shocked you." Most people had heard of the book, but few had read it. It had been extensively banned for its forthright language and extremely modern—some would say indecent—ideas.

He hurried to reassure me. "No, no. Your aunt shocked me. I wouldn't imagine most ladies would send an affianced bride such a book."

"My aunt isn't most ladies," I said darkly. "She's my father's sister, and they're all eccentric. They're famous for it, and because they're aristocrats, no one seems to mind. Of course, Mother nearly had an apoplexy when she found the book, but I'd already read it by that point, and I knew what I had to do."

"And what was that?"

"I had to seduce Gerald."

This time the curate clipped the edge of a kerb, bouncing us hard before he recovered himself and steered the motorcar back onto the road.

"I shocked you again," I said sadly.

"Not in the slightest," he assured me, his voice slightly strangled. He cleared his throat, adopting a distinctly paternal tone in spite of his youth. "Go on, child."

"Well, it was rather more difficult to arrange than I'd expected. No one seems to want to leave you alone when you're betrothed, which is rather silly because whatever you get up to can't be all that bad because you're with the person you're going to be getting up to it with once you're married, and it's all right then. And isn't it peculiar that just because a priest says a few words over your head, the thing that was sinful and wrong is suddenly perfectly all right? No offence to present company."

"None taken. It does indeed give one pause for thought. You were saying?"

"Oh, the arrangements. Well, I couldn't manage it until a fortnight ago. By that time I was fairly *seething* with impatience. I'm sorry—did you say something?"

"Not at all. It was the mental image of you seething with impatience. It was rather distracting."

"Oh, I am sorry. Should we postpone this discussion for another time? When you're not driving perhaps?"

"No, indeed. I promise you this is the most interesting discussion I've had in a very long while."

"And you're still not shocked?" I asked him. I was feeling a bit anxious on that point. I had a habit of engaging in what Mother called Inappropriate Conversation. The trouble was, I never realised I was doing it until after the fact. I was always far too busy enjoying myself.

"Not in the slightest. Continue—you were seething."

"Yes, I was in an absolute fever, I was so anxious. We were invited to the Madderleys' main estate in Kent—a sort of 'getting to know you' affair between the Madderleys and the Hammonds. It was very gracious of Gerald's mother to suggest it, although now that I think about it, it wasn't so much about the families getting to know one another as about the viscount and my stepfather discussing the drains and the roofs and how far my dowry would go to repairing it all."

I stopped to finish unpinning the veil and pulled it free, tearing the lace a little in my haste. I shoved my hands through my hair, ruffling up my curls and giving a profound sigh. "Oh, that's better! Pity about the veil. That's Belgian lace, you know. Made by nuns, although why nuns should want to make bridal veils is beyond me. Anyway, the gentlemen were discussing the money my dowry would bring to the estate, and the ladies were going on about the children we were going to have and what would be expected of me as the future viscountess. Do you know Gerald's mother even hired my lady's maid? Masterman, frightful creature. I'm terrified of her—she's so efficient and correct. Anyway, I suddenly realised that was going to be the rest of my life—doing what was perfectly proper at all times and bearing just the right number of children—and I was so bored with it all I nearly threw myself in front of a train like Anna Karenina just to be done with it. I couldn't imagine actually living in that draughty great pile of stone, eating off the same china the Madderleys have been using since the time of Queen Anne. But I thought it would all be bearable if Gerald and I were compatible in the Art of Love."

"The Art of Love?"

"That's what Mrs. Stopes called it in *Married Love*. She says that no matter what differences a couple might have in religion or politics or social customs, if they are compatible in the Art of Love, all may be adjusted."

"I see." He sounded strangled again.

"So, one night after everyone had retired, I crept to Gerald's room and insisted we discover if we were mutually compatible."

"And were you?"

"No," I said flatly. "I thought it was my fault at first. But I chose the date so carefully to make sure my sex-tide would be at its highest."

"Your sex-tide?"

"Yes. Really, you ought to know these things if you mean to counsel your parishioners. The achievement of perfect marital harmony only comes with an understanding of the sex-tides—the ebb and flow of a person's desires and inclinations for physical pleasure."

He cleared his throat lavishly. "Oh, the sex-tides. Of course."

"In any event, Gerald and I were most definitely not compatible." I paused then plunged on. "To begin with, he wouldn't even take off his pyjamas when we were engaged in the Act of Love."

The curate's lips twitched into a small smile. "Now that shocks me."

"Doesn't it? What sort of man wants a barrier of cloth between himself and the skin of his beloved? I have read the *Song of Solomon*, you know. It's a very informative piece of literature and it was quite explicit with all the talk of breasts like twin fawns and eating of the secret honeycomb and honey. I presume you've read the *Song of Solomon*? It is in the Bible, after all."

"It is," he agreed. "Quite the most interesting book, if you ask me." Again there was a flash of something wicked as he shot me a quick look. "So, was your betrothed a young god with legs like pillars of marble and a body like polished ivory?"

I pulled a face. "He was not. That was a very great disappointment, let me tell you. And then it was over with so quickly—I mean, I scarcely had time to get accustomed to the strangeness of it because, let's be frank, there is something so frightfully silly about doing *that*, although you probably don't know yourself, being a member of the clergy and all. But before I could quite get a handle on things, it was finished."

"Finished?" he said, his hands tight on the steering wheel.

"Finished. At least, Gerald was," I added sulkily. "He gave a great shudder and made an odd sort of squeaking sound."

"Squeaking sound?"

"Yes." I tipped my head, thinking. "Like a rabbit that's just seen a fox. And then he rolled over and went to sleep just like that."

"Philistine," he pronounced.

"Then you do understand! How important the physical side

of marriage is, I mean. Particularly with a husband like Gerald. One would need a satisfactory time in the bedroom to make up for—" I clapped a hand to my mouth. He smiled then, indulgently, and I dropped my hand, but I still felt abashed. "Oh, that was unkind. Gerald has many sterling attributes. Sterling," I assured him.

"*Sterling* is what one wants out of one's silver. Not a husband," he said mildly.

I sighed in contentment. "You are good at this. You understand. And you haven't made me feel guilty over the sin of it, although you mustn't tell anyone, but I don't really believe in sin at all. I know that's a wicked thing to say, but I think all God really expects is a little common sense and kindness out of us. Surely He's too busy to keep a tally of all our misdeeds. That would make Him nothing more than a sort of junior clerk with a very important sense of Himself, wouldn't it?"

"I suppose."

"Oh, I know you can't agree with me. You make your career on sin, just as much as anybody who sells liquor or naughty photographs. Sin is your bread and butter."

"You have a unique way of looking at the world, Miss Hammond."

"I think it's because I've been so much on my own," I told him after a moment. "I've had a lot of time to think things over."

"Why have you been so much on your own?" he asked. His voice was gentler than it had been, and the air of perpetual amusement had been replaced by something kinder, and it seemed as if he were genuinely interested. It was a novel situation for me. Most people who wanted to talk to me did so because of my stepfather's money.

"Oh, didn't you know? Apparently it was a bit of a scandal at the time. It was in all the newspapers and of course they raked it all up again when I became engaged to Gerald. My parents divorced, and Mother took me to America when she left my father. I was an infant at the time, and apparently he let her take me because he knew it would utterly break her heart to leave me behind. He stayed in England and she went off to America. We're practically strangers, Father and I. He's always been a bit of a sore spot to Mother, even though she did quite well out of it all. She married Mr. Hammond—Reginald. He's a lovely man, but rather too interested in golf."

"Lots of gentlemen play," he remarked. His hands were relaxed again, and he opened the car up a little, guiding it expertly as we fairly flew down the road.

"Oh, Reginald doesn't just play. He builds golf courses. Designing them amuses him, and after he made his millions in copper, he decided to travel around the world, building golf courses. Places like Florida, the Bahamas. He's quite mad about the game—he even named his yacht the Gutta-Percha, even though no one uses gutta-percha balls anymore."

He shook his head as if to clear it and I gave him a sympathetic look. "Do you need me to read maps or something? It must be fatiguing to drive all this way."

"The conversation is keeping me entirely alert," he promised.

"Oh, good. Where was I?"

"Reginald Hammond doesn't have gutta-percha balls," he replied solemnly. If he had been one of my half-brothers, I would have suspected him of making an indelicate joke, but his face was perfectly solemn.

"No one does," I assured him. "Anyway, he's a lovely man but he isn't really my father. And when the twins came along, and then the boys, well, they had their own family, didn't they? It was nothing to do with me." I fell silent a moment then pressed on, adopting a firmly cheerful tone. "Still, it hasn't been so bad. I thoroughly enjoyed coming back here to go to school, and I have found my father."

"You've seen him?" he asked quickly.

"No. But I made some inquiries, and I know where he is. He's a painter," I told him. I was rather proud of the little bit of detection I had done to track him down. "We wrote letters for a while, but he travelled extensively—looking for subjects to paint, I suppose. He gave me a London address in Half Moon Street to send the letters, but he didn't actually live there. You know, it's quite sad, but I always felt so guilty when his letters came. Mother would take to her bed with a bottle of reviving tonic every time she saw his handwriting in the post. I didn't dare ask to invite him to the wedding. She would have shrieked the house down, and it did seem rather beastly to Reginald since he was paying for it. Still, it is peculiar to have an entire family I haven't met. Some of them kept in touch—my Aunt Portia, for one. She sent me the copy of *Married Love*. When I came to England for the little season, I asked her where Father was. She promised not to tell him I'd asked, but she sent me his address. He has a house in Devon. He likes the light there, something about it being good for his work."

"I see."

"It's very kind of you to drive me," I said, suddenly feeling rather shy with this stranger to whom I had revealed entirely too much. "Oh!" I sat up very straight. "I don't even know your name."

"Sebastian. My name is Sebastian Cantrip."

"Cantrip? That's an odd name," I told him.

"No odder than Penelope."

I laughed. "It's Greek, I think. My mother's choice. She thought it sounded very elegant and educated. But my father called me Poppy."

Sebastian slanted me a look. "It suits you better."

"I think so, but when I was presented as a debutante, Mother insisted on calling me Penelope Hammond. Hammond isn't my legal name, you know. It gave me quite a start to see the name on the invitations to the wedding. Mr. and Mrs. Reginald Hammond cordially invite you to the wedding of their daughter, Penelope Hammond. But I'm not Penelope Hammond, not really." I lifted my chin towards the road rising before us. "I'm Poppy March."

"Well, Poppy March, I suggest you rest a bit. We've a long drive ahead of us, and you must be exhausted."

I snuggled down into the seat, eyelids drooping, then bolted up again. "You're sure you don't need me? I am an ace reader of maps."

"I think I can find my way to Devonshire," he assured me. "If I get to Land's End, I'll know I've gone too far."

TWO

It was dark by the time we reached Sidmouth, and darker still by the time we turned off the main road to the small byway leading to the village of Abbots Burton. I had provided him with an imperfect address, but Sebastian had an excellent sense of direction and the wit to stop twice and ask the locals. A garage mechanic put him on the right road to carry us to the end of the village, and an avidly curious woman walking her Pomeranians pointed out the cottage.

"That's it, Cowslip Cottage. There's an artist that lives there," she told him, edging around to get a proper look at me—the girl in the wedding dress sitting silently in the fancy motorcar.

Sebastian thanked the woman and nipped back into the vehicle, slamming the door sharply to put an end to the conversation. The woman tutted to her dogs as I smothered a laugh.

"Laugh now," Sebastian told me dryly. "It will be all over the village by morning that your father has a visitor. If you wanted to keep your whereabouts a secret, I'm afraid you'd have been better off hiding out in London."

I shrugged. Now that we were actually here the fight seemed to have gone out of me, and the look Sebastian gave me was decidedly worried.

"Damn, I'm a brute. I didn't even think to feed you," he muttered.

I smiled. "It doesn't matter," I assured him. "I couldn't have eaten a bite."

Just then my stomach rumbled loudly, as if to prove me a liar, and Sebastian grinned. "I'm sure your father will be more than happy to feed you up. Now, are you ready?"

I nodded, taking his hand as he helped me out of the motorcar. I'd come too far to turn back now, and I made a point of striding purposefully through the little gate at the front of the cottage and straight up to the door.

It wasn't until I raised my hand to the knocker that I hesitated. But Sebastian was behind me, solid and reassuring, and I felt better for having him there. I suddenly realised I had never actually felt better for having Gerald around.

"I did the right thing in running away," I murmured to myself. But still I did not knock.

"Allow me," Sebastian said. He didn't give me time to think. He simply lifted the knocker and dropped it into place with two sharp taps.

I barely had time to take a breath before the door opened. A man in a canvas apron stood on the threshold, scowling.

"What the devil do you want? Do you have any idea what time it is?" he barked.

I felt myself wilt, and Sebastian stepped forward, his expression livid.

"I say, that's no way to talk to the young lady," he began.

But before he could finish, the man in the apron was prodded aside by the business end of a walking stick. It was wielded by a tall gentleman with a head of thick silver hair and a primrose-striped smoking jacket. Father.

"Shut up, George. That isn't how we welcome guests," Father said. He came forward, rather slowly but with a very straight back. He peered at us and drew in his breath sharply.

"Poppy," he breathed, and it sounded like a prayer. "Are you a mirage, child?" He put out his hand, a gnarled old hand with traces of rose madder across the knuckles. The skin on the hand was wrinkled and the fingers were twisted like the roots of an oak. An old hand, but still a graceful one.

I caught it in my own. "Yes, Father. It's Poppy."

He coughed hard, smothering what might have been an involuntary sound of emotion. He glanced sharply away, but when he looked back, he had recovered himself.

"Come in, child. You must be chilled to the bone. George, fetch tea and whisky. And sandwiches while you're at it. I suspect our guests haven't eaten," he added.

He had not released my hand, and with it still grasped in his, he drew me into the sitting room of the cottage, where a bright fire burned upon the hearth. A pair of comfortable chairs had been arranged by the fire, but we did not sit.

"Father, I am sorry for just landing on you like this, and I will explain everything."

"I already know," he said mildly. "I get the newspapers even buried down here. You're married." He turned to Sebastian with a bland look. "I suppose I ought to offer you congratulations, young man. The heir to the Viscount Madderley, is it?"

I gave a strangled sound of horror, but Sebastian rose smoothly to the occasion. "I am afraid I do not have that honour, sir. I am Sebastian Cantrip."

"Ah, yes. I see the dog collar now."

I cut in before things could get entirely out of hand, muddling the introductions. "Mr. Cantrip, this is my father, Eglamour March, third son of the late Earl March, known to his friends and familiars as Plum. Father, Mr. Cantrip was the means by which I—that is to say—" I faltered, and turned pleading eyes to Sebastian.

He rose smoothly to the occasion. "Miss March, perhaps you would like to excuse yourself to wash your hands after the journey. I can explain matters to your father."

Father gave Sebastian an assessing look, then flicked me a glance. "Back through the hall and up the stairs, my dear."

I slipped out, hesitating outside the door. I could just hear them from my vantage point, Sebastian's firm baritone underscored by Father's rather more demanding aristocratic tone.

"Well, young man?" Father asked.

Sebastian hesitated, and I wished I could see their expressions.

"I'm afraid Miss March found herself disinclined to go through with the marriage. She was seeking a place of refuge," he said solemnly. "I hope I have done right to bring her here."

To my surprise, Father's voice was tight with something that sounded like anger. "I suppose you didn't think you had a choice."

"No, I didn't," Sebastian countered, his own voice amused. "I daresay there will be a hue and cry and all sorts of bother before it's all sorted, but these things can't be helped."

"What do you think you're doing eavesdropping?" I jumped to find the manservant George lurking behind me, a laden tray in his hands.

"I dropped my handkerchief," I lied coolly.

"I see no handkerchief," he retorted.

"That's because I haven't found it yet," I replied. I swept past him before he could make heads or tails of that answer, and fled up the stairs. I returned a few minutes later, face washed and hands clean, and smoothed out the crushed skirts of the

wedding gown, wishing desperately that I had something—
anything—else to put on.

"Next time I run away, I'll plan better," I muttered. I hurried into the sitting room to find Father and Sebastian sitting
companionably. Food and drink had appeared in my absence
but had not been touched. As soon as I took a chair the sandwiches and cakes were passed. I loaded my plate and dived
in, scarcely breathing between bites. The sandwiches were
dainty but stuffed with perfectly roasted ham, and the cake
was light as a feather.

"George is quite something in the kitchen," Father said,
eyeing my rapidly emptying plate.

I swallowed and shot Sebastian a dark look as he helped
himself to the last of the cherry tarts. The cherries had been
brandied and glazed to look like jewels and the first two had
melted in my mouth.

"He's an interesting fellow," I said politely.

Father arched a brow. "By that you mean he's a boor, and
you're entirely correct. But he's a devilishly good manservant
and his company suits me. He frightens away all of the casual
callers, and I am left to my work."

His tone was light, but I felt the sting of loneliness in his
words. I put my plate down, the cake suddenly ashes in my
mouth.

"I don't blame you," he said softly.

I looked up into green eyes that were very like my own.
Father was smiling. "It was your wretched mother's doing.
She's the one I blame."

A sharp blow sounded at the front door, and I started. Sebastian jumped to his feet, but Father sat serenely. "That will
be the harpy now," he said mildly.

"Most likely," Sebastian agreed. "I drove fast, but I suspect they saw us getting away, and Mr. Hammond has a beauty of a Lagonda. I glimpsed it a few times on the road behind us."

I threw Sebastian a horrified glance, and he stepped in front of me as if to act as my shield. From his seat, Father gave us a curious glance and was watching us still when George appeared.

"Shall I answer that, sir, or send them to Coventry?"

"By all means, answer it," Father said, waving an airy hand. "Might as well get it done with now. I have too much experience of Araminta's temper to think it will sweeten by morning."

I rose to my feet, my hand sliding neatly into Sebastian's. At the warm touch of his skin, I jumped, pulling free and thrusting both of my hands behind my back. All proper behaviour seemed to have flown out of my head, and I found myself wishing I could faint or fall into a fit, anything to avoid the next few minutes.

"She'll be frightfully angry," I warned Sebastian. "This is far worse than the time I kept a pet frog in the bidet at the Ritz."

"Courage," Sebastian murmured.

I nodded and took a deep breath as George returned. "Mr. and Mrs. Hammond, sir. And I didn't get the names of all the rest of them. There were too many," he added nastily. He stepped aside to let Mother and Reginald into the room, and behind them came an avalanche of people.

"Good God," Father pronounced. "Am I to be invaded by a whole tribe of Americans?"

"It's just the family," I assured him. "That's my stepfather, Mr. Hammond, and of course, you know Mother, and those are the twins, Petunia and Pansy, and I think those must be the boys back there, Reginald Junior and Stephen. There's my maid, Masterman—she's the one looking disapproving. And oh, yes, there's Gerald. Hello, Gerald," I said as calmly as I could manage. "You haven't met my father, Eglamour March. Father, Gerald Madderley."

Father took a deep breath and rose slowly from his chair. He greeted Gerald, then put out his hand to my stepfather. "How do you do, Mr. Hammond. I believe we have something in common," he said, his voice acid on the last word as he glanced at Mother.

She was not pleased. Her tone was just as cold as his as she watched her two husbands shake hands. "Yes, let's all be marvelously polite about this, shall we? In the meanwhile—"

"In the meanwhile, Araminta, you've had entirely too many children for my sitting room to accommodate," Father said firmly. "Now, those boys will have to go as well as the girls with the appalling flower names. Madderley, I suppose you have a dog in this fight, so you may stay. Hammond, since you paid for the affair, you are welcome to stay, as well. And let's have the maid in case anyone decides to succumb to the vapours. Araminta, you will stay only so long as you can keep a civil tongue in your head."

Mother opened her mouth to reply then snapped it closed. "Very well," she said through gritted teeth. "Children, out to the car. And mind you don't get out and go walking about. These English villages are full of typhoid. They have very bad drains."

Father gave a short laugh. "Good God, how could I have forgot your obsession with drains?"

"I think we have more important matters to discuss," she told him, her voice icy. She turned to me. "Poppy, do you have anything to say for yourself?"

I looked from my enraged mother to Gerald's mild face and back again. "Only that I am very sorry for behaving quite so badly. I ought to have said something sooner—"

"Sooner!" Mother's voice rose on a shriek. "You mean, you knew? You *knew* you had no intention of marrying Gerald and you let this all play out like some sort of Elizabethan tragedy—"

"Oh, for God's sake, Araminta, a pair of people who probably weren't terribly suited didn't get married. I would hardly call that a tragedy," Father put in.

"Of course you wouldn't," she replied. "You are the very last person who would understand about keeping one's sacred promises."

He raised a silver brow. "A hit. A palpable hit," he said, his tone amused. "I was waiting for that, and I'm so glad you didn't disappoint." He turned to Reginald with an appraising gaze. "You must have the patience of Job, good sir. I salute you." He raised a glass of whisky in Reginald's direction.

"I play a good bit of golf," my stepfather told him. "It teaches patience like nothing else."

Mother opened her mouth, no doubt to blast Father again, but she suddenly seemed to catch sight of Sebastian. "Who are you? I recognise you. You were at the church today. Do you mean to say—" She broke off, her expression one of mounting horror. "Oh, my dear God. I cannot believe it. Not even you, Penelope, would be heartless enough to elope on your wedding day with another man."

Sebastian opened his mouth, but before he could get out a word, Gerald stepped up and clipped him under the chin with one good punch, snapping his head back smartly. Sebastian kept his feet for a moment, then his eyes rolled back into his head and he slid slowly to the floor.

Gerald stood over him, shaking out his hand while Father called for George to bring cold cloths, and the children, hearing the uproar, dashed in from outside. As they crowded into the sitting room, Reginald attempted to calm Mother as she hysterically berated me while I stared in horror at Sebastian's closed eyes.

Father threw up his hands. "It seems we must surrender to pandemonium," he said to no one.

George brought the cloths as I shoved Gerald out of the way to kneel over Sebastian. Father guided Gerald to the fire and gave him a glass of whisky while I held a cold, wet cloth to Sebastian's jaw. His eyes fluttered open, wide and very dark. I leaned over him, one hand on his chest, and he reached up to clasp my hand as my face hovered inches from his.

"Can you hear me?" I pleaded. "Are you all right?"

His mouth curved into a smile.

"Lovely," he murmured. "Just a bit closer."

I gasped. "You fraud!" I muttered just loudly enough for him to hear. "He didn't knock you out at all."

Sebastian rolled his eyes. "No, but I wasn't about to give him the chance to try again. This way he keeps his pride, and I don't make a mess of your father's sitting room carpet by shedding Madderley blood all over it."

I pushed off his chest, sitting upright and handing him the cloth. "You can hold your own compress," I told him tartly. I didn't even bother to explain to him that Gerald had been the boxing champion of his year at Harrow. There was something rather endearing about Sebastian's faith that he could trounce Gerald, and I had learned enough about men to let him keep his illusions, although I had to admit the chest under my palm had been very firmly muscled.

A quarter of an hour later, order had been restored. Sebastian was sitting upright in one of the chairs, nursing a large whisky and making a show of holding a cold compress to his jaw. Mother had ordered the younger children to return to the motorcar, which they did under violent protest, and Father had opened a bottle of his best single malt to share with

Reginald—a sort of reward for the job he had done soothing Mother's hysteria. Masterman the maid simply stood out of the fray, her expression inscrutable as a Buddha as she watched the chaos unfold.

I sipped at my own whisky as Mother regarded me coldly.

"I do not approve of young ladies drinking spirits," she said.

"Considering the circumstances, it's a wonder she isn't sniffing cocaine," Father put in. He poured another measure for an appreciative Reginald and settled himself back into his chair.

"Now, I think we can all agree that physical violence is not called for under the circumstances and that we ought to discuss matters like adults," Father began with a dark look to where Gerald sat nursing his sore knuckles in the corner. Gerald flushed but said nothing.

"Too bloody late for that," Sebastian muttered.

"Yes, well," Father said, trailing off with a vague smile. "Now, I think it is quite clear that Poppy did not in fact elope with Mr. Cantrip. He obviously thought he was carrying out some act of chivalry, for which his only payment has been a rather lucky blow from Mr. Madderley."

Sebastian glowered at Gerald, who studied the carpet with rapt fascination.

Father went on. "Now, there are many things to be settled, but the first is one of the law. Mr. Cantrip, you are entitled to bring charges against Mr. Madderley for the assault to which we have all been witness. Do you wish me to send for the police so that you may do so?"

There were shocked gasps from around the room, but Gerald lifted his chin, ready to do his duty manfully.

All eyes were fixed on Sebastian. "God, no," he moaned.

"Very well," Father said, his expression one of grudging admiration. "Now, Poppy, your former fiancé has travelled down here, clearly with an eye to carrying you back to London and into the bonds of holy wedlock. Do you wish to go with him?"

"God, no," I said, echoing Sebastian as I dropped my head into my hands.

"Very well. Mr. Madderley, you are excused."

Gerald bolted to his feet. "Now, see here—"

"No," Father said pleasantly. "I don't have to see anything. What you must see is that you have intruded upon the peace and tranquility of my house by bringing violence into it. The young man you assaulted is good enough to overlook your bullying, and my daughter wishes to have nothing to do with you. Therefore, you have no further business here. Go away. And next time, choose a girl who actually loves you. My daughter clearly does not."

I raised my head to watch as Gerald opened his mouth a few times, but no words came. He turned wordlessly on his heel and left.

Father gave me an appraising look. "If that's the sort of man you chose of your own free will, your mother has done a far more tragic job of bringing you up than I would have credited."

"Oh, that is like you, Eglamour," Mother began.

Father lifted an elegant hand. "I'm sure you did your best, Araminta. But it is quite clear that you've raised a daughter who has absolutely no idea how to speak to you, otherwise she would have told you ages ago she had doubts about this wedding."

Mother's eyes narrowed. "How do you know she had doubts about this wedding?"

Father's look to me was kindly. "Because she went to the trouble to find out my address some weeks back. I'm sorry, child, but your Aunt Portia has never been particularly good at keeping secrets. She told me you asked for my address, and I hoped you would come to me if you needed me."

"Thank you, Father," I said, almost inaudibly.

"Now, I know you want to abuse her further, Araminta, and I won't say she hasn't acted quite badly. I'm sure you, Mr. Hammond, are out quite a few of your American dollars on this wedding that almost was," Father said.

Reginald looked uncomfortable as he always did where money was concerned. "Well, if it made her happy," he said, trailing off.

"Yes, well, I think we can all agree it did *not* make her happy. In fact, I daresay the child doesn't know what will. But she needs rest and time to discover that."

Mother gathered up her resolve and opened her mouth, but Father lifted his hand again.

"No, Minty. I will give you full credit for raising a lovely girl. She's audacious and brave and passably clever, I'd say, and, like all Americans, beautifully groomed. But she's also limp with exhaustion, and a scene with you is the last thing she needs. Leave her here with me. For one month. At the end of that time, I will deliver her to London myself to face the consequences of her actions."

The fight seemed suddenly to go out of Mother and I stared, rapt. I had never known anyone, not even Reginald, to handle her so deftly. I could see him paying close attention—I only hoped he was taking notes. Mother sniffled a little, capitulating under Father's masterful handling. "I don't know what to do with her, Plum. I never did. She's exhausting, always asking questions and never satisfied just to *be*. There's always something new she wants to do, some new scheme to try. Cookery classes and psychology courses and driving lessons, and none of them ever finished. It's one mad idea after another and so much…she's just so…so *March*."

Father smiled thinly. "Blood will out, dear Minty. Now, go back to London with your appallingly healthy and boisterous brood of Americans and let me sort this out. Perhaps you could send down some clothes for her if you think about it. She can't totter about like Miss Havisham in her wedding finery."

Mother rose. "Naturally, I've already thought of that. Her trousseau trunk is in the car." She turned to my maid. "Masterman, we cannot expect you to continue in service with Miss Hammond after today's debacle. We will naturally give you an excellent reference, a month's wages, and a ride back to London. It was good of you to come this far."

Masterman stirred. "On the contrary, madam, I should like to remain with Miss Hammond."

Mother blinked. "Whatever for?"

Masterman's expression did not change, but I had the strangest feeling Mother might have more easily shifted the Pyramids than moved Masterman from her decision. "Because it suits me, madam," she replied quietly.

Mother shrugged. "Very well, but do not be surprised if you find you can't stick it after all. Miss Hammond can be extremely trying to one's nerves." Mother turned and gave me a long look. "One month, Penelope. You have one month to figure out what it is that you want. This is the last time I will clear up a mess you've left behind."

She turned on her heel and swept from the room. Reginald stepped forward, putting a kindly hand on my shoulder as I stared after her in dismay.

"Don't fret, honey. I'll settle her down. You just rest and don't worry about anything. And I'll put some money into your account," he added softly. Dear Reginald, always solving everyone's problems by throwing cash at them.

I summoned a smile and rose on tiptoe to press a kiss to

his smoothly shaven cheek. "You really are a very nice man, Reginald."

He ducked his head and shook hands with Father before following Mother out the door. Father sat back in his chair with an air of satisfaction.

"That man ought to be sainted," he mused. "For miraculous fortitude."

"Mother isn't so bad," I began automatically.

"She's a nightmare," Sebastian observed in a dry voice.

"Dear God, I almost forgot you were still here," Father said, perking up. "It's grown late. I suppose we shall have to offer you a place to sleep tonight. George can show you over to the inn. They've always a room in reserve for one of my guests, and they'll be happy to accommodate you. As for you—Masterman, was it? There is an extra bed in the guest room upstairs. Help your mistress, there's a good girl. I think Poppy is half-asleep on her feet."

I started to protest that I could very easily make my own way upstairs, but Masterman had taken charge of the situation. I didn't know if she was more put out at having to share a room or Father calling her a girl, but she pushed me firmly up the stairs and put me to bed with ruthless efficiency. I gave myself up to it, letting her bully me a little since it suited us both. She turned out the light and undressed swiftly, settling herself into the narrow extra bed.

"You didn't have to stay on," I told her sulkily. There had been a certain guilty glee in ridding myself of Gerald, but it was a little blunted with Masterman still there to make certain I didn't do anything interesting.

"Yes, I did," she said, her voice almost fierce in the darkness.

"But why?"

"My reasons belong to me, miss. Now go to sleep or you'll look a fright in the morning," she said.

So I did.

THREE

The next morning Masterman busied herself unpacking my trunk while I found Father at breakfast. I murmured a greeting and slid into a chair, smiling widely at a glowering George who banged a pot of tea on the table in front of me and trudged off for a fresh rack of toast.

"Poor soul," I said quietly. "I imagine he was in the war. Is it shell shock?"

Father lowered his newspaper and gave me a thoughtful look. "You mean his foul moods? No, no. George is a flat-footed Quaker, entirely unsuited to the soldiering life. He's just churlish. But he is an excellent cook and I've never had whiter linen," he finished. He went on looking at me intently.

"I behaved very badly, didn't I? It all seemed so remote yesterday, as though it were happening to a stranger, but today..." I trailed off.

"Today it is news," Father said, passing the newspaper.

There it was, in black and white for all to see. Viscount's Heir Jilted By American Society Girl. I shook my head. "How awful it sounds. And I'm not really American," I protested.

Father smiled. "Thank God for small mercies. At least you sound like one of us. It's been quite a few years since I've seen you. You have a look of the Marches about you. Puts me quite in mind of your Aunt Julia when she was your age, although your hair is fairer."

"If it weren't for my aunts, I wouldn't be in this frightful mess," I said darkly.

Father raised his brows inquiringly, and before I knew quite what I was saying, the entire story tumbled out, starting with Aunt Portia's gift of *Married Love*. I paused only while George brought in the toast, but as soon as he returned to the kitchen, I carried on.

"And that's it, minus the gruesome details," I added. I alluded to a fundamental incompatibility with Gerald, but there had been no actual mention of sex-tides. Some things a girl cannot share with even the most liberal of fathers. I gave him a smile. "You've been truly marvellous, and I know it can't have been easy, not with Mother descending like all the plagues of Egypt yesterday."

Father smiled again. "I can cope with Araminta. And I must say, I'm very glad you felt you could come to me. I know I'm little more than a stranger to you really."

"But you aren't," I protested. "I had your letters. At least Mother let us correspond. And I always think letters are terribly intimate, don't you? I mean, you can tell the page things you can't ever say to a person's face."

"Heart's blood in place of ink?" he asked, his eyes bright.

"Precisely. Although I seem to be doing a rather good job of telling you what I'm thinking now. I probably shouldn't have told you any of it, but it seems that once I told it all to Mr. Cantrip yesterday, I can't stop talking about it. Very freeing, I find." I plucked a fresh piece of toast from the rack and buttered it liberally. "Of course, now I have to decide what to do with myself."

"Surely that won't be difficult."

"Not for a person like you," I said, nodding to the exquisite framed landscapes on the walls. "You've always had your painting. I'm simply hopeless. I was expensively educated to be decorative and charming and precious little else. Mother was right, you know. I never stick with anything because I don't seem to be good at anything."

"What have you tried?"

I shrugged. "All the usual nonsense they make you do at school, at least at schools for young ladies. Flower arranging, painting, music."

"And none of those suit you?"

"My flower arrangements look like compost heaps, my paintings all look like bogs, and as for music, I have the keenest appreciation for it and no ability whatsoever to understand it. I think it's because of the maths."

"Maths?"

"Music is all mathematical, at least that's what our music master told us. And I was frightful at maths, as well."

"Rather a good thing your Uncle Lysander isn't alive to hear you say it. He was a gifted composer, you know. You would have crushed him thoroughly."

I gave him a sympathetic look. "I know I wrote at the time, but I really am quite sorry. I should have liked to have known him. Perhaps I can meet Aunt Violante and the children whilst I'm here."

Father stared into the depths of his teacup as if looking for answers. He said nothing, and I moved on, my tone deliberately bright. "In any event, I'm hopeless at all the usual female things. All I seem to be good at is poking around into people's lives. Headmistress used to say I could take a First in Gossip if it were on offer at Oxford."

A ghost of a smile touched Father's lips. "Your Aunt Julia is precisely the same. I sometimes wonder if Mr. Kipling met her somewhere and used her as the basis for his inquisitive mongoose. 'Go and find out' will be etched on her gravestone. But she has ended up doing well enough for herself."

I rolled my eyes. "I should say. It is rather grand having a duchess in the family since I threw away my chance at being a peeress."

"Believe me, child, being a duchess is the least of her accomplishments, and it was entirely unexpected. If it weren't for peculiar Scottish peerage laws and half a dozen young men getting blown up in the war, her husband would never have succeeded to the dukedom. No, I wasn't thinking of her rank, child. I was thinking of her work. She struggled with many of the same feelings you have. She found purpose in joining her husband's work. I know it's practically revolutionary to suggest it, but I don't think idleness is good for young people— particularly not young people with money. It grinds away at the character until there's nothing left."

I tipped my head, thoughtful. "You think I ought to take a job? Like something in a shop?"

He smiled again. "I doubt a shopkeeper would want you if you're hopeless at maths. I was thinking of something that excited you, stirred your sense of adventure. You need to be challenged, child. You need to see something of the world, and from some vantage point other than your stepfather's yacht. Oh, I've seen the society columns," he went on. "I know what it means to be the stepdaughter of a man like Reginald Hammond. You think you've seen the world because you've been to New York and Paris and Biarritz, but what have you really seen other than a pack of useless people exactly the same as the ones you left behind? Same old faces, same old places," he pronounced.

I nodded. "You're right, of course. There are times I want to simply scream with boredom. But I wouldn't even know where to start to look for something useful to do." My glance fell to the newspaper, and I grinned as I pointed to an article. "How about this? Apparently the famous aviatrix Evangeline Starke has disappeared in the Syrian desert. Perhaps I should give flying lessons a bash," I added.

Father lifted an elegant brow. "I was thinking of something a trifle less life-threatening."

I was about to suggest rally-car driving when George appeared in the doorway. "It's that Mr. Cantrip," he said darkly.

Father smoothed his turquoise waistcoat. "Very well. Send him through, George."

I was still immersed in the article about Evangeline Merryweather Starke when Sebastian entered and Father greeted him coolly.

"Good morning, Mr. Cantrip. I trust you had a good night's sleep at the inn?"

"Very good, thanks. Good morning, Miss March." The name took me aback for a moment then I grinned to myself. I had played at being Miss Hammond for too long. It was time to reclaim my own name once and for all.

I looked up and flashed him a quick smile. "Good morning." My face fell as I took a closer look at him. A spectacular bruise was blossoming on his jaw, and I jumped to my feet.

"Oh, heavens! It's worse than I thought last night. I still can't quite believe Gerald did that to you. He's always seemed so mild-mannered."

Sebastian touched his jaw ruefully. "Yes, well, apparently still waters run deep in his case." He glanced down at the newspaper on the table. "I see you've the morning edition there. I suppose they've been rude about you?"

I pulled a face. "Brutal. As expected. One doesn't just jilt a peer's son with impunity," I said with an attempt at lightness. "But I'm far more interested in this story about the aviatrix who's gone missing in Syria."

I handed the newspaper to Sebastian, who skimmed the article quickly. He gave it back without a word and I looked at him curiously. "Are you quite all right, Mr. Cantrip? You've gone very white under that bruise."

Sebastian summoned a smile that didn't quite meet his eyes. "Have I? I suppose it's just the delayed effects of yesterday's dramatics. Shock and all that. I'll be right as rain in a bit."

"Won't you have some breakfast?" Father asked him, his expression thoughtful.

"No, sir, thank you. They fed me quite heartily at the inn. I merely wanted to pay my respects on my way back to London."

"You're going back? Already?" I masked the pang I felt with a quick smile. "Of course you are. You have a parish there, and I've managed to drag you away from it and through the muck. Shall I see you out?"

He followed me to the front door of the cottage.

"I know what you're worried about," I said, pitching my voice low. "But you aren't named in the newspaper piece," I assured him. "They haven't any idea how I got away, and I won't tell a soul. I ought to have realised what awful trouble you could get into by helping me, and I won't forget it. Really, I owe you most dreadfully and I never forget a debt."

He shook his head, his expression dazed. "You are a unique young woman, Miss March." He hesitated on the doorstep. "I wish I didn't have to dash away."

"So do I," I told him. "I feel as if I've just imposed on you horribly and haven't had the chance to make it up to you."

For an instant the buccaneer flash was back in his eyes, and I wondered just how hard he found it to be a properly behaved member of the clergy. "Would you like to make it up to me?"

I felt a thrill at his audacity, but I primmed my mouth, remembering propriety for once.

"Thank you. For everything." I put out my hand, but he ignored it. Instead he settled both of his hands on my shoulders, leaning down to brush a quick kiss to my cheek. He hadn't shaved, and his whiskers rasped a little against my skin. Before I could respond, he was gone, out the door and out of my life as quickly as he'd come.

I closed the door behind him feeling a little deflated and oddly nostalgic. He had been a perfect companion in my little adventure, and I could never have managed my escape without him. After months of Gerald's chilly affections, being around Sebastian had been like basking in summer sunshine. It was absurd, I told myself firmly. I had only just met him. One couldn't get homesick for a person.

When I returned to the breakfast table, Father was looking thoughtfully at the newspaper I'd left behind.

"Everything all right, Father?"

He gave me a bland smile. "Quite, my dear. Now, finish your breakfast and perhaps you and Masterman would like to take a nice walk and get acquainted with the village. This will be your home for as long as you like."

It took fewer than twenty minutes to walk completely around the village, and by the time I finished I had a pebble in my shoe and had counted precisely seventeen front curtains twitch as we walked past.

"It seems the entire village has already heard about our arrival," I told Masterman.

She pursed her lips. "People are the same wherever you go,

miss—interested in gossip and scandal, and you've given them meat enough to feed on for a year."

We had just come to the pond on the village green and I stopped. I had been considering how to approach her ever since she had told Mother she would stay with me. It wasn't that I didn't like Masterman, not exactly. But she was my last tie to Gerald's family and my near-miss as the future Viscountess Madderley. The sooner I severed that connection, the better. Besides, there was something uncanny about her, a quiet watchfulness I didn't entirely understand.

I cleared my throat. "It's really very good of you to stay on, all things considered." I chose my words carefully. "After all, working for me won't exactly count in your favour when you apply for a new position."

She said nothing as we walked on, and I decided to push just a little further. "I mean, you won't want to go on working for me forever. I don't even know what my plans will be."

"I am certain you will figure it out," she said mildly.

I suppressed a sigh. She was going to be difficult to dislodge, I decided. And the only solution was a more direct approach.

"See here, Masterman—"

She turned to look at me, her hazel eyes placid. There was a slightly greenish cast to them, like a mossy stone on a riverbed. "I am not leaving, miss."

I gaped at her. "How on earth did you know that's what I was about to suggest?"

She shrugged. "It's only logical. Mrs. Hammond suggested it last night and you lit up like Bonfire Night."

I ducked my head. "That wasn't very kind of me. I apologise, Masterman. And it isn't that I don't like you. You mustn't think that."

"I don't," she replied with that same unflappable calm.

"Oh, well, good. Because I do," I assured her with a fatuous smile. "It's just that—"

"I make you uncomfortable," she supplied.

"That's not at all what I meant to say," I said, feeling my cheeks flush warmly.

"But it is what you feel," she said. There was no malice in her voice and her gaze was calm and level. I heaved a sigh.

"Very well. Yes. You make me uncomfortable. I'm afraid you'll always be a reminder of how badly I behaved."

"But I don't think you did behave badly," she told me.

I stared at her a long moment. "That might be the nicest thing you've ever said to me."

"It happens to be true," she said. She began to walk and I hurried after, suddenly eager to talk to her. There was something curiously topsy-turvy about the mistress chasing after the maid, and I grinned as I caught up to her.

"You don't think I ought to have married Gerald?"

"Absolutely not. Miss March, what do you think a servant's chief responsibility is?"

I thought of the endless round of brushing clothes and whipping hems and pinning hair and shrugged.

"It's to be watchful—to see all and understand what we see. I watched you with Mr. Madderley, and I could tell from the first moment I saw you together you were entirely unsuited."

"You might have told me," I said, kicking a pebble.

"You did not ask," she returned mildly.

I grinned again. "All right, Masterman. I'll give you that. And you can stay on if you like."

She gave me a brisk nod to indicate her acceptance. We walked on in silence for a little while, taking a turn around the pond. A few apathetic ducks bobbed on the glassy surface and a limp lily floated along. There was no one else on the village green, and even the smoke coming from the chimneys drifted in lazy circles.

"Masterman, with your gift for watchfulness what do you make of our present circumstances?"

She looked around the village, taking in the quiet shops and tranquil, sleepy air of the place.

"I think, miss, we are in very great danger of being bored."

She was not wrong. After that, our days settled into a pattern. Masterman and I went for long walks each morning, and after luncheon Father painted in his studio while I tried to make friends with George, although he remained stubbornly unmoved by my charms. I asked him to teach me to make his clever little soufflés or roast a duck or let me polish the silver, but each attempt was met with a firm rebuff. "That's your side of the cottage," he would state flatly, pushing me out of the kitchen and back into the hall. It was too bad really, because I was bored senseless and genuinely interested in acquiring a few new skills. It might come in handy to be able to roast a duck, I thought, but George was unwilling to oblige.

So I occupied myself with brooding. I wrote no letters and received only one—a curt message from Mother stating that she had returned the wedding gifts but that I had been remiss in returning my engagement ring to Gerald. It was an enormous pigeon's blood ruby, a relic from the days of the first King George and worn by every Madderley bride. The viscountess had been particularly resentful at giving it up, and I was abashed I hadn't thought to give it back to Gerald when he left the cottage. I made a note to take it with me when I went up to London next; I couldn't possibly trust such a valuable jewel to the post. But London held no charms for me in my present mood. I had given up reading the Town newspapers after the second day. They were vitriolic on the subject of my almost-marriage, and going up would mean facing people who had decided I was only slightly less awful than Messalina.

So I buried myself in books, raiding Father's library for anything that looked promising. There were a handful of Scarlet Pimpernel books and an assortment of detective stories, but beyond that nothing but weighty tomes on art history. I had almost resigned myself to reading one of them when I discovered a set of books high on a shelf, bound in scarlet morocco. They were privately printed, that much was obvious, and I gave a little gasp when I saw the author's name: Lady Julia Brisbane. She was Father's youngest sister, and the most notorious of our eccentric family. After a particularly awful first marriage, she had taken as her second husband a Scot who was half-Gypsy and rumoured to have the second sight. The fact that he was distantly related to the Duke of Aberdour hadn't counted for much, I seemed to recall. There had been scandal and outrage that a peer's daughter had married a man in trade. Nicholas Brisbane was a private inquiry agent, and Aunt Julia had joined him in his work. Ending up a duchess must have been particularly sweet for her, I decided. Father had talked about them my first morning at the cottage, and as near as I could guess, these books were her memoirs.

I turned the first over in my hands. *Silent in the Grave* was incised in gilt letters and a slender piece of striped silk served as a bookmark. I opened to the first page and read the first line. "To say that I met Nicholas Brisbane over my husband's dead body is not entirely accurate. Edward, it should be noted, was still twitching upon the floor." I slipped down to sit on the carpet, the books tumbled in my lap, and began to read.

I did not move until it was time for tea, and only then because Father joined me. He beckoned me to the table by the fire, giving a nod of his silvery-white head to the book in my hands.

"I see you've discovered Julia's memoirs."

I shook my head, clearing out the cobwebs. I had spent the whole day wandering the fog-bound streets of Victorian London with my aunt, striding over windy Yorkshire moors and climbing the foothills of the Himalayas. I took a plate from him and sipped at my tea.

"I can't believe I never knew she did all those things."

His smile was gentle. "It's never been a secret."

"Yes, I always knew she went sleuthing with Uncle Brisbane but I had no idea the dangers they faced. And you—"

I broke off, giving him a hard look.

He burst out laughing. "There's no need to look so accusing, child. Yes, I did my fair share of detective work, as well."

"I can't believe Aunt Julia almost killed you once with her experiments with explosives."

"Once?" His eyes were wide. "Keep reading."

He urged sandwiches and cakes on me, and I ate heartily, suddenly ravenous after missing luncheon entirely.

"That's what I want," I told him.

He had been staring into the fire, wool-gathering, and my voice roused him. He blinked a few times and looked up from the fire. "What, child?"

"I want what Aunt Julia has. I want a purpose. I want work that makes me feel useful. I don't just want to arrange flowers and bring up babies. Oh, that's all right for other girls, but it isn't right for me. I want something different."

"Perhaps you always have," he offered mildly.

"I think I have," I replied slowly. "I've always been so different from the others and I never understood why. My half-sisters and -brothers, my schoolmates. Don't mistake me—I've had jolly enough times, and I've had friends," I told him, pulling a face. "I was even head girl one year. But as long as I can remember, I've had the oddest sense that it was just so much play-acting, that it wasn't my real life at all. Does that sound mad?"

"Mad as a March hare," he said, his lips twitching. He nodded to the mantelpiece, where a painting hung, a family crest. Our family crest. It was a grand-looking affair with plenty of scarlet and gold and a pair of rabbits to hold it up. "Family lore maintains the old saying about March hares is down to us, that it isn't about rabbits at all. It refers to our eccentricity, the wildness in our blood. And the saying is a tribute to the fact that we do as we dare. As do you," he finished mildly.

I started. "What do you mean by that?"

A wry smile played over his lips. "I know more of your exploits than you think, child."

"Exploits! I haven't done anything so very interesting," I protested.

He gave me a sceptical look. "Poppy, give me some credit. I mayn't have been a very devoted father, but neither have I been a disinterested one. Every school you've been to, every holiday you've taken, I've had reports."

"What sort of reports?" I demanded.

"The sort any father would want. I had little opportunity to ascertain your character myself, so I made my own inquiries. I learnt you were healthy and being brought up quite properly, if dully. Araminta has proven herself a thoroughly unimaginative but unobjectionable mother. At first, I thought it best, given the sort of family we come from. I thought a chance at normality might be the best thing for you. But the more I came to discover of you, the more I came to believe you were one of us. They do say that blood will always tell, Poppy."

I gave him a look of grudging admiration. "I'm torn. I don't know whether to be outraged that you spied upon me or flattered that you cared enough to do it."

His smile was wistful. "I always cared, child. I cared enough to give you a chance at an ordinary life. And if you think that wasn't a sacrifice of my own heart's blood, then you're not half as clever as I think you are."

His eyes were oddly bright and I looked away for a moment. I looked back when he had cleared his throat and recovered himself. "I'm surprised you found me clever from my school reports. The mistresses were far more eloquent on the subject of my behaviour."

"No, your marks were frightful except in languages. Looking solely at those I might have been forgiven for thinking you were slightly backwards. It was those reports of your behaviour that intrigued me, particularly the modest acts of theft and arson."

"But those were necessary!" I protested. "I broke into the science master's room to free the rabbits he'd bought for dissection. And the fire was only a very small one. I knew if the music mistress saw her desk on fire, she'd reveal where she'd hidden the money they accused the kitchen maid of stealing."

He clucked his tongue. "Impetuous. Instinctive. Audacious. These are March traits, child. We've been living by them for the past six hundred years. There have been epic poems written about our oddities, and more than one king of England has had cause to be grateful for them. And now you are one of us."

I gave a little shiver as if a goose had walked over my grave. "Rather a lot to live up to."

He shrugged. "I should think you would find that consoling. You have an ancestor who eloped with her footman, another who rode his horse into Parliament, a great-grandmother who used to dance with a scooped-out pumpkin on her head because she found it cool and refreshing. And those are the ones I can talk about in polite company," he added with a twinkle. "Don't be put off by your legacy, Poppy. Embrace it. Follow your own star, wherever it leads, child."

"Follow my own star," I said slowly. "Yes, I think I will."
The only question was, where?

The next day I had my answer. I had gone to the pantry
to try yet again to help George with the washing up, deter-
minedly cheerful in the face of his resistance.

"You will come to like me," I promised him.

"I have my doubts," he replied shortly. I put out a hand to
wipe a glass, and he flicked the glass cloth sharply at my fingers. "Leave that be."

"I could read to you while you work," I offered. I picked up
the book he had stashed on a shelf in the pantry—*Northanger
Abbey*.

I sighed. "It's not Austen's best, you know."

He snatched the book from my hand. "It's Austen and that's
good enough for me."

He replaced the book lovingly on the shelf, and I took it
down again. "Very well. I apologise. But why do you like it so
much? Don't you find Catherine Morland appallingly naïve?"

"It seems to be a common failing in young ladies," he said,
giving me a dark look.

I burst out laughing. "Oh, George. You do say the nicest
things." I flipped to where he had carefully marked his place.
He had almost reached the end of the first chapter. I cleared
my throat and read aloud. "'But when a young lady is to be a
heroine, the perverseness of forty surrounding families cannot prevent her. Something must and will happen to throw
a hero in her way.'"

I looked up, giving George a thoughtful look. "Do you suppose that's true, George? Do you think when a young lady is
supposed to be a heroine, her hero will appear?"

"Certainly," he said, polishing an invisible spot from one of the glasses. "If Miss Austen says it, it must be true. But not all young ladies are meant to be heroines," he added pointedly.

"That's very hurtful, George," I told him. I turned back to the book. I read the next paragraph, then slowed as I came to these words, "'…if adventures will not befall a young lady in her own village, she must seek them abroad.'" I looked up again. "'She must seek them abroad,'" I repeated slowly.

George kept on with his polishing, but he flicked me a glance. "An excellent idea. You should go abroad."

I smiled in spite of him. "Why are you so eager to get rid of me, George? Surely it's not that much extra work to scrape a few more carrots for dinner. And I've seen Masterman doing heaps of things for you, so it's clearly just me you don't like. Why can't we be friends?"

I turned up the smile, giving him my most winsome look. He turned and put down the glass, folding the cloth carefully.

"I'll not have you hurt him," he said plainly.

I blinked. "George, what on earth are you talking about?"

"I'll not have you hurt Mr. Plum."

I felt my throat tighten with anger. "The very idea! I have no intention of hurting Father at all. I can't believe you would even suggest such a thing."

"I don't say as you would mean to do it," he allowed. "But things happen. He'll get used to you if you stay on here. And then you'll go away and it will break his heart. I don't think he could stand that again."

My anger ebbed. I had not considered what a wrench it must have been for him when Mother took me away. "You've been a good friend to him, George."

George scowled. "I'm his manservant, and don't be forgetting that, for I'm not. But I'll not have him hurt again. His heart isn't what it was. He has spells with it. Not serious," he said, noticing my start of alarm. "But he needs calm and we've had that here. That was when he moved down to the country and left London for good. He keeps regular hours here and paints. And there's no more detective work."

"Detective work? George, what are you talking about?"

"Your father's work in London. He was part of your uncle's private inquiry agency. Among other things."

I blinked. "But that was decades ago! Uncle Brisbane and Aunt Julia gave that all up well before I was born."

George snorted. "Publicly, they did. But privately, they carried on just as they had. And your father was a part of it. They did government work, and if it weren't for them, we'd have had a war with Germany twenty years earlier than we did."

"George, are you seriously asking me to believe that my family were involved in some sort of global espionage?"

He shrugged. "You haven't read all of your auntie's memoirs yet, have you? Believe what you like, miss. It matters nought to me. But the work was demanding. They had friends killed, and your father had a close shave or two, I don't mind telling you. That's how he met me, in fact, and no, I'll not tell you the story, but I will say your father saved my life, he did, and I'll serve him until the end of mine. But all of that is behind him. He's got a pleasant way down here, just his painting and his garden. He's right old, miss, and he's not got many years left. I mean to see they're peaceful ones."

"Of course," I said automatically. There was a pang in my heart when he said Father hadn't many years left, and I thought of how drastically my little drama must have upset Father's routine. "I'll do everything I can to make certain he's not upset," I promised. "And I will find something to do with myself. I won't make him regret having me here. You have my word, George."

He gave me a grudging nod and turned back to his washing up.

I thought of the ruby ring nestled in my underclothes up-stairs and took a deep breath. "I'll go to London. I have a few things I ought to attend to, and I'll take Masterman. She's looking peaky from all this country air."

George nodded again, this time with slightly more warmth, and I smiled. "Besides, who knows what will happen? Perhaps I will seek an adventure."

FOUR

The next morning I dressed carefully in one of my honey-moon travelling ensembles, a beautifully cut suit of salt-and-pepper tweed with an emerald silk shirtwaist. There was a daring green feather in my cloche, and green gloves to match. My feet were neatly shod in high French heels and my stockings were the sheerest silk. I had planned on wearing a plain dark grey affair with very little embellishment, but Masterman had firmly squashed that notion.

"I think not," she said with a decisive air. "What if you should run into Mr. Madderley or any of his circle? Do you want them to see you looking like a whipped dog? No, miss. You go up to London with your head held high and wearing something smart." I didn't have the will to argue, and as I turned this way and that in front of the mirror, I had to admit, Masterman knew exactly what she was doing.

"A stylish outfit will do wonders for a girl's pride," I murmured.

Masterman pretended not to hear, but I saw her satisfied expression. She dressed herself in a sober costume of dark blue tweed with a discreet gold watch pinned to her lapel and hurried us off to the tiny train station with five minutes to spare.

The train made good time, and we stopped first at the bank where Gerald's family kept their valuables. There was a brief, painful interview with their banker, who took the ring from me as if he were receiving a holy relic and issued a receipt, which he handed to me with just his fingertips.

"Did you see that?" I fumed to Masterman as we emerged from the bank. "He didn't even want to touch my hand. It's as if I were a leper."

"What did you expect, miss?" she asked reasonably. "He's the Madderleys' banker and you're the woman who threw over Mr. Gerald."

"I suppose," I grumbled. "It's still rude."

"You'll be in for worse," she warned. "So you might as well steel yourself and get it over with."

"How would I do that?" I asked, narrowing my eyes at her.

"Lunch at the Savoy," was the prompt reply.

I shuddered. "I'd rather walk naked into a pit of vipers."

She gave me one of her inscrutable looks and lifted her shoulders in a small shrug. "As you wish, miss. But the sooner you face them down, the sooner you'll know what you're made of."

I opened my mouth to argue, but I couldn't. She was right, of course. They were just a pack of society gossips. The only whip they wielded was the lash of disapproval. And what sort of adventuress would I be if I couldn't stand a little gossip?

I squared my shoulders. "Very well. But there's something else I need to do first."

I had made an airy mention of adventure to George, but I hadn't understood my real reason for going to London until my feet turned automatically towards the church. I owed Gerald the return of his ring, but that did not matter as much as seeing Sebastian again. I had thought of him ceaselessly since he'd left the cottage, and I couldn't imagine why.

Of course there was his kindness, I told myself. And those rather gorgeous dark eyes. And what I suspected might be a spectacular pair of shoulders under his cleric's garb. And a superbly noble profile, which suited his waving dark hair. The combination was very nearly Byronic. I ticked his attributes off on my fingers. He was cool in a crisis. Most men wouldn't have had the steely nerve to help me escape from my own wedding, much less to do it with a smile. He'd been terribly understanding when I had prattled on about the troubles I'd had with Gerald in the bedroom. He must have been dreadfully shocked, but he hadn't made me feel the least bit awful about any of it. And he'd been a perfect sport about letting Gerald punch him without hitting him back and complicating everything. He had been an absolute brick, a thorough hero when I needed him, and I hadn't even thanked him properly.

It was only to thank him that I wanted to see him, I decided. It was just good manners, after all, and I had been brought up to know what was right even if I didn't always do it.

None of which explained why I didn't tell Masterman where we were going. I just knew I was in no mood for questions, and Masterman's were invariably uncomfortable ones. I only wanted to see Sebastian and thank him once and for all and that was it, I told myself firmly.

As we walked to the door of the church where I was to have been married, I turned, giving Masterman a pious look.

"Masterman, I'd like you to wait in the park just opposite. I wish to step into the church for a bit of private reflection."

Her eyes narrowed. "Unless you plan to reflect aloud, miss, I would hardly be in your way."

"Private," I repeated gently. She huffed a little but took herself off in the direction of the park.

I went into the church and crept quietly into a back pew. It was one of the great churches of London, stately and ancient, the stone smelling of incense and time. There was something comforting about the old stone walls, and I felt the strain of the past months ease a little as I sat. The choir was in the stalls, practising something restful, and before I knew it, my chin was bobbing on my chest, my breathing soft and slow.

"Pardon me, miss." There was a gentle hand on my shoulder and I awoke with a horrified start to find a clergyman with a kindly face standing over me

"Oh, I am sorry! I don't know what came over me."

The kindly face smiled. "Don't tell the vicar, but it happens to me more than you'd think."

"That's very gracious of you," I said, smothering a yawn. "I say, I don't suppose you could help me find someone? I actually came to speak with the curate."

The smile deepened. "Then you're in luck. You have found him. I'm the curate, Mr. Hobbs."

I blinked. "I'm sorry, I mean the other curate, Mr. Cantrip."

"There is no other curate, miss. I am the only curate for this parish."

I shook my head. "No, I'm sorry, but there was a Mr. Cantrip here. He said he was—" I broke off, thinking furiously. *Had* Sebastian said he was the curate? Or had I simply inferred it from the dog collar?

Mr. Hobbs' gentle expression turned thoughtful. "I say, aren't you Miss Hammond? The young lady—"

"Who ran out on her wedding to the heir to Viscount Madderley? Yes," I said automatically.

"I was going to phrase it a little more delicately than that," he told me with only the mildest hint of reproach.

"Oh, it's all right, I understand it's what everyone is saying." I was still thinking hard. Perhaps I had misunderstood. Sebastian might not be curate of *this* parish, but he must be associated with another.

"Mr. Hobbs, do vicars ever lend their curates?"

The smile was back, this time a shade rueful. "Well, we are men of the cloth, you know, not books in a lending library, but I regret to say some vicars do indeed treat us as such."

"You mean a vicar who had an important service to perform might request help from another parish?"

"Yes, these things do happen."

I brightened. "That must be it. Sebastian Cantrip is another parish's curate and he was simply borrowed for the wedding."

"I beg your pardon, Miss Hammond, but if you are referring to your—er, wedding," he said with a cough, "there was no borrowed curate. It was my job to assist the vicar at your nuptials."

I resisted the urge to light a cigarette. "Do you mean no one from outside your parish was expected?"

"No indeed," he said proudly. "We took great pride in our ability to execute everything to the viscountess's specifications."

His last remark proved his involvement, I thought grimly. Mother had planned everything to the smallest detail, but Gerald's mother had come from a family populated with bishops and her pet hobby was all matters ecclesiastical. The viscountess had expressed no interest in the wedding whatsoever except when it came to texts and hymns and vestments.

"And you don't know a Mr. Cantrip?" I persisted.

"Indeed not, although if I did, I should think it a very great joke," he said, the smile once more in evidence.

"Oh, why?"

"Well, as it happens, I am a fancier of unusual names. I collect them, as it were, and Cantrip is most singular."

"In what way?"

He shrugged. "I should presume it was a pseudonym. Have you never heard the word before? A *cantrip* is an old Scots word. It means a witch's trick, a spell. The very word means *deception*."

I rose slowly from the pew and fished in my bag for a note. "For the collection plate, Mr. Hobbs. Thank you for your time."

I went out into the street, blinking at the weak sunlight. The church had been a haven of cool security, but now I felt oddly off balance, as if someone had just proven the sky was green. I walked slowly across to the park and sat on a bench, thinking hard.

"Private reflection my eye," said Masterman as she slid onto the bench next to me.

"I beg your pardon?"

"If you wanted a nap, there's many a place better than that," she told me.

I shrugged. "I nodded off. It's been a very trying time," I replied to her, but my mind was elsewhere.

I had been overwrought that day, but it wasn't as if I had *imagined* him. In the first place, too many other people had seen him. And in the second, how had I got myself down to Devonshire without him driving me?

"Of course he drove you," Masterman was saying.

I blinked. "Was I talking aloud?"

"Muttering more like. Something about that Mr. Cantrip and imagining. What's this all about?" she demanded.

I took a deep breath and plunged in. "I came to London today to thank Mr. Cantrip for the spot of rescuing he did when he drove me down to Devon. But I cannot find him.

In fact, the curate in the church seems to think no such person exists."

Masterman pursed her lips. "Of course he does. We all saw him."

"Exactly. But who was he, if not Sebastian Cantrip, curate of this parish? And more to the point, what was he doing at my wedding?"

Masterman was thoughtful. "My money is on reporter. They're a nasty lot, those journalists. Probably infiltrated the wedding party to get some exclusive information to publish in his newspaper."

"He is not one of those filthy reporters," I countered with some warmth.

"How would you know?"

"Because he just isn't," I retorted stubbornly. "He's kind."

Her eyes narrowed. "You're smitten with him."

"Don't be vulgar. I'm nothing of the sort. It's only good manners to thank people when they do you a good turn, and he might have got into real trouble helping me run away." I paused, horrified. "You don't think that's why he's disappeared, do you?"

Masterman gave a short bark of a laugh, the first I'd ever heard from her. "I hardly think so. What do you expect, miss, that the Archbishop of Canterbury keeps a special prison just for wayward priests? Locks them up with only bread and water, never to see the light of day?"

She laughed again and I gave her a sour look. "You needn't be so foul, Masterman. It was an idea. I never said it was a good one."

She sobered and her expression was a little kinder. "Miss, don't take it like that. I was only having a bit of fun."

"At my expense."

"Well, you were the one being silly," she pointed out reasonably. "Now, why don't you work backwards? That's what I do whenever I've misplaced something. Where was the last place I know it was, and where before that?"

"He isn't a misplaced hat or bit of knitting, you know." It felt pointless, but I hadn't a better idea, so I obliged her. "The last place we saw him was in the cottage. He said he was returning to London."

"And where before that?"

"In the motorcar," I began, but as soon as the words were out of my mouth, I knew. "Oh, Masterman, you utter genius!" I clasped her hand in excitement. "I saw a garage ticket in the glovebox when I was looking for a packet of cigarettes. A garage ticket fell out, a ticket with a—oh, drat. I can't remember the name now."

"Of course you can," Masterman said confidently. "It only requires a bit of concentration. Close your eyes."

I obeyed, burrowing in my memory for the name. Something Irish, of that I was certain. And an address in Hampstead.

"O'Loughlin's," I said, my eyes popping open. I regarded Masterman with real admiration. "You are quite useful."

She gave me a thin smile. "You are not the first to make that observation, miss. Shall we go?"

In a very short while we found ourselves in Hampstead, standing on a main road. It seemed logical that a shop or post office would best know the garages in the area, and a quick visit to the latter provided the exact address. The garage was in the next street, and we hurried there, growing more excited with each step.

The garage man was wiping his hands on an oily rag when we appeared, looking a little out of place amongst the spanners and grease. I flicked Masterman a look indicating she should stay behind me. She obeyed, keeping a little distance as the garage man came forward.

"Can I help, miss?"

I put out my hand, then thought better of it when he apologetically showed a soiled palm.

"I hope so. Are you the proprietor, Mr. O'Loughlin?"

He grinned. "Naw, miss. I'm Wilson. Never has been an O'Loughlin here. I gave the place that name because the quality do like their Irish chauffeurs, don't they?"

I returned the smile. "Clever of you, Mr. Wilson. I've come because I'm trying to find an acquaintance of mine, a gentleman who assisted me under some very trying circumstances. He gave me a ride when I rather desperately needed transportation. I'm afraid I didn't have a chance to thank him properly and it's rather got under my skin. It would have been about a week ago. He drives a pretty little Talbot tourer. Painted blue? Quite fast?"

The garage man's face brightened. "Ah, yes, a right little beauty, isn't she? And Mr. Fox is a good customer, he is. Always ready with a pleasant word and what matter if he forgets a bill now and then? He always pays it and a little more when he realises. A real gentleman."

"Mr. Fox, you say? I'm afraid I didn't catch his name when he gave me a ride."

"Sebastian Fox," the garage man said promptly. "He lodges in the next street with Mrs. Webb what keeps the big house on the corner."

I thanked him and followed his directions to the corner house with Masterman trotting alongside.

"Honestly, I don't see what all the fuss with being a detective is," I told her. "It's quite easy, really. But did you hear the garage man? The curate was right. Sebastian's name isn't Cantrip at all. It's Fox. Why on earth would he lie?"

"Perhaps he's a criminal," Masterman said blandly.

"He's nothing of the sort. I think he was hiding from some-one," I told her. "Perhaps he is in some sort of trouble."

She snorted. "What sort of trouble would a man be in that he changes his name and lies about his identity rather than going to the police? He's a criminal," she repeated slyly as we reached the corner house.

I noted that the front steps were freshly scrubbed and the brass knocker had been polished to a blinding shine. I used it to rap briskly, and the door was opened almost immediately by a tall, imposing woman with a wealth of iron-grey hair bundled into an old-fashioned snood. She wore a black dress with a crisp white collar, and everything about her spoke of respectability.

"Have you come to inquire about the room?" she asked pleasantly.

I was caught off guard. "Oh, no, I—" I broke off, thinking wildly. I couldn't very well explain who Masterman was. Ladies who could afford maids didn't live in boarding houses. I felt a sudden jolt of inspiration and smiled winsomely at Mrs. Webb. "That is to say, not just a room. My, er, friend and I would need a pair of rooms." I flicked a glance at Master-man, who must have been surprised but kept her expression perfectly impassive.

Mrs. Webb nodded. "Well, I've only the one, I'm afraid, but it is large enough for two. I could put in a second bed, no trouble at all. It's only just come available, but I assure you it's in very good condition. The gentleman who occupied it was not always tidy, but he was clean, if you take my meaning."

"Show us," I said, amending it hastily with a fervent, "please."

Mrs. Webb escorted us up the stairs and unlocked a door from the ring of heavy keys at her belt. "There you are, miss?" She let the word dangle hopefully.

"Cantrip," I said promptly. "And this is my friend, Miss Smith."

Mrs. Webb nodded. "I'll leave you both to look around. I have a sponge in the oven. If you will make your way down when you are finished, you'd be most welcome to a cup of tea."

"Thank you, Mrs. Webb."

The landlady withdrew and Masterman gave me a grudging nod, her expression speculative. "You've a talent for lying, miss."

"I always have had," I admitted. "Learnt in more boarding schools than I can count. Now, let's have a good sniff around and see if we can discover anything about our mysterious Mr. Fox."

Masterman busied herself with the wardrobe while I circled slowly, taking in the room. It was large with a bow window that gave onto the street. I flicked aside the crisp white curtains with a gloved finger. There was a perfect view of the comings and goings of the neighbourhood from this room, although something at the back overlooking the garden would certainly be quieter. Interesting.

I turned and inspected the rest of the room. There was a small sitting area by the fireplace, a deep armchair, and a little table just large enough to hold a cup of tea and a book. The fender was well-polished and the leather cushion on top showed a bit of wear. I could just imagine Sebastian there, slouched comfortably in his chair, stockinged feet propped on the fender as a fire crackled merrily away.

Masterman finished with the wardrobe and wandered to the bookshelf, touching the books idly. "Not so much as a pin in the wardrobe, miss. It's been thoroughly cleaned."

There was nothing else to search save the bed and bookshelf. The bed was stripped to the mattress, narrow and freshly turned, and the bookshelf was nearly empty. Only half a dozen volumes stood upon it, and I motioned for Masterman to move as I took each one down, riffling through hastily.

Most were classic novels of the sort anyone might have, Dickens and the ubiquitous Austen, but I was intrigued to find the last book was *Peter Pan in Kensington Gardens*. I held it up to Masterman. "See? Not a criminal. No criminal would have a copy of this. It's a child's adventure book." I thumbed through to find my favourite picture, the Rackham illustration of Queen Mab, the queen of the fairies in Kensington Gardens.

And there it was, on the flyleaf in neat copperplate script. "Sebastian Fox," I said, tracing the handwriting with a fingertip.

"Do you suppose it's his real name?" she asked.

"I suspect so. It's dated 1911, the year the book was published, and the handwriting is a boy's. So, confirmation he lied to me but told the garage man the truth."

I looked up at Masterman with fearful eyes. "This book is very nearly falling apart. It's been read to pieces. Look where he's mended it, here and here. And he's underlined passages. This was no ordinary book to him, Masterman. It was a treasure. He would have had to have been in a very big hurry indeed to leave without it."

She nodded. "I'm beginning to think you're right, miss."

I shoved the book back onto the bookshelf with reluctant fingers. "I think his leaving this behind is a sign that we are onto something here."

Masterman said nothing as I prodded her downstairs to find the landlady. Mrs. Webb was in the kitchen finishing laying the tea things, and she gave us an apologetic look.

"I've nearly done here if you would go through to the sitting room, my dears."

I hesitated. We had passed the sitting room on our way up

the stairs. It was precisely the sort of room a proper landlady would keep—chilly and formal with an ancient Victorian horsehair suite of furniture and too many china ornaments. It was not a place for confidences. No, one wanted a kitchen for that. Many secrets could be exchanged in a warm and cosy room over a fat brown teapot and good bread and butter.

"That is so kind of you, Mrs. Webb, but I wonder if you would mind very much if we had our tea in here? It's just that I seem to have twisted my ankle a little in these wretched shoes and I shouldn't like to take my shoe off in your lovely sitting room."

With that little confession, Mrs. Webb dropped her formal manner and began to fuss like a mother hen. She insisted on making up a basin of hot water liberally dosed with salts for soaking my ankle and settling me in front of the welcoming fire. She had cut generous slices of bread and butter and we ate these companionably as Mrs. Webb poured out from a fat brown teapot precisely as I had expected. There were slices of feather-light sponge to follow with homemade raspberry jam, and I had to resist the urge to lick my fingers.

"I promise you, Mrs. Webb, I haven't had such a lovely tea since our last English nanny left," I said. As soon as the words were out, I could have bitten my tongue. I hadn't intended to reveal anything true about myself, much less that I came from a family of means.

Masterman darted me a quick glance, but I dropped my eyes and affected a little break in my voice. "I oughtn't talk of better days," I said softly. I gave Mrs. Webb a look from under my lashes. "The family has come down in the world," I murmured. "Financial reversals."

Mrs. Webb gave me a kindly smile. "I do understand, dear. And little wonder you enjoyed it then. I was a nanny for twenty years before I married. I missed all the little ones ter-

ribly when I left service. Mr. Webb did always say I fussed
too much, but I do so like to look after my guests properly."

I seized my chance. "And did you fuss over the gentleman
whose room you showed us?"

"Well, bless you, my dear, I did. Such a thoughtful young
man was Mr. Fox. Mind you, I didn't much care for him coming in all hours as he used to do. Far too much coming and
going, and that's a fact. But he was never once late with his
rent and never disturbed the others with noise or bad language.
I shall miss him, and there's no doubt about that."

I waited until Mrs. Webb had poured out another cup of tea
before picking up the thread of her inquiry. "Why did your
nice Mr. Fox leave? I shouldn't think any tenant would want
to leave this house unless he had to."

Mrs. Webb beamed at me. "Bless you, dear, but it's a fact
my tenants stay far longer than those next door at Mrs. Campbell's." She lowered her voice to a conspiratorial whisper.
"Tinned sauce on her puddings," she murmured, shaking her
head. "But you are quite right about Mr. Fox. He had to leave
us, and it was a sad day for me when he did."

I accepted another slice of sponge, thinking it was a wonder Sebastian hadn't been fat as a tick with eating Mrs. Webb's
cooking. "Business, I suppose?" I asked casually.

"Indeed. Mr. Fox is a scholar, you see. Biblical texts and so
forth. It was all quite over my head. I asked him once about
his work, and I don't mind to tell you, the explanation he gave
was more than I needed to hear. Quite too much for me to
understand! But he was a clever young gentleman, our Mr.
Fox. His studies were naturally interrupted by the war, but
now that peace has come, he has the chance to join an expedition in the Holy Land."

"Indeed?" I asked faintly, my hopes beginning to fade. I had traced him to Hampstead only to find I now had the whole of the Holy Land to search instead.

Masterman asked quietly, "Whereabouts in the Holy Land?"

Mrs. Webb spread her hands, her lips thinning a little with distaste. "Oh, bless you, dear, I couldn't say. I don't believe I know one of those foreign places from another! Geography was never my strong suit."

She folded her hands over her belly and gave me a piercing look. "Now, dear. About that room?"

Mrs. Webb was not at all pleased with our excuses for not taking the room. She expressed again her willingness to put in an extra bed and take something off the rent, but it wasn't until I told her quite firmly that I could only live in an east-facing room on account of my morning devotionals to the Egyptian sun god Ra that we were hurried out onto the front steps and the door closed behind us with a bang.

"Rather quick on your feet, aren't you, miss? I thought you'd given away the game when you mentioned a nanny, but you turned up trumps. You even got your chin to tremble," she said in admiration.

"Contrived contrition," I said with a brisk nod. "An entirely useful skill honed in far too many boarding schools."

"Still," she went on, "you rather burnt that bridge, didn't you?" Masterman asked mildly. "What on earth possessed you to tell such a whopping lie? Sun god Ra indeed."

I shrugged. "It got us out of there. Useful lies aren't that great a sin."

"Well, if we're on the subject of sins, I ought to confess I took this." She reached into her handbag and took out the copy of *Peter Pan in Kensington Gardens*.

"Masterman!"

Her expression was impassive. "I'm sorry, miss. I ought not

to have done it, but when I nipped back up to..." She paused delicately to allude to bodily functions. "Anyway," she hurried on, "when I came out of that room, I thought I would just have another look around while you were busy getting along with Mrs. Webb like a house afire. And I thought we ought to take it. It's a connection to him, do you see? It's the one piece of proof we have of his real name. We haven't even an idea of where he is except the Holy Land, and that's a mighty big haystack for a single needle, if you ask me."

"Of course it is, but we can approach it logically," I told her automatically.

She stood on the pavement, regarding me with something between suspicion and admiration.

"Are you always like this, miss?"

I blinked at her. "Like what?"

She sketched a gesture taking me in from head to toe. "This. You're the original optimist, aren't you?"

I shrugged. "I suppose. I always think things will turn out for the best, and somehow they usually do. Besides, what if we are able to find out where he went? Do you realise what it means, Masterman? It's the Near East—Richard the Lion-heart and Saladin in the Crusades, it's Lady Jane Digby riding off on a camel, and *djinns* on flying carpets, and Scheherezade spinning her tales, and Ali Baba with his thieves, and Lady Hester Stanhope perched on a mountaintop."

I had taken her arm in the course of my little speech, and she disengaged my fingers gently.

"I'm quite certain some of those aren't real people," she said darkly.

"Of course not. That isn't the point. The point is that some of them *were* real. They lived there, and they were legends, larger than life because they gripped life with both hands and looked it right in the eye. That's the sort of life I want."

I squared my shoulders as I gripped the book, feeling a rush of savage, untrammelled certainty. "This is it, Masterman. This is the adventure I've been looking for. The chance I've wanted to make something more of myself. I owe Sebastian a debt. And I mean to repay it. I'm going to find him. And if he truly is in trouble of some sort, I'm going to help him, just as he helped me."

Masterman stood toe to toe with me, and there was resolve in her eyes. "Not without me, miss. Not without me."

FIVE

And somehow, through our mutual resolve, a partnership was born. I had made up my mind to find Sebastian, and Masterman had made up her mind to help. The first order of business was to make inquiries at the steamship offices, and since it was already past teatime, we arranged to spend the night in London at a small but respectable hotel. Masterman booked the room and I hurried in with my cloche pulled low to avoid being recognised. It wasn't likely that any of Mother's friends would frequent such a quiet place, but I was in no mood to take chances. We left early the next morning to divide and conquer. We separated with conspiratorial nods, and I took the offices of the five largest companies, smiling sweetly and asking to see the passenger lists for departures to Palestine, Syria, the Lebanon, the Transjordan, Turkey, and Egypt. I thought I had narrowed the search considerably, but there proved to be far more ships departing than I had expected. The tiny printed names blurred together as I reached for yet another list from yet another bored clerk.

I worked on, studying the endless lists and pushing through

a headache and stiff shoulders. I stifled a yawn and just as I was about to put aside the last list, a name jumped out at me. *Fox, Sebastian*. I yelped, earning myself a dark look from the clerk, but I blew him a kiss and asked him for paper and pencil. He sweetly obliged, and I copied out every scrap of information, the name of the ship, the date of departure, the class of cabin he had booked.

Beckoning the clerk over, I showed him the list. "Can you tell me exactly where this ship stops?"

Bored once more, the clerk silently handed over a slim pamphlet with the ship's itinerary shown on a small map as well as a list of amenities and attractions. I thanked him and left, mind whirling. It was time for lunch and Masterman and I were not supposed to rendezvous until teatime. It was the perfect opportunity to take her advice and brave one of society's favourite hotspots. I made my way to the Savoy, forcing myself to think of the rather delectable *Poulard de France Dorothy* instead of the stares and glares I was bound to attract. I was just about to enter the restaurant when I heard a voice behind me.

"I don't believe it—Penelope Hammond!"

I whirled around, wincing a little at the sound of my name echoing through the lobby, but as soon as I saw the source, I broke into a grin. "Cubby Ashley!"

Lord Edward Ashley, known to his friends by his childhood nickname of Cubby for his resemblance to an amiable bear, kissed me swiftly on the cheek. "It's good to see you in person," he told me. "The direst rumours are going round about you at the clubs."

"I can imagine," I said dryly. "Don't tell me you're listening to such nonsense."

"Nonsense? My dear girl, I've got a fiver on you being covered in scales under all your clothes."

I tweaked his arm. "Ass." But I said it with affection. "It

is good to see you, too, Cubby. I do feel rather awful about the wedding."

"Yes, well, you didn't just run out on Gerald, you know. There I was, all got up in my rig for standing up with him—and dashed splendid I looked, too. It isn't every day I make the effort," he added with a twinkling smile. Before I could speak, he darted a glance around. The lobby of the Savoy was a crowded place and we were already beginning to attract attention. "I say, Penelope, I would like to catch up. I don't suppose you'd have lunch?"

"Of course," I said promptly. "But not here. I'm afraid my nerve has rather deserted me. I've just seen Lady Knapely walk in, and she's one of Mother's chums. I couldn't bear running into Mother just now."

With the furtive hilarity of children on holiday we hurried out and down the street to a quiet little corner house, where we ordered quickly and settled down to the business of catching up.

"All right, Cubby. Out with it. I know why I didn't want to stay at the Savoy, but why were you so eager to get out of there. What's afoot?"

To my astonishment, the gentle giant actually blushed.

"Cubby! You've got a girl," I deduced. "And you didn't want to be seen in public with a scandal like me in case your girl heard about it. Confess all—I'm right, aren't I?"

The blush deepened. "More than a girl. I've got a fiancée."

"How wonderful!"

"Not really," he said with a grin. "You see, Father had a bride all picked out for me."

I held up a hand. "Don't tell me. Some heiress to shore up that castle of his."

Cubby nodded. "You know how it is. The Ashley title is

five hundred years old but we haven't a bean. The whole north tower actually collapsed last month."

I winced. "Oh, dear. And I suppose your father found a nice girl with pots of nice money, did he? What was she—American? Railroad heiress?"

"South American with a squint and mouse-brown hair. And it's not railroad money at all. Nitrate mining," he told me between spoonfuls of soup.

"What is a nitrate and why does one want to mine it?"

He shrugged. "Something to do with arms. Her father made a bloody fortune in the war, which I think is quite low really."

I smiled into my soup bowl. "Cubby, you're one of the nicest people I've ever met. For you to say something is low, it must have been awfully vile."

"Yes, well, you know how it was. I was over there in the trenches. I lost friends, more than I care to count. And to marry a girl whose father made his money that way—" He broke off, wincing. "I hadn't the stomach for it. At least, not until you."

I put down my spoon. "Until me?"

"When you had the courage to leave Gerald at the altar. Serves him right, the pompous prig."

"Cubby, Gerald is your best friend and your cousin," I reminded him. "And what I did wasn't courageous. It was the rankest cowardice."

"It was not," he said stubbornly. "If you knew you had doubts, the right thing, the only thing, was to get out before it all became official. I call it good sense."

"Good sense, bad form," I murmured.

"Yes, well, society doesn't know everything," he said firmly.

I tipped my head thoughtfully. "Cubby, tell me about your new fiancée. Does society not approve?"

"It does not," he told her. He put down his spoon and

leaned forward, his eyes bright. "She's the prettiest girl in the world. She's kind and thoughtful, and well, I simply wouldn't want to live if I couldn't have her."

"You're quite the romantic, Cubby," I said, smiling. "But if she's so wonderful, why the objections to the match? Hasn't she any money?"

"Not tuppence to rub together, I'm afraid. She's the vicar's daughter," he said with a rueful face. "Mother is about to have an apoplexy, and Father's threatened to cut me off without a shilling, but I don't care. I love Gwen, and I'll marry her or no one. It's been the most terrible secret, utterly awful not to be able to talk about it, and you've always been so friendly. I feel somehow you understand that I mean to do this. I must do this." Cubby's chin had taken on a decidedly mulish cast, and I tried not to imagine the outrage of the Marchioness of Drumlanrig at having a daughter-in-law called Gwen.

"I'm sure they'll come around," I said, certain of no such thing. But it seemed the only polite remark to make under the circumstances, and Cubby brightened noticeably.

"But you see, Gwen is a bit uncertain of me just yet," he went on. "She's feeling out of sorts at how awful my family are being, and it's made her doubt herself. If she were to find out I'd been lunching with someone as notorious as—"

He broke off, blushing again as I gave an indignant screech. "I'm not notorious! A moment ago, you said I was courageous."

"And I meant it. But people do say things about you. I mean, what sort of girl leaves a viscount's heir at the altar?"

"And what sort of man throws over a nitrate heiress for a village maiden?" I retorted.

But I could never stay mad at Cubby, and having at least one friend to talk to made me feel marginally less like a pariah. By the time we had tucked into large plates of apple tart with cream, we were perfectly friendly again—friendly enough that I ventured to give him an almost truthful response when he asked about my plans.

"I mean to travel," I told him. "I'm thinking of someplace nice and sunny. Perhaps the Holy Land."

He sat back, patting his rounded belly in satisfaction. "Rather a long way just for some sun."

"Yes, well, I've always been mad about Biblical antiquities," I said blithely. "Nineveh and Bethlehem and Sodom." At least I hoped those were real places. Cubby blinked and I hurried on. "Anyway, now that the war's over, I can see the region properly."

"Ah, taking a Cook's tour or something?"

I thought quickly. A Cook's tour would cost the earth, and I doubted my funds would stretch to passage for me and Masterman, as well. I could have asked Reginald and he would have given the money happily, but something in me rebelled for the first time. If I asked Reginald, it meant involving Mother, who would ask endless questions and even, possibly, insist upon coming along. But if I found the means myself, I was answerable to no one. I could go as I please. I could be truly independent for once. The thought was as intoxicating as the finest champagne, and I blurted out before I could stop myself, "Actually, I mean to get a job."

Cubby blinked. "A job? Really? Well, that's splendid," he said, a shade too heartily. "What sort of job?"

I shrugged. "Companion, I suppose. It's what I'm fit for. I can answer letters and walk dogs and arrange flowers. I don't think I should make a very good governess or nurse," I finished with a shudder.

"No, I don't think so," he agreed with a kindly smile. His expression turned thoughtful. "I say, it's the strangest coincidence, but I might know of something."

"Really?"

"My great-uncle on Mother's side, curious old chap. Always haring off to parts unknown. He was a great explorer in years past, but now he's content to potter about his old haunts. He was quite ill this past winter, as a matter of fact, we were certain he was a goner. But he's pulled through and wants to go back to the Levant. Apparently he had a roaring time of it when he was younger and wants to see it all again before he dies."

"And he needs a companion?" My heart began to beat quickly, tightly, like a new drum.

"Not exactly. He means to write his memoirs and his handwriting is truly awful. Even worse than mine and no one has read a word I've written since 1912. I don't suppose you can type?" he finished hopefully.

I smiled thinking of the secretarial course I had very nearly completed. "As a matter of fact, I can. After a fashion," I added in a burst of honesty.

"Well, that's just ripping," he said with a hearty chuckle. "I do love when things work out so neatly, almost as if it were meant to be. Now, if I know Uncle Cyrus, he's using this memoir as an excuse to have someone younger to come along on the trip. He's very fond of young people," he advised. "You see, Uncle Cyrus likes to tell stories, bang on about the old days. My theory is he's told them all too many times and his valet won't listen anymore. He wants a fresh pair of ears," Cubby finished with a nod.

"I have fresh ears," I told him. I was suddenly quite desperate to go to the Levant with Uncle Cyrus. "Would you mind asking your uncle if he still has a position open?"

He shrugged. "Not at all. Always happy to do a good turn for a pal."

I hesitated. "And when you ask, can you tell him my name is March?"

Cubby's spaniel-brown eyes widened as he shaped a soundless whistle. "I say, a bit of intrigue there. Going incognita, are you?"

"No, as it happens. Hammond isn't my legal name. Mother was divorced from my father, you know. His name was March."

"Not one of the Sussex Marches?"

"The same."

He gave another bark of laughter. "But they're all mad as hatters."

"Yes, well," I said dryly, "sometimes I think this particular apple mayn't have fallen far from the tree. But it will damp down the scandal if I start using my real name again, don't you think?"

He shrugged. "How the devil should I know? I have no intrigues. I am pure as the driven snow," he added, pulling a face.

I gave him a suspicious glance. "Oh, I don't know, Cubby. I should think you were capable of an intrigue or two if you put your mind to it."

He paled for a second, but as soon as the colour in his face ebbed it flooded back, and he took a quick sip of his coffee. I grinned.

"Only joking. I am sure Miss Gwen can be certain of your fidelity. You're the last fellow to have a señorita tucked away on the side."

He threw me a grateful look. "Yes, quite. Where are you staying?"

I wrote down my details on a bit of scrap paper and handed it to Cubby. "Thank you, Cubby. I won't forget this."

He laughed. "Don't thank me. You haven't met Uncle Cyrus."

★ ★ ★

Cubby was as good as his word, and the following afternoon I appeared punctually at the Langham Hotel. It didn't have the glamour and swing of the Savoy, but the staid Victorian solemnity of it was reassuring. It occurred to me as I stepped into the lift that this was the very first time I had interviewed for a job, and I squared my shoulders and rapped smartly on the door. I ought to have been alarmed, but what was finishing school for if it couldn't give a girl confidence and prepare her for any eventuality?

The door swung open and so did my mouth. Standing on the other side was a man so handsome even the queen would have looked twice. He was the sort of man you could just imagine carrying you from a burning building or duelling for your honour, all broad shoulders and chiselled jaw with a pair of fathomless blue eyes that looked me over as he gave me a slow smile of appreciation.

He got his mouth under control more quickly than I did mine. He dropped the smile and cleared his throat, although his eyes—dark blue as a summer sky and fringed with thick, sooty lashes—still danced.

"Miss March, I presume."

I snapped my mouth shut then realised I needed it to speak. "Colonel Archainbaud?"

He laughed. "Not by half. I'm the valet, Talbot. Hugh Talbot. Come this way, miss. The colonel is expecting you."

He didn't look behind to see if I was following, but it wasn't necessary. I would have followed him to the gates of hell, I thought stupidly. He conducted me to an inner room where the colonel waited and announced me.

"Yes, yes, come in, child!" the colonel instructed.

I darted another glance at Talbot, and he turned, giving me an almost imperceptible wink as he left.

"Colonel Archainbaud, how kind of you to see me," I began. I crossed to where he was seated.

"Forgive me for not rising," he said, tapping his leg. "Dicky leg since the war. Doesn't do what I want some days. But you understand, I'm sure."

"Of course." He waved me to a chair and I took the opportunity to look him over. He must have been a fine figure of a man once. He had stooped shoulders and white hair, but I could see the remnants of a tall frame and a soldier's regal bearing. I'd met a dozen like him before—no-nonsense, plain-spoken, and full of love for king and country. His cheeks were ruddy and his brows, thick and woolly as white cater-pillars, wriggled when he spoke. They were extraordinary, those brows, and I tried not to stare.

While I had been looking him over, he had been doing the same to me, assessing me with a gimlet eye.

"You're not what I expected," he said bluntly.

"In what way, Colonel?"

"You're a damn sight too young, for starters. Are you even twenty?"

I paused. Ancient colonels fell into two camps, those with utterly no sense of humour and those who prided themselves on their banter. I gambled that he was the latter. "Surely you don't expect a lady to tell her age," I said demurely.

I had gambled and won. The colonel let out a sharp bark of a laugh followed by a wheeze.

"That's told me, hasn't it? Always did like a girl who could keep me in my place. Well, so long as you remember there's a time for raillery and a time to be serious," he added with a narrowed eye.

"Of course," I promised, smoothing my skirt over my knee.

"Well, you might be far too young, but at least no one will assume I'm misbehaving when they see us together. They'll think you're my granddaughter," he said, breaking into more of his peculiar barking laughter. "Now, tell me about your references," he commanded, watching me slyly.

"References?" My voice was hollow. It hadn't even occurred to me to forge any, and I wondered then if finishing school had been a colossal waste of time when it came to equipping a girl with the skills that really mattered.

I had paused too long. The colonel knew I had none and laughed again. "Now, now, don't look so downcast. I heard all I needed from young Cubby. The boy's an ass, but he has nice friends, and all he tells me about you is that you're in a spot of bother."

His eyes were kindly, and I hurried to reassure him. "Nothing important, Colonel. But I do find myself in need of a job and there isn't much I am qualified to do."

"Why not nursery governess?"

I shuddered. "I don't much care for babies. I mean, I might like one if it were mine, but as I've never had one I can't say for sure. My mother had four after me, and I never much liked them as infants."

"Too froggy-looking," he agreed. "Why not shop assistant?"

I smiled. "I don't think I have the temperament to deal with difficult people."

"Ha! And what makes you think I won't be difficult?" he asked, leaning forward, his eyes alight under those caterpillar brows.

"Because you are a gentleman," I returned sweetly.

He preened and puffed a little, and that's when I knew the job was mine. We fell to discussing terms. The salary was not ungenerous, and the responsibilities were simple ones.

"Handwriting is a bit untidy these days," he said ruefully, "so deciphering it might be a bit of a bore, but you can always ask. Chances are, I won't be able to read it myself and we'll just have to make something up," he added with a jolly smile. "I've been working on the memoir for years and I've made a pig's breakfast of it. It needs a steady hand and clear eye to bring some order to it. Aside from that, just a bit of light secretarial work—writing the odd letter and so forth, keeping me company with a bit of chess. And of course helping out with Peeky when Talbot isn't around," he added.

"Peeky?"

As if on cue, the door opened and the beautiful valet entered bearing an armful of moth-eaten rug.

"Peeky," the colonel told me. Talbot deposited the dog onto his master's lap, and it looked at me with disdain. It was a Pekinese of middle age and uncertain temperament. But Pekes were Mother's particular favourite, and I knew precisely how to handle them.

"That won't be a problem," I promised.

Talbot slipped out again, and Peeky looked after him longingly. I sympathised.

The colonel's hand absently stroked the Peke's fur. "The truth is, Miss March, I could get a fellow to handle these things. For that matter, I could have Talbot attend to them. He's a competent enough chap. But the truth is, I like young people, and there's something about having a female around that just—" he broke off, his manner slightly uncomfortable as he made his confession. "Dash it all, I just think a lady makes it all nicer."

"I understand," I told him. And I did. There was something infinitely depressing about a bachelor establishment, I had always felt. Actually, there was something infinitely depressing about finishing schools for that matter. Too much of one's own sex was a dangerous thing.

"Well, then," he said gruffly, putting out his hand. "Welcome aboard, Miss March."

I shook hands with him and stayed to tea, and attempted to make friends with Peeky, who stared down his nose and loathed me quietly. I would have to work on that one, I decided as I rose to leave. The colonel had slumped a little in his chair, snoring gently, and it was Talbot who showed me out.

We paused at the door. "Looks as if he's taken quite a shine to you," he said, jerking his head back towards the colonel's sitting room. "Can't say as I blame him."

The eyes were dancing again, and I pulled a serious face. "Mr. Talbot, am I going to have trouble with you?"

"No more than you ask for," he told me with a grin. Then he put out his own hand for me to shake. "You mustn't take me too seriously, Miss March. I'm simply giddy with delight that there will be a prettier face than mine around here. It gets rather lonely with just us elderly bachelors, the colonel, Peeky and myself."

I shook his hand, and he held it the merest second too long.

"Thank you, Mr. Talbot."

He shook his head. "No, miss. The colonel won't like that. You might work for him, too, but he knows you are a lady. To you, I'm just Talbot."

"That hardly seems right," I protested.

His expression was rueful. "You'll find out soon enough—he might be a splendid old fellow, but this is not a democracy, Miss March. Good afternoon."

"Good afternoon, Talbot," I said. I made my way out of the hotel and into a watery grey afternoon. A spring storm had blown up while I was inside, and the pavements were wet. The clouds were low and ominous, the wind cruel as only a March wind can be. I had forgot my umbrella and my coat was impossibly thin. Within minutes I was soaked through, but I didn't mind. I was leaving for the Holy Land in a week's time. I had done it.

Masterman was less impressed when I told her I had taken the post. We met in our little room at the hotel she had found, and I was crackling with excitement. Masterman was considerably more subdued as she hung up my wet coat and stuffed newspaper into my shoes.

"You cannot seriously mean to work for this man," she protested. She set the shoes well away from the fire to dry slowly.

"I can and I do," I told her firmly. "Now, we haven't much time to make our arrangements. The colonel expects me to begin work the day of our departure, so that gives us only a few days to travel down to Father's and pack up my things, and we still have to book your passage."

She shook her head. "I feel peculiar."

"Take a bromide."

"It's not indigestion," she said. "And you mustn't be flippant. It's gone too far now."

I blinked at her in astonishment. "Masterman, this is what we have been working towards. How can you possibly say it's gone too far?"

She spread her hands. They were surprisingly elegant hands, but capable. They knew how to do things and do them well. My own hands seemed silly and childish by comparison.

"I thought you were merely having a little adventure, a grand little adventure."

"And what did you think would happen when it was finished? How did you think it would end?"

"I thought you would realise you haven't a hope of finding Sebastian. I thought it would all just…stop. I expected you would go back to the life you came from."

I felt a surge of anger. "This isn't just a lark, Masterman.

Sebastian could be in trouble—injured or even dead for all we know."

"And you really think you can find him?" she asked evenly. I had the strangest feeling she was testing me, and I rose to the bait.

My hands fisted at my sides. "Why not? Why should it fall to someone else to care what happened to him? He was kind to me when I needed it. He went out of his way to help me, and I owe him a debt, Masterman. I can't just walk away now. I've spent my entire life walking away from things."

Her expression was curious. "Miss?"

"Oh, very well! Gerald wasn't the first," I confessed miserably. "I've been very nearly engaged twice before. I've managed to avoid committing myself, but it was frightfully awkward. I've left schools, half a dozen of them. I've taken on pets and causes and friendships and let them go the moment they asked too much of me. I've never once in the whole of my life finished anything. Don't you see, Masterman? If I don't finish this, this one thing, I'll never finish anything. I'll never see anything through to the end. My family think it's funny. They joke about the hobbies and romances and projects I've left undone. But it's not a joke anymore. Because it's become who I am, what I've become. I don't want to be a joke, Masterman. I want to see this through. Not just for Sebastian—for me. Oh, never mind. I can't explain it. I only know that this is something I have to do. Saying it aloud only makes it sound silly and melodramatic, but the truth is, it feels like a calling."

"A calling?"

"Yes, isn't that what clergymen say about their work? They're called to it? Well, that's how I feel about this. It's not just Sebastian, Masterman. Can't you see? It's something much bigger, and I don't understand it yet, but I know I have to go looking."

Masterman said nothing for a long moment. Then she took a deep breath and exhaled it very, very slowly, and the fight seemed to go out of her. "Very well, miss. We'll go."

"You don't have to—" I began.

The expression on her face was so fierce I flinched. "Yes, I do. However long it takes, wherever it takes us. 'Whither thou goest,'" she finished.

I smiled weakly. "You'll be my Ruth, then?"

"However long, wherever it takes us," she repeated.

SIX

A week later, I stood at the rail of the ship, watching the southern coastline of France recede, butterflies hurtling around in my stomach like bees in a jar. I was always slightly unsettled when I started a new sea voyage, but this time the feeling was largely one of pure elation. I had done it. Seizing every opportunity that had come my way, I had secured a position as companion to the elderly Colonel Cyrus Archainbaud, packed my bags, and set sail for the Holy Land. It had been a whirlwind of activity, from the first interview with the colonel to boarding the train in London. And in the meantime, there was Masterman to argue with. After an initial ding-dong that nearly had her marching straight to Mother to Reveal All, she gave in and packed my small trunk with perfect precision and very bad grace.

I had intended to talk her out of coming—the passage was eye-wateringly expensive and consumed almost all of the salary the colonel had advanced me—but she refused to let me go alone, and with a little careful extortion, she persuaded me that it would be far better for her to come along.

"I can keep an eye on things," she said firmly.

"Masterman, a companion cannot travel with a lady's maid," I pointed out acidly. "How can I be in the colonel's employ when you are in mine?"

She shook her head. "I won't be in your employ, at least not publicly. I will go on my own, as an independent traveller. That way I can be at hand if trouble comes, and I can go and find things out. Two pairs of eyes and ears are better than one," she added slyly. "And if it means we find poor Sebastian sooner, well, miss, it would be criminal not to try. As you said, what if he is come to some harm? What if he's in need of friends to aid him? Just think of it, that poor fellow, perhaps chained to a wall somewhere in those heathen lands—"

I held up a hand. "There is no need for melodrama, Masterman. And I thought you believed he was a criminal."

She drew herself up. "No lad who reads *Peter Pan* can be all bad."

And that was that. I would not give her the satisfaction of knowing that I was secretly glad to have her along, but the notion of being so far from everything and everyone I had known in pursuit of adventure had been the slightest bit daunting. It would be good to have her play Watson to my Holmes, although I was quite sure she would have taken umbrage at being the sidekick.

The only fly in the otherwise satisfactory ointment was leaving Father behind. I crossed my fingers behind my back as I explained that friends had invited me on a nice long sea voyage, and since Masterman was accompanying me, the lie made perfect sense. Father said little, but our last evening together had been marked by his silence. He had turned in early, and it had been left to George to bid us farewell at the station the next morning with a whistled tune and even a semblance of a smile as he waved us off. I told myself it was for the best. The cottage was small and Father's health was precarious. George had been right to insist on my being respectful of Father's privacy, and I reasoned to myself that the sooner I learned to stand on my own two feet, the sooner Father and I could establish a mutually respectful relationship of equals. It had been lowering to throw myself on his charity, although his response had been heroic. Now it was time to show him what I could do on my own.

Mother was a different affair altogether. I didn't trust her to accept my decision to leave the cottage as gracefully as Father had, so I waited until the morning we departed for France to post a letter giving her the same vague lie I had offered Father. I calculated it was only a matter of time before Cubby managed to spill the beans, but in the meanwhile it would buy me a bit of breathing room.

Breathing room. I drew in great draughts of sweet sea air and blew them out slowly. The rushing to and fro of the past weeks vanished, and I stood on the deck for ages, watching the sun stretch its last reaching rays over the horizon before it fell away. There was a short purple twilight and then the stars began to shimmer to life.

A quote—something from *Peter and Wendy*—teased at the edge of my mind, and I whispered it aloud, just to hear a voice in the midst of all that shimmering darkness. "'Stars are beautiful, but they may not take an active part in anything, they must just look on forever…' But what is the next bit? Something about old stars seldom speaking but the little ones still wondering."

"Enjoying yourself, my dear?" I turned at the sound of a voice in the shadows behind me.

"Good evening, Colonel. Did you need me?"

He emerged from the gathering darkness, walking heavily with the aid of a stick. He seemed a little fatigued from the journey so far, although his spine was still straight as a lance. From what I had learned, his life had been a series of losses. First the family fortunes, then a young wife and infant child, then a succession of battles that had left him the worse for wear. But there was still something vital about him, and he had proven far more shrewd and alert than what I had expected from Cubby's description and our brief meetings in London.

He waved off the question. "Not a bit of it, child. I thought it might be nice to come out and see the stars. First night on the open sea is always the start of the journey, I feel. That's when you get right away from everything, don't you think?"

I smiled. "I do."

I decided I quite liked my new employer. He was delicate as a cat in his habits, tidy but not fussy, and Talbot took care of the donkey work. The colonel had decreed that we could not possibly begin on the memoir until we were well out to sea and perfectly settled, so all that was left to me was a bit of letter writing on the colonel's behalf and to amuse him. This usually took the form of mealtime conversation, some reading aloud, and the occasional game of chess. I started out with a few modest successes but I'd become quite proficient in the few days we had been travelling together. But even with my improved game, I could not hope to best the colonel. His gentle chivalry did not extend to letting me win, and whatever gains I made in the game were always hard-won. Occasionally I caught him watching me closely as we played, and an inscrutable expression would pass over his features. I wondered if I reminded him of someone he once knew, but I did not like to ask.

He was wearing that expression again as he approached the rail, his stick tapping gently on the deck. "Ah, see that constellation there? That's good old Cancer, the crab. You know, of course, how it got its name?"

The question wasn't really a question, and I knew it. The colonel was entirely capable of asking and answering with no help from me, and so I said nothing as he went on.

"When Heracles, the son of Zeus, was battling with the water-serpent Hydra, his jealous stepmother, Hera, sent Cancer the crab to aid the serpent and vanquish her stepson once and for all. But Heracles crushed the poor old crab with a single blow of his foot, shattering its shell. For his devotion even unto death, Hera reassembled him and placed him in the stars to honour his loyalty." He was silent a moment as we stared up at the glimmering stars.

"Ah, well," he finished, "tales from my schoolboy days. I don't suppose they teach much mythology nowadays, but that's what started me on my love of travel, you see. I wanted to see these places out of myth for myself—Mount Olympus and Sparta and the gates of Troy. Of course, those stories were replaced by real history as I grew up. I learnt about the Crusades, about Richard the Lionheart, our soldier king, and I wanted to be a soldier just like him. And when it was over and done, I remembered those stories I'd known as a boy, of faraway places and great warriors, and I thought it must be time at last to see them. Made seventeen trips to that part of the world, all told. All around the Mediterranean, and although you'll never hear me say there's any of them that can touch England, there is much to be seen, my dear. Much indeed."

His breath was coming quite fast, and I realised he was growing a little overexcited by his reminiscences. I was just wrestling with whether or not I should call Talbot when the man himself appeared, impeccable in his evening clothes. He cleared his throat quietly and the colonel turned.

"Time for your medicine, Colonel," the valet told him. Like his master, the valet had splendid posture, and he wore his evening clothes with all the elegance of a gentleman. He did not look at me as he addressed the colonel, but I knew he would have taken in every detail of my appearance. Nothing escaped him, at least nothing about me, and I felt myself preen a little at his nearness. He just had an effect upon people, particularly women. More than once I had seen ladies giving him the glad eye as our little party passed. Even Masterman, during our brief snatches of conversation, had pronounced him "a bit of something."

The colonel fussed a little but tottered off, giving himself up to Talbot's attentions. I turned back to the rail, chin in hand, peering into the inky-black nothingness beyond. If it weren't for the stars and their darting reflections in the waves, I would have thought myself entirely alone in the universe. It was nothing but a fancy, of course. I could hear the faint, nostalgic sweep of the orchestra playing for the smart after-dinner crowd, and somewhere in the distance a deckhand was singing, low and off-key, something mournful. It had a keening quality to it, as if he were grieving for something lost, and I gave a shudder.

A whisper of velvet slid around my shoulders. "You forgot your wrap."

It was Talbot, wrapping my stole about me, and standing a scant inch too close for comfort.

"Thank you, Talbot. That's very kind," I told him.

His eyes were glittering in the starlight, and I thought—not for the first time since I had met him—that he really was the most stunningly handsome man I'd ever seen. Particularly when he smiled that irresistible smile. "I think you'll find I'm not kind, Miss March. I seldom do things except for my own amusement."

"And I amuse you?"

"I think you could."

"I think I won't," I returned, but with a smile of my own

to soften the words. "You forget I have to keep my reputation intact, Talbot. I am in the colonel's employ."

"What I have in mind won't tarnish your reputation," he assured me. "At least, not much."

He held out his hand. "Dance with me."

I laughed. "You must be joking."

"I never joke about dancing, Miss March. Listen to that orchestra," he coaxed. "They think they're playing for the rich, the titled, the masters of the universe. But really they're playing for us," he said, stepping very close, his lips brushing my ear as he spoke.

"I suppose one dance wouldn't hurt," I told him, joining in with enthusiasm.

He was an expert dancer, and as he executed one particularly deft bit of footwork, leading me perfectly in time, he gave a soft laugh, squeezing my waist for an instant. "I can tell you're surprised. I may be a valet, but I do have my accomplishments," he assured me.

"I have no doubt," I replied. "But I don't think I should experience any more of them tonight," I told him firmly. I slid out of his arms and wrapped my stole securely about my shoulders. "Thank you for the dance, Talbot." I held out my hand to shake his and he took it, his expression grave while his eyes were alight with mischief.

"Such beautiful manners you have, Miss March," he said silkily. "And how I should like to see you forget them."

"Good night," I said, turning on my heel and making my way inside. From behind me, I heard his soft laugh echoing in the shadows of the starry night.

The rest of the voyage passed swiftly with each port of call proving more memorable and exotic than the last. The odours of wood smoke and coal fires mingled with those of donkey and spices and ripe fruit on the sea air, and I was enchanted with it all. My days were spent in undemanding attendance on the colonel, taking a bit of dictation and occasionally typing up a few pages of his memoir notes, and reading everything I could get my hands on about the Near East and its inhabitants. I had maps, guide books, biographies of Lady Jane Digby and Lady Hester Stanhope, and the memoirs of Lady Hester's doctor, Charles Meryon, as well as Kinglake's *Eothen*. I devoured them all, and once, in a moment of sweet madness, I pulled out Sebastian's copy of *Peter Pan in Kensington Gardens* and read it for the first time in a decade, noting the passages he had underlined. "'In this world, there are no second chances,'" I read aloud. And I wondered if that was what had driven him to the Holy Land. Was he chasing a second chance?

Increasingly my evenings were spent with Talbot. The colonel retired earlier and earlier as the ship neared its final port of call, and we were often thrown together. More than once the colonel told us to go ashore and enjoy the sights and sounds as he rested, sipping bouillon in his deck chair, or playing endless games of shuffleboard with one or two of the acquaintances he had found amongst the passengers. So Talbot and I danced and talked and took Peeky for endless walks around the ship's decks as we steamed ever eastward.

Our destination was Beirut, and we were among the last to disembark. I saw Masterman making her way ashore, with only a single backwards glance to show she was thinking of me. She was swallowed up by the throng of people while we waited on the deck. The colonel did not care to be jostled and preferred to wait until the crowds had dispersed to make his way carefully down the gangway. I followed close behind Peeky while Talbot brought up the rear laden with attaché case, travelling rug, and assorted newspapers and books. Halfway down the gangplank, I stopped dead in my tracks. I did not move, not when Peeky tugged impatiently at his lead or when Talbot stopped behind me.

"Miss March? Is everything all right?"

I opened my mouth, but for an instant I made no sound, and I was reminded of those horrible dreams where one's feet were rooted to the spot or one's screams were silent. I collected myself with a shudder and forced a smile.

"Fine. So silly of me. I have a touch of vertigo," I lied as I looked down at the green water swirling below. A little slick of oil lay on the top, glistening pink and blue and black against the sea, and overhead a gull screamed. I threw Talbot an apologetic look and hurried on, not telling him the truth, not telling him that I stopped because I had had a premonition of disaster. He would have laughed and said I was silly, that it was nothing more than a goose walking over my grave. But I knew better. And as I set foot on the sturdy dock, landing in Asia for the first time in my life, I wondered what disaster would befall me here.

In spite of my premonition of gloom, Beirut proved a lovely city, cosmopolitan and sophisticated in the extreme. I would have liked to have spent time there, but the colonel had other ideas.

"No, it's on to Damascus!" he insisted. "There are interesting times afoot," he had added with a finger to the side of his nose. "History is being made there as we speak."

I blinked. I hadn't looked at more than the society pages of the newspaper in ages, and the colonel gave me an indulgent nod and patted my hand.

"Don't trouble yourself, my dear. No one expects the ladies to know these things." I opened my mouth to protest, but realised I would learn far more if I pretended to be merely decorative.

The colonel went on. "You see, after the war, the native Arab fellows thought they'd like to have a hand in running their own country. But we know best, of course. They wouldn't have the first notion of how to manage their own affairs. So we settled with the French to divide things up amongst those of us who know what we're about. We Brits have taken the Transjordan and Palestine—the French have Syria and the Lebanon. We've split Mesopotamia between us, and there were a few Turkish bits left over for the Russians. Best to keep them quiet, although one certainly cannot say they've conducted themselves like gentlemen," he finished, going rather red in the face.

I was appalled, as much because I hadn't known what was going on in the Levant as for what the colonel had told me. It all seemed horribly high-handed, but I knew I could never say as much to the colonel. He was far too convinced of the rightness of British imperialism.

He warmed to his theme. "And now the French don't seem to be able to handle the native fellows at all. This local lad, Feisal, has proclaimed himself king of Syria, and seems bent on throwing the French out altogether. Going to be a bit of a dust-up," he added, rubbing his hands together.

I smothered a sigh of exasperation. He was like a small, mischievous boy. He didn't mean anything malicious by it; he simply thought it was all good fun, like playing at toy soldiers. Rather an odd attitude for a man who had actually seen bloodshed, I thought with a shiver.

"And this is where we are going?" I asked pleasantly.

He reached over and patted my hand again. "Now, don't you worry, Miss March. I would never let you come to danger. I travel with my service revolver, you know."

I did know. The thing had accidentally discharged twice already, shattering a hotel vase and my nerves in the process.

"And young Talbot is a good man to know in a tight spot," he added.

"Is he?"

The colonel pitched his voice to a conspiratorial whisper. "Mentioned in dispatches during the war. Wasn't publicly decorated because his work was pretty hush-hush stuff, but he's the stuff heroes are made of."

My eyes were wide. "Do you mean he was a *spy*?"

My voice rose on the last word and the colonel looked around to make certain we weren't overheard.

"I can't say more. Even now it's all classified. But there were cloak-and-dagger goings-on, make no mistake about it. He's a fine lad," he added with a touch of emotion in his voice. "A fine lad." The colonel pulled out his large red handkerchief and blew his nose while I looked away tactfully.

He gathered up his composure and gave me a wink. "Don't you worry, my dear. We might be going where there's a bit of a dust-up, but he won't let you come to harm. And if it comes down to it, I've still got a bit of fight left in me, as well," he added with a determined nod.

I did not dare smile. "Thank you, Colonel," I said gravely. "That's very reassuring."

"I am a good man to know," he added without a trace of irony. "I have friends in the city, well-connected friends. The best of them is the Comtesse de Courtempierre. She's a house in the old part of the city, very historic and all that. We're to dine with her when we arrive in Damascus. No doubt you'll enjoy seeing a bit of local colour."

Being dragged about like a prize pet to visit the colonel's friends sounded about as enticing as an afternoon with Gerald's mother, but I had no choice in the matter. I merely smiled and said it sounded ripping, and the colonel turned back to his newspaper.

The train journey ought to have been a short one. The distance on paper wasn't very great—I had traced it on a map with my fingertip. But I hadn't counted on the relaxed attitudes of easterners when it came to travel, and the afternoon was drawing to a close as we pulled into the station in Damascus. Long rays of sunshine slanted over the city, gilding the stone and causing it to shimmer on the flat plain. Mount Hermon, newly carpeted in soft green on its lower flanks, rose to snowy heights in the distance, and I could smell the mingled scents of freshly turned earth and fruit blossoms and smoke on the air.

When we stopped in the station, I handed Peeky over to Talbot and gave the colonel an apologetic look. "Terribly sorry, won't be a moment. I just need to visit the er—"

And since no gentleman would ever dare question a woman's intentions when she states a need for the "er—," the colonel simply waved me off with a gruff gesture and I hurried on to the ladies' retiring room. I didn't look back to see if Masterman followed me, but it would have been the most natural thing in the world for any lady disembarking from a long and dusty train journey to avail herself of the necessary facilities at once.

I brushed off my clothes as well as I could, washed my hands, and by the time I powdered my nose, she had joined me. She took off her hat and brushed her hair although I'd never seen her with so much as a strand out of place.

In a low voice I gave her the name of the hotel. "I've not dared make inquiries myself, but I'm sure you can find a single room there. Don't contact me directly. Just sit in the lobby wearing your blue hat if there's any trouble. If you wear your brown, I'll know all is well. We needn't speak."

"You're very cautious, miss," she said, shooting her cuffs.

"Yes, well, I suppose I could introduce you as an acquaintance from back home, but the less we're seen about together, the better," I reminded her. "How was your voyage?"

"Seasick," was the crisp reply. "Stayed in my cabin the better part of it, but once I got my sea legs, I managed well enough. Entered the shuttlecock tournament and won five pounds."

"Remind me not to play against you."

She smiled an enigmatic smile. "But better than that, I have found something that will put a smile on your face. Sebastian Fox is in Damascus."

I gaped at her. "Masterman, you're a witch! How did you find out?"

"I would like to say it was skill, but the plain truth it was the sheerest dumb luck. I spoke with one of the railway fellows. I told him I was supposed to meet up with my brother out here but that his letter with all of the details had gone astray and had he seen him? I described Sebastian and the fellow remembered him straight away. Said he had taken that very train not a fortnight before."

I gripped her hand. "I can't believe we've done it. We've actually tracked him here."

She gave a nod of satisfaction. "That we did, although it'll be the devil's own work to find him now, if you'll pardon my language."

I flapped a hand at her. "Piffle. We had the whole world to choose from and we followed him this far. We can certainly find him within the confines of a city. Just wait."

Her expression was doubtful, but she merely nodded. "I will begin inquiries at the hotel. I don't imagine it will be difficult to find the cafés the expats like to frequent. Perhaps he's been seen in one or two of those."

"Excellent plan. I'll settle in at the hotel and sniff out what I can. The colonel mentioned friends in Damascus. If any of them are in the diplomatic corps they might have an ear to the ground for new visitors. Shall we meet in a few days' time to exchange information?"

Masterman dived into her enormous handbag and pulled out a Baedeker guide to Palestine and Syria. In it she had already marked a page. "The Great Mosque, miss. It's one of the highlights of any traveller's visit to the city. No one will think it at all strange if you want to go there."

"Superb, Masterman, but why the mosque in particular? It looks enormous," I said, skimming the description of the place. It was not a simple mosque but rather a compound, holding the tombs of Saladin and John the Baptist, among other attractions. "We might have the devil's own time trying to find one another."

She gave me her cool, competent look. "Not in the ladies' corner," she said, pointing to a particular passage.

I nodded. "That will do very nicely. Two days. Shall we say midmorning? I must be getting on now before the colonel has an apoplexy."

I went to give her the guidebook, but she waved me off. "Keep it, miss. Study the maps. You might find it useful to know your way around a strange city."

I smiled. "Little you know. I've spent most of the voyage reading that very guidebook as well as half a dozen others. I'll wager I know more about getting around Damascus than any casual traveller has a right to."

"Good," she said, tucking the bag away with crisp efficiency. "You never know when such knowledge will come in handy."

We parted then, and I hurried to the colonel, full of apologies. He harrumphed a little and I trotted off after him. I glanced back only once to see Masterman emerging from the ladies' retiring room, her hat once more pinned securely atop her head, her capacious handbag in hand. And it gave me some comfort to know that I had a friend in the city. I hoped wherever he was, Sebastian knew he did, as well.

SEVEN

I trotted obediently behind as the colonel forced his way through the crowds and towards the waiting taxis. The languor of old age seemed to have fallen away from him. His steps were brisk and even his cane was used more often to prod people out of the way than to keep him from falling. I exchanged quick smiles with Talbot.

"He always gets like this when he travels," he told me, pitching his voice low for my ears only. "In England he seems to waste away, but when he gets abroad, he comes alive again."

"I can see why," I breathed. I had travelled before, rather frequently. But nothing about our trips to fashionable resorts had prepared me for the East. The station was teeming with people in all forms of native dress. There were Frenchmen neatly attired and Englishmen whose London tailoring put them to shame. There were Damascenes dressed in their native robes, and here and there a Bedouin with the customary headdress and long boots, eyes rimmed in kohl to prevent the desert sun from burning their eyelids. I could even see a Turk or two with their fezzes, remnants of an empire that had crumbled to dust in the last war, gambling on a German victory. The colonel had explained that now the Turks had only themselves to rule, their *vilayets* broken up and handed to the victors. Damascus had been the ripest plum of all. Since time immemorial it had been the great city of jasmine, the pearl of the desert, revered by Julian the Apostate as the "eye of the East" the jewel of many a conqueror's crown. This time it had been given to the French, but now the native Syrians were intent upon wrestling it back, and a sense of expectancy hummed in the air.

"Let's not linger," Talbot prodded. "I won't be easy until we get a feel for what's really happening here."

I turned to him in mingled alarm and excitement. "Surely you don't think they would turn on the English?"

His expression was grim. "I don't think anything yet. It's early days, and things could get ugly. I mean to be ready if they do."

With that he tucked a firm hand under my elbow and guided me out, into the waning sunlight and the city beyond. The taxis were assembled haphazardly, but with a good deal of arm waving and shouting the colonel finally managed to make himself understood. His Arabic was nonexistent and his French execrable, but he resorted to the time-honoured tactic of waving bits of money around and suddenly things began to happen. We were bundled into a taxi with the baggage slung onto the back, held with ropes and dumb good luck. The driver was free with his horn and freer with his hands, gesturing wildly as he shouted abuse at pedestrians and donkeys and other drivers.

In spite of the chaos, it somehow worked, and within a remarkably short period of time we had arrived at our hotel. Once the palace of a Turkish pasha, it had been taken in hand by a Frenchman with exquisite taste and piles of money. He had retained all that was best of the East and added sufficient comforts that even the most exacting westerners would find nothing to complain of. Only the plumbing was a bit temperamental, but I certainly didn't have the heart to fuss—not when my view was of the old city, minarets and tiled roofs and gardens thick with oleander and bougainvillea, shimmering under the setting sun. As I stood in the open window, I could hear the call of the *muezzin,* summoning the faithful to prayer. Allah was good, Allah was merciful. And I was in the heart of it all.

After wrestling a bit with the uncooperative taps, I finished my toilette and descended to the lobby. In the corner I saw Masterman, hair tucked neatly under her hideous brown hat, reading a newspaper. She did not look up as I passed, and I breathed a little easier knowing all was well with her as I went to meet the colonel. Talbot had done him proud, dressing him in his evening best without a speck of dust or stray hair of Peeky's to ruin his grandeur. Masterman had insisted upon packing two evening gowns for me, and I had reached for the more stylish of the two—a straight-sided frock of peacock silk embroidered with a feather motif. A fringe of feathers floated about my knees, tickling my legs. It was a dress for making mischief, and the colonel saluted me smartly when he saw it.

"Very pretty indeed," he assured me. "Now, I know you're bound to feel a mite out of your depth with the *comtesse,* but don't let that put you off. You look quite fetching, my dear, and it wouldn't be suitable for you to try to ape a lady of her sophistication."

I smiled, wondering what the colonel would say if he knew the dress I was wearing had cost twenty guineas or that my youth had been spent reconciling the various demands of *Debrett's* and the *New York Social Register* for arranging seating at Mother's dinner parties. Clearly Cubby had given him a highly edited account of my past if he thought dinner with a mere *comtesse* would put me off my game.

The *comtesse* had sent her own car and driver for us, and if they were any indication, we were in for a treat. Both were luxurious and highly polished, and I wondered if the driver's few minutes of tardiness could be put down to having stopped to wipe it clean. I scraped my shoes carefully as I stepped into the pristine interior.

"I am Faruq," the driver told us. "I am at your disposal while you are in our city."

The colonel gave a nod of satisfaction. "That's Sabine for you," he told me with a finger to the side of his nose. "Madame la Comtesse de Courtempierre. She's half-Damascene—her mother was a rare beauty, a rare beauty indeed," he said with a touch of wistfulness. "And her father was French, a member of the Castries family. Sabine married another Frenchman, but he's been dead twenty years. She came back here to her mother's people, but she lives as a European. For the most part," he added.

I was eager to meet our hostess, and as the car wended its way through the teeming streets, it occurred to me that a quiet private home might come as a welcome change. Damascus was not the easiest city to navigate, but Faruq did an admirable job of it. We passed through the merchant quarter and into a more peaceful residential area in the suburbs. This was where wealthy Damascenes had built their homes for generations, away from the din of the *souks*. The streets were lined with thick walls pierced here and there with ornamental gates and laden with tangled vines of jasmine. The walls gave away no secrets, and it was not until one of the gates opened and the car glided inside that I realised just how remarkable the houses were.

We drove into a large court paved with stone and surrounded on three sides by buildings. One of these was clearly an old stable, now refitted to house the motorcar, although I could just see the top of an ornate old carriage tucked away inside. The other two buildings were wings of the house: one for servants, the other, taller and more lavishly decorated, for the family. The colonel clearly knew his way, for he went directly to a wide double door that stood open, spilling warm golden lamplight over the paving stones. We passed through an arch and into another court, but this one was not plain and serviceable like the entry court. It was grand and imposing, with galleries on four sides whose tall arches overlooked a fountain that shimmered and danced in the light of dozens of glass lamps. Endless pots of flowers and herbs filled the courtyard, perfuming the air thickly, and here and there long stone divans had been fitted with silken cushions to make comfortable places to rest. Gilded birdcages hung from the arcades and tall stands of beautifully wrought iron, and each was filled with an assortment of songbirds, twittering amongst the leaves.

"Rather nice, what?" said the colonel.

"It's magnificent," I told him truthfully.

"I am so glad you like it," said a woman's voice, low and musical. A figure that had been sitting in the shadows of one of the jasmine vines rose and came towards us. "Cyril, how good to see you again," she said, holding out her hands.

The colonel took them in his, clearly delighted to be in her company, and I could well see why. I don't know what I had expected, but when the colonel told me his friend was a widow of twenty years, I could have been forgiven for thinking she would be white-haired and stooped.

This woman was a vision. Straight as an oak and very nearly six feet tall, she carried herself with the posture of a queen. But her exquisite carriage was the least of her attractions. She was, quite simply, the most beautiful woman I had ever seen, and even that word does not do justice. Beauty suggests mere perfection of face and form, but the *comtesse* had something more—an indefinable elegance and purposefulness to her gestures that made me feel positively bovine in comparison. She was dressed in flowing Eastern robes of dark emerald silk figured in gold, no doubt of local origin. The Damascene looms were some of the finest in the world, and she had made good use of them. Her arms were loaded with slender gold bangles, and a tangle of chains and pendants lay on her breast. She wore a light veil of sheer gold gauze, and even that was held in place with two dainty pins of gold. In spite of her height, she gave the impression of delicacy and grace, and she was the most marvelous creature I had ever seen.

I hated her on sight.

It wasn't mere feminine vanity at work. The beauty, I could see, was only skin-deep. The eyes that looked into mine were fathomless and cold, and the hands that reached for me gripped me so hard the bones ached.

"This must be the charming Miss March of whom I have heard so much," she said, smiling. But the smile did not reach her eyes, and I wondered how I could possibly have made an enemy of her so quickly.

Just then, a passing breeze lifted her veil and I could see the first suggestion of softness at her jaw and a faint webbing of lines at her eyes. The goddess was aging, then, and I understood exactly why she disliked me. She was obviously fond of the colonel, and if she had any designs on him at all, it must rankle for him to turn up with a companion in tow—a companion young enough to be his granddaughter.

I smiled widely to put her at ease. "*Comtesse*. You have such a beautiful home."

She spread her arms. "And you must consider it open to you for the duration of your stay in Damascus. All that I have I share with my guests. It is the way of the East. And now you must meet my son."

She turned and beckoned with a graceful gesture. A shadow detached itself from the leafy corner of one of the galleries and glided forward. As he came into the light, I gulped audibly. If I had thought Talbot was handsome, he was nothing compared to this beautiful boy. But he wasn't a boy, I realised as he came near. He was a man, fully grown, but with the slender grace of David walking out to meet Goliath. There was an air of beautiful tragedy about him, and I saw his mother's eyes linger on him with unmistakable pride. She had a right to be proud, I thought. Any woman would have been happy to claim him.

He inclined his head to greet the colonel, but when he came to me, he reached for my hand, bowing low from the waist and letting a single lock of black hair tumble over his smooth brow. I don't remember giving my hand to him, but when he rose, he held it between both of his as if it were a trapped bird—lightly, gently, just a whisper of his lips against my fingers before he brushed his thumb across my pulse and released it.

He was smiling. He had felt the rush of my blood under his thumb and he knew exactly what it meant. "Miss March. We have heard so much about you. Welcome to our home. I am the Comte de Courtempierre, but you will please call me Armand."

I nodded. It was the most I could manage, and he smiled again as he turned away.

We settled into one of the alcove divans for a drink before dinner. The *comtesse* might have been half-Damascene, but she was clearly not a devoted Muslim. She served a spectacularly good wine, sweet and golden, and I held it up to the lamp-light in admiration.

"It is from Syrian grapes," the *comtesse* told me loftily. "From our country estate. If you like it, you must permit me to make you a gift of a case."

"That's too kind of you," I demurred.

"Nonsense," she said, dismissing my objection with a wave of her hand. She had a way of brushing my conversation aside as if I were a tolerable nuisance, and as the evening progressed, it amused me to see how easily she combined graciousness with superiority.

The *comte* was a different matter altogether. "This is your first time in Damascus, Miss March?" he asked. "You must have a long list of sights you wish to see."

"Indeed," I said promptly. I had made a list of such places during the voyage as I pored over the maps and tour books.

"In that case," he said, his tone suddenly silky, "you must permit me to guide you."

He was lounging subtly against the cushions, his pose relaxed, and I wondered if he always looked as if he had just stepped from a sculptor's plinth.

But he came by the theatricality honestly. His mother raised her arms just then to bid us to the table, lifting them with all the grace of a pagan priestess summoning her acolytes.

It was only the four of us at dinner. The *comtesse* and her son seemed to live alone. I didn't ask what happened to the previous count, and no one volunteered. The atmosphere was strangely charged, with odd undercurrents, unspoken conversations that seemed to eddy and swirl around me without ever settling.

The *comtesse* looked often at her son, her eyes resting on him with great fondness. But her gaze sharpened each time she turned it on me, and I wondered then if she disliked all young women or only those to whom her son showed particular favour. Armand's attentions were marked, and if it hadn't been

.

for the graceful combination of Eastern customs and French ways, I would have been embarrassed. He pressed each dish upon me, insisting I try everything, and even sent back the second bottle of wine, ordering a better one to be uncorked for my pleasure. He talked smoothly of anything he thought might interest me—fashion and music mostly—while the *comtesse* picked at her food and the colonel ploughed through several courses with diligence.

At last the strange meal drew to a close. "Come," said Armand, rising from his cushion with practised ease. "I wish to show you the fountain court by moonlight. I think you will find it very lovely."

I turned to the colonel, but he flapped a hand, his lids heavy. "Yes, yes. You young people ought to stick together. The *comtesse* and I will only be talking about old times and that's never amusing for others."

The *comtesse*'s eyes narrowed and her son gave her a dazzling smile. "Just for a little while, *maman*."

His mouth twitched as he said the words, and in spite of herself, she returned the smile. "As you wish, *chou*."

"Cabbage," I murmured as we made our way out to the court. "Your mother calls you *cabbage*."

Armand spread his hands in a particularly Gallic gesture. "She still thinks of me as a child. But what can a man do?"

He asked the question lightly, and he expected no answer. He walked me to the center of the court where the fountain stood, the water trickling peacefully over the stones making a sort of music of its own. The birds were still twittering in their cages, but sleepily now. A long tendril of jasmine snaked overhead and the blossoms were white and starry against the dark, glossy green of the leaves. I pinched one off and a cloud of perfume rose, sweet and sensual.

"It's an aphrodisiac, you know, the flower of the jasmine

vine. My mother's people are from Grasse, where the purest jasmine is grown for perfumes. And in those legendary flower fields where the most beautiful French perfumes are born, the farmers refuse to let their virgin daughters into the fields when the jasmine is ripe for fear they will be lost to sensuality."

Armand was looking at me intently, the beautiful mouth curved into his habitual half-smile. It was as much a part of him as the Eastern clothes he wore, but it suddenly occurred to me that it seemed affected. That the lips smiled, but something darker and more secret lay behind and unrevealed.

Just then a bird called sharply and I realised I had crushed the blossom to bits in my palm. Armand turned my hand over and brushed the bruised petals from my skin. He lifted my hand, pressing his nose into my palm and inhaling deeply.

"Ah, the perfume of jasmine mingled with the skin of a woman. What could be more intoxicating? Have you heard of the golden peaches of Samarkand? So luscious is this fruit that the Emperor of China sent men across all of Asia to fetch them. They are blushing and sweet and delicious," he said.

As he spoke, his finger stroked the back of my hand in tiny circles, almost unconsciously. I breathed in sharply and he grinned, baring his teeth in something that was almost but not entirely a smile. He flicked his eyes to the left. "Do you see that staircase, little flower? That leads to the *harim*. It was there that my ancestors kept the most beautiful, the most delectable women. It was there that they engaged in the most exquisite of pleasures. Would you like to see it?"

I squared my shoulders and gave him a friendly smile as I stepped away. "I think not, but it's darling of you to ask."

His jaw went slack in astonishment, and then he threw back his head and laughed, suddenly more natural than he had been all evening.

"My God, you English girls do not disappoint! How you

have wounded my *amour propre*," he said, giving me a look that was half-admiring.

"Come now," I said briskly, "does that really work? The moonlight and the jasmine and the songbirds?"

He stroked his chin. "More often than you would think."

"Shame on you! And in your mother's house."

He dropped a friendly arm around my shoulders, and this time I did not sidle away. "Forget what I said before. My mother knows that I am a man—a man who likes beautiful things."

I rolled my eyes. "I am not a thing, Armand."

He dropped his arm, putting his hands in front as if to ward off a blow. "How you wound me with your misunderstanding! It is as if you do not wish for us to be friends."

"Of course I'd like to be friends. My employer is a very close friend of your mother, and I am sure we will see quite a bit of one another whilst we are in Damascus. It would be awkward if we were uncivil."

"Uncivil! Oh, how I love the English. I could teach you a warmer word than that," he said with a playful leer.

"I have no doubt. But I'm long practised in the art of fending off unwanted advances," I warned him.

He dropped his head so that his lips barely skimmed my ear. "Oh, I intend to make you want them."

In spite of the warmth of the evening, I shivered a little. There was something almost menacing in his words, in the long, slow stroke of his fingertips as they brushed over my arm, raising gooseflesh in their wake.

"I think it's time we rejoined the others," I managed, slipping away from him.

Behind me, he laughed in the shadows but did not follow. I smelled the mossy, greenish scent of the fountain water as I passed, and beeswax and hot metal from the lamps, but always afterwards it was the smell of jasmine that conjured that strange night for me in the fountain court and my first meeting with Armand.

The next morning I rose and washed and presented myself at breakfast to find the colonel sitting alone with a stack of newspapers and a pot of coffee. An empty basket still held a few crumbs of bread rolls, and as soon as I arrived, the waiter whisked the empty basket out of sight and brought fresh rolls with a pot of quince jam and coffee.

The colonel looked up from his newspapers in disgust. "It's vile stuff, that coffee. Turkish and thick as honey. Full of grit, too," he warned me. I slathered a roll in jam and bit into it. Heaven.

"What do you mean to do today, Colonel?"

He tossed aside a newspaper and retrieved another, skimming the headlines with a distracted air. "Hmm? Tour of the city. Always best to get the lay of the land, so to speak, as soon as one arrives. A spot of sightseeing is just the thing."

"What do you want to see?"

His woolly caterpillar eyebrows jerked upwards in surprise. "Not me, child. I've seen every hole in Damascus twice over. I meant you. The *comtesse*'s driver, the fellow with the bull neck—Fareeq? Whatever his name is. He's to take you and young Talbot around."

I said nothing, wondering what had happened to Armand's plan of showing me the sights of Damascus. Perhaps he'd decided English *sangfroid* was not as attractive as he'd initially thought. Or perhaps he had business to attend to. Whichever, if I wondered about his absence that morning, Talbot most certainly did not. We settled ourselves into the *comtesse*'s plush motorcar with Faruq behind the wheel, and Talbot gave a sigh of relief.

"Thank God," he murmured. "I heard the little *comte* offered to take you to see the city and I have to say I didn't much like it."

I grinned. "The colonel's been telling tales out of school. But whyever should you mind? He's a lovely fellow."

"He's a cad," he said brutally. "He's trying to muscle in on you, and I don't care for it one bit."

I tried to lift a brow at him, but I think I only ended up wriggling it a bit. "Muscle in? You've seen too many pictures. You're talking like an American gangster."

He shrugged. "I don't think much of him."

"He's very handsome," I teased.

Talbot was in no mood to joke, but he must have realised then how grim he was being. He covered my hand briefly with his own and gave me a dazzling smile. "Forget it. I just think, well, you know what I think. And I can't say I like other men thinking the same thing about you. Although I do certainly understand it."

I pulled my hand away gently. "Let's forget all about the count and enjoy ourselves, shall we?"

"I would enjoy myself more if you could bring yourself to call me Hugh," he suggested. "Not when anyone else is around, of course, but like this. When we're alone."

I nodded towards the back of Faruq's head. "Not quite alone."

"You know what I mean," Hugh said in a conspiratorial whisper. I knew exactly what he meant. Faruq was a servant, and as such, didn't matter. It was a curious attitude for a valet to take, but if anyone understood the way things worked, it would be Hugh. A superior servant like a valet or lady's maid or driver saw everything and talked about nothing, at least that was the expectation. I could call Hugh by his given name or even let him put his arm through mine and Faruq wouldn't care.

But as tempting as it was to stroll arm in arm with Hugh, hanging on to his firm muscles, I resisted. It was a foreign country, after all, and we were representing England in a fashion. I knew the customs of Syria were different; here the women went veiled and walked sedately behind their menfolk. And in motorcars, the women sat apart. It seemed prudent to respect their ways as far as I understood them, and so I walked a few feet apart from Hugh most of the time as we trotted obediently after Faruq.

He was a fount of information, all of it delivered in a plain monotone. He was an enormous, muscled fellow, with a neck as thick as a bull's, and wherever we parked, he looked around, giving threatening glances at any street urchins who dared to so much as look at the motorcar. Hugh and I took ourselves around the sights while Faruq stood guard, polishing the vehicle with a bit of chamois skin and the air of a fanatic. To my distinct pleasure, the tour included a visit to the Protestant cemetery to see the grave of Lady Jane Digby.

"How did you know I wanted to see this?" I demanded as Faruq negotiated with the caretaker to open the gate for us.

Hugh gave a modest shrug. "I saw you reading a book about her on the voyage out. I don't know much about her, but she seems your type of personality."

"I don't know whether to be flattered or insulted," I told him. The caretaker accepted the coins Faruq pressed on him and opened the gate, waving us through and pointing in the general direction we were to take. We picked our way carefully over the stones and stood at the foot of the simple granite slab. The top was marked with a cross and inscribed on the stone at her side were the words:

Jane Elizabeth Digby,
daughter of Admiral Sir Henry Digby GCB.
Born April 3rd, 1807. Died August 11th, 1881.

"It isn't enough," I said mournfully.

Hugh had come to stand at my elbow. "What isn't?"

"Such small words to hold such a large life. She was a force of nature," I told him. "And a famous beauty, the loveliest woman in Europe by all accounts. She was an English aristocrat and had four husbands and twice as many lovers, including the King of Bavaria. But her real claim to fame is that for the last thirty years or so of her life, she lived as the wife of a Bedouin sheikh, a Mezrab, one of the tribe who guard the desert between here and Palmyra."

"She married a native fellow?" he asked, his brows arching upwards.

I nodded to the pink slab of limestone at her feet. "It's a rock from Palmyra. And that is her real epitaph."

Hugh leaned closer to read aloud, "'Madame Digby el Mezrab.'"

He straightened. "Fancy that. All the English blokes to choose from and half of Europe and she ends up with a desert chieftain."

I tamped down a flicker of irritation. "He wasn't just a desert chieftain," I protested. "He was a very well-educated, highly respected fellow."

"If you say so." He gave me a grin. "But as far as these native chappies go, give me Saladin any day. He's one of the colonel's favourites, you know."

He clearly was not interested in the exploits of Lady Jane Digby, so I gave it up as a lost cause and picked up the thread of conversation.

"You're fond of the old fellow, aren't you?" I asked. "The colonel, I mean."

He shrugged. "In my way." He was modest, but I had seen how quick he was to jump to the colonel's side with a brandy flask when the old gent grew agitated and needed a bit of settling down. He was forever fussing with travelling rugs and water bottles and walking sticks, and I realised there was something terribly attractive about a man who could take care of others.

As if sensing my mood, he tucked a hand under my elbow as we left the cemetery. "Stay close, if you don't mind," he said quietly. "I told Faruq I thought we could walk just a bit, but I don't want you wandering too far afield."

"I thought it best if we kept our distance. We aren't related, after all. I wouldn't like to offend anyone. Besides, the city seems calm enough," I told him.

He shrugged. "For now. But it's a powder keg, Poppy. The slightest spark will set it off and there will be hell to pay. And they won't mind us walking together. They don't expect us to abide by the customs. They know we're different."

We wandered into a neighbouring *souk*, where I was entranced to find a scene straight out of ancient history. As they had for centuries, merchants and craftsman created and sold their wares here, everything from silks to spices, although I was later to learn that each trade had its preferred *souk*. The markets were crowded with people and animals, and the noise was staggering. Canopies of silk and wool had been tacked overhead to provide shelter from the sun, and the twisting streets and alleyways doubled back on one another in a labyrinthine sort of configuration. As closely as I had studied my maps, I only had the general outline of the main streets. The narrow alleyways of the *souks* were hopeless. We walked for some time, before deciding to turn back to the motorcar and

Faruq. I had not paid much attention to the direction we took, but we wound through a few rather unsavoury passages, and after a moment or two I was rather certain Hugh was lost.

"Of course I'm not," he said testily. "I just thought we'd go back another way. Get a bit of local colour."

I smiled to myself. No man ever admitted he was lost, and I had just resigned myself to an afternoon of sore feet and worn shoe leather when a beggar loomed out from the shadows.

He was sinister looking, with his robes streaked with filth and a long, twisting scar that started at his brow and puckered his eyelid, scoring his cheek almost in two. I felt my stomach churn at the sight of him, and one soiled hand reached out as he gabbled something at me. He moved closer still and I could see only one disgusting foot peeping out from under his robe as he leant heavily on his stick.

He made a beckoning motion with his hand, asking for alms, and I thrust a hand into my pocket to find him a coin.

"For God's sake, don't," Hugh said, gripping my elbow tighter. "You'll only encourage him."

"He's lame, Hugh. What greater encouragement does he need to beg in this part of the world?" I pressed a coin into the beggar's hand, and he began to recite some sort of verse or prayer of thanksgiving. I gave him a quick nod and made to step around him, but he reached out with one wretched hand and closed it about my wrist.

I gasped, but he stared into my palm and pressed a dirty fingernail to one of the lines there. He said another word, a word I did not understand, and repeated it urgently.

Hugh raised a hand in warning and the fellow cowered, cringing away. His one sandal flapped against the stones as he left us, his walking stick scraping slowly. Hugh turned to me.

"Are you all right? The villain didn't hurt you, did he?"

"Don't be silly. He only touched my hand."

Hugh took out his handkerchief and scrubbed at my palm. When he was finished, he bent and pressed a swift kiss to it, his lips brushing so lightly over the skin I almost could have imagined it. He straightened with a smile. "All better now."

"Thank you."

Hugh had wiped my palm clean, but for a long time after I could feel the beggar's fingers on mine.

EIGHT

We returned to the hotel to find matters in a bit of an uproar. The colonel's leg had given out as he had been coming down the stairs for luncheon, and he had taken a tumble. Nothing serious, he insisted, but he would keep to his bed for the next few days with the leg wrapped and propped on a pillow.

"A good chance to work on the memoir," I said brightly, cursing the bad luck that had laid him low. I was meant to meet Masterman the following day, and it seemed I should be stuck in the hotel instead, shackled to the typewriter or playing games of chess to amuse the colonel.

But he waved me off. "Can't possibly concentrate with this leg wrapped up. Itches like hellfire, pardon the expression. No, you go out and amuse yourself tomorrow. See more of the city."

I tried to hide my elation, but I was turning cartwheels in my head. "That's very kind of you, Colonel."

He waved me off. "Talbot will stay here and look after me. But mind you take Faruq. Talbot told me there was a bit of trouble in the *souk* today. You'll need someone sturdy to look after you."

I suppressed a sigh. Of course Hugh had told him.

"That really isn't necessary," I began. I was not entirely pleased at the idea of a bodyguard.

There was a flutter of silk in the doorway and the *comtesse* entered the room, apparently having heard the tail end of our conversation. I hadn't realised she was hanging about, but I supposed it made sense that she should call upon the colonel since he was too indisposed to visit her.

"But how unfortunate that you should have such an experience in my city. I feel responsible," she said, her eyes wide with outrage. "No, the dear colonel is quite right. You must take Faruq with you. I am only bereft that Armand cannot accompany you. Unfortunately, his business will detain him further, I am sorry to say."

She didn't look sorry in the least. In fact, she looked extremely satisfied with the situation, like a sleek cat with a plump fish to eat. She took a seat as a little maid brought in a tray with a pot and two cups.

"White coffee," she murmured to the colonel. "I ordered it special from the hotel kitchen. Made from cardamom and very soothing." She poured out the two cups and looked pointedly from the pair of them to me.

I didn't miss the hint. "I'll just be going then, Colonel."

He waved me off and I left. It was late afternoon, almost evening, and I decided to go and read for a little while in the lobby. I found the stack of newspapers the colonel had been reading and helped myself. I settled down on a bench near the fountain, listening to the pleasant music of the water as I read.

Much of it was old news, for the situation in Damascus seemed to change almost daily. But one story caught my eye.

Famed Aviatrix Found Alive. Aviatrix Evangeline Merryweather Starke, who had disappeared into the Syrian desert a few weeks before, had been recovered. She had returned to Damascus after her exotic adventure, and refused to comment on her experience except to say that she had got herself lost when she wandered away from an archaeological site she was visiting and had been cared for by the Bedouin.

A photograph accompanied the article, a publicity picture of Mrs. Starke. She was not, strictly speaking, beautiful. She had strongly marked brows and a mouth that was too wide to be a fashionable little Cupid's bow. But her eyes were strikingly beautiful, and she looked as if she knew how to wring the most out of life. I felt a frisson when I looked at the picture, the same as I had felt when I had disembarked at Beirut, and then I realised why.

I had been reading the story of her disappearance the morning after I had run away. I had dropped the newspaper when Sebastian came in, and it was when he spotted the headline that his face had gone white. He had covered it smoothly, but it was that moment that he began to excuse himself and explain he must return to London.

Was Evangeline Starke the reason he had come to the Holy Land? Was he somehow mixed up in her disappearance? I scoured the article for clues, but there was nothing else of importance. I learned that she was a widow, her husband having been the famed explorer and archaeologist Gabriel Starke, lost in the *Lusitania* disaster just a few months after their marriage. The article mentioned her war work and how she had learned to fly from the pilots she nursed in a convalescent home in England. After the war, she had embarked upon a Seven Seas tour, flying her aeroplane across the seven seas of antiquity. During the tour, she had taken the opportunity to visit Damascus and expressed an interest in seeing a proper archaeological expedition—no doubt a relic of her husband's influence. It was rather sweet, really, the fact that she was still interested in archaeology five years after her husband's death.

But there was nothing else. No hint of scandal or intrigue or anything else that might bring Sebastian dashing down to Syria upon learning of her disappearance. And it was ridiculous to think her story could have provoked him to come, I reasoned. Evangeline Starke was famous and there had been people out searching for her. Surely, even if they were friends, Sebastian's best course was to remain in London, where he would be easily accessible by wire or telephone to hear the latest news. Haring off to Damascus himself was something only a lover would do....

I sat back in the chair, feeling suddenly quite bloodless. Her lover. That would explain everything. If he were in love with the dashing Mrs. Starke, it made perfect sense that he would throw all else aside and rush to find her.

"Oh, Poppy, you utter fool," I muttered. Why hadn't I considered before the possibility that Sebastian might be in love with someone? "He just can't be," I said firmly. "I won't believe it until I hear it from his own lips." I was determined to find him, but for the first time in the course of my adventure it began to occur to me that Sebastian Fox might not want to be found.

By the next morning my usual high spirits had returned, and I couldn't wait to tell Masterman what I'd discovered. I dashed through breakfast to be on my way and found Faruq waiting for me by the motorcar.

I gave him a broad smile. "Hello, Faruq. Lovely day, isn't it?"

He gave me a slow blink in return and opened the door. "Where shall I take you, miss?"

"The Umayyad mosque, please," I said, brandishing my

Baedeker at him. "I wish to pay my respects to Saladin. Salāh al-Dīn," I corrected quickly. He gave a nod, content that I should think so highly of his countryman, and without another word he delivered me to the mosque. I scurried inside and took up a heavy black robe. It was expected of all women to go veiled into the holiest places of the mosque, and I draped myself in the rusty black head covering. There was ritual hand-washing and footwashing to be done as well, and by the time I reached the ladies' corner, it was quite late in the morning, and I was desperately afraid I had missed Masterman.

I sat for a long moment in quiet contemplation of the mosque. It was peaceful here, with the sound of trickling water from the fountains and the low voices of women in private conversation. I found it all quite tranquil and was just dozing off when I felt a sharp poke.

"Wake up, miss," Masterman hissed.

I rubbed my arm. "I wasn't asleep. And how on earth did you know it was me through all this?" I asked, nodding towards the encompassing black. If I hadn't heard her voice, I certainly should not have known the creature next to me as Masterman. She had adopted a far more conservative costume than I had, with a veil and robe that concealed everything except the smallest portion of her face, two round greenish-brown eyes made darker with the heavy application of kohl. She had even darkened her eyebrows.

"That's quite impressive. I think under the right circumstances, you might be mistaken for a native," I told her.

"I endeavoured to blend in," she told me with an air of satisfaction. "Tell me what you've discovered." I plunged into my story, telling her at once of what I had discovered in the old newspaper I had found.

"She's alive?" she asked sharply. "Well, that's unexpected."

"You know who she is?"

"Of course," she returned promptly. "I have followed her career with a great deal of interest. A great deal of interest indeed. I shouldn't have thought there was a connection with Sebastian Fox, though."

"But why not?" I reasoned. "They're both English, after all. And she worked in a convalescent home for pilots during the war. We don't know what Sebastian did in the war. He might have been a flyer. Or they could have met any one of a hundred other ways," I finished.

"I suppose they could," she said slowly. "And you think she might know something of his whereabouts now?"

"I certainly think she is connected to his coming here. It stands to reason he has made some effort to get in touch with her. Goodness, he might even be staying with her! For all we know, they're lovers."

She gave a short, sharp laugh, smothered by her veil. "I cannot see it."

I shrugged. "Neither can I. Evangeline Starke is so daring, so glamorous, and Sebastian is attractive enough, I suppose, but he's—" I broke off, not entirely certain of how to describe him.

"He is?" she prompted.

I struggled. "Well, he's quite good-looking really, didn't you think? In the right clothes he'd be downright handsome. If he were a character in *Peter Pan and Wendy*, he would be John—all seriousness and rectitude. He's jolly nice—I just think he's frightfully conventional. I suppose a curate must be. He could hardly get on in the church if he went about flexing his muscles."

"Hiding his light under a bushel," Masterman pronounced.

"Precisely. And that's hardly the sort of man to appeal to a daredevil like Evangeline Starke, particularly when you consider what her husband was. But I suppose the mysteries of the heart are entirely impenetrable," I finished in a cryptic voice.

"Quite," she said, clipping off the word. "Well, then I suppose I shall make inquiries on the whereabouts of Mrs. Starke. She shouldn't be difficult to find. I should guess every newspaper in the city would want to interview her about her experiences in the desert. Was that all, miss?"

I hesitated. "Not entirely. It hardly seems worth mentioning, but I suppose it's best if we share everything." Hastily, I told her about my experience of the previous day, and as I related the tale, there was an almost imperceptible change in her face. All I could see were those eyes, but they grew chillier and more forbidding as she listened to my story of the beggar in the *souk*.

"The East is a cunning place," she said slowly.

I sighed. "Masterman, it's no worse than any place in England. Tell me you could walk down by the docks in London and not be accosted by beggars."

"Yes, but I might at least understand what they are saying. Besides, there are no harems in London. You might have been stolen right off the street."

I rolled my eyes. "*Harims* are a Turkish invention, and in case you hadn't noticed, the Turks have been thrown out of here." I thought it best not to mention Armand's allusions to his ancestors' proclivities. I hurried on. "Besides, there might not be harems in London, but there are certainly brothels, and you cannot tell me they are better."

"A nice girl wouldn't know such things," she said darkly. "I wonder what that word was, the one the beggar said," she mused.

I shrugged. "I can't imagine."

"What did it sound like?" she persisted.

I closed my eyes, conjuring in my memory the smell of the

sun-warmed stone and the pungent scent of donkey and beggar. His hand had been firm but not painful on mine, and
there was urgency in his voice.

"Al mawt," I said suddenly, opening my eyes. "Or something like that."

Her eyes went very wide and she did not blink.

"What is it, Masterman? You look as if you'd seen a ghost."

She shook her head. "There's a little maid who cleans my
room at the hotel. We've got friendly, and as her English is
quite good, I have had her teach me a few words of the native lingo."

"And did she teach you that one?"

She nodded slowly. "Yes, miss." She paused. "It is the Arabic word for *death.*"

After a long moment I burst out laughing, then smothered
it immediately, remembering I was in a holy place. "Oh, Masterman, you can't seriously think it was a threat."

"No, miss. I think it was a warning."

"A warning of what? I know nothing about anything."

Her eyes hardened. "I think it means you do know something. I think it's about Mr. Fox."

"Oh, do be serious. First of all, no one could possibly con-
nect me with him. We have nothing whatsoever to tie us together except that he drove me down to Devon."

"We've been asking questions in London," she corrected.

I shrugged. "Then why weren't you the one who received
the frightful warning of Death? You've asked a far sight more
questions than I have. No, Masterman. It was a beggar, a sim-
pleton who wanted a bit of money."

"But why try to frighten you after you'd already given it
to him?" she demanded.

"Heavens, I don't know. Why does anyone do anything? I

already told you he seemed half-witted. He clearly wasn't in his right mind, that's all. There's an end of it."

"I don't like it," she said coolly. "Perhaps we should go home."

"Go home!" I was aghast. "Masterman, I see that this has shaken you, and I'm sorry. But do be sensible. We have no real connection to Sebastian, and there's no reason for anyone to be alarmed by the questions you've been asking. This was simply a poor beggar who amused himself at my expense. Now, get hold of yourself and let's have no more nonsense about going home."

She gave me an inscrutable look. "Very well."

I gave her a miserable look. "Don't be like that, Masterman."

"Like what, miss?"

"All po-faced and perfect. We agreed that for the duration of this trip, we're partners of a sort, not mistress and maid. Only now you've gone all distant and formal again, and it's not a bit of fun."

"Some things are more important than fun, miss," she said, unbending a little. "Your safety is one of them. I wonder if I haven't made a very grave mistake in letting you come on this lark."

"Letting me! I like that. I'm a grown woman," I reminded her. "I came on my own, with no one's permission. Let me, indeed. What a thing to say. Now, you start to work on finding out what you can about where Mrs. Starke has gone since she's been found. If we can locate her, perhaps we'll find Sebastian."

I could tell from the stiff way she carried her head she was not happy, but I ignored it. "Where shall we meet next?"

She motioned for me to take out the Baedeker, and flipped quickly to a map where she drew a small *X* with a pencil.

"That is a Turkish *hammam*, baths for women only. It won't be suspicious if you go in there without the driver or Mr. Talbot. Every tourist lady likes to take the baths there, and we can speak alone."

We set a date for our next rendezvous, and I put the Baedeker away as I rose. "Excellent work, Masterman. You may have a real talent for subterfuge," I told her.

"Thank you, miss," she said. But her voice was grim, and after I walked away, I turned back to find her still sitting on the bench, lost in thought.

As I emerged from the mosque, I saw Faruq standing next to the motorcar, chatting to someone. The *comte* turned as I reached them, a smile spreading slowly over his face.

"Miss March. I am enchanted."

"Hello, *Comte*."

"Armand," he said with a faint air of admonition. He was dressed in European clothes, the best Savile Row could supply, tailored to within an inch of indecency, and I wasn't surprised that heads turned as people walked past.

"Armand," I said slowly.

He extended his arm. "I am delighted that I have run you to ground. That's one of your English hunting metaphors, is it not?"

"It is," I said, taking his arm. "It's what the dogs do right before they tear the fox apart."

He gave me a look of mock horror. "What a terrible thing to suggest! No, Miss March, I can think of far better things to do with you if I had in mind to punish you. For example, you must lunch with me."

"I would hardly call that a punishment."

He smiled broadly, revealing beautiful even white teeth. "Only a few days in the East and already you have learned the art of the compliment."

"Surely the easterner doesn't have a monopoly on that," I argued. "The Frenchman must at least be his rival in the art of flattery."

"And I am both," he said, giving me a long look from under his thick lashes. "So you are doubly in danger."

He laughed then and waved me into the motorcar. Danger indeed.

We lunched at one of the fashionable, expensive hotels that had been built by French hoteliers since the war had dropped the city into their manicured hands. Like my own hotel, this one had once been a private residence.

"It used to be a palace," Armand told me, waving his arm in a gesture that sketched the whole of the beautiful dining room and beyond. "You can still see traces of the pasha's excesses."

"Pasha? So it was a Turk's palace?" I asked.

"The Turk held sway here for a long time," he replied. "But his day is done. It is time for the native Syrian to rule his own country."

"You support King Feisal, then?"

He did not answer as waiters scurried around, bringing glasses and plates full of tasty, costly morsels of beautifully crafted French food. There was nothing of the Levant here, no heaps of couscous and stewed meats studded with pomegranate and dripping with sauces. Instead we had cuisine straight from Paris, lobsters dressed in frills and drawn butter, and aspics with vegetables quivering inside like tiny museum specimens. It wasn't the sort of food I enjoyed, but the *comte* applied himself to it with enthusiasm. He ate beautifully, with delicacy and refinement, just as he did everything else. I looked at the elegant hands holding the heavy silver knife and fork and I wondered what else those hands did well.

As if he guessed my thoughts, Armand put down his cutlery and gave me an assessing look. "I owe you an apology. I thought you were just asking to be polite, but I believe there is more to you than I first anticipated. So I will pay you the compliment of a complete reply. I do not support Feisal. A king of Syria ought to be Syrian. Feisal is a Howeitat Bedouin."

"And the Howeitat are not Syrian?"

"No," he said, his face flushing a little with emotion. The colour crept slowly up his skin, touching first the smoothly shaven cheeks, rising up the sharp cheekbones until it crested them and passed onto the plain of his wide, unlined brow. "The Howeitat are Arabian. His father is the Sharif of Mecca, a very important position in the Islamic world, but not one calculated to find loyalty here. The Bedouin are not a single group, Miss March. They are like the Indians in America, tribes fractured by rivalries and warfare and blood feuds. They do not wish to be united, and even if they did, how is the Bedouin to understand his city-dwelling brother? It is like asking a fish to understand a cow. They are different species, and their language, their customs, their very values are not the same."

I mused over this while he returned to his aspic, spearing a bit of asparagus through the quivering jelly.

"And you don't think Feisal can unite them, not even for the chance at having their own country for the first time?"

He gave me a thin smile and patted his lips with his napkin. "My dear Miss March, he hasn't the slightest chance of success. The French will sweep him away like..." He paused then flicked a crumb from the table with his forefinger and thumb. "Like that."

"If you believe that, why are you here?" It was a bold question, but it did not displease him. Instead, he gave me a smile, perhaps the first authentic smile he had given me yet.

"Because there are fortunes to be made upon the backs of desperate men," he said simply.

He waved the waiter over to bring more champagne and I returned to my lobster.

While I ate, he talked on, telling me of his plans for building a villa outside the city. By the time they brought plates of mint sherbet, I found myself distracted, toying with my spoon.

Instantly, his mood shifted. He pushed away his plate and levelled a look at me that seemed calculated to provoke a reaction.

"Forgive me, Miss March. I have droned on about my plans, and you are bored."

"No, not at all," I said, almost sounding convincing.

He clucked his tongue. "I don't like liars," he said, drawing out the last word like a caress. "Remember, we did discuss my penchant for punishment."

I summoned a thin smile. "Really, I am sorry. I was just wool-gathering."

"It is I who should apologise. I have gone on and on about myself, but you must understand, it is only because I dare not say the things I would wish to say, the things I would say, if only—"

He broke off, his face twisted with emotion. I watched as he mastered himself with what seemed an heroic effort. "As I said, I apologise. I have already said too much. Your employer is a friend of my mother's and you are a guest in our country. I would not violate the laws of courtesy for anything, no matter how great the temptation," he assured me, his voice lingering again on the last word.

I blinked at him. As far as seductions went, it was masterfully done. He hadn't promised anything, hadn't revealed anything. In fact, he had made a point to tell me he *couldn't* promise anything. But the suggestion was there all the same. It was in his voice, the hands that rested, palms upon the table, supplicating. And it was in the eyes that rested warmly on my face. The eyes that never left mine as he waited for a response.

It was an almost perfect performance. If he could have mastered his mouth, I would have believed it. But the little half-smile still tugged at his lips, and I knew this was nothing more than a gambit in a game.

Well, if seduction really was on his mind, he'd be vastly disappointed if I capitulated now, I reasoned.

I gave him a wide smile. "Think nothing of it, *comte*," I said brightly. "I promise you, I won't."

With another little prick to his *amour-propre*, he conceded the field. He gave me a gracious nod and summoned the waiter to bring the bill.

NINE

That evening after dinner, I pleaded a headache and excused myself early. Dinner had been served on trays in the colonel's room, and the atmosphere had been stuffy. The truth was, the colonel and the *comtesse* seemed entirely happy to be left alone, and I wondered if a budding love affair was in the offing. It seemed only tactful to leave them to it, and so I excused myself and went to my room. But it was no night to be alone. I opened the shutters. It was a glorious night, the sort made for lovers and thieves, and I stood at the window for a long time, smelling the heady scent of the jasmine that bloomed under my window.

The scent clung to my skin and I walked out onto the balcony that joined my room with the others, restless in the soft night. I heard the *muezzin*'s call to prayer and somewhere a Christian church's bells chimed the hour. It was very late, and a cloud crossed the moon, throwing the balcony into heavy shadow. The songbirds in the courtyard below had tucked their heads under their wings and gone to sleep, but I heard a soft sound that might have been a dove coo. A frisson of awareness shivered my skin. For just a moment I fancied I was not alone. I opened my mouth to call a name, but stopped. I was letting the moon and the heady fragrance play havoc with my common sense, I told myself firmly. There was no one in the shadows. I went to my bed then, leaving the shutters open to the jasmine-scented night, but I did not sleep. Not for a very long time.

The next morning, the colonel dictated a chapter of his memoirs, reciting endless details about the First Boer War until I wanted to scream with boredom. I considered faking a faint, but just as I put the back of my hand to my brow, a better notion occurred to me.

"Colonel," I said quickly. "I do hate to interrupt you— really, it's all been *most* interesting, but I must get on with the typing soon and I've just remembered the typewriter needs a fresh ribbon. Do you suppose there's a stationer's shop or something where I could find one?"

The story was the rankest lie. I had changed the ribbon only the week before. But it was as good an excuse as any, and he nodded.

"Yes, yes, of course" he said, waving a hand. "Bound to be one. You must ask Talbot to go with you," he added slyly, and I wondered, not for the first time, if he were deliberately playing the matchmaker.

I gave him a prim smile and tamped the pages of notes and tucked them away. In spite of the colonel's attempt to throw us together, I was rather glad of a little time to myself and slipped out of the hotel alone. Damascus was teeming with life, perhaps more so than any city I had ever seen. A quick chat with the hotel porter had provided the address of the stationer's shop, and I made my way there on foot, taking in the sights and smells as I walked. A vendor in the street sold kebabs, the meat juicy and succulent and wafting the most extraordinarily delicious aromas, while others hawked cooling sherbets or roasted nuts. A pack of small boys chased a stray dog past a woman who sat on the kerb, crafting paper roses with nimble fingers. I stopped for a moment to watch. Her hands were gnarled but somehow supple, moving swiftly to transform a square of rough paper into something beautiful if fleeting. She scented each with a mist of rosewater, just to heighten the illusion. Behind her, the doors of a local coffee house had been thrown open, and the noise of friendly arguments—in French and Arabic and Turkish—spilled out into the street. I stood a moment longer before I felt a light touch on my shoulder.

I turned to find Armand looking down at me with rueful amusement. "Miss March, what a delightful surprise to find you out and about in my city."

I lifted a brow. "Is it a surprise?"

To his credit, he laughed. "Not at all. Faruq delivered me to your hotel just as you left. I saw you ask the porter for directions. It took only a very small coin to ask him where he sent you."

"And now you have found me."

"That I have." He indicated the direction of the shop. "Will you permit me to escort you to the shop?"

I felt a flutter of irritation. I was vastly enjoying my time alone, but I couldn't very well insult a connection of the colonel's. "Oh, I couldn't ask you to disarrange your day on my behalf," I said.

"But it is the greatest pleasure," he assured me.

He took my elbow and we began to walk. "Tell me, Miss March, what do you think of my city?"

"I like it," I told him truthfully. "Very much."

"Is it so? But it is very different to London," he said.

I darted a look at him, wondering for one mad instant if

he knew my real identity, but his face betrayed nothing. He had not mentioned New York, I reminded myself, and if he'd known the name Penelope Hammond, he would have.

He was waiting for a response, and I smiled. "Very different, and that's what I like. London is very polite and beautiful, of course, but Damascus is full of life and so colourful."

"You are very kind," he murmured. "Ah, here is the shop."

He gestured for me to go inside, but did not follow. "I will await you here, unless you would care for some assistance in making your purchase?"

"No, thank you," I replied. I pushed my way into the shop, pleased to find it was a wonderful mixture of old and new. There were beautiful marbled papers, so thick and lovely it would have been a crime to write upon them. Wide shelves held finely-tooled leather blotters of every description with portfolios and cases. Another set of shelves held bottles of ink, shimmering like dark jewels in the dim, cool light of the shop. I paused to admire them and the proprietor approached.

"*Assalam aleikum, mademoiselle.* Good day to you," he said.

He was an elderly gentleman, bald as an egg but with a luxuriant beard and eyebrows even more lavish than the colonel's.

"*Aleikum assalam,*" I returned.

He broke into a wide smile. "Your accent is very good, but you are not a speaker of Arabic, I think."

"You've just heard the only two words I know," I confessed. "I'm very glad you speak English."

"But of course, *mademoiselle,*" he said gravely. "It is a courtesy to my customers. Will you permit me to show you my shop?"

He took me on a tour then, pointing out the beautiful pens from France, the exquisite workmanship of the blotters—"Crafted here in Damascus by the finest leather workers, *mademoiselle!*"—and opened bottles of scented ink to waft under my nose. "Can you smell the rose in this one? And here, you must try this. It smells of violets, a favourite scent of Napoleon, you know," he advised as he held out a bottle of ink the colour of crushed blackberries.

"They're divine," I told him. "But I really only need a typewriter ribbon."

He spread his hands. "Yes, this I have, but first you must be cared for. Tea, *mademoiselle*," he pronounced. He made a quick click of his tongue and a boy scurried out of the back room bearing a tray with a pot and two glasses. The proprietor gestured towards the corner of the shop, where he had arranged a small seating area. "Here we will drink tea together," he told me as he plumped up a cushion for my comfort. The seating area was cosy and it afforded an excellent view of the street. I glanced out to see Armand standing, smoking a thin black cigarette. He looked as if he were brooding, and I turned to the proprietor with an apologetic shrug.

"It's so kind of you, but I'm not sure I ought to. You see, I have a friend waiting," I told him with a nod towards Armand.

The proprietor smiled. "Is he a Damascene?"

"Yes."

"Then he understands the proper way that things must be done," he informed me. He poured out the tea—mint and heavily sweetened. "You see, *mademoiselle*, it is very important that all things are civilised. You come to my business to purchase a typewriter ribbon. This is a small thing. I could give you the ribbon and take your money and it would be the matter of mere minutes. But I do not like this way. It is impersonal. Now you have seen my shop. You have been made comfortable and been given tea and a place to sit to refresh yourself. The boy will bring your ribbon when we have finished and I will send a bill later. This is civilised," he finished firmly.

"Very much so," I told him. "And if you're sure the gentleman won't mind—"

The elderly man's eyes twinkled. "It does not hurt a man to wait on a pretty girl."

He refreshed my tea then and we sat and talked for some time. He told me about his wife of forty years and his four sons—"Three of them are handsome and stupid. One is clever and has the face of a dog." He asked many questions about England in turn, and was particularly interested in Queen Mary. "I think she is a fine figure of a woman. She looks very like my wife," he told me, his eyes bright with amusement.

"Then you are a lucky man," I said in a slightly strangled voice. I had never heard anyone call Queen Mary a fine figure of a woman, but the old fellow was very kind and when we had finished our tea, he summoned the boy again and in a very few minutes the ribbon appeared, neatly wrapped in a paper parcel and tied with wax string.

"As you requested, *mademoiselle*," the proprietor told me, presenting it with as much ceremony as if it were a jewel.

"Thank you—" I hesitated. "I'm afraid I don't know your name."

He put his hand to his heart in a courtly gesture. "I am Mohammed, *mademoiselle*. And you are Mademoiselle March at the Hotel Palmyra," he recited. "You see, I remember. I am an old man, but I do not forget."

"And I won't forget you, *monsieur*. Thank you for a lovely introduction to your shop."

"You must come again," he said, bowing once more. He glanced out the window to where Armand had been standing. "And I was right. It has made your gentleman friend no trouble to wait. He has met an acquaintance," he pointed out.

I looked past him to see Armand in conversation with Hugh. The conversation did not appear entirely friendly. Ar-

mand was listening with a raised brow, his lips thin with irritation. But whatever Hugh said, it must have struck home,
for Armand finally lifted his hand in annoyance and made a
gesture as if to swat away a fly.

By the time I said goodbye to Mohammed and made my
way onto the street, they had smoothed things over. Hugh
was looking a trifle flushed, but smiled when he saw me, and
Armand was wearing his usual unruffled expression.

"My dear Miss March, I hope you found all that you required?" he asked.

"Yes, I'm terribly sorry to have kept you waiting for so
long," I began, but he brushed away my excuses.

"This is the gateway to the East, Miss March," he said
lightly. "All transactions take time. It would be uncivilised
to do otherwise."

"So I've been told. Hullo," I said formally.

Hugh inclined his head. "The colonel sent me to find you.
He seemed to think he'd instructed you to take me along on
your errand today and seemed a trifle put out to find you'd
left without me."

"Did he?" I asked, opening my eyes very wide. "How curious. I must have misunderstood." That excuse seldom worked
with Mother, but Hugh seemed pacified.

"Yes, well, now that I've found you, I've just been explaining to the *comte* that I was planning on taking you to lunch."

He gave the *comte* a defiant look as if daring him to object,
and Armand gracefully ceded the field. He bowed slightly to
me. "A charming notion. I can think of no finer luncheon
companion than Miss March, as I have reason to know," he
added with a touch of malice.

He lifted his hat and walked away without waiting for a
response.

"I do not like that fellow," Hugh said, his hands tightening into fists.

I tucked my hand into his elbow. "Never mind. I suspect you're just feeling irksome because you're hungry. I know I'm famished, and if you really mean to take me to lunch, the proprietor of the stationery shop suggested the most wonderful restaurant just around the corner. Come on!"

It was scarcely two minutes' walk to the restaurant, and I was a little surprised to find that we were standing in front of a shabby wooden door where a legless beggar held out a bowl.

Hugh gave me a doubtful look. "Are you quite certain about this?"

"Quite," I said firmly. "Mohammed's cousin owns it. It is a traditional restaurant, and he says it serves the most authentic luncheon in the city." I lowered my voice. "He also said to pay no mind to Selim, the beggar. Apparently, he is here every day. Mohammed said we're just to step over his stump." Hugh did exactly that, ignoring the fellow completely, but I managed to drop a few coppers into his bowl on the way in.

Hugh pushed open the wooden doors and I caught my breath. Beyond was a courtyard, very like the *comtesse*'s but even more magnificent, and past that was the restaurant, part of an extensive palace, but now serving patrons the most delicious food in Damascus, at least the owner insisted so. Mohammed had apparently sent word ahead that we were coming and the owner gave us a perfect table under the centre of a high golden dome. There were no proper chairs, but silken cushions scattered around, and I smiled as Hugh folded his tall body into something more compact.

He was graceful as an athlete, and too polite to notice my own struggles with a slim skirt. But I managed, and by the time I had arranged myself, he had already given in to the owner's insistence on bringing us his own choices.

What followed was one of the most memorable meals of my life. There was stewed meat of four different varieties, each heavily spiced, and couscous bejewelled with pomegranate seeds and heaped onto a platter. There were bowls of softly cooked vegetables and tiny savoury pastries, hot with spice and crisp. A succession of sweets followed, each more decadent than the last, ending with a bowl of rosewater sherbet with a pistachio sauce and biscuits made with anise served alongside strong coffee scented with cardamom.

"That was magnificent," Hugh said, patting his stomach with a sigh.

"I won't ever forget it," I agreed.

He touched my hand briefly. "I hope you won't forget anything about this trip," he said softly.

Before I could respond, he pulled his hand away, smiling a devilish half-smile. "Now, let's walk off this feast, shall we?"

We moved into the street where things were beginning to stir to life again. There was always a quiet period after the luncheon hour, but we had lingered so long with our coffee and biscuits that the merchants had returned to their shops and the artisans to their crafts. We wandered into a *souk*, and Hugh's hand stole into mine.

He paused by another old woman making paper flowers and bought me a rose. "There," he said in satisfaction. "A proper Damascene flower to wear in your lapel. May I?"

I let him pin it in place and took a deep whiff of the light rosewater scent. "I'll press it in a book of poetry tonight so I will always remember this day," I told him lightly.

He lowered his head so only I could hear. "I'd far rather you remembered it because it's the day you decided you couldn't live without me," he teased.

"Hugh, I—"

He shook his head. "Don't speak. Poppy, I know I am only a valet now, and I have no right to speak to you this way, but you must believe I am not what you think I am. Dash it all, I wish I could tell you the truth. No, don't ask it of me. It would mean putting you in the gravest danger, and I won't risk it. I can't talk about it now, but one day, one day very soon, I won't be a valet anymore. I hope then I can…well, dammit, a man can hope, can't he?" he asked, his expression pleading.

I had just opened my mouth to respond when I heard a shriek, and then a horrific commotion as one of the braziers where the coppersmiths worked blazed up and out of control. There were shouts in a dozen dialects and pushing and shoving as people tried to get out of the way. Smoke billowed through the *souk*, thick and choking, and I blinked hard, wiping soot from my eyes.

I peered through the cloud and realised I had lost sight entirely of Hugh. Before I could panic, there was a tug on my skirt.

"Miss! Your friend went this way," said a small boy, pointing towards a hole in the wall I had not noticed before.

I peered at it, but the smoke kept drifting into my face. I dug into my handbag for a handkerchief to wipe my eyes. They were streaming so heavily I couldn't see a thing, and the boy reached for my hand.

"Come, miss. Shall I show you?"

"Oh, yes, please!" He towed me along, through the narrow doorway and into what seemed to be another alley. Here the smoke was thinner, but my eyes still streamed and I allowed my little guide to navigate our way through the market.

"Are you sure this is where my friend went?" I demanded. We had walked for some time and I had seen no sign of Hugh. I had seen little sign of anyone, I realised with alarm.

"Miss has red eyes. I am bringing you to fountain so you may bathe them and they do not hurt," he told me solemnly.

"Well, that's kind of you," I managed. And just at that moment we turned into a small private courtyard where a fountain stood in the centre. He motioned for me to bathe my eyes, and I dipped my handkerchief into the water, pressing it to my face.

"I must look a fright," I began, but as I looked around, I grasped that my little guide had disappeared. I assumed he had gone to find Hugh and settled down to wait, but as the minutes ticked past, I began to understand I had been abandoned—left entirely alone in a place I could not hope to find my way out of.

"Oh, this is maddening," I muttered. Just then, I caught sight of something floating in the fountain. It was a little bird fashioned of paper, and as I watched, it floated near to me. I stretched out my hand for it, and it skimmed backwards, just out of reach.

But I forced myself to wait a moment, and the motion of the fountain pushed it back to me again. This time I waited until it was near enough to lift from the water, and to my astonishment, I saw that it was a bank note. A British bank note.

I unfolded it with trembling fingers. I was fluttering with excitement, and I was so persuaded I was on a great adventure, I wasn't entirely surprised to find a message scrawled upon it.

FOLLOW ME.

I jumped to my feet, peering around, and just at the edge of the court, deep in the shadows, I saw a flutter of a white robe disappearing around a corner.

I took to my heels, running hard to catch up. I hurtled around the corner blindly, and just as I rounded it, I saw a door closing. I yanked hard, and it opened. I dashed inside, only comprehending what I had done when the door slammed shut behind me, and I heard the sound of a bolt thudding home.

I was in a small room, deep in the heart of the *souk*. The shutters were closed tightly, and not even a sliver of sunlight penetrated them. The floor and walls were stone, and the room was bare save for a table and a single hard chair. The sole light was a bowl of oil with a rag for a wick, heavily shaded so that only a sliver of light shone around it. Feeble as it was, the light from it dazzled my sore eyes, and I scurried to put the table between me and the figure that had just bolted me inside with him. He wore native robes, with the traditional headdress pulled low over his brow. The end of the headscarf had been draped over his face and pinned in place, throwing his face into darkness. He wore only black, and the impression he gave was of a shadow come to life.

The shadow spoke in a low, rough voice, heavily accented in the Damascene dialect.

"Please, make yourself comfortable and sit."

I did as he told me for the simple reason that it didn't seem as if anyone advising me to make myself comfortable would be intent upon killing me—at least not immediately. I was afraid, of course. Anyone who had just been abducted in a strange country would be. But I was not bound or gagged, and the feeling I had from the shadow was not one of menace. In fact, there was something rather thrilling about it all, and I didn't stop at the time to think how unspeakably stupid it was to find it exciting. I was as bad as my Aunt Julia.

So I sat down and folded my hands in my lap.

"Do you think I might have a glass of water?"

"Not in this city," the voice said tartly. "Or haven't your travelling companions taught you anything?"

"You know Colonel Archainbaud? And Mr. Talbot?"

"I know all," said the shadow.

"Really? I doubt that," I said, thinking of Masterman and our quest to find Sebastian.

"I know that you have come to this city to seek something... someone to be precise. And I am telling you to seek no more."

I caught my breath sharply. "Why don't you want me to look for what I came for?" I demanded.

"Because there is no need. Your friend is safe and well and that is all you need know. He would send you his regards if he could."

"If he could! There, you see, he is not safe and well or he could speak to me himself."

The shadow made a little noise of exasperation. "It is not possible. He has business here and you must not interfere. It might be dangerous."

"I'm not worried about danger to me," I said proudly, tossing my head.

"I mean danger to him."

My hands fisted at my sides. "If you have harmed him, I promise you there aren't enough devils in hell to protect you from me," I swore.

The shadow laughed. "He is entirely unharmed. I give you my word, and in this city, my word is worth a great deal." He paused a moment. "But why should you care so much what happens to the Englishman you seek?"

"He—he is my friend," I said simply.

"Ah! So you have known him a very long time, then?"

"No, not exactly." I hesitated, suddenly understanding how utterly stupid it sounded to say it aloud. "We've only met once."

The shadow laughed again. "And yet you come all this way to seek him out?" He made a tutting sound. "The women of this country would scorn you for such unladylike behaviour."

"I don't care about being unladylike," I told him, my temper rising. "I owe a debt."

The shadow tipped his head. "What debt? Do you owe him money?" he asked eagerly. "I could convey it to him."

"I should hardly trust an abductor with my money," I returned tartly. "But no, nothing like that. It's a debt of honour. I owe him for rescuing me."

The shadow gave a little snort. "Rescuing you? What sort of peril do you have in England? There are no desert bandits there to carry you off, no brigands to steal your purse or your virtue."

"You haven't been to the docks," I told him, remembering a similar conversation with Masterman. "But it wasn't like that, either. I was running away and he helped me."

"Here it is a criminal thing for a girl to run away from her family."

"Yes, well, then I'm bloody glad I'm an Englishwoman."

The shadow laughed again. He seemed to be enjoying the abduction thoroughly, and I wondered if he made a career of it.

"So the Englishman helped you to run away? This is the great act of heroism that caused you to chase him halfway around the world?"

"I didn't chase him," I corrected. "I thought he was in danger. I still think it," I added. "You haven't exactly convinced me, you know."

He spread his hands. "You must forgive the melodrama. But these things are sometimes necessary, dear lady. And I am sorry I have not persuaded you. It is the truth—your English friend is alive and well and wishes you to be the same. You must not seek him further, I beg you. And he begs you, as well." The shadow's voice was low, almost pleading.

"But he's my friend," I said simply.

The shadow nodded slowly. "Yes, it is good to have friends.

I hope that you will believe me when I tell you that your Englishman is also a friend of mine. And I will convey your concerns to him. But you must not seek him further."

He gathered his robes and prepared to rise. "I do not propose to warn you again. If you disobey me, there will be consequences."

"Consequences like these?" I asked, spreading my hands to indicate the barren room.

"Oh, these are not consequences, my lady. They do not leave marks."

I gave a squawk of alarm. "Are you threatening me with violence? I'll have you know my grandfather was the Earl March, and my stepfather—"

He rose to his full height, looming over me. "Do not threaten me, my lady. Beyond the walls of this city lies the *Badiyat ash-Sham*, the great Syrian desert, where a person could be left alone to wander until thirst and madness claim all life and the sun bleaches the bones from now to the end of time itself. I think you would not like to find yourself there."

My breath caught in my throat and I sat, paralysed as a rabbit in front of a snake as he stepped backwards into the shadows.

"Now you have heard my words. You are free to go," he said, lifting one hand in a gesture of farewell.

I scurried past him and out the door before he could change his mind. The room gave directly onto a small alleyway, part of a vast complex of buildings, each looking very like the others. I started forward, then understood I would never find my way back to this room again. It was too similar to the others, and the passages were labyrinthine, twisting back on themselves and making it impossible to know one from another. I had to discover whatever I could about my abductor, and this was my only chance.

I turned back to the room. I had the element of surprise and

I meant to use it. He could not have left—the windows were barred and there were no other doors. And despite his threats about the desert, I did not think him a killer. He had had the chance to do me any number of mischiefs when I was in his power and he had not taken it. If I could just peer through the door, he might reveal enough to show me some distinguishing feature, something I could use to identify him again.

I crept back, my shoes silent on the stones. I put my eye to the keyhole, blinking hard. The little flame still burned in the crude shaded lamp, and the table was precisely where I had left it. The windows were still barred from the outside and nothing had been moved.

But the room was completely empty.

To my relief, the boy appeared again then, and even though I gave him a tongue-lashing that ought to have blistered his skin, he kept a cheerful smile as he led me through the *souk*. After several minutes I rounded a corner to find he had disappeared again, and just as I opened my mouth to scream in outrage, I understood where I was. The scorched façade of the coppersmith's shop was in front of me. He had delivered me to the precise location he had found me, and as soon as he had, he melted away again into the crowded *souk*.

A hand clamped around my arm and I let out a shriek.

Hugh crushed my arm as he whirled me around. "My God, where have you been? I've been frantic!"

I gave him a feeble smile. "I got lost in the commotion," I told him. "I followed a little boy, who took me to a fountain to bathe my eyes. I couldn't see anything in the smoke."

It was almost entirely true, but his eyes narrowed. "I think we've had enough excitement for one day. Let's go." I was only too happy to oblige, and as soon as we arrived back at the hotel I went straight to my room to take off my sooty frock and have a good scrub. I went to unpin the paper Damascene rose Hugh had given me, but when I looked, there was nothing left but a slender stem, each petal having been torn off in the drama of the day.

TEN

The next day the colonel was feeling peevish and absolutely not inclined to settle to work. I looked in on him after breakfast, but he flapped a hand at me as if he were shooing away a goose.

"Go and amuse yourself, my dear. Talbot will attend me."

Hugh said nothing, but I could tell from the set of his shoulders as he tidied the colonel's room that he was irritated. I gave the colonel a quick smile and darted away, as anxious to avoid Hugh as I was to meet up with Masterman.

I snatched up my trusty Baedeker and hurried down the stairs and out the lobby only to find the *comtesse*'s motorcar waiting at the kerb.

Faruq was waiting. "Good morning, miss," he said serenely.

"Good morning, Faruq." I made to go around him, but he stepped neatly in front of me. For such a large fellow, he moved surprisingly fast.

"I am under orders to take you wherever you would like to go," he told me.

"Oh, that isn't necessary," I protested. Once more I tried to step around and once more he blocked me.

"It is the wish of my mistress, the *comtesse*. I must obey."

"Well, naturally," I said, giving him a wide smile. "But surely someone else will have greater need of you. It seems silly for you to spend your time hauling me around."

He did not answer. He merely walked to the door of the motorcar and opened it for me. He stood aside and waited, and with a sigh I got in.

"Where to, miss?"

I gave him the address of the Turkish bath Masterman had set as our meeting place.

"Very good, miss."

He said nothing more. I stared at the back of his sturdy head as he deftly navigated the motorcar through the narrow streets and rolled to a stop in front of a high wall. There was a wooden door but no sign and Faruq got out to open my door.

"Are you sure this is the place?" I asked.

He inclined his head, and I pulled a face. Faruq was clearly never going to be one for conversation.

I went in, noting the shabbiness of the exterior and wondering exactly what I'd got myself into. But the anteroom alone took my breath away. It might have been a rich man's home at one time, *must* have been, I decided with a glance at the gilded ceiling overhead. The floors and walls were tiled and the air was thick with steam that smelled of cinnamon and cedar and something else I couldn't quite identify. An attendant hurried forward and led me to the disrobing area where I was stripped and given a small towel to cover myself with. From there I was guided to a small room with a low ceiling where I was told to sit and breathe in the billows of steam caused by another attendant whose sole job was ladling water onto hot coals strewn with herbs. I was utterly relaxed and rather light-headed when they took me to the next room—so light-headed I didn't even protest when they slathered me in a mixture of hot beet sugar thinned with lemon juice. They applied thin muslin strips then, rubbing them firmly over the syrupy concoction before tearing them off, taking the sticky solution and other things with it. I gave a little shriek of protest, but they paid me absolutely no attention, and what they did next did not bear thinking about.

When it was finished, they rubbed me down with scented oils, stretching my muscles until they were sleek and gleaming. They wrapped me in wet sheets and beat me lightly with herb branches before scrubbing my hair and fingernails until everything shone. When they were finished with their elegant tortures, they sent me into the main bath to recover.

I tottered to one of the pools and slid in. The water was heavenly, warm and gently scented from the flowers that floated on the surface. There were several women already there, as naked as I and completely unconcerned with it. I thought of hiding behind a convenient lily, but there seemed little point. The women enjoying the baths came in all shapes and sizes, from a tiny teenage bride preparing for her nuptials to a great-grandmother whose breasts stretched down to her hips. Nobody else seemed to mind, so I gave myself up to the experience and floated as lilies bobbed past.

After a long while, an attendant prodded me, and I climbed into the dry sheet she held. She guided me to a divan and thrust a glass of mint tea into my hands. I couldn't remember ever feeling so utterly unconcerned with anything at all, and my head was nodding a little as I noticed a woman leaving one of the baths. She had a spectacular figure, and she moved slowly and gracefully, rising from the perfumed water like Venus emerging from the foam. The water broke over the curve of her breasts, rolling back from a long, smooth expanse of stomach and lapping at a pair of beautifully rounded hips and shapely legs. I blinked through the steam.

"Masterman?"

The vision gestured towards an attendant for a dry sheet and came towards me. Her hair was hanging loose, waving damply about her shoulders.

"Hello, miss. Enjoy the bath?"

I blinked again. Without her severe hairstyle she looked years younger, and I gaped at the long, supple limbs and spectacular breasts.

I narrowed my eyes at her. "Masterman, how old are you?"

She gave me a slow, heavy-lidded stare. "Forty, miss."

I swallowed hard. "Golly."

"Golly?"

"It's American," I told her. "It's one of those words you use when you don't quite know what to say. Masterman, I think Sebastian isn't the only one hiding a light under a bushel."

"Miss?"

I waved a hand in her general direction. "You're stunning. You just need the right clothes. Those dark tweeds you wear don't do a thing for you. And that hair—you need to have it cut right off. I've never noticed your cheekbones before, but you could cut glass on them."

She looked down her nose. "I think not, miss."

"But it's true. You just need a little help. If there's one thing I know, it's how to dress. Green, I think. We'll find you something in green to bring out your eyes. And maybe some heels. You always wear those awful clumpy shoes but you have perfect ankles."

Masterman tucked her feet underneath the divan. "I am quite satisfied with my appearance, miss."

"That's because you don't know the power of a good frock," I told her seriously.

"Perhaps not, but I'm satisfied just the same. And you never answered. Did you enjoy the *hammam*?"

I narrowed my eyes again. "Most of it was utter heaven. But you might have warned me about that sadist with the beet sugar."

Masterman grinned. "It does take one by surprise, doesn't it? Now, what have you discovered?"

Over more tea and sherbet I related the events of the previous day in the *souk*. She grew pale and then dark red by turns as I told her about my encounter with the shadow.

"I don't like it," she said flatly.

"Don't like it? Masterman, it's our first real clue!" I said, dropping my voice to a whisper.

"You were warned off by some strange shadowy figure that can apparently disappear into thin air to stop looking for Sebastian."

"And?" I prompted.

"And I think you should listen to the shadow."

She gestured for more mint tea, heavily sweetened, and watched as I drank it all. "It's good for shock."

"I haven't had a shock," I protested. "I've had an epiphany."

"You are not normal. A normal girl would have swooned or gone into hysterics."

"I'm made of sterner stuff," I said proudly. "Remember I told you about my Aunt Julia? She once confronted a murderer—"

She held up a hand. "I'm not interested in any more of your family's tall tales."

"They aren't tall tales," I told her sulkily. "They're memoirs. They're perfectly true, I'll have you know. My Aunt Julia was a proper detective at one time. And my father, as well." It was on the tip of my tongue to tell her about their experiences in espionage, but I wasn't certain how many people knew of their exploits, and a little discretion for once seemed prudent. "It's in my blood. I'm cool in a crisis and I have excellent deductive skills."

"And these deductive skills have led you to believe that Sebastian came to the aid of his *inamorata* Evangeline Starke when she went missing in the desert?"

I shrugged. "It's as good an explanation as any. And it suits his character. He came to my aid when I needed him. Perhaps he has a complex of sorts."

"A complex?"

"Psychological complex. Some sort of disorder where he has to help ladies in need. What do you suppose such a complex would be called?"

Her expression was dark. "I'd call it a Galahad Complex."

"Galahad! Yes, that's it precisely. He was the youngest of Arthur's knights, wasn't he? And the only one to achieve the Grail?"

"And a virgin," she added. I looked closely to see if she were joking, but not a muscle of her face twitched.

"Yes, well, he is a clergyman, so one would presume his conscience spotless. Although I suppose he can't be entirely like Galahad if his quest is a glamorous widow instead of the Sangreal, but the similarities are there. And I am convinced that glamorous widow is the one responsible for my warning from the shadow yesterday."

Masterman gaped at me while I gave her a smug smile in return. "How do you account for that, miss?"

"It's quite simple. If the message were from Sebastian himself, why not just come and say 'Hello, I believe you're looking for me. I'm quite all right. Cheerio then,' instead of all this melodrama? Because it didn't come from him at all," I told her, warming to my tale. "It must have been her. She somehow deduced I was following him. Perhaps he spotted me in

Damascus and made mention of the fact that he helped me to run away or something. Her jealousy is piqued. Determined to get rid of me, she hires someone to play the role of the shadow and give me that warning to leave Sébastian alone."

"It does make a certain ridiculous sort of sense," Masterman allowed.

"Of course it does. And what's more, I'll lay money on it being correct."

Masterman sighed. "As a matter of fact, you're not correct. I had a reply to my inquiries this morning. Mrs. Starke left Damascus in the company of her elderly aunt. Before we arrived."

I gaped at her. "Are you quite certain?"

"Quite. I heard it from three sources just to be sure."

"Drat," I said, sulking a little. "It was such a pretty theory, too. Now I don't have the vaguest notion of who the shadow might have been."

"Don't you? I mean, if you put your imagination to work…" she said, trailing off.

I thought a moment. "As I said before, it can't be Sebastian or a friend or he wouldn't have gone to all the trouble of the theatrics. No, it must be someone who is a third party. An enemy would hardly take those sorts of pains to—" I drew in a sharp breath. "Unless he is working with Sebastian's enemies and wants to keep us away because he knows we're here to help. He doesn't want to harm us because we're Englishwomen and that would create a terrific international incident. So, he stages that ridiculous bit of mummery to get our attention and persuade us to give it all up. It was meant to frighten us off so he can get back to his filthy plan to harm Sebastian."

"What filthy plan?" she asked, eyes narrowed.

I flapped a hand. "The one we don't know about. But he must have one, otherwise why trouble us?"

Masterman looked doubtful. "Say for a moment you're right," she said slowly. "What now?"

I shrugged. "I go on until I've found Sebastian."

Masterman gritted her teeth. "But the shadow said he was fine."

I looked at her through narrowed eyes, my tone pitying. "Masterman, the shadow is in league with a villain. How do we know he is telling the truth? No. Until I see Sebastian for myself, I cannot simply take the shadow's word for the fact that he is all right. I will go on searching until I find him."

She made a gesture of surrender. "Very well. And so long as you are searching for him, I will help—you know that. Someone has to keep an eye on you," she added with a sour smile. There was the old Masterman, I thought with a grin. The hectoring, bossy lady's maid still lurked under the exquisite skin of this lovely woman.

She looked around at the bath, from the tiled floors and gilded dome to the clouds of perfumed steam. "I'm glad you enjoyed this. I thought it might prove informative."

"Informative?"

"This is the *hammam* where Evangeline Starke bathed just before she went off and disappeared in the *Badiyat ash-Sham*."

I stared at her in astonishment. "Is it? How very extraordinary."

Masterman shrugged. "I thought perhaps we might discover something useful. I asked around before you arrived. The attendants remembered her, but she didn't come back."

"You might have asked without going through all of this," I pointed out, gesturing towards the elaborate setting. "I think you hoped to be struck by inspiration, a bit of lightning to illuminate the way."

"Perhaps I did," she said slowly.

"Then you're a revelation, Masterman," I told her. "You're far more fanciful than I anticipated."

She gave me a sad, faraway little look. "Some would consider that a failing."

"I think it makes you human."

She grinned in spite of her moment of melancholy and rose, adjusting her sheet so that it fell in stately folds. "I shall go now, miss. I'll be in touch. Give me a quarter of an hour's start, then dress and leave, if you please."

I waved her off. I was perfectly happy to recline on my divan and order another glass of sherbet. As I was swallowing the last of it, I watched another woman emerge from the pools. Women had come and gone as Masterman and I had talked and I'd taken little notice of them. But, like Masterman, this woman seemed to command attention. She emerged on the far side of the bath with her back to me, moving gracefully up the steps, and if I'd thought Masterman was stunning, she couldn't hold a candle to this woman. Long black hair waved to a narrow waist, stopping just above the point where her hips flared, lush and shapely. Her thighs were long and slender and the backs of her knees were dimpled. She turned then, the water cascading down her smooth flesh, and I gave a little gasp.

It was the last place I had expected to see the Comtesse de Courtempierre.

Mercifully, the *comtesse* hadn't seen me, and by shrinking down into my divan, I was able to avoid her notice until she had passed into the dressing room. I gave her a full half an hour to dress and leave, and by the time I had hurried into my own clothes, Faruq was pacing the pavement in front of the *hammam*.

"I am sorry to have taken so long," I told him. "But the baths were just heavenly."

He gave me a sour look and moved to open the door. I stepped back smartly.

"I think not, Faruq. You're very kind, but the heat from the baths has left me quite sleepy. I need a good, brisk walk to clear my head."

He opened his mouth, but I had anticipated his refusal. "I will walk through the *souk* and meet you in two hours outside the Palace Hotel," I told him firmly. It was the hotel where Armand and I had dined, so I knew Faruq was familiar with it, and I brandished my Baedeker at him so he would understand I had no intention of getting lost.

His mouth thinned into an unpleasant line, but he gave me a short, sharp nod and got into the motorcar. I was astonished he had let me go so easily. And as I walked away, I wondered exactly where his mistress was and why he made no mention of seeing her. Moreover, why had she sent her car to haul me around the city when she clearly had need of it? It was a peculiar sort of attention to pay the employee of an old friend, and it all felt a bit Gothic. Except for the short walk to the stationer's and the first hour in the *hammam*, I hadn't been properly alone outside the hotel since I'd arrived in Damascus. Between Hugh's impassioned efforts and Armand's attentions, I was in demand, I thought as I turned away from the *hammam*. It was interesting to weigh the two men on the basis of what they wanted from me. Hugh had hinted at something permanent and respectable, even if he couched it in cryptic phrases about his standing in the world.

But Armand's intentions seemed a trifle less conventional. Conversation with him felt like a fencing match, all strategy and innuendo. He was sophisticated—most Frenchmen were in matters of seduction—and he had the exoticism of the East to strengthen his charms. Did he think I was sophisticated, as well? That I would play along for the duration? Or was that part of *my* charm? Would it amuse him to pick up a naïve English girl and play a few games until someone else took his fancy?

My thoughts weren't particularly nice ones, but it all made sense. If Armand was bent solely on bedding me, it explained everything—from the *comtesse*'s coolness to the colonel's insistence on getting me out of the hotel under Faruq's chaperonage. The *comtesse* would feel responsible for her son's misdeeds, but a doting mother always blamed the temptation, not the sinner. And the colonel couldn't very well warn me off directly even if he suspected Armand's intentions. It would be too insulting to his dear friend, the *comtesse*. No, he had no option but to be watchful and keep me as far away from Armand as possible by sending me out into the city to see the sights. I wondered if he and the *comtesse* had discussed the possibility of a misalliance between myself and the heir to the Courtempierre name. The very idea of it made my cheeks burn with indignation. The thought that they might have discussed it over tea and pastries…

My stomach gave a little lurch. I was hungry in spite of the tasty sherbets in the *hammam*. If I hurried, I would have time for a luscious luncheon at the hotel before I headed back to the house with Faruq. I walked, Baedeker in hand, down the street called Straight, determined to see the most historic byway in the whole city on my way to the hotel. It was at a house in this street where Paul's eyesight had been restored to him, and since the time of the Romans, spice merchants had traded their wares under the colonnades. It was invariably crowded, thronged with fabric pedlars and their customers, tradesmen plying their wares of leather and incense, and errand boys weaving through the press of bodies.

Just as I stepped off the kerb, my shoe felt loose, and I stopped to check the buckle. Without warning, I felt a blow to my back, and I flew into a bale of unspun cotton, landing hard but unharmed. I blinked hard, hearing shouts, and struggled up just in time to see a donkey cart out of control, the animal plunging and braying as its driver struggled to direct it. It was standing precisely where I had just been, and between us was Faruq, panting heavily, sweat pouring down his face. At the last moment, it swerved to the side, grazing him only a little as it plunged on.

He reached out a meaty hand. "Miss, are you all right?" he demanded.

"I—I think so. Oh, heavens, Faruq, what happened?"

"The driver lost control of his cart and it plunged down the street. Did you not hear me shouting for you?"

I shook my head. "I'm sorry, Faruq. I was wool-gathering, I'm afraid."

His expression was stern. "What does this mean?"

"It means I wasn't paying attention."

"This is not acceptable, miss. Damascus is a dangerous place for those who are not careful. Come now. I have left the motorcar in the next street."

He guided me back to the car. As he opened the door, I paused and looked up at his impassive face.

"Faruq, we were supposed to meet at the hotel. Why did you come looking for me here? Were you following me?"

The expression in his eyes did not change. "Some things only Allah himself knows," he said. And no matter how much I pestered him, he would say no more.

The colonel was horrified to hear of my close call, and he closed his newspaper with a decisive snap. "That tears it, my dear girl. You can't possibly go out again without Talbot. And furthermore, I think we must accept your kind offer, Sabine," he added, turning to the *comtesse*.

"Kind offer?" I asked.

The colonel turned back to me. "The *comtesse* has graciously invited us to stay with her. Now, I refused at first because I don't like to put an old friend out, but this hotel is not up to my standards, and with this nastiness happening to you today, I think we have no choice but to decamp to the villa."

I started to protest, but I understood immediately it was futile. The colonel's colour was high, and the *comtesse* backed him up. "Unrest grows in the city," she said as gloomy as any pythoness at Delphi. I resisted the urge to pull a face at her. "You will be far safer at my villa."

Little wonder she was gloomy. As a hospitable friend to the colonel, she must make the offer, but as a mother she couldn't much like the idea of my staying under the same roof as her son.

"Colonel, really, please don't change your arrangements on my account. It isn't necessary."

"'Course it is," he said flatly. "You don't know what it means to lose a soldier under your command," he added, emotion making his woolly eyebrows dance up and down. "It's not a thing I care to repeat. You're under my protection here, and I won't take any chances with your life, child."

The *comtesse* gave her a thin smile. "Is it such a trial to be forced to spend time with us, Miss March? Or to be escorted by the handsome Talbot? I assure you, not many young women would think it a tribulation." She finished on a peal of laughter, and I hated her cordially for her casual vulgarity.

I excused myself with icy politeness and went straight to my room to pack. I had just enough time to slip down to the lobby and leave a note for Masterman explaining my whereabouts before Faruq arrived to whisk us away to the Courtempierre villa. A guest suite in the *comtesse*'s wing had been put aside for the colonel's use, but Hugh and I were given rooms in a second, smaller wing, closer to the entry court and just over the archway leading into the main fountain court.

"I suggest you unpack," the *comtesse* said coolly. "And have a little rest. I will put dinner back. Something simple tonight, Cyrus. I worry about your digestion," she said with a fond glance at his ruddy cheeks. The colonel was only too happy to agree to the plan and I was left with a sulking Peeky and a soft-footed maid to lead me to my room. The girl was even younger than I was, and clearly in awe of her mistress. She never looked around once but hurried to my room, throwing open the door and making no attempt at conversation.

"*Pour vous,*" she told me in halting French.

"*Merci,*" I started, but before I could continue, she was gone, closing the door softly behind her.

"So much for the welcoming committee," I said to myself. "Come along, Peeky. Let's inspect."

Peeky claimed a cushion for his own and refused to budge another step, but I spent the next few minutes surveying my little corner of the villa. It was up on a corner of the first floor, perfectly situated to take in the breezes from either direction. It was a comfortable enough suite, with a small bedroom and a tiny boudoir. Both were furnished in the French style with loads of gilding—a little out of place in such a warm climate, but the gauzy curtains that stirred at the windows helped. The carpets were Turkish and pretty but very nearly thread-bare, and I was not entirely surprised to find Eastern plumbing. There were pale patches on the walls where I fancied art had once hung but been removed. And the bedcover was silk but positively ancient, shredded a little at the seams. At least the bed was comfortable, and to my delight, I found a small stone staircase leading directly from my rooms to the entry court we had first driven into. It would make slipping away so much simpler, I decided. And slip away, I intended to. The villa's location beyond the walls of the old city was a nuisance, and I had little doubt I would be chaperoned everywhere I went, but if they thought they were going to keep tabs on me all the time, they were sorely mistaken.

I fluffed up my hair and went down to dinner, a little surprised and more than a little relieved to find Armand was not in attendance. The *comtesse* seemed pleased as well, and I anticipated our stay was going to be punctuated by her attempts to keep us apart and his to throw us together. It promised to make for interesting times.

The colonel was peevish, having bashed his bad leg about a few times in the move, and the *comtesse* clucked and fussed over him until he purred like a cat. I settled Peeky with him, and he waved me away, just as happy to be alone with his beautiful companion. I could well see what he admired in her—all the more since I had spied her in the *hammam*. It was the attraction on her side I couldn't quite understand. The colonel was a dear old fellow, but he was thoroughly and decidedly English and a soldier at that. His life had been one of activity and purpose and now that he was aging, he felt his limitations keenly. I had seen him carp at Talbot when he had hefted a trunk easily or managed some other bit of manliness the colonel was no longer capable of. Did it soothe his ruffled vanity to have a lady as lovely as the *comtesse* play up to him? And what did she hope to get out of the bargain? Surely she had plenty of admirers. The colonel could not be the only one to notice her considerable gifts—beauty, a title, a lovely home.

But it was the home itself that suggested a motive for her friendship with the colonel. My suite was not the only place where I noticed faded grandeur and new economies. There were empty niches and stripped alcoves all over the villa. Marks in the carpets showed where furniture had once stood before being hauled away, no doubt to a sale room. The little maid was the only servant I saw in a house that ought to have had at least twenty indoor staff to maintain it.

"All the more reason for the *comtesse* to dislike me," I murmured to myself as I went to my suite. "She wouldn't half like her son to marry a secretary companion. That wouldn't go far to refilling the family coffers." If he were the marrying sort, I thought darkly. There was still a significant doubt in my mind that his motives were anything other than illicit.

My thoughts were tangled as I closed the door of my suite and dropped the slender bolt. Damascus was particularly ravishing that night. It was unseasonably warm, and the shutters had been thrown back to reveal a large pearly moon hanging over the minarets of the city like a jewel. The air was thick with the scent of orange blossom, and the calls of the faithful to prayer were exotic as the city itself. I stood on the balcony, where the vines from the courtyard wound their way upwards, watching the moon rise and the stars wink to life.

Suddenly, just as on the balcony of the hotel, I felt I was not alone. The balcony ran across my room and down the length of the arcade, joining all the rooms on that floor. I turned my head, and there, in the shadows was a deeper darkness, a figure of a man. Hugh emerged, his coat discarded and his shirt open at the throat.

"It's frightfully romantic," I said lightly.

"Yes," he said. He stopped just short of touching me. "I'm a fool. I shouldn't have come out here. I should have stayed in my room and closed the shutters and pretended I didn't smell the jasmine and couldn't see you standing in the moonlight. Instead here I am with you, alone."

"Is it so bad being alone with me?" My heart was taut in my chest.

"It's torture," he said savagely. He reached out, his hands clasped hard on my shoulders. "Are you really that blind, my darling?" His kisses were nothing like Gerald's. His had been timid, polite. Hugh's were nothing of the sort. His technique was experienced, and he held me firmly with one arm while the other hand slid up into my hair, stroking my neck intimately. He moaned endearments as my arms came to settle at his waist. It was a very good performance on his part, and it seemed only courteous to offer him something in return.

From the jasmine a nightingale gave a short, sharp burst of song and it sounded like a laugh.

"Well, I suppose that's a commentary on my lovemaking," he said. He attempted lightness, but his voice shook and I could see the pulse beating hard at his throat.

"If so, it's mistaken," I told him. "Your lovemaking is quite practised."

He presumed it was a compliment. He pressed another kiss, this one more chaste, to my temple, murmuring more sweet words against my skin.

I slipped nimbly away from his groping hands and pointed to the stars.

"It was a star that told Peter Pan when to fly away with Wendy," I said idly.

Hugh tipped his head. "Come again?"

"Peter Pan," I explained. "When he goes into the nursery window and coaxes the children to come away with him. It's a naughty little star that warns him the grown-ups are about to come and spoil his fun. That's when they all fly away together, all because a little star shouted a warning."

His expression was blank. "I'm afraid I don't know it."

"You don't know Peter Pan! You must have been a grown-up for a very long time not to know it," I teased.

His face was serious in the half-light of the rising moon. "I think I have been," he said slowly. "It's been a long time since I felt anything other than a thousand years old."

"The war?" I asked.

He shrugged, giving me a lopsided smile. "It meant the end of childhood for a lot of us. There were things I did that I cannot possibly explain to the boy I once was."

I said nothing. He turned to me then, lifting his hands to grip my shoulders. "I wish I could explain them to you. There's so much I want you to understand, so much I can't tell you."

"Why not?" I whispered. It seemed a night made for whispering, and in the vines against the wall, I heard rustling. Doves, exchanging confidences of their own.

His hands tightened. "Because I'm afraid you'll despise me. And I couldn't bear that. Not from you." A pause stretched between us, taut and expectant, and just as he bent his head to mine, the rustling in the vines grew louder. "Bloody birds," he muttered.

I smothered the urge to giggle. Something about his mood told me he wouldn't appreciate frivolity on my part, and I looked up at him as demurely as I could manage. His expression was tortured.

"Dear God, darling, if only I could tell you everything, make a clean breast of it all. But now it seems my past is catching up with me. I'm not afraid for myself, but I think it may be putting you in danger." It was almost word for word what he had told me in the street, and I wondered how often he had rehearsed it. The little speech seemed designed to evoke sympathy and add a dash of mystique, and I didn't much blame him. Wooing must be hard enough for a fellow, but to have only a valet's wages to offer a girl would be a difficult thing indeed. Better men than Hugh Talbot had probably invented richly embroidered pasts to make themselves seem glamorous to the girls they courted.

But there was a new urgency to his approach, and I pushed at his chest to see him better.

"What on earth are you talking about?"

"The cart today. Do you really think it was an accident?" he demanded.

"Of course it was."

"My poor naïve little love," he murmured. "I am so sorry to have involved you in all of this. If I could have spared you, but how was I to know? It seems my old ghosts are coming home to roost."

I thought of the colonel's hints, and stared up at Hugh with dawning certainty. The hints and innuendoes hadn't been a bit of flummery to impress a girl he liked. He *had* been a spy. My own little adventure seemed suddenly quite small compared to his daring deeds. "What ghosts?" I demanded.

"I can't tell you, my darling girl. I've been sworn to secrecy. But I can tell you I will protect you. With my life if I must," he promised.

And to seal it, he bent his head and kissed me again.

It was a thorough kiss, expert and sensual and extremely impressive. He pulled back after a long moment, his voice husky as he looked down into my eyes.

"My adorable girl. I think it's time to tell you."

"Tell me what?" I asked, widening my eyes.

"About Sebastian Fox."

ELEVEN

I caught my breath. "You know him?"

He gave a small, tight smile. "I see you know the name, too. Yes, I do. I'm afraid our paths crossed during the war. I should have put him out of commission then, but I lost my chance. It was either remove him or save a dozen lives, and I chose...well, I still don't know if I chose wisely. He disappeared for a while, and I hoped he was dead. God knows the monster deserves to be," he said vehemently.

I shook my head, trying to reconcile the idea of Sebastian as a monster with the friendly, accommodating curate who had rescued me from my own wedding. "What did he do?"

"Unspeakable things," he said swiftly. "Things that would give me nightmares if I could dream anymore. But I will never tell you. I won't sully you with the sordidness of what he did."

I shook my head. "But Sebastian is so...so—"

His face was grim. "Don't underestimate him, my love. That perfectly cordial, English public-school persona of his is precisely why people get into trouble. They trust him, and before they understand what he is, he shows his true colours. You've had a narrow escape, but this time he's gone too far."

He gave a dramatic pause to allow me to react. I said nothing, and my lack of response must have goaded him. He gripped my shoulders. "I know where he is now. He over-played himself with this little stunt with the donkey cart. And now I'm onto him. And I think you deserve to be there when I confront him." He had the air of a man conferring a great favour, so I gave him an appreciatively breathless little gasp.

"Me? Do you really think so?"

"I do. You deserve to look that bastard in the face and tell him what you really think of him. And then my assignment will be finished."

"Your assignment?"

His half-smile was back. "Did you really think I was a valet, darling?"

I shrugged and he laughed softly, pulling me into his arms.

"My poor little love. You're shivering. I hope it isn't from fear. There's nothing to be afraid of now. I'm going to get him tonight, with your help. And then it will all be over."

There was a sudden rustling in the shadows. "Oh, for God's sake, that was the most revolting display I've ever seen," said a familiar voice.

One of the shadows detached itself and moved towards us, stepping into the pool of moonlight. It was Sebastian, but not the Sebastian I had known. His long black cloak was thrown back to reveal native dress instead of his shabby curate's suit—a slim robe over snug trousers that had been tucked into tall boots. A wide belt bound his narrow waist, and his shoulders seemed very broad in comparison. He wore a native head-dress, also black, and he was bearded—a new development since I had last seen him, and this addition brought his fea-tures into crisp focus. I could just see his mouth, set in an unpleasant line, as he regarded Hugh. His nose and cheekbones were sharply prominent now, like a profile from an ancient coin, and his eyes had been lined with kohl, darkening them to blackness. He looked every inch the desert prince, and I stared from him to Hugh.

"Fox," Hugh said grimly. He put a hand into his pocket and pulled out a pistol, aiming it squarely at Sebastian's chest.

Sebastian gave a mocking half-bow. "I hear you've been looking for me. No need to draw poor Miss March into things, old boy."

He crossed his arms coolly over his chest and gave Hugh a superior stare.

Hugh's expression was one of pure contempt. "You're the one who pulled Miss March into this. I swear, if you harm a hair on her head—"

Sebastian coughed. "Really, that's uncalled-for. I don't make a habit of harming women."

"Really?" Hugh gave a thin, mirthless laugh. "What about the donkey cart?"

Sebastian blinked at him. "What donkey cart?"

"The donkey cart that very nearly killed her today!" Hugh said, eyes blazing. His hands were fisted at his sides.

"I don't know anything about that," Sebastian said evenly.

"I don't believe you," Hugh said, lifting his chin. "You're just monstrous enough to try to harm her to get to me. And all for your filthy gold."

I spoke up for the first time. "What gold?"

"The Ashkelon gold," Hugh said.

I gave a short, sharp laugh. "Lady Hester's gold? You can't be serious."

"Oh, but I am. It is the most fabulous treasure in all of history."

"It would be if it were true," I countered. I had learnt about the gold in the biography of Lady Hester I had read on the ship. A cache of Crusader gold brought here by the Templars, it had been lost for five centuries.

"It is true," Hugh insisted. "It was rediscovered by Lady Hester Stanhope in the early nineteenth century. It's worth more than any other find in all the world, enough gold to fill the holds of a hundred ships. And now he has come for it," he finished.

Sebastian rolled his eyes. "Oh, for God's sake. It's a myth, a fairy story invented by treasure hunters to keep themselves warm at night. It doesn't exist. It never did. And even if it did, do you honestly believe a dilettante like Lady Hester Stanhope could have unearthed it? And if she did, how do you possibly imagine she could have kept the find quiet? It beggars belief that people like you are really stupid enough to think—" It was a spectacular rant. He kept on in that vein for quite some time, taunting Hugh's intelligence, courage, common sense, and even his manhood. All the while, Hugh came closer, until finally, at the height of his rampage, Sebastian struck out with his foot and kicked the pistol out of his hand.

They were of similar height and build and I would have expected them to grapple for some time. Instead, it was over in a single blow. Sebastian clipped him neatly under the jaw, and down he went like an empty suit of clothes, folding over himself quietly.

Sebastian bent to assess his condition and gave a nod of satisfaction as he kicked Hugh's gun under a potted plant. He turned to me and put out his hand. "Are you coming with me willingly or shall I abduct you properly?"

"What, you mean throw me over your shoulder and carry me off like an old carpet?" I retorted.

"Something like that."

"I could just throw my head back and scream like a banshee."

Sebastian rolled his eyes. "Do you want me to gag you?"

"Not particularly. But I would dearly love an explanation."

"No time, I'm afraid." He glanced down at Hugh's motionless form. "We only have about five minutes before your gentleman caller comes to and decides to pay me back for that. If you're coming, it's now or never."

He held out his hand again and I didn't hesitate. I took it as I stepped lightly over Hugh. "By the way, where are we going?"

Sebastian gave me a half-smile. "After the Ashkelon gold, of course."

We fled down the stone stairs as quickly as we dared. The outer door in the stone wall was still locked, but it scarcely slowed Sebastian. He took a run at it and vaulted, putting one foot high on the wall and launching himself onto the top of it. If I hadn't seen it with my own eyes, I would hardly have believed it. But there was no time to marvel. He put his hands out and hauled me up to the top of the wall with him.

"Wait!" I put a hand to his sleeve. "What about the colonel? The *comtesse*? Hugh is clearly a danger. We have to warn them."

"Not a chance," Sebastian said flatly. "They don't know a damned thing about the gold, so they're safe. It's me he wants, and if you don't mind, I'd rather not give him a second opportunity to point that gun at me."

With that he grabbed my wrists again and tossed me lightly down the other side of the wall. I landed in a bougainvillea—an extremely uncomfortable experience—but he avoided it entirely. He pulled me free, and I dusted the leaves off my dress.

"Do you think just once we could spend time together without you throwing me into shrubbery?" I demanded.

But he wasn't listening. He was looking around, assessing the situation as he peered into the darkened street. "Come on."

He took me by the hand and turned the corner, plunging into a nearby alleyway. We walked for hours, changing direction and doubling back. Even if Hugh had managed to follow us, he would never have kept to our trail. We climbed more walls, nipping through sleeping gardens and crossing private courts. One was festooned with washing hung out on a line, and Sebastian pulled down a long black robe for me along with a veil.

"Put these on over your clothes. If we encounter anyone it would look damned strange for a native bloke to be out with a European woman."

I dragged them on, immediately regretting it. I had worn a similar costume at the Great Mosque. It was required of female visitors, and I hadn't liked it any better there than I did now. The robe was heavy wool and suffocating even in the coolness of the night.

"You can lift up the bottom of the robe until we see anyone. Then drop it and shuffle your feet. It wouldn't do for anyone to see those wretched heels of yours."

I was wearing my evening slippers—pale pink silk with high heels. They were heavenly, but I had to agree with Sebastian; they weren't the most practical footwear for dashing through stone streets.

"Where exactly are we going, by the way? Not that I'm not having an absolutely marvelous time," I assured him.

He flicked me a small grin. "I've a bolthole not far from here."

"A bolthole! How exciting. Do you have many?"

"Enough. Now stop talking. The only thing worse than anyone spotting those ridiculous shoes would be hearing you speak English."

I did as he told me and trotted after him, cursing under my breath at the costume. I don't know how Sebastian managed native robes so beautifully. I was forever tripping over the hem or getting the veil twisted sideways so I couldn't see anything at all. But after another eternity of stone passages and sleeping courtyards, we came to a small door hidden in the shadows. He eased inside, pulling me after him. It was pitch-black on the other side, but he struck a match and I saw we were in a storeroom. The place was lined with bolts of fabric of every variety, mostly silks, and all of them beautiful. They shimmered crimson and cerulean and the most vivid shade of violet I had ever seen. It was like being in Aladdin's cave, only the jewels had been spun into cloth.

I put out my hand to touch a length of it, and Sebastian tutted. "Don't even think of it. Demetrius will have my head if so much as an inch of his inventory is moved." He bolted the door behind us and lit a small lamp. He went to the corner where a large cabinet stood, ancient and decrepit-looking, the wood riddled with worm.

It seemed a curious choice for a man so fastidious about his inventory, but before I could ask, Sebastian had vanished into the cabinet, taking the light with him.

I screeched and he put his head out again, haloed in the soft light. "Good God, I've known monkeys that couldn't make that noise. Hush and follow."

I obeyed, climbing into the cabinet after him. I didn't much relish the idea of hiding out in a fusty cabinet, but to my astonishment, it wasn't a cabinet at all. The back of it was actually a stout door, and beyond that was a narrow, twisting stair. I could see from the glow that Sebastian was descending and I followed, gathering my skirts in my hands.

We emerged into a small storage room, this one comfortably fitted with a sleeping pallet, another lamp, a few books, and a few tins of food with a crooked table and a pair of decrepit chairs.

"Not much, but it will do in a pinch," he said by way of explanation. He waved to a small trunk in the corner. "There are bits and pieces for disguise there, and we can probably find better shoes for you as well as some kohl to darken your eyes."

While he talked he set to work, extracting things from the trunk as deftly as any magician as I stripped off the fusty black robe.

"I do feel bad about the colonel," I began. "He'll worry so. Unless Hugh tells him the truth."

"He might," Sebastian conceded. "But it makes far more sense for Hugh to keep his mouth shut and claim he knows nothing about your disappearance. If he plays dumb, the colonel will have no reason to doubt him."

"I suppose. But what's to stop the colonel from launching a hue and cry about my disappearance? Surely we don't want him scouring the city for me. That would only get in our way," I pointed out.

"You can write a note. There's paper and pencil on that shelf. I'll see he gets it. That's the best I can do," he warned.

"I suppose it will have to do. I could tell him I left to tend a sick friend or something."

"Feeble. Why would you leave your things behind?"

I shrugged. "I could tell him I left in haste and would he please send my things along, perhaps to the hotel."

"You can't go near the hotel. If Hugh has any sense, it's the first place he will check."

"Then I'll just have to be resigned to the loss of my things, at least for now. The hotel will keep them in storage," I said stubbornly.

He sighed and seemed to look at me for the first time. "Poppy, I know I said we ought to go after the gold, but I must have been mad. I was so outraged at seeing that devil pawing at you that my first thought was just to get you away. Now that I've had time to think on it, the smartest thing is to get you right out of the city altogether."

I felt a chill whisper in my marrow, raising the hairs on the back of my neck.

"You want to go on without me."

"I don't want to, but you must see that it's safer for you. Do you think I want to be responsible when something worse happens?"

"But you saved me," I pointed out evenly.

He groaned. "I got lucky. Poppy, I've been in situations like that more times than I care to count. I know how to handle myself, but having another person in the same sort of danger, it changes things. If Talbot gets his hands on you, he won't hesitate to use you as a hostage to draw me out again. Do you have friends in the city? Anyone I can take you to who would look after you, get you safely back to England so I can get on with this?"

His voice was very nearly pleading, and it scorched me to see such a proud man almost begging. I thought of Masterman then, with her quiet competence. She would have been cool in the face of Hugh's violence. She could get me safely back to England, I had no doubt. I thought of her sitting in her room at the hotel, waiting for word from me.

And I slipped my hands out of his and crossed my fingers behind my back. "No one," I said brightly. "I'm afraid you're stuck with me."

I wasn't cruel enough to leave Masterman dangling. I scrawled a note to her as well and slipped it into my pocket, determined to find an opportunity to send it to her.

When I had finished writing my notes, Sebastian disappeared for a moment back down the darkened stairs. I heard the faint murmur of voices and then he returned, this time with a tray full of food. I fell on it, as ravenously as if I hadn't just eaten a splendid dinner at the *comtesse*'s villa. It seemed a hundred years ago, and I said as much to Sebastian.

He nodded. "This sort of work takes some people that way."

It seemed as good a time as any to ask. "So this is your work, then."

His gaze was level and calm. "It is."

"Are you even a priest?"

He looked affronted. "Of course I am. I'd never lie about taking Holy Orders. But I don't have a parish and I'm not a curate."

I looked him over again from bearded jaw to broad chest, scarcely able to believe my eyes.

"You look so different."

He gave my evening frock an appreciative glance. "As do you. I must say I like this better than the wedding gown. Now, we haven't much time, so let's clear the air, shall we. You go first. Why did you come after me?"

"I thought you might be in trouble of some sort. You see, I went to thank you for rescuing me from my wedding, only the curate at the church had never heard of you. And then I got curious, wildly so. I couldn't imagine why anyone would lie about such a thing, so I began to trace your whereabouts."

"How?" he asked, quirking up one heavy brow. The gesture was surprisingly effective.

"I remembered the name of your garage from the ticket I found in your glovebox. I went there and the garage man told me where you lodged."

"Impressive," he told me. "But Mrs. Webb didn't know exactly where I was bound. How did you trace my route to Damascus?"

"Sheer hard graft. I searched the passenger lists of all the liners bound for the Holy Land. At length I found your name."

"My real name?" He cocked his head. "And how did you discover that?"

"It was the garage man actually," I told him. I didn't bother to mention that Masterman had stolen his copy of *Peter Pan in Kensington Gardens* from his lodging as confirmation of his name. It seemed like an intrusion somehow that I had the book, and I only hoped I could recover it eventually and re-store it to him.

He'd fallen silent, his expression pensive. "This isn't just about an old myth of Crusader gold, is it? What are you doing here, Sebastian?"

His jaw hardened. "For me to know and you to find out, dear child."

"That's not a proper answer!"

"It's the only one you'll get for now."

"That isn't fair."

"Fine. You go first. You had a choice back there—Talbot or me. He was making tepid love to you under the jasmine blossoms and feeding you a ripping yarn about what horrors I'd got up to. You had no reason to choose me over him. Why did you?"

I struggled to put it clearly into words. "Because when I was with Hugh, none of it felt real. He was playing a part with me. I don't know how I knew it, but I did. There was more genuine emotion in riding in your car with you than any kiss he ever gave me."

Sebastian's eyes gleamed, but he said nothing for a long moment. Then he swallowed hard.

"Thank you for that."

"Your turn," I prodded. "Why are you here?"

"Later."

I opened my mouth, but he held up a commanding finger. "No more. At least not yet."

"When, then?"

A ghost of a smile touched his lips. "Persistent, aren't you?"

"It's my best quality," I told him modestly.

He sighed. "Like water on a stone. But it's too dangerous yet. People have disappeared—people have died because of this gold. If I tell you everything now, it will put you at risk. Now, I've got you safely out of Talbot's clutches, but that's as far as I'm prepared to take you. You simply have to get out of Damascus, but I'm damned if I can figure out how to make it happen. My connections aren't what they used to be."

Masterman's name was on the tip of my tongue. But the moment I told him the truth about her, he would pack me off on the first ship out of Beirut and that would be the end of it—my wonderful adventure, finished before it really began. I wondered what my Aunt Julia would have done under the circumstances, and I knew what I had to do.

I smiled apologetically, giving him an angelic look. "I'm dreadfully sorry, Sebastian. Is it so terrible being stuck with me? Perhaps I could help? This hoard sounds intriguing."

"It's more than intriguing. I'm beginning to think the damned thing is cursed," he said slowly. "I'd take you home myself, but I'm so damned close…." He trailed off.

"If you're close, you mustn't give up," I insisted. "And I might be of assistance," I pressed. "I have lots of skills that might come in handy."

"Oh, really?" He was clearly amused. "Of what sort? Cryptography? Cartography? Forgery?"

"Well, perhaps not those," I admitted. "But surely I can be useful in some capacity. If nothing else, I could provide you with a bit of cover."

"Cover?"

"Yes, it's what spies call the story they use to keep their disguise," I told him.

"Is that right?" He was amused again, but before I could push further, there was a noise, so slight I almost didn't hear it.

But Sebastian did. He dived for the lamp and blew it out. He was like a cat in the dark, moving swiftly and silently so that when the secret door opened, he was ready. There was the sound of an almighty scuffle, and several blows being struck. I heard a groan and a thud, and then, unmistakably, an outraged English voice that wasn't Sebastian's.

"For God's sake, Slightly, don't be such an ass!" followed by a string of rich profanity.

I struck a match and it flared to life, illuminating a scene I would never forget. Sebastian and his assailant were heaped together in a tangle of muscled limbs and Eastern robes, both streaming blood and detaining each other in holds that looked excruciatingly painful. As they took stock of each other, recognition dawned. The newcomer released Sebastian, who promptly rolled to his feet and vomited in the corner. When he was done, he took a long draft from a wineskin and wiped his mouth on his sleeve, wincing as he put a hand to his ribs.

"Goddammit, you might have warned me you were coming," he said brutally. He waved towards me. "This is Poppy. March," he said with emphasis on my surname.

The newcomer smiled broadly and spat out a mouthful of blood. "How do you do, Miss March?"

Sebastian turned to me and lifted a shaking finger to the other man. "Poppy, say hello to Gabriel Starke."

TWELVE

"But you're dead!" I exclaimed. It sounded stupid even to my own ears but he was gracious enough to smile.

"*Dead* is a relative term out here, Miss March."

The application of a few cold water compresses and copious amounts of new wine seemed in order, and I watched as they assessed the damages. Sebastian prodded a cracked rib or two and a bruised solar plexus while Starke had a bloody lip and a spectacular bruise coming up on his cheekbone. He also had a dislocated finger which he forced back into the socket in a manoeuvre that left me feeling queasy.

"You ought to have taken notes," he told me as he wrapped a cloth soaked in cold water around the swelling digit. "It's a useful skill to have out here." His eyes were a peculiarly opaque shade of brown, uncanny and not particularly attractive.

"Miss March isn't in our line of work," Sebastian said quickly.

Starke gave me an appraising look, blinking furiously. "Do pardon me, Miss March. This isn't the most pleasant thing to watch." He reached into his pocket for a small tin and flicked it open. With a deft gesture, he levered something out of his eye, holding it out for my inspection. It was a piece of glass, the centre of it painted a muddy-brown. He removed the other and blinked again, shaking his head a little. "God, I hate those things." He peered at me again, thoughtfully, and I saw that his eyes were actually the most startlingly beautiful shade of blue. Little wonder he was forced to disguise them. No one, having seen them, would soon forget Gabriel Starke's eyes. He tipped his head as he studied me. "Not in our line of work? You surprise me, Slightly. She looks like she might like an adventure."

I dimpled at him, and he smiled back, a pirate's smile, and I passed him a plate of nut-studded pastries. "Eat these. You'll need to keep up your strength."

"Don't mind if I do," he said, helping himself to a handful. Sebastian sulked in the corner.

"Those were mine," he said pointedly.

"Don't begrudge me, lad," Starke said calmly. "I haven't eaten in two days. I just got in from the *Badiyat ash-Sham*."

"The desert?" I asked, my ears perking up. I had read of it in the Baedeker guide. The vast stretch of desert reached from just beyond Damascus to the border of Mesopotamia. Within it lay Crusader castles and ruined monasteries, desert oases, and the fallen glories of Palmyra.

"The same," Starke said. "I was with our friend Hamid," he added to Sebastian.

Sebastian unbent a little. "How is he? It's been a long time."

"He is well. Another wife, this one even prettier than the first two," Starke told him. He turned to me. "Our friend Hamid is a Bedouin chieftain."

"A *sheikh*! How marvellous. Can we meet him?" I asked Sebastian.

"No," he said sternly. "Gabriel, I'm trying to get Miss March out of Damascus and back to safety, but she's reluctant to go. I don't need you swanning in here with tales out of Arabian Nights to make it more difficult."

Gabriel shrugged, and I might have pointed out that in his Eastern robes with his kohl-rimmed eyes and extremely snug trousers, Sebastian was doing quite enough to showcase the romance of the place. I primmed my mouth.

"Pay no attention to him, Mr. Starke. He's just cranky because I want to go with him to find the Ashkelon gold."

Starke's expressive brows shot skyward. "That's what this is about? The Ashkelon hoard? Is that why you've been looking for me?" he demanded.

Sebastian folded his arms over the breadth of his chest. Anger simmered in the air between them. "Yes. Of course, the main reason I came was to make sure you were still alive, but since it didn't seem to bother you to play dead without explanation, we'll assume the friendship is of secondary importance and focus on the treasure, shall we?"

His words were coldly clipped, and Gabriel answered him softly. "It bothered me, Slightly. More than you'll ever know."

I looked from one to the other. "Slightly?"

"Don't ask," Sebastian ordered. He waited, and Gabriel took a breath, steeling himself it seemed. He let it out slowly, and with it came the story.

"I regretted it, Sebastian. I regretted every decision I made, from the moment I let Evie think I went down with that bloody ship. Everything I did after that was a lie. Except the friendships. Those were real," he said, giving each word slow purpose. "The lot of you were the only family I had left besides the Bedouin. And when I saw how badly I was letting them down with that ridiculous charade, I realised I was letting the rest of you down, as well."

"What charade?" I asked.

He turned to me. Every word seemed forced through his lips, as though he were heaving each one like a stone out of his heart and offering it as penance. "I presume you have heard of Colonel Lawrence's exploits in Arabia?"

"Of course! The newsreels were absolutely spectacular," I enthused. But his eyes were shadowed, and his mouth was set in a grim line.

"Yes, well, it was nothing like that glamorous in real life. Lawrence was tasked with uniting the southern Arab tribes and using them to harass the Turks wherever he could, mostly in the area of Aqaba and the Hejaz Railway. The rest of us were busy in the north, wreaking our own havoc on the Turkish border."

I blinked. "But Lawrence was a legend! How is it you were doing the same in the north and no one knew?"

He smiled thinly. "Politics is a nasty business, child. There are competing offices and bureaus and ministries that don't much care to talk to one another. And if two of them should happen to hit upon the same strategy at the same time, neither one will give ground to the other lest they get the glory. The Arab Bureau in Cairo directed Lawrence's efforts, largely at his instigation. After he and I had a rather instructive meeting in Jerusalem," he added.

I gaped. "You mean Lawrence stole the idea of using an Englishman to unite the Arab troops to fight the Turks?"

He shrugged. "Lawrence and I disagreed on the fundamentals. He felt the tribes would come to support Prince Feisal as their natural leader. I thought it was madness. The Bedouin of the *Badiyat ash-Sham* would never rally behind a Howeitat from Mecca like Feisal. The Bedouin are very like our Scots, all rival clans and blood feuds. Expecting them to rally to a single flag simply because they happen to speak Arabic and worship the same god is as preposterous as expecting a Campbell and a MacGregor to sit down to supper. It cannot be done." He paused, a faraway look in his eyes, and Sebastian poured himself another drink and I thought of the similar conversation I had had with Armand on the very subject.

"But," Starke went on, "there was something to be said for rallying the northern Bedouin around a figurehead of their own choosing, a legend from their own folklore. There was an Englishman, a rather bright lad with a head stuffed full of legends and poetry, who remembered that the Bedouin of the north had a fellow rather like Robin Hood in their mythology. A fellow called the *Saqr*, the falcon. And that was how we came to create our own legend," he said, finishing the last word with a bitter twist of his lips.

I turned to Sebastian. "The legend of the *Saqr*—you were the one who knew of it."

He gave a mirthless laugh. "I have a gift for useless information. Languages, history and folklore. Those were the talents I was recruited for, among others."

"Recruited?" I looked from one to the other. "By whom?"

They exchanged glances and Sebastian gave an almost imperceptible shake of his head.

Starke spoke again, smoothly this time. "The exact organisation is unimportant. But Sebastian and I were amongst a very select group of young operatives deemed unsuitable for more conventional activities."

"Unsuitable? But why?"

Starke's mouth quirked into a grim smile. "I made the mistake of eloping just before I was due to begin training. That spontaneity made me suspect in the eyes of our superiors. They questioned my judgment and my ability to keep my wife safe from the complications of our work. As it happened, they were right."

"And that's why you pretended to go down with the *Lusitania*," I said, piecing it all together. "You were trying to keep her out of harm's way."

"Oh, I was crueler than that," he said, his eyes gleaming with guilty malice. "I told her I was going to divorce her. I broke her heart before I left her just to make certain she wouldn't have a reason to regret me when I was gone."

My eyes stung with sudden tears. "That's the most romantic thing I've ever heard."

Starke gaped at me. "How can you think so?"

"You sacrificed your own happiness for her safety," I said simply. "It's heroic."

His mouth worked a moment, but nothing came out. Finally, he managed a simple grunt and a nod.

"Has no one ever put it to you like that?" I asked gently.

"No," he said, his voice rasping. "No one except Evie."

"Then you have seen her," Sebastian put in.

Gabriel nodded. "She came to Damascus to find me. I was in the *Badiyat ash-Sham*, working on an archaeological expedition."

"How did she know where to find you?" Sebastian asked evenly, but there was an icy edge to his question.

"Because I sent her a photograph with my general location on the back," Starke answered. "I needed to make amends. I brought her out here because I had something to give her, something she would stand a far better chance than I would at getting out of Syria."

Sebastian's jaw tightened and his hands curled into fists. "You gave her the gold."

Gabriel held up a hand. "Calm yourself, Slightly. I've no wish to be on the receiving end of your temper for a second time tonight. I didn't give Evie anything that belonged to the Lost Boys."

"The Lost Boys?" I asked.

Sebastian's hands relaxed. "That's what our little band was called. There were seven of us who didn't fit into any other work the bureau wanted. We were the leftovers, the flotsam and jetsam of the department. It was Gabriel who called us the Lost Boys the first time we met and the name stuck."

"Where are the others?" I wondered.

Starke shrugged. "Dead, missing, scattered by the war. I'll admit I didn't make it my business to find out."

"No, you were too sunk in self-pity and recrimination to wonder about the rest of us," Sebastian shot back. He rose, wincing only a little. "I'll be back in a minute. I want to make certain Demetrius' shop is still secure." He let himself out through the little door in the wardrobe, and I turned to find Starke smiling after him.

"The boy looks good. He still had a bit of puppy fat the last time I saw him. Glad to see that's been worked off."

"He's rather hard on you," I ventured.

Starke swiveled his head, fixing me with those devastating blue eyes. "I only found out recently that when the war ended and I walked away from it all, he was rotting in a Turkish prison. I don't think I'd blame him if he had slit my throat the minute I walked in the door." My stomach gave a lurch as he went on, softly, "I don't know what they did to him. But I know what they did to Lawrence, and those are things I wouldn't do to a rabid dog. The fact that he's still alive and sane means he's a far stronger man than I am. He's got the heart of a lion, that boy. And the rage of a Viking berserker," he added with a knowing wink.

I blinked. "But he's a clergyman," I said.

Starke grinned his pirate's grin. "Clearly you've never seen him in a knife fight." Before I could decide if he were joking or not, there was a rustling at the door and Sebastian appeared with a fresh skin of wine. He tossed it to Starke, who opened it and poured out a full measure for all of us.

"So what did you give Evangeline if not the gold?" Sebastian asked, settling into a chair.

I darted a surreptitious look at him from under my lashes. There were no scars, at least none I could see, and I wondered what horrors he had endured at the hands of his captors.

Starke was speaking. "The abandoned monastery outside Ashkelon, the last night we were all together, do you remember? It was the night before we went our separate ways to take up our roles in the great charade. There was a storm outside, raging, and we took refuge in that old wreck up on the hill. But the roof was gone, and the wind and rain drove us down through the crypts and into the old temple of Venus. We burned whatever we could get our hands on to stay warm, furniture and barrels and packing crates. And that's when we found the manuscripts, cached there when the monks abandoned the place." His words were directed at Sebastian, but he did not look at him. His gaze was soft and unfocused, and I knew he was seeing the scene in his head, unrolling like a moving picture. The storm raging outside, the little band of spies, brothers, gathered together one last time before they embarked upon a mission that could destroy them all.

"We didn't know what they were at first, not until you deciphered them. But they were ordinary, lists of caravan goods and orders for chapel goods. Until you came to the one that told of the Templar treasure, Crusader gold brought to this land to finance the wars of the Middle Ages, the wars between gods and men, a treasure lost to time. But this document was more than a history. It was a map, and someone recognised it as being a copy of the same manuscript Lady Hester Stanhope had purchased on her travels."

"Jocasta," Sebastian said softly. "It was Jocasta. She specialised in modern Levantine history."

Starke gave a quiet laugh. "Jocasta. How could I have forgot? She was giddy as a schoolgirl when she realised what we had found. A treasure map detailing the location of the Ashkelon hoard, the gold that Lady Hester spent her fortune in search of."

I shook my head. It seemed fantastical that they were discussing Lady Hester so casually. She was a real historical personage, but her story was straight out of myth. She had served as society hostess to her bachelor uncle, the younger Pitt, when he was Prime Minister, but a disappointment in love had driven her to travel. She had struck out for the East, adopting the dress of a Turkish man and Eastern customs as they suited her. She had established the first modern archaeological dig at Ashkelon, looking for ancient art and, according to rumour, something more fabulous—a cache of gold pieces hauled to the Holy Land by the crusading Templars.

"Did she ever find it?" I asked.

Starke roused himself, seeming to see me for the first time. "No one knows. She retired to a sprawling house on a hillside, and lived out her days in splendid squalour. But that doesn't mean anything. She may well have found it and hidden it again. All her family were famous eccentrics. It would have amused her to keep the secret."

"It would," Sebastian agreed. He turned to me. "We know at Ashkelon she unearthed a priceless statue of Zeus, the greatest archaeological discovery to date. And she ordered it smashed and the pieces hurled into the sea."

I remembered the incident from the book I had read. "It was outrageous," I said hotly.

Sebastian nodded. "That it was. And what for? Sheer bloody-mindedness? Desire to thwart the Turks, who would have claimed it for themselves? No one knows. But if anyone was capable of discovering a treasure of Templar gold and never telling a soul, it was Lady Hester."

I looked at Starke. "What did you do with the map?"

He smiled, and it was a ghost's smile. "We did what any group of people facing their own mortality would do. We put it back. It had clearly lain undisturbed for a few hundred years. We made a pact to leave it in peace until the war was over. When it was finished, then we would claim it and share it out—a pact I have not broken," he added with a meaningful look at Sebastian.

"Then what did you give Evangeline?" Sebastian returned.

"There was another document, a second map," Starke said. "This one led to a very different sort of treasure."

"What treasure?" I asked, eyes round with anticipation.

"The True Cross." I shook my head stupidly.

"The True Cross? You mean the actual Cross, the one that— Oh, my heavens," I said weakly.

"Exactly," he said with a shadow of a grin. "The document detailed what happened to it after it was removed from Golgotha, tracing its movements throughout history. It suffered in the process and bits of it were burnt or hacked off, but a sizeable portion remained. To most historians, it was lost after the Battle of Hattin."

"Hattin? Wait, I know that name," I said quickly. "How do I know it?"

"Because it was fought here," Sebastian supplied. "On a desert plain between two peaks called the Horns of Hattin. The army of the King of Jerusalem clashed with that of Salāh al-Dīn—known to our historians as Saladin. The Bishop of Acre himself carried the Cross into battle. They were crushed by the heat and the Mohammedan army. Salāh al-Dīn picked it up and carried it in triumph here to Damascus. He had it paved into the stones of the place as his greatest trophy, but it was lost to history."

Starke broke in. "Lost to Western history," he corrected. "As it happens, easterners have known all along what happened to it. Their chronicles explain that the Cross was badly damaged in the Battle of Hattin, and Salāh al-Dīn brought what was left to Damascus—a fragment of the original, but still the largest piece left anywhere in the world. He had it embedded in the floor of the Great Mosque, and it didn't leave again until 1400 when Tamerlane sacked the city. He had the mosque burnt and prised up the Cross, carrying it back to Samarkand. After a century, it was recovered by a group of Christian monks whose monastery was in the *Badiyat ash-Sham*. They reset it in gold and crystal, preserving what was left. They kept the secret of its existence—a little too well. One of the usual tribal wars erupted, and the monks scattered. One of them hid the Cross and documented its whereabouts. But he and his brethren died, and the Cross was lost again."

"Until you," Sebastian said thinly.

"Yes, well," Starke said. He cleared his throat. "As it happens, I did find it. And I gave it to Evie. Or at least, I meant to."

"Where is it now?" Sebastian demanded.

"Burnt in an aeroplane crash," Starke answered cheerfully. "There was someone else after it, and he was rather tenacious. He crashed his plane in the *Badiyat ash-Sham* and the Cross was melted in the fire. Nothing left but a puddle of molten gold, although I suppose the Bedouin have helped themselves by now," he finished, stroking his chin.

"And you would have kept it for yourself," Sebastian said, his tone clipped.

Starke held up a hand. "I did not break our pact, Slightly. We all gave our word not to go after the Ashkelon hoard alone, and I didn't. I went after something altogether different. And I'm happy to relinquish my claim to the Ashkelon gold if it's ever found," he added. "That's more than enough to make up for taking the Cross for myself."

"How much is the Ashkelon gold worth?" I asked as a matter of curiosity.

Starke gave me a cool smile. "Three million."

"Three million *pounds*?" I squeaked.

Sebastian shook his head. "No, child. Three million pieces."

I stared from one to the other. "You can't be serious. Three million separate pieces of gold. But it must be worth—"

"Fairly incalculable," Starke said gently. "And I wash my hands of the business. My seventh is to be shared out amongst the rest, however many there may be left. If they can find it."

Sebastian's gaze sharpened. "What makes you say that?"

Starke sighed. "I had to go back to the monastery to retrieve the map to the Cross. The Ashkelon document was missing, Slightly. It's been taken. And without it, you'll have the devil's own time finding the gold."

Sebastian's face was livid. "I don't believe it."

Starke was gentle. "You must. I've come to terms with it, and so must you. One of our merry band is a traitor."

"In that case—"

Starke held up a hand. "In that case, the likeliest suspect is me. But I didn't take it. I give you my word. And whatever else I've done, I think we both know that's still worth something in this part of the world."

Sebastian flushed. "I know, Gabriel."

Starke rose and drained the last of his wine. He held out his hand for mine, and when I gave it to him, kissed it. "My dear Miss March, it has been a most unexpected pleasure. Most unexpected indeed."

He smiled at some secret amusement, then turned to Sebastian, hesitating. He put out his hand slowly, and Sebastian took it. They clasped each other's hands, then leaned in, resting their foreheads together in an Eastern gesture of respect for a brief moment before Starke withdrew, clearly in the grip of strong emotion.

"I don't know if I'll see you again, Slightly. I've told you all I can. Rashid is in Damascus. I can spare him for a few days if you need him. And mind you take care of Miss March," he added with a significant glance at me.

And then he was gone, disappeared through the secret door.

I turned to Sebastian, feeling as though the air had gone out of the room. And without warning I began to laugh.

He turned his head. "What is it?"

"I've only just puzzled out why he calls you Slightly. You were the Lost Boys, Peter Pan's band of adventurers," I said through peals of laughter. "And you are Slightly Soiled."

Sebastian did not find the remark nearly as funny as I did. He gave me a sour look and threw a length of wool at me, gesturing towards a straw pallet on the floor as he did so.

"You need rest now. So do I, for that matter." Beyond the kohl darkening his eyes, I saw shadows, crescents of purple smudged just above his cheekbones.

I wrapped myself in the wool and lay down on the rough pallet.

"Haven't you slept?"

He shrugged. "Not much. Too busy chasing down leads on where I might find Gabriel." He folded a bit of wool and eased himself down into a corner, still wincing slightly.

"Should you have a look at those ribs?"

He gave me a faint smile. "Only bruised, my dear Miss March. If they were broken, I would know."

"You sound as if you have experience with that sort of thing."

"I do. Now go to sleep."

I closed my eyes, but sleep was the furthest thing from my mind. A kaleidoscope of pictures tumbled in my mind, splintering and chasing and breaking again as they formed new images. I could not believe so much had happened in so little time. I saw Hugh's face, twisted with avarice, and Sebastian dashing to my rescue like something straight out of myth. He was exhausted, but still he sat up, attentive to every noise, waiting for danger.

I forced myself to sit up, rubbing my eyes.

"Can't sleep?" he asked.

I shook my head. "I keep seeing it all over again."

"It takes people like that sometimes, their first experience with this sort of thing."

"I hope it's not my last," I told him solemnly.

He cocked his head, taking me in from tumbled hair to impractical shoes. "Do you really think you're cut out for this sort of thing?"

"I don't know," I said slowly. "But I should like to try."

"Why?" His voice was blunt. "It's dangerous and dirty, and if you're only in it for a bit of fun, you'll get yourself killed."

I thought and chose my words carefully. "It's because I've never really belonged."

He quirked up a brow. "The society debutante with the millionaire stepfather has never belonged?" The words were cutting, but he had the grace to say them gently.

"That's just it," I explained. "Reginald's money opens doors, but what I do when I go through them is up to me. And usually I've just made a mess of it all. I can't ever seem to settle down to doing what other people expect of me. That's how I ended up running out on poor Gerald. I thought I was doing what was right, what I'd been bred for, but I just didn't fit. I never have. Not in school, not even in my family. Mother had the twins and then the boys came along, and through it all Reginald was really rather wonderful to me. He has always treated me as his own, but I don't look like them. I don't speak like them. I'm not one of them. I am the cuckoo in the nest."

"And now you'd like to fly your own way, is that it?"

"Precisely. Only I never knew what that way might be until recently."

His gaze sharpened. "What happened recently?"

"I discovered my Aunt Julia's memoirs. She was a detective, you know. Not on purpose, you understand. She fell into it. Her husband was the one with the inquiry agency, but he made her a partner, a real partner. And she learned to be herself. That's what I want."

"You think international intrigue is the way to go about that?"

"Heavens, no! That bit is your fault."

He choked a little. "My fault?"

"By disappearing so dramatically. I thought there must be something terribly wrong. I was worried about you," I told him.

Suspicion seemed to dawn then, and he lowered his chin, fixing me with an icy stare. "Do you mean to tell me you came out here on a rescue mission? You thought you were saving me?"

"Well, yes, actually."

He said nothing for a long moment, and then the words came in bursts. "Of all the— I can't imagine— The most insulting, infuriating—"

"Of course, that's before I knew you," I said. But he wouldn't be placated. He clamped his jaw shut, the muscle in his cheek working furiously.

"Sebastian?"

"Go to sleep."

"I didn't mean to insult you, really I didn't. I thought you were just an unprepossessing clergyman who had been abducted or assaulted, and I honestly believed—"

He cut in with swift brutality. "I am not at all interested in your beliefs, Miss March. Now go to sleep."

He rose and flung his bit of woolen fabric around his shoulders as he strode to the door.

"Where are you going?"

He turned, giving me a cold stare. "I am going to keep watch. Don't worry. If I get into any trouble, I'll shriek for help."

He stalked out, closing the door carefully behind him.

I lay back down, cursing my own chattering tongue. I hadn't meant to make him sound so much like a milquetoast, but I *had* thought I was coming on a rescue mission. How was I to know he was some sort of spy, I asked myself irritably. I punched and thumped the lumpy straw into something passably comfortable, but it was a long time before I slept. I had come to know Sebastian well enough to know that he would be racking his brain to find some way of getting me back to England safely. If I wasn't lucky, I would find myself packed onto a steamer the very next day.

Of course, that was before I knew about the murder.

THIRTEEN

I woke stiffly, groaning a little as I moved my limbs.

"What's the matter? Accommodations not to your liking, princess?" asked Sebastian coolly.

He was sitting at the table, eating a plate of cold meat and flatbread. I pushed myself onto my elbows with a sigh. Clearly he hadn't forgiven me for my lapse the night before.

There was a bucket of cold water in the corner and I washed my face and hands hastily before joining him at the table. He shoved the food at me with bad grace, and I began to eat. The meat was tough and the bread stale, but it was delectable. There was more wine, and I drank a little of that to clear my head.

"Feeling better?" he asked. His earlier irritation seemed to have faded a little, and I smiled.

"Yes, actually. It's a new day, Sebastian. Why don't we forget our differences and make the best of things? I've been thinking it over, and I believe I can help you. I know Gabriel said the map to the gold was gone, but what if we go back to the monastery? He might have been mistaken. It's been a few years since the group of you were there, and what if he didn't look thoroughly enough?"

Sebastian regarded me thoughtfully. "A logical plan, I'll give you that. But how far do you suppose we will get when I'm wanted for murder?"

I stopped eating, my hand halfway to my mouth with a piece of bread. I put it down and wiped my mouth carefully. "That isn't a very nice joke, Sebastian."

He pushed a newspaper towards me. "I was going to wait until you finished, but it's best you know."

And there it was. In lurid black and white. The body of an Englishman had been discovered in the old quarter. He had been shot to death and left where he fell. The body, discovered in the middle of the night by a watchman making his rounds, had been identified as Hugh Talbot, valet to Colonel Cyrus Archainbaud.

"It's not possible," I murmured.

He poured another cup of wine and pushed it towards me. "Drink."

"Oh, my God," I moaned. "I don't understand."

"At some point, friend Hugh must have shaken off the blow I gave him and given chase. And somewhere along the line, it ended badly for him."

"Pickpockets—" I began, but he gave me a pitying look.

"Pickpockets don't shoot men to death, not in Damascus. Besides, his papers were still on him as was his money," he pointed out.

I moaned again and dropped my head to the table, but as soon as it hit I jerked it up again.

"There's no mention of me," I said suddenly.

Sebastian gave a nod of satisfaction. "I wondered when that would occur to you. As far as the colonel knows, you're missing."

"But why? The colonel must know I'm gone. Oh, God, he must think I've been abducted by the villains who killed Hugh. He must be frantic."

"So frantic he didn't tell the police?" he asked gently.

"But it doesn't make sense," I protested. There was a sense of watchfulness about Sebastian, as if he had already puzzled it out but meant to give me time to catch up. I gave a sudden gasp. "Unless he thinks *I* did it. If he thought I killed Hugh he wouldn't tell the police. He'd try to protect me by hushing it all up. But what possible reason would there be for me to kill Hugh?"

Sebastian gave me a pointed look. "He did come to your room last night. Perhaps someone saw him."

"He did not come to my room. He came to my balcony, as did you," I said coldly. "And if anyone had seen him come, they would have seen me leave with you."

"Not necessarily. They mightn't have liked to pry." His cool detachment was maddening, but it made a horrible kind of sense.

"I suppose," I said slowly. "Someone might have seen him come to my room, but then what?"

"He could have persuaded you to go out with him. I believe you've been out in public with the fellow several times since your arrival in Damascus," he said, widening his eyes innocently.

"Yes." The word was as clipped and sharp as I could make it. "We were friendly."

"And you've been seen out with the *comte*, too, haven't you?" he asked in the same sweetly insinuating voice.

I looked up, horrified. "But it sounds so sordid. As if I were carrying on with both of them! And I wasn't carrying on with either of them, not really," I finished roundly.

"But, in fact, you did—what was the phrase you used—

'carry on'?—with Hugh," he said, his voice gentle. He was watching me closely, and I made every effort to keep my voice calm even though my fingers were shaking on the newspaper.

"It's very simple," I told him. "Hugh made overtures towards me. I thought he might be useful, so I didn't discourage them. I thought a man of action might be helpful if matters proved complicated with regard to finding you." Sebastian's face darkened, but I went on. "So, I didn't put him off. I temporised. Women have been doing it for centuries, you know."

He tipped his head thoughtfully. "Why?"

"Because some men don't take kindly to being rejected," I told him a trifle waspishly. "They're like overgrown toddlers. You have to take them by the hand and lead them into doing what you want in order to avoid a fuss. Oh, I could have thrown him over, but he would have sulked. He was just the type. And I didn't want scenes and an atmosphere when I was trying to work. So I humoured him."

"And that meant kissing him," he said, idly scraping a knife under his fingernails. "Of course, I can hardly blame you when he was doing precisely the same."

I narrowed my eyes. "What do you mean?"

His expression was thoughtful. "Doesn't it seem a trifle coincidental to you that Hugh should try to make love to the one girl he thinks is capable of leading him to me? To the Ashkelon hoard?"

"You think he only kissed me because he was using me to get the gold?" I demanded.

He gave a half shrug, wincing when he remembered his tender ribs. "Granted, you're alluring enough, I suppose he might have been inclined to have a go anyway, but let's just say I don't like coincidences."

I ground my teeth together and he waved a finger. "That's

very bad for your teeth, you know. I'm sure your mother wouldn't approve."

I opened my mouth long enough to ask a question. "If you don't like coincidences, how do you account for the fact that I just happened to be in the colonel's employ at the same time as Hugh Talbot?"

Sebastian considered this a moment. "How did you come by the job? Advertisement in the newspaper?"

"No, actually it wasn't. Cubby Ashley, a friend of mine, happens to be the colonel's nephew. He put me onto it."

"A grown man going by the name of Cubby? You can't be serious. He ought to be horsewhipped."

"It's a pet name, and I hardly think someone called Slightly ought to be throwing stones."

Sebastian gave me a glowering look from under his brows but decided to let that one pass. He spread his hands. "But there you go. I suspected for some weeks before my departure that I was being watched. Talbot or a confederate of his could have very easily seen us leave the church together. And given the unorthodoxy of our departure," he added, his dark eyes gleaming, "they might have put entirely the wrong construction upon our relationship and assumed it was far more intimate than it is. They could have traced me to the steamship office and lost the trail there. The most logical thing was to backtrack and pick you up to use as their pointer."

"And then he could have had a word with Cubby," I said slowly. "He could have suggested it first to the colonel, convinced him he needed someone else to help with the travel. And then he could have worked on Cubby, persuaded him to put the plan to me, knowing I'd be desperate to find a way to the Holy Land. It's rather diabolical, isn't it?"

He gave me a thoughtful look. "Does your unfortunately named friend need money?"

"Pots of it. He's expected to marry well, and he's fallen in love with a girl who has nothing. He could easily have been bribed to suggest the job to me. And Cubby's not terribly bright. He would have bought any story, thought it a great lark. Oh, the fool!" I said bitterly. I gave him a cold look. "Go on. Say it. Cubby's a fool but not as big a one as a girl who thinks trips to the Holy Land just happen."

He gave me a thin smile and said nothing.

"The poor colonel," I murmured. "I must get that note to him."

"Not a chance," Sebastian told me flatly.

"But he's worried! He thinks I've been abducted. Or worse," I said darkly.

He fixed me with an inscrutable look. "I've been abducted, Poppy. There *is* nothing worse." I stared at him, mouth agape, but he merely went on speaking in a calmly matter-of-fact tone. "The colonel is in no danger from Hugh's conspirators, whoever they may be. There's clearly been a falling-out amongst thieves—or perhaps they decided Hugh's usefulness was outlived since he managed to bring you out here and flush me from my cover. And one less conspirator means one less share of the gold given out." He paused and I wondered if he were thinking of his own Lost Boys and the traitor amongst them. "Besides," he went on, "you cannot contact the colonel because the note would be handed over to the authorities and would serve no purpose. You are just as much a possible murderess as potential victim in this case."

I spluttered. "But that's impossible! They can't really believe I killed Hugh."

"Why not? You had an intimate friendship with the man and then he ends up dead the same night you disappear? Looks suspicious enough to me, and I'm inclined to give you the benefit of the doubt."

"The benefit of the doubt?" My voice had risen to a screech and he held up a finger, wincing. "Why shouldn't you," I hissed, "when you were with me the whole time? You know I didn't kill Hugh."

He shrugged. "I assume you didn't kill Hugh, but I wasn't with you the whole night. I stepped out to keep watch, remember?"

"You were keeping watch. You would have seen me go," I pointed out acidly.

"Not necessarily. Sometimes a gentleman has bodily functions to attend to," he told me, batting his eyes modestly.

It was the batting of the eyes that tipped it. "You're joking! You think this entire affair is some great jest," I accused.

He sobered. "No, I don't. A man is dead, but he's not the sort I'll weep salty tears for, and I don't see you reaching for the sackcloth and ashes, so spare me the indignation."

I shook my head. "I have never been so wrong about a person in my entire life. I thought you were *nice*."

"I am nice," he returned, giving me a hurt look. "If I weren't, would I have rescued you from his clutches last night? Would I let you stay here even though I could collect a generous reward for your return?"

I pointed to a significant sentence in the newspaper. "I think not. You are wanted just as fervently as I am."

He shrugged. "There are ways to manage these things. I have friends, you know. I could simply put one of them forward to claim the reward and share it out. I'm generous like that."

I screeched again, and he put up a hand in protest. "For God's sake, Poppy. My grandmother had a parrot that didn't make noises that off-putting."

I crossed my arms over my chest. "Fine. What do you want out of all this? What is your grand plan?"

He folded one booted leg over the other. "I've had considerably longer to think this over than you have, and I have a bit more experience of what to do when the authorities would like you to do something you really, really don't want to do." He rubbed his hands together gleefully. "Putting you on a train for Beirut is obviously a non-starter since they'll be watching the station, and the last thing we need is for you to be taken into custody now. So we'll have to leave Damascus another way."

I blinked. "Wait. You're taking me with you?"

His gaze was marginally kinder. "I am. I told you, I've thought it over. So long as you don't mind the newspapers saying nasty things about you for a few days, the best plan is to get right out of Damascus. Whoever killed Hugh is looking for the gold, Poppy. That means they're looking for us," he finished gently.

"Oh. OH," I said, putting it together. "You mean we're in danger, then. But how do you know Hugh was killed by someone after the gold? It might have been a robber or—"

He shook his head. "It won't do, Poppy. I told you I don't like coincidences, and that would be a monstrous one. He comes here as part of a conspiracy to recover a fabled treasure and just happens to get murdered? I can't believe that. He wasn't robbed. He was shot at very close quarters, in the heart. That implies it was someone he trusted to get close to him, a confederate. He might have told them about me, and if he did, we're in even more trouble. Our only choice is to stick together."

"I'm surprised you don't want to hand me over to the police," I said. "It seems the reasonable thing to do."

"If we were in England, I would. But have you been questioned by Syrian police? I have. It's not an experience I care to repeat, and it's not one you should have. Ever," he said flatly.

"First things first—we need to get out of the city. We'll need to plan a route and secure disguises."

It seemed logical enough and I told him so.

"Thank you," he said dryly. "It is what I do, you know."

"I'm beginning to wonder if I know you at all," I said.

He threw me an enigmatic smile. "Then here endeth the lesson."

We finished the remains of the cold meat and flatbread and I asked him if he had specifics in mind with regard to our next move.

His expression was thoughtful. "I'm not thrilled about our prospects, but for now the best thing will be to lie low and get out of Damascus. Somehow I have to get you out of the country and into the hands of the British authorities."

"I'm rather surprised you don't plan to go straight to them," I said mildly. I hated to give him ideas for getting rid of me, but I was quite certain he'd already thought of it.

"Almost as difficult an option as the Syrians, but for very different reasons. The situation here is delicate. There's a revolution afoot, in case you hadn't noticed," he told me. "God only knows what's going to happen, but right now the British authorities here are in no position to hold off the Syrians if they want you for murder. Or me for that matter. We'd put them in a devil of a bind if we simply turned up. No, we need to get you somewhere else entirely."

He fell silent a moment, then reached into a cupboard and pulled out a map. He spread it over the table, using the cups and plates to anchor the corners. "Here we are," he told me, pointing to a large dot labelled Damascus. It sat serenely next to the pointed peak of Mount Hebron and beside the long brown sweep of the *Badiyat ash-Sham*. A little distance away was the coastline with Beirut and Sidon marked at the edge of the blue fringe of the Mediterranean. The coastline ran straight down from the Lebanon through Palestine, then curved as it led westward, skimming its way towards Africa. To the east, the vast stretches of desert pointed the way to Mesopotamia, the capital city of Baghdad labelled in a tidy hand.

"Any preferences?" he asked casually.

I was startled. "What do you mean?"

He pointed to Cairo, far to the west, and then east, to Baghdad. "I have contacts there and there. People who might actually listen if we explain we didn't murder Friend Hugh. Which do you fancy?"

The fact that he had asked for my opinion was astonishing; the possibility that he might actually listen to it was miraculous. I bent and studied the map, looking it over carefully, scouting the dangers and difficulties along the way.

I straightened, pointing to Egypt. "Cairo. Definitely."

He had been watching me carefully as I scrutinised the map and now his eyes were coolly assessing. "You seem adamant. Explain your reasoning, if you please."

I pointed again to the map. "Baghdad is a good option, but not an excellent one. We cannot take the train—therefore the fastest and most secure route across the desert is cut off for us. To cross the desert, particularly as the days are growing warmer, would require a very fast motorcar with excellent suspension or horses. Motorcars can break down and horses must be changed if you're riding fast. And then there are the Bedouin."

"Go on," he urged.

"They are at war with one another, tribal conflicts, and so forth. I would imagine crossing the desert would require an escort. That would take time and money and draw attention to us." I pointed to the map, tracing out the route along the coast. "But if we make for Cairo, we can go by sea if we like to Alexandria. The distance to the coast is not significant, so

missing out on taking the train wouldn't be nearly as much
a handicap as not taking it to Baghdad. We could make for
Sidon and turn south from there, either using the coastal roads
or by ship," I finished.

He gave a grudging nod. "Sound logic, dear girl. Very
sound."

"How long will it take?"

He shrugged. "Sixty miles would be a good day's riding,
but the Anti-Lebanon Mountains lie between. They're not
tall, mind you—you crossed when you came on the train from
Beirut. But we'll want to avoid the usual checkpoints. We'll
have to go around a longer way and slip over the border at
one of the unmanned crossings."

"I thought Syria and the Lebanon were both under French
control."

"For now," he said dryly. "The boundary is roughly where
Mount Hermon lies. But the French do love their bureaucracy.
You wouldn't have noticed much on the train, but crossing
via the roads can be a different matter, and with the Syrians
making noises about supporting Feisal, things could change at
any minute. Far safer to take the long way around and make
camp tonight."

I was pleased he had taken my suggestion of travelling to
Cairo—pleased enough to press my luck just a bit further.
"You know, if we were heading to Cairo, Ashkelon is prac-
tically on the way."

I kept my tone casual, but he burst out laughing. "You don't
give up, do you?"

"No, I don't," I told him stubbornly. "At least, not anymore," I amended. "I've spent the whole of my life giving up,
and that is not who I am now."

"And who exactly are you now?"

"I am a woman who follows through, who knows her mind

and has a single-minded purpose to direct her," I said, lifting my chin. "And don't let your silly male pride get in the way of what is an excellent plan. They'll be looking for us in the larger cities, near train stations and steamship offices. No one will think to look in a tiny backwater like Ashkelon for us. We could stop along the way."

"And do a little searching for the gold in the meantime," he said shrewdly.

"Why not? It's the last thing anyone would expect of us."

"You do have a point there," he said, stroking his chin thoughtfully. "But if we do this—"

"And we should."

"*If* we do this," he repeated, "it means that much longer that your reputation is in shreds. Your family will hear of this, Poppy. There's no way to keep it out of the newspapers once the wires pick it up. It will be in every London and New York paper because of your father and your stepfather. You will carry the weight of this for the rest of your life."

I weighed my words carefully. "My reputation is not my character, Sebastian. People can say what they like, but are they the people who matter? There's been a boundary around my whole life, and it was the question of what people would think. Throwing over Gerald was the first time I did what I wanted, not what they expected. And it was the best decision I have ever made. What more proof do I need that I must do what I feel is right, even if I'm the only one in the world who believes it?"

He said nothing, but his expression was thoughtful.

I pushed on. "Would the notion of what people say about you put you off from what you wanted?"

"No."

"Then why should it stop me?" I leaned closer, pressing the point. "The newspapers will not make the connection to

my stepfather or my father for a little while. I never told the
colonel the truth about my family, so it will take a very enter-
prising reporter to piece it all together. With a little luck we
might have reached Cairo by the time the story breaks and I
can wire Mother immediately."

I sat back and let him think.

"You can't possibly pass for Syrian," he told me finally. I
felt a rush of exhilaration, which I tamped down. *Best to keep
myself calm and cool*, I thought. But inside I felt as if the finest
champagne was bubbling through my veins.

"I could veil," I said helpfully.

He shook his head. "It won't do. We'll have to say you're
Circassian."

"Circassian?"

He grew animated as he talked, the ideas coming together
swiftly. "From the Caucasus. They've been largely displaced by
the Turks, but there's a fair number of them in Syria. They're
fairer-skinned than some and they've often got blue or green
eyes. They also have their own language, so it won't seem all
that strange that you can't speak Arabic."

He rose and went to the door, disappearing through the little cupboard. A moment later he returned with a very refined-
looking gentleman, a Damascene with elegant hands and the
most perfect posture I had ever seen.

"Poppy, this is my friend Demetrius. He is the silk merchant
whose shop is above us. Demetrius, Miss March."

Before I had a chance to acknowledge the introduction,
they were in conference, heads together as ideas flew between
them. They made me stand and circled me while they discussed Sebastian's idea of passing me off as Circassian.

Through it all, Demetrius sucked his teeth, turning his head
this way and that as he scrutinised me. "She is too short for a
proper Circassian," he said finally. "But she has good bones

and the eyes are very beautiful. The complexion is perfect. Can she speak Adyghe? What about Kabardian?"

"She can't even speak Arabic," Sebastian told him flatly.

Demetrius cocked his head. "Can you make her a mute?"

I opened my mouth to protest sharply, but Sebastian was smiling. "No chance of that. She chatters like a monkey."

I snapped my teeth together and Sebastian's smile deepened. One of Demetrius' brows shot up. "I see what you mean. It will be difficult," he explained. "Circassian women are known for their grace and their beautiful posture." He turned to me. "You will walk, please?"

He gestured across the little room, and I bit my tongue to keep from putting it out at Sebastian. I had had enough deportment lessons in finishing school to know what was expected. I rose ever so slightly onto the balls of my feet and glided forward. I crossed the room and turned back again.

Demetrius nodded. "It is not bad. But if you will permit, Miss March," he said as he approached. He put his hands to the tips of my ears and pulled up.

"Ow!"

"Always you must pretend there are strings attached to the ears, pulling them upwards," he instructed me. "And think light thoughts as you move, butterflies and sparrows, skimming on the air."

I rubbed my ears and tried again as he watched.

"Better." He turned to Sebastian. "It will do from a distance. Do not let her speak. But she must do something about her eyes."

"What's wrong with my eyes?" I demanded.

Demetrius turned back with a pained expression. "Miss March, it is obvious you did not have the benefit of a convent education."

"I beg your pardon?"

"Demetrius' daughters are all convent girls," Sebastian explained.

"What does that have to do with the price of butter?" I asked crisply.

Demetrius gave a patient sigh. "Miss March, in the convent, a girl is taught the principle of custody of the eyes, to keep them directed at one thing and one thing only. During the Mass, it is the priest."

I blinked. "You're Catholic?"

He bowed slightly. "Greek Orthodox. Now, if you will attend, Miss March. I was explaining custody of the eyes. It is customary during Mass, but it is essential for you to adopt a similar habit if you are to be convincing as the wife of a Syrian."

"The what?" I looked from him to where Sebastian was standing casually, one booted leg crossed over the other.

"Demetrius, will you give us a moment?" he asked. Demetrius bowed again.

"Of course. I will go and secure the necessary costumes," he assured Sebastian.

As soon as he had gone, I turned on Sebastian. "What did he mean, wife?"

"Surely you understand there was no other way," he said evenly. "We'll be travelling in remote areas. A woman does not travel in a Muslim country without the protection of a male relative."

"Then why can't I be your sister?"

"Because I'm not going to be disguised as a Circassian," he said with an effort at patience. "I already have another identity established as a silk merchant, and I'm going to use it. You cannot pass as a Syrian, so you will have to be my new Circassian bride."

"But—"

"And I will not have you sleeping alone," he added flatly.

"What do you mean sleeping alone?"

"If we were to pass ourselves as brother and sister, we would be separated at night in any lodgings we take. You would be taken to stay with the women while I would be shunted over to sleep with the fellows. There's no way I can protect you if I'm not there, Poppy."

I temporised. "What if I disguise myself as a boy?"

He gave me an odd look. "Have you ever seen your walk? It's all hips. You'd be spotted inside a minute. Besides, have you ever slept in a group of men? It will be eight hours of bodily noises and smells to which no lady should ever be subjected. Now, I know you want to do this, but you haven't the faintest idea what sort of danger is involved. I'm acting against all my better instincts in even agreeing to do this, but you must let me do some things my way. And I will insist on being with you. At all times."

He spoke quietly but with such authority I knew there was no possible way to refuse.

"I accept your terms," I told him.

He gave a nod of approval. "Good. I'll go and see if Demetrius needs a hand."

I called him back just as he reached the door. "What would you have done if I'd refused?"

"I would have tied you up and dropped you off at the nearest police station," he replied. And with a rakish grin he was gone.

FOURTEEN

Two hours later, we were dressed and ready for the journey. Demetrius, whom I gathered was a contact of Sebastian's of long standing, supplied him with a fresh set of robes. Sebastian had lined his eyes again with kohl as well as rubbed a little soot on his chin to darken his beard. The effect was startling. His eyes, dark enough to begin with, were now fathomless, and nearly black. His thick, expressive brows looked exotically appropriate under his native headdress, and the flowing robes gave him the glamour of an Eastern prince. I tried not to stare, practising my own version of custody of the eyes, but Sebastian showed no such reluctance when I finally emerged dressed in my Circassian costume.

The first point of contention between Demetrius and me had been my hair. He had approached me with a bowl full of what appeared to be black mud as he gestured for me to sit. He threw a towel about my shoulders, and I was just about to ask him what he meant to do when he dropped a dollop of the cold mud onto my head.

I squawked and would have jumped up but he pushed me back into the chair. "It is necessary," he said shortly.

"What is it?" I asked through gritted teeth. It smelt like dirt, and I could only hope there was nothing more unsavoury mixed in.

"Black henna. To further disguise you." He continued to slap mud on my head as I wriggled in discomfort.

"But Sebastian said Circassian women often have light hair," I protested.

Demetrius sighed and dribbled more mud onto my head. "It will be worth it," he promised.

"Well, if it was good enough for Lady Jane Digby," I muttered. She had dyed her own corn-gold hair to black with the stuff to better resemble her husband's Bedouin relations. If I were going to play the adventuress, I might as well be hanged for a sheep as a lamb, I supposed.

After the mud had sat for a little while, congealing nastily, Demetrius took me to a hole in the floor and bade me lean over it. He brought can after can of water, cold but freshly drawn, and poured it over my head. After endless rinsings, he pronounced it acceptable and brought towels to dry it.

"It ought to be long," he told me severely as he eyed my crop of curls. "But the headdress will cover the rest of it. At least the hairline is dark now. It makes a difference," he observed, handing me a small looking glass. He was not wrong. My light brown hair, usually shot through with a bit of red, was now black as a raven's wing. The change was startling. It made my skin look milk-white in comparison, my eyes large and much greener.

"I suppose it's all right," I said grudgingly. The truth was, I rather liked it, but Demetrius and I were soon at loggerheads over the Circassian costume. I nearly squealed aloud when he had brought it to me. It was the most spectacular costume I had ever seen, and it had taken me the better part of an hour to assemble the pieces in the correct order. There was a corset, intricately laced, and fiendishly uncomfortable at first. I had never worn one before, and Demetrius brought his wife to lace me into the thing. But even I had to admit it whittled my waist down spectacularly. Over it went an undergown of fine linen and a pair of slim trousers of thin, silky chamois. Atop this went an overgown that buttoned tightly at the waist to show off the narrow lines of the corset. It was black silk, figured heavily in white, with scarlet-lined sleeves that swept to the ground. The bodice of the gown was clasped with heavy silver buttons, and shafts of carved bone decorated the front like a sort of glamorous breastplate. There were soft crimson leather boots, and a small headdress to secure the long veil of fine white gauze. The effect was stupendous, and I discovered as I moved that Demetrius needn't have bothered with the deportment lessons. Between the corset and the tight buttons, there was no possible way to move in the costume that wasn't queenly.

Sebastian scrutinised me from head to toe, looking so closely that I felt myself beginning to blush.

"Will I do?" I asked tartly.

"I suppose," he said, his tone casual. He turned to finish packing a saddlebag with essentials while Demetrius tweaked bits of my costume.

"Very becoming, Miss March," he told me.

"And devilishly uncomfortable," I confessed. "I'd just as soon not have this wretched corset."

He looked shocked. "But the whole effect of slenderness and beauty would be lost."

I started to explain that women had thrown their corsets out in order to show the embracing of new freedoms, but Demetrius merely stared at me with lips pursed in disapproval.

"Freedom is very well, Miss March, but no woman without a corset will ever look so regal," he said grandly. He pitched his voice lower. "Besides, there is a lovely Circassian tradition. On the wedding night, it is the task of the bridegroom to free his bride from her corset using only his dagger. If so much as a nick appears in the perfection of her flesh, he is disgraced. Is that not a lovely tradition?" he asked, his eyes a little dreamy.

"It sounds dreadful." I shuddered, imagining all the things that could go wrong. I wondered how many Circassian brides had been accidentally disfigured on their wedding nights.

Demetrius was mournful. "You have not the soul of a poet," he said.

"Perhaps not, but I am grateful to you," I told him by way of making amends. "It really is a lovely costume, and I will take excellent care of it."

He waved a hand. "It is yours now, dear lady. I have been well-paid for it."

He nodded towards Sebastian, who had finished his packing and was hefting the saddlebag to his shoulder.

"Come along, Poppy. Time to mount up."

I followed him outside and into the alleyway as hastily as my beautiful dress would allow.

"The animals are tethered in the next little alley," he told me softly. "I didn't want to attract any more attention to Demetrius' shop."

He took long strides in his native robes and I hurried after, holding my long skirt in one hand. The city was just coming to life, with the smells of kindling fires and roasting meats filling the air. I anticipated a pair of beautiful matched Arabian horses or even a couple of milk-white Bedouin camels to carry us out of the city. Instead there was one horse and a donkey that was as sturdy as he was short. Holding the reins of both animals was a young man whose posture was even more gorgeous than mine. He was wearing a striped robe and he held the leather reins with a lazy grace. He sketched me a polite salaam as we approached, and he reminded me of nothing so much as a faun out of myth. Sebastian bent to mutter in my ear.

"This is Rashid, a Bedouin friend of Gabriel's. He's playing the part of our servant, at least until we reach the coast."

It made sense, now that I thought of it. Sebastian was posing as a prosperous businessman. No such fellow would travel with his bride and no manservant.

I smiled at Rashid and inclined my head as much as the tight headdress would allow.

"How do you do?"

Sebastian hissed through his teeth. "For God's sake, haven't you learned anything? It's *assalam aleikum*."

But Rashid merely grinned, and it was the impish grin of a faun. *"Aleikum assalam, sitt,"* he said politely.

I looked at the little donkey he was holding.

"Sebastian, how on earth is that poor little beast going to carry you?" I asked.

"Oh, he isn't for me," he said, strapping his saddlebag to the Arabian. "Climb on, and mind that's a sidesaddle."

I stared at him. "You must be joking."

The alleyway behind the shop was deserted apart from us and Rashid, but he glanced around. "Poppy, this entire operation depends upon you doing what I tell you when I tell you without question and without argument. Now, mount the bloody donkey or I will leave you here."

He spoke in a calm, conversational tone so that anyone overhearing just the sound would think us having a pleasant discussion. But there was a distinct lack of humour in his eyes, and I hurried to the side of the donkey. Rashid made no move to help, and I remembered that, aside from Demetrius,

Eastern men did not make a practise of touching women to whom they were not related.

I stared at the little donkey, realising that it suddenly seemed much taller than I had anticipated when I was expected to mount it—particularly in my elaborate Circassian robes.

"Er, Sebastian," I began. But there was no chance to finish. I had started to raise my foot and before I could complete the sentence, Sebastian had laced his fingers together and cupped my heel, vaulting me up into the saddle. I landed heavily, but the donkey merely sighed and Sebastian took the rein. I thought he would give it to me, but he held it as he leapt into the saddle of his Arabian with all the grace of a centaur.

"Surely you don't mean to lead me around like a sack of potatoes," I protested. He didn't bother to answer. He merely threaded my rein through a loop on his saddle and touched his horse lightly with his heels. Rashid followed us on foot as Sebastian gave a quick command in Arabic to the horse. She tossed her head, prancing on beautiful feet as she led us out of the alleyway and into the crowded streets of Damascus. At last, I thought, my heart rushing into my throat, it was beginning.

The trip through the city took longer than I would have imagined, but this was largely due to the fact that Sebastian took a route that included the busiest thoroughfares. At first, I was aghast, but I soon discovered it was a clever strategy. The authorities would never look for us to be travelling in native costumes, and a merchant leaving the city would not keep to tiny alleys and hidden byways. Rashid brought up the rear on foot, occasionally casting glances behind to make certain we were not followed. Tethered by the rein, my little donkey plodded on behind the beautiful horse, and since I was attempting to keep my eyes carefully fixed upon my "husband," I had little choice but to study Sebastian's posture. Something about wearing Eastern dress had changed him completely. Gone was the friendly, affable curate, and in his place was a man who wouldn't have looked out of place in any royal court. His posture was perfectly straight, his chin held high with a stateliness that bordered on arrogance. He did not turn his head right or left, but kept it steady, expecting others to move out of his path, as any gentleman of wealth and power might do. From my perch behind, I saw the scurrying motions of people moving aside to let us pass, and I began to relax. Sebastian's air of command was so thorough no one would have dared to question him. With him leading, we eventually reached the edge of the city, where the sprawling suburbs gave on to the countryside, orchards of lemon and pomegranate, and fields of melons. The earth smelled new after the odours of the city, and I breathed as deeply as the corset would let me. Sebastian clicked again to his horse and she shifted up into a trot, which my donkey immediately imitated.

"Oh, dear God, no," I muttered. I turned back to find Rashid had broken into an easy lope and was grinning at me. For the next few hours I was bounced around mercilessly as the donkey jounced after the brisk Arabian. I didn't protest, partly out of pride and partly because I assumed it wouldn't do me any good. Sebastian had shown he meant to be in control of our expedition, and since I hadn't told him about Masterman, the least I could do was follow obediently. I felt terribly guilty about the omission, not least because I suspected Masterman would be frantic if she'd read the newspapers. I could just imagine her, breakfasting with her single boiled egg and the newspaper, reading the sordid details, going very white about the lips, perhaps spilling her tea.

And then I thought of something truly horrifying: Masterman knew who my family were. I had persuaded Sebastian to travel to Cairo by way of Ashkelon by convincing him it would take some time for the reporters to make the connection between Poppy March and Penelope Hammond, stepdaughter of American millionaire Reginald Hammond. But Masterman could do it in an instant. One word in the wrong ear, and my story would be splashed from Damascus to Dubuque, and God help us both if Mother herself decided to come to Syria to find me.

I nibbled the inside of my cheek, wondering how to break the news to Sebastian. He would no doubt be furious that I had kept the secret of Masterman's existence in the first place. And in the second...

I turned in the saddle to look behind us. Rashid still loped along behind, taking the distance easily as an athlete. Beyond him, Damascus lay like a postcard city, gleaming white in the late morning sun. She seemed to shimmer on the flat plain, a mirage that would prove heartbreakingly real if Sebastian decided to return me. And I knew he would. He had stated more than once and in painfully blunt detail what his course of action would be if he believed things had got too far out of hand. I would be handed over to the authorities. He had talked glibly of trussing me up and dropping me at their feet, but I knew that was nothing like what would happen. He had been bluffing to get his way. The truth was, if he had no choice but to turn me over, he would go as well, taking the blame for Hugh's death and clearing me entirely. I had no doubt he would lie himself blue in the face to swear he had abducted me and killed Hugh. There was no other story the authorities could hear that would put me firmly in the clear— unless we knew and could prove who had really done it, and that would be like looking for a particularly nefarious needle in a very large haystack. Who knew what low types he had consorted with in Damascus? Hugh might have had an entire network of dangerous confederates who had turned on him.

Or, I reasoned, he might have simply been the victim of circumstances, wrong time and wrong place. Damascus was a city in the process of remaking itself, and there were dangerous corners especially for foreigners. Who was to say he had not wandered into one of them when we left him?

No, finding out who had killed Hugh would have been a Herculean task, one much better suited to the police, who could sleuth out his associates and question people thoroughly. I only hoped they would throw their nets further afield than merely looking for Sebastian and me. It would be tempting for them to insist we must be the villains of the piece—to begin with, it kept victim and killer from the same group of foreigners. It might reflect badly on them that it had happened in Damascus, but no real blame could be attached to them. If, however, it could be proved it was a Syrian who had killed him, they opened themselves up to an international incident when they could least afford it. Admitting one of their own had killed an Englishman, just when they needed English support in throwing off the French and installing their own king was unthinkable. Even if they found proof Hugh had been killed by a Syrian, it would be impossible for them to admit it. Far easier to put the blame on a pair of English fugitives. Who knew? They might even be able to parlay that into a bit of gentle extortion in getting the English to look the other way while they threw out the French.

We rode on, and I continued to work it all out even as the donkey shook my bones to aspic. We were the best suspects in Hugh's death, from circumstance and also from the perspective of the Damascene authorities. If nothing else, failing to present ourselves promptly would make us look thoroughly guilty. There was no way at all to explain what had happened with Hugh and why we had not come forward.

Unless Sebastian fell on his sword. I looked ahead to that

proud back, rising in the saddle at the top of the trot, strong
legs working like pistons, robes flowing behind him in the
wind. Something in him reminded me of Gabriel Starke, that
same self-sacrificing nobility hidden by a veneer of deprecation
and wry humour. They played at being villains, but there was
some finer metal in both of them. Gabriel had sacrificed every
bit of his own happiness for Evangeline's safety, and although
I was merely an acquaintance to Sebastian, I had no doubt he
would do the same for me rather than allow me to be taken
into custody as a suspect in Hugh's death. No, in his version
of events, I would be his victim, an innocent party, and that
would be his story, no matter how long and how hard they
pressed him to tell otherwise.

I knew then that I had to keep Masterman's existence a
secret—but not for my sake. For his.

By the time the sun was high overhead, Sebastian stopped
in the cool green shade of a pomegranate orchard. He drew
his horse a little off the road—enough to be discreet but not
suspicious. He dismounted lightly and did not bother to tether
his horse as he slid the rein from mine out from the saddle.
He flicked me a glance as Rashid trotted up, scarcely winded
after his long run. His beautiful skin gleamed in the sunlight
with the sheen of fresh perspiration and he smiled broadly.
He at least was having the time of his life.

Sebastian looked up at me. "Aren't you getting off?"

I blinked. "I don't think I can."

"Whyever not?" He took the precaution of tying the donkey, but apparently trusted the horse not to bolt. She merely
stood by, batting long lashes at Sebastian as Rashid stroked
her nose.

"He isn't exactly an easy mount."

Sebastian grinned. "Shook you a little?"

"Rattled my teeth like castanets," I told him. "And now I've clung on to him so long, I don't think I can get off."

With a smothered laugh, Sebastian strode to the donkey's side, raising his arms. "Come on, princess," he ordered.

I turned stiffly in the saddle and tried to slide down, but somehow my boot got caught and I ended up slithering down Sebastian's chest until he caught me. My legs were jellied, and he held me up a moment before I could support myself.

I looked up to thank him, but he dropped my arms. "Walk it off," he instructed briskly. "The more you move, the faster the blood flow will come back. Rashid, my friend, you need water."

He turned away to share his water with Rashid and attend to his horse and the donkey. I began to pace the orchard. I hobbled to the end of the row, but by the time I had turned and made my way back, I was moving a little more smoothly. When I returned, I found they had watered the animals, and Sebastian was murmuring endearments to the horse.

Rashid approached then, smiling in triumph. "I have found pomegranates. The windfall from after the last harvest. These will be the last of the season," he told me. He broke open one of the fruits and showed me the seeds, glittering like jewels.

He gestured for me to turn over my palm and when I did, he tapped the skin of the fruit sharply, causing the ruby seeds to rain out of the soft white flesh. I ate a few and he smiled.

"The Prophet Mohammad, peace be unto him, taught that eating the seeds of the pomegranate would purge hatred from the soul and sweeten the temper," he told me.

"Then feed her plenty," Sebastian told him.

I resisted the urge to put out my tongue at him.

"And speak Arabic to her, Rashid. She's appallingly badly educated."

That time I did put my tongue out, but I turned to Rashid

with a smile. "He isn't entirely wrong, though. I don't speak Arabic and I ought to learn. How does one say *thank you*?"

"*Shukran,*" Rashid replied.

I repeated it, and Rashid took his responsibility seriously, repeating the phrase twice more as I mimicked him. He lifted his brows. "Very good, *sitt*." He turned to Sebastian. "Her accent is better than yours, my friend."

Sebastian curled a lip. "It's one word, Rashid. Let me know when she can actually put a sentence together."

Rashid and I settled down in the shade of one of the slender trees to enjoy our fruit. "You are Bedouin, is that right?"

He lifted his chin proudly. "I am, *sitt*. My tribe is from the north, near Palmyra. Our winter pasturage is very close to the ruins of the great city."

"I should love to see it," I breathed, thinking of the vast stretches of columned ruins, once the playground of the fabulous warrior queen, Zenobia, vanquished only by Rome and led through the city streets in golden chains.

Rashid grinned. "Many ladies like Palmyra. It is because of the great queen."

"No doubt," I mused. "And now you have a king. What of your own people? What do they think of Feisal?"

He shrugged. "He is a Howeitat, a southerner. He is not one of us."

"I have heard others say the same. So, he does not speak for your tribe?"

Rashid's smile was patient. "That is not our way, *sitt*. A man is responsible for his family, and the family is responsible for the tribe. There is much discussion and much cooperation because the rules are not written. They are understood. As a man, I am answerable to my kinsmen, the men of my own blood. How can a Howeitat hold me responsible for my actions when they are not my kin?" He did have a point, and

I thought it interesting that his views should be so similar to those of Armand. Rashid went on. "But the rule of an Arab over his own people is preferable to that of a foreigner," he said firmly. "The French, the English, they have no place here except to help us become what we must be."

"And what is that, Rashid?"

"Masters of our own fate," he told me. We talked a bit longer, sharing fruit and chatting idly until he rose. "I will go and find more pomegranates. Take the last, *sitt*," he insisted, pressing two of the fruits upon me.

Sebastian was still murmuring endearments to his horse, stroking her long nose.

"What is her name?"

"Albi. It means *heart* in Arabic," he told me.

"She's utterly gorgeous," I said, holding out a pomegranate on my palm. She gave me a long look then snuffled her velvet lips over my hand, taking the fruit up as daintily as a princess.

"She knows it," Sebastian said seriously. "That's her trouble."

She crunched on the pomegranate and I held the other out to the donkey. "And this one is an utter menace."

Sebastian shrugged. "I looked his feet over when you were playing with the pomegranates. He's going lame." He held out a goatskin full of water. "Drink up. We'll have to get on again as soon as Rashid returns."

I groaned but did as I was told and in a very few moments Rashid appeared, carrying a bag stuffed with late pomegranates. Sebastian stowed the goatskin and together they looked the donkey over and discussed the options. Rashid seemed deeply upset, talking rapidly and sketching wide gestures of dismay with his arms.

Sebastian soothed him down and after a long moment, took the rein from the little donkey and handed it to Rashid.

Rashid bowed in a gesture of *salaam*. "We must part here, *sitt*. I am to return this worthless animal to the city."

Sebastian's jaw was set—I could tell that much from the mulish expression of his beard. "If we push him onto the coast, it will only get worse, and he'll hold us back. Better we travel fast even if we have to go alone."

I started to put out my hand, then remembered the customs of the land. "I am sorry to lose your company, Rashid."

He smiled his beautiful faun's smile. "And I yours, dear lady."

He brushed his fingertips to his mouth and made a graceful gesture of farewell. I felt a little flutter in my stomach as I watched him go.

"If you're quite finished mooning over Rashid, we ought to be going," Sebastian said, his words clipped and icy.

"Oh, for heaven's sake, I wasn't mooning," I protested. "But you have to admit he's a beautiful boy. Besides he's already got two wives."

Sebastian rounded on me. "How the devil do you know that?"

I shrugged. "We chatted. He's a trifle worried about the second wife. Apparently she's expecting her first child and having a wretched time of it."

He gaped at me. "I've known Rashid for the better part of five years and he's never mentioned a wife."

"What can I say? People tell me things."

He gave me a dark look and carried on. "Can you ride astride?"

"Yes, actually, I can."

"Good," he said, and as he had done before, he put his hands under my heel and tossed me into the saddle. This time the perch was much higher, and as I sat there astride the gorgeous horse, she bobbed her head a little, making the bells on her headstall ring.

"I can ride her?" I asked in delight. He didn't answer. Before I could protest, he shoved me as far back in the saddle as I could go, perching me uncomfortably on the very top ridge of it. "Sebastian, I don't think—"

As was becoming his custom, he ignored me and did as he pleased. He mounted Albi swiftly, careful not to knock me off as he did so, settling himself neatly into the space just in front of me. As he sat, I slid down off the top edge of the saddle and ended up wedged snugly against him, hip to hip.

"Oh, you cannot be serious," I muttered.

He turned his head slightly. "It's either this or walk. And frankly, I don't much care."

I sighed. The boots were gorgeous, but they were a trifle tight and I didn't relish a long dusty walk to the coast. "Fine."

"Then mind you hold on. I'm going to give Albi her head and if you fall off, I'm not going back for you," he instructed.

He touched her lightly with his heels and gave a single command in Arabic. She sprang forward and I clasped my arms about Sebastian's waist. It was smaller than I expected. The baggy clergyman's suit he had worn in London had hid a multitude of things, I decided. Among them a pair of rather impressive shoulders and a narrow, athletic waist.

I held him tightly as we rode, the wind blowing our veils behind us, the dust of the road billowing as we went. It was all I could do not to let out a whoop of sheer joy as we rode. This was adventure at last.

FIFTEEN

We stopped twice more, both times to rest and water the horse. Sebastian drank deeply but took no food although he forced me to eat.

"You're not accustomed to this sort of travel, and I won't have you fainting like a Gothic heroine," he warned me. "Try these."

He passed me a sticky paper twist. I stared into it suspiciously. "What are they?"

"Raisins. Soaked in honey. If you don't want them, give them back," he ordered.

I nibbled one and gave a little moan. "Oh, they're heaven. I hope you bought enough for yourself, too."

He pulled a face but let me keep them as we set off again.

As the afternoon wore on, the roads became smaller and narrower as we wended our way up into the Anti-Lebanon. The triple peaks of Mount Hermon stood guard to the south as we picked a path into the hills, turning slightly to the north and skirting the edge of Mount Lebanon. Albi's brisk pace meant that a breeze fanned my cheeks under the veil, but I was thirsty and tired by the time we turned off the last road and onto a narrow track that wound upwards through a rocky landscape that seemed to lead nowhere.

"Where are we going?" I asked. Sebastian shrugged, the muscles of his back rolling under my clasped arms.

"Looking for a suitable site to camp for the night."

We'd been riding for hours, and although I would have died rather than admit it to Sebastian, I was thoroughly exhausted. I gave a sigh of impatience and dropped my head to his back. He jerked, nearly throwing himself off the horse. His sudden lurch irritated her and she tossed her head, crossing her feet sideways.

"For God's sake," I muttered irritably. "What's the matter with you? Anyone would think *you* were the Gothic heroine."

He reseated himself and calmed the dancing Albi. "Don't do that again," he ordered through gritted teeth.

I sighed again. He was getting touchier and more irritable the longer we spent together, I decided. Perhaps rough travel didn't agree with him. Or perhaps he wasn't as comfortable with fieldwork as I had expected from someone who had spent his war years actively engaged in espionage.

For that matter, I reasoned, he might not have been that active at all. His specialty had been languages. Clearly he had been sent to Syria to be close at hand if Gabriel needed assistance maintaining his cover as a dashing Bedouin hero out of folklore, but it seemed likely to me that Sebastian had spent his war years tucked away in an office waiting for Gabriel's field reports and preparing memoranda for the London office. Even Gabriel's remark about Sebastian's prowess in a knife fight seemed like a joke. After all, he certainly hadn't knifed Hugh when he had the chance. He'd merely incapacitated him and left as quickly as possible. I began to wonder if he was afflicted with a bit of genteel distaste for violence.

It wasn't entirely fair either, I decided. After casting off the shabby garb of an impoverished English curate, he looked like a hero out of myth. The least he could do was behave like one.

I was still happily occupied in dissecting his character when Albi pulled us up over the lip of a rise onto a small plateau. Part of the plateau was rock but most was a narrow meadow with fresh grass for the horse and a thin stream trickling down from the snowy peaks in the far distance.

"Where are we?" I asked.

Sebastian half-turned in the saddle. "In the Lebanon now. We slipped over the border some distance back. We've made good time in spite of riding double. We're very near Sidon." He lifted his hand and pointed. "And over there on that ridge is Djoun."

I gaped. "Lady Hester Stanhope's home! But can't we—"

He knew exactly what I was about to ask. "We can't stay there. The place is deserted now, but there's a village at the base of the ridge full of curious folk who'd make note of travellers poking about." He gave me a quick grin. "Besides, I've already been inside. It was a long shot that there would be anything of note left in the old ruin, but I made a point of breaking in and making a thorough search of the place."

"And there's nothing left?" I shaded my eyes to make out the sprawl of the distant compound. "It looks simply enormous."

"Big enough," he agreed. "And packed to the rafters with rubbish, not surprisingly. It's changed hands a dozen times since Lady Hester's death, and it gets more derelict with every new owner. Someone ought to pull it down and start over."

It was a disappointing coda to the thrill of stopping so close to Lady Hester's old home. It seemed too cruel to be so near the place and not be able to step foot inside. I must have been fairly vibrating with excitement, because Sebastian flicked me a sideways look.

"There won't be gold here, Poppy. If she did find it and brought it here, it would have been discovered by now. But I thought you'd like to see it for yourself, and this little plateau will be as good a place as any to shelter for the night. Now, hush. I want to make certain there's no one around before we get too comfortable."

But no sooner had he spoken than I felt him stiffen in the saddle. Just behind us, emerging onto the plateau was a party of horsemen. Sebastian wheeled Albi smartly and hissed through gritted teeth, "Let me handle this. Eyes down. No English."

He adopted a relaxed pose as he watched them pick their way towards us. There were three horsemen, and to my surprise, I saw as they came near they were Europeans—explorers of some sort. They wore unflattering khaki garb and their horses carried bulging saddlebags. They rode slowly, no doubt held up by the little donkey tethered to one of the horses, its back heaped with various cases and boxes.

"Hello, there," hailed the fellow in front. "I say, hello! *Assalam aleikum*," he said, drawling the words heavily as he waved.

Sebastian inclined his head with slow grace. *"Aleikum assalam,"* he returned.

They closed the distance, and as they reached us, I realized the second horseman was in fact a woman. She rode astride like the men, and her costume was every bit as plainly serviceable.

The last man was more preoccupied with getting the donkey where he was supposed to be, and the woman looked frankly bored, but the first man gave a wide smile and stood in his stirrups, gesturing broadly towards the plateau.

"Did you mean to camp here, friend? Only it's the best

ground for miles, and we thought we'd do the same. D'ye speak English?"

Sebastian inclined his head again. "I do. But my wife does not."

I suppressed a flicker of irritation and concentrated on looking mystified by the conversation.

"Oh, splendid. I'm afraid my Arabic isn't all it ought to be," the man said. He removed his hat, showing a stripe of bright white skin above the flaming pink of his sunburnt brow. "My name is Johnson, Richard Johnson. This is my wife, Rosamund. And bringing up the rear back there is Alec MacGregor, Old Lecky we call him. We're archaeologists on our way to a dig near Palmyra."

Sebastian gave him a long, cool look. "You are a long way from Palmyra, my friend." He had adopted a slightly accented version of English with Rashid's soft vowels. It was astonishing how different that little trick of the voice made him sound. He was suddenly quite foreign to me, and I understood then how far I had come from the girl who had run out on her wedding only a few short weeks before.

Mr. Johnson laughed, a quick barking sound, like a fox. "Yes, we are. But it's the missus' first time in this part of the world. Thought she'd like to see where I spent my bachelor days," he added with a wink.

Sebastian nodded towards the end of the plateau. "There is a stream there with fresh water for your horses."

"And you don't mind if we share the camping?" Mr. Johnson asked. The other two seemed to have no opinion on the matter. Mrs. Johnson was studying her nails and Old Lecky was trying to wake up the donkey, which seemed to have fallen asleep standing up.

"Not at all," Sebastian told him.

"Very kind of you," Mr. Johnson said. "You must share our

meal as soon as Rosamund has prepared it. Perhaps your wife would lend a hand?"

I kept my expression carefully blank but poked Sebastian in the back as he nodded. "Of course," he said graciously. "You will permit us to wash first and water our horse?"

"Absolutely, my dear fellow. Come along to our camp. We'll pitch the tents now and start getting things in order."

Sebastian clicked to Albi and she surged forward. By the time we reached the stream, I was seething.

"Are you quite mad?" I asked softly as I slid stiff-legged from Albi's back. "You expect me to be able to keep up the fiction of not understanding English for an entire evening with those people? And since when do I cook your supper?"

"Since I want to know more about our coincidental strangers," he said with a grim look.

"Coincidental? You don't believe them?" I trotted behind as he led Albi to the water to take a deep drink.

"I think their appearance is a little too timely. We've been out of Damascus for exactly one day and already we encounter a party of fake archaeologists?"

"How do you know they're fakes?"

He shrugged. "Intuition."

"Intuition? That's not very spylike," I grumbled.

He rolled his eyes as he unstrapped Albi's saddle. "What do you know of it? Intuition is nothing more than swift observation and calculation so rapid your mind doesn't even register it. My instinct says they're not what they seem. If you want particulars, you've no further to look than Johnson's complexion."

"What's the matter with his complexion?"

"He's badly sunburnt. An archaeologist who's spent time in the field—as he claims he has—wouldn't burn so badly. He would also have quite a collection of lines about his eyes from a lifetime of squinting at the sun. He's got none in spite of his

age. Neither has his portly little friend. They're no more archaeologists than I am."

"All right, you've persuaded me. But what are they really
doing here and why lie about it?"

Sebastian shrugged. "They might be doing surveys secretly
for the oil companies. You can't ride a mile out here without
stumbling over a group of them. And none of them ever tells
the truth about what they're doing for fear of tipping off the
others to a likely spot."

I glanced about the meadow with its soft spring grass. "Is
this a likely spot?"

"No, but they said they were on the way to Palmyra. Much
more promising landscape for that sort of thing. And Mesopotamia is heaving with the stuff. You can't throw a rock without hitting a geyser of it."

"I think you might have chosen the wrong line of work,"
I mused.

He shot me a dark look as he tended to Albi, rubbing her
down and supplementing her grass with fodder he had brought
from Damascus. When we had washed our hands and faces
and Sebastian had rigged up a small tent, we made our way to
their campsite. They had accomplished a remarkable amount
in so short a time. They had pitched tents—three, I was interested to see. Apparently the Johnsons' marriage was not a
demonstrative one. And they had arranged picnic rugs around
a merrily crackling fire to make a sort of seating area. A flat
rock had been cleared for Rosamund Johnson to use to prepare the food.

I gave her a quick smile to show my friendliness, but she
sized me up coolly. "You don't look remotely useful in that
costume," she said. "Sit there."

She pointed to another rock and I gave no sign of understanding anything she said, only the gesture, which was un-

mistakable. I seated myself and watched as she expertly mixed up flour and water to make flatbreads and assembled a sort of stew made of meat and spices. She moved with an economical grace, every movement efficient and tidy, her long white hands stirring and shaping and reaching as she worked. She must have been aware of my scrutiny, but she said nothing, merely continued her preparations with the same chilly precision. Her hair was black, but not the flat hennaed black of mine. It was a rich black, glossy as a crow's feathers, with a blue sheen in the depths, but scraped back into an unflattering style, old-fashioned and heavy, plaited tightly and pinned at the nape of her neck. Her eyes, when they turned on me, were an odd grey, almost silver, and her brows were highly arched and might have been expressive if she had not been so perfectly detached. Her features were lovely, and it occurred to me that she had deliberately downplayed her beauty with her choice of clothing and hairstyle. A little powder and rouge and she would be devastating, I decided, and I wondered whether I should offer her a bit of Sebastian's kohl as an improvement.

She finished assembling the food then turned to me, her generous mouth curved into a sweet, sudden smile. She held out a bowl of oranges. "Would you mind carrying these, you stupid whore?"

I smiled broadly, holding out my hands as her husband came over to where we stood.

"Well?" It was a single word, but it carried a world of meaning.

Rosamund Johnson shook her head. "He was telling the truth. She doesn't understand English."

He smiled at me and reached out to take an orange from the bowl. "Excellent. He's a merchant from Damascus. He and his bride are going to visit family at the seaside. Thought he'd take her the scenic way round," he told his wife with a lip that curled faintly into a sneer.

"Quite the honeymoon," she said lightly.

"Quite," he returned. "But better than ours," he added with a meaningful look.

She gave him a smile as honeyed as the one she had offered me. "If you attempt to come into my tent again, I will kill you. And I won't bother to make it look like an accident. If you want my help, get rid of these two in the morning."

He gave her a speculative glance. "When you say 'get rid of—'"

She made an impatient gesture. "I mean let them leave. They're no use to us."

He held her eyes a long moment then nodded. "As you wish, *darling*," he said, drawing out the last word in an exaggerated caress.

He walked back to where Sebastian stood chatting with Old Lecky. My face hurt from smiling, but my winsome expression hadn't slipped so much as an inch.

Rosamund Johnson gave me a cynical look. "Keep smiling, little one. I just saved your life."

The rest of the evening passed so conventionally, I almost believed I had dreamt the entire conversation. Rosamund was an excellent cook and they were heavily provisioned with everything from tins of French pâté to smoked oysters. We ate heartily before finishing with coffee and oranges, and finally Sebastian, with flowery compliments and much grateful *salaam*ing, said our goodbyes and escorted me to our tent at the edge of the stream.

He gave me a little push and I collapsed inside the tent, every muscle of my body aching.

"I would sell you to anyone who offered to take you if I could get a hot bath in exchange," I told him.

"If they'd bathe me, too, I'd let you," he said, falling onto the makeshift pallet with a heavy groan. "Well, I was right about their not being archaeologists. The portly fellow doesn't even know the word *lithic*."

"I don't know the word *lithic*," I pointed out.

"It means stone, you poor undereducated ninny. But no one expects you to know. You're not trying to pass yourself off as a digger-up of priceless antiquities."

I propped myself on one elbow to see his face. His eyes were closed and the shadow at his jaw was much darker than it had been that morning. He wouldn't need to darken it with soot again.

"I may not be a digger-up of priceless antiquities, but I am a winkler-out of secrets," I told him.

He opened one eye. "Even as the mute wife of the merchant Talal?"

"Oh, is that your name? I don't like it. Why not Hussein? Or Rashid? I like Rashid."

"I noticed," he said dryly. He closed his eye. "What secrets have you winkled, wife of mine?"

"I know that the Johnsons are most probably not married. I know he is after something that he can only get with her help. And I know she would love nothing better than to stick a knife in his ribs," I said pleasantly.

Both of his eyes flew open. "You're joking. When did you learn all that?"

"Right after she called me a whore."

He pushed himself to a sitting position, all fatigue quite fled. He was alert and commanding. "Tell me. From the beginning," he ordered.

I related the conversation as I had heard it, not omitting my impressions of them, as well. "Old Lecky is a sort of sidekick, I think. Clearly Johnson is driving the whole plot, whatever it is. And she doesn't like it one bit, but he has a hold over her. I can't imagine what it is, but it's left her furiously angry, only she hides it rather well. I'd never have known she was so enraged if she hadn't had a go at him. But he must need her because he stood for it. That means whatever they're after is bigger than her anger and his pride."

"Something like the Ashkelon hoard," he said, his face grim.

I shivered.

"Goose walk over your grave?" he asked.

"Something like that. I don't want to stay here, not now that we know what they're like."

"We don't know for certain they're after the treasure. And Mrs. Johnson, if that is her name, has persuaded them we're harmless. If we leave now, it will make them suspicious. Much better to sit it out and leave at first light as we planned."

"They could slit our throats while we sleep!" I protested.

Sebastian looked affronted. "Do you actually think I'd let that happen?"

"I don't think you'd have much choice if you were dead," I grumbled.

But I rolled over with my back to him and within moments, I was fast asleep.

The next morning, just before dawn rose over the ridge, Sebastian shoved me awake.

"You don't have a knife in your ribs," he informed me tartly. "I checked. Now get up and look sharp. I want to be out of here."

Before I could get my bearings he had disassembled the little tent and packed it swiftly onto Albi's back. He shoved a handful of dried apricots at me. "Breakfast," he informed me as he tossed me into the saddle.

We were gone just as the sun touched the edge of the ridge, chasing the long purple shadows of morning from the meadow. I thought of the guidebooks I had read. "In another month, this whole area will be covered in poppies," I told him, "a vast carpet of scarlet as far as the eye can see."

His only response was a grunt, and I sighed, shoving another apricot into my mouth. I had obviously insulted him by my doubts of the previous night, and Sebastian clearly had a gift for sulking. I entertained myself by peering closely at the Johnsons' camp as we rode past. The fire had burnt out and it had a cold, shuttered look, and I was glad to put them behind us. The sudden appearance of the sun, warming the stone landscape with its golden-pink light filled me with sudden confidence. I pinned my veil into place, and he touched Albi's flank, commanding her to move out onto the plateau and down the long dusty track towards the sea.

SIXTEEN

Sebastian insisted upon taking a circuitous route once again, winding up and down the hills of the Anti-Lebanon until at last we reached Sidon, once the great Phoenician port with its citadel by the sea. While I kept my eyes properly downcast, Sebastian manoeuvered the horse through the teeming throng of townsfolk and passengers and merchants, all making their way somewhere. The bright salty tang of the sea hung in the air, and with it less savoury smells—oil and rotting fish and coal fires. Sebastian left Albi at a stable, paying out what seemed a substantial sum for the privilege.

"Rashid will come and fetch her," he assured me softly. I must have looked anxious, but he gave me a quick nod and a pat to the waist. I ought to have realised he wouldn't have overlooked making arrangements for her. I stroked her neck in farewell and hurried after Sebastian, trotting obediently behind as he made his way unerringly towards a small steamer that stood rocking at its berth. Sailors hurried to and fro, doing various and important things with ropes and coal and ballast, while passengers stood around looking bored. I kept my gaze firmly on Sebastian as Demetrius had instructed, and I was impressed with his quiet authority. He paid the captain in cash for our fares, extracting a number of notes from a small purse at his belt, and apparently negotiating firmly, as any good merchant would do. We were shown to a small cabin with a leer from the captain, and I remembered we were supposed to be playing the parts of newlyweds. I could only guess what he was thinking, and I felt my cheeks flush as I turned away to follow Sebastian.

The cabin was small and spare, and I looked around curiously. There were charts on the wall, and a few antique instruments on a shelf along with a photograph of a stern-looking woman and two extremely ugly children.

"It's the captain's own cabin," Sebastian told me. "He's full up, but was willing to take us on when I pleaded a bride's necessity for privacy."

"More like a bride's necessity for a bath," I corrected.

He shrugged. "We can't manage that, but at least there will be food. Ah, that's it now," he said as a knock came at the door.

Sebastian admitted a cabin boy who brought in a tray of covered dishes. Sebastian gave him a generous tip, which seemed to thrill him, and he hurried away, ducking his head in a gesture of thanks and respect.

"You've made a friend there," I told him. I uncovered the dishes, nearly weeping as I saw meatballs and rice and dishes of vegetables, hot and savoury along with a whole fish cooked in a broth of spices.

"What is it?" he asked, peering over my shoulder.

I was already sticking a fork into the fish. "I don't care, but if you wait any longer, there won't be any for you," I warned him.

We settled down and dug into the food, not even speaking until every bowl and plate was scraped clean.

"God, that was delicious," he said at last as he pushed the last of the dishes aside. "You don't often get proper fish in Syria, not like that." I must have looked puzzled because he nodded towards the porthole. "This coast isn't a gentle one. There's a very narrow bit of ledge running alongside the land and then it drops off into very deep waters."

"And no shallow water means nothing for the fish to feed on," I reasoned. "Ergo, not much fishing about."

"Compared to other ports? No." He cocked his head, giving me an appraising look. "You're a quick study, I'll give you that."

I shrugged. "I like to learn. There's nothing quite so exciting as finding out something you didn't know before, don't you think?"

"I can think of one or two things more exciting," he said with a flash of something wicked in his eyes. But his tone was bland and he looked again to the porthole. "Here's something new for you then—did you know the first mermaid was said to have swum in these very waters?"

"No! Tell me," I urged, and he settled back into his chair, hands laced behind his head. With his long boots and elegant robes he looked like nothing so much as an Eastern pirate lord.

He told me the story, his voice a lazy drawl as he recounted it. "Long ago, Syrians worshipped a goddess named Atargatis, the Great Mother, the source of all fertility and life. Her priests were so devoted they would work themselves into fits of ecstatic worship and emasculate themselves. But the goddess loved a mortal, an unworthy youth, who was untrue to her. When she bore his child, she flung herself into the sea in a fit of despair and shame, intending to turn herself into a fish. But so great was her beauty that only half of her body changed. She had the tail of a splendid fish but the breasts and face of a beautiful woman, the very first mermaid. Sailors who ply these waters still hope to catch glimpses of her on moonlit nights, swimming alongside their ships."

"Atargatis? I've never heard of her."

"You have," he said with a smile. "Some call her Astarte, others mingle her myths with those of Aphrodite and Venus, goddesses born of the sea. They say the center of her cult was in Ashkelon."

"Ashkelon! That name does keep cropping up, doesn't it? Sebastian," I said, adopting my most winsome smile, "I don't suppose—"

"No," he said flatly. "We've already discussed it, Poppy. The most dangerous bit is behind us. We're at sea now. A few stops along the coast and we'll be in Alexandria—just a short train journey from Cairo and my contacts there. I'm not changing my mind, and that's an end to the matter."

"You can't blame me for trying," I pointed out cheerfully.

"I should be greatly disappointed if you hadn't," he agreed.

He rose and put the tray outside the door, locking it carefully, placing the single chair underneath the knob.

"You're very cautious," I observed.

"This wouldn't have been my first choice," he said soberly. "There are too many other people on board, but I didn't dare hire a private boat. That would have attracted too much attention. I hoped by masquerading as honeymooners, we might persuade the captain to be discreet. Although, from the looks of that photograph, it's been a while since he was a bridegroom," he added with a flick of a glance to the captain's wife.

My lips twitched. "She might be a perfectly lovely woman," I said with an attempt at severity. "Perhaps she takes care of orphans or nurses the sickly."

"Poppy, her whiskers are thicker than mine. Furthermore, she's pinching the boy, and the girl looks as if her braids are so tight her scalp is about to bleed. Clearly the woman is a misery. No wonder the poor fellow seems so happy to be going to sea," he said.

"True enough. I wonder why he married her." I took the photograph, scrutinizing the unlovely face and the severe expression. There was nothing about her that seemed kind or generous or loving, and yet she had a husband and a pair of children and a purpose to her life.

I put the photograph back abruptly.

"It was your choice," he said, his voice oddly gentle.

"What was?"

"Leaving that lordling at the altar." He removed the headdress that had confined him all day and ran his hands through his tumbled hair. "Christ, that feels better." He eyed my gown. "You haven't had that corset off in two days. You must be in misery."

"A bit," I admitted.

He slipped a knife from his boot and sat on the edge of the narrow bed. "Well, I'm no Circassian bridegroom, but I'll do the best I can."

I hesitated. "How will I lace it again in the morning? I haven't spare laces and I can't fit into the gown without the corset."

"Demetrius anticipated that. There's a set in my bag," he assured me. I went to him, surprised to find that as I approached, he dropped his eyes. I stood with my back to him, waiting for the prick of the knife. It wasn't that I didn't trust Sebastian, but Demetrius had explained how delicate the cutting of the corset was, and it was a measure of my discomfort that I was willing to risk modest disfigurement rather than let the corset stay on a minute longer. I opened the outer dress, unclasping the wide buttons and dropping it to the floor. Then off came the underdress, leaving only the narrow pair of trousers and the corset itself laced over a whisper-thin chemise.

I took a deep breath, steeling myself, and Sebastian gave a little laugh, his breath warm on my neck. "That doesn't speak much to your confidence in me," he told me.

Before I could respond, I felt a quick tug and heard the whisper of steel against silk and it was done. The corset hesitated a moment, then dropped to the floor, and I felt a flood of relief.

"Oh, that's bliss," I moaned. I stretched my arms over my head and wriggled in pure pleasure. I turned to thank Sebastian but he was sitting with his eyes closed on the bed, waiting.

There was an expression of such perfect resignation on his face that I thought of a painting I had once seen.

"You look exactly like your namesake," I told him.

He opened his eyes slowly. "My namesake?"

"Saint Sebastian. Suffering but prepared for holy martyrdom. Determined to do the right thing even if it kills you."

I was watching him closely, and that was the only reason I saw him swallow hard. His expression was calm and his voice was even. I wondered how much effort it cost him to choke down whatever emotion he was feeling and give me nothing but the patient martyr.

"That is what Nanny taught me, you know," he said softly. "'Be good, think good, do good.' Rather difficult to escape your cradle training."

"Sebastian—" I began. He rose to his feet, folding his arms over his chest as if to ward me off.

"Unless you're planning on planting an arrow in my chest and ending my misery, perhaps you'll be good enough to leave off playing at torturing me," he said.

"Torturing you! I would never torture you," I protested.

"Then put your clothes on," he said coldly. He moved across the small cabin and opened the porthole. The sun was shedding long golden rays over the sea, gilding it like a Renaissance painting as we left Sidon and turned down the coast towards Cairo.

He watched the sea as I slipped back into the underdress. I couldn't fasten it properly, but at least I looked respectable again, and when he eventually turned around, I was the very picture of propriety. I sat on the bunk with my knees firmly together and my lips prim.

His mouth twitched in response, but he said nothing.

I looked about the small cabin and spied something of interest in the corner. I darted over and dived to retrieve it. "Is this what I think it is?" I demanded.

"It's a hookah," Sebastian answered. I had seen men smoking them in the coffee houses in Damascus, but none had seemed as fine as this one. It was a marvellous piece, fashioned of bright brass with a blown-glass bowl and a long, curving snake of a mouthpiece fitted with more brass.

"Can we smoke it?" I asked.

Sebastian seized it from me and put it firmly aside. "No, we cannot."

"Why not? If the captain has a pipe, he must have something to put into it. Where's the tobacco?"

I started to rummage through the various drawers and cupboards fitted into the cabin, but Sebastian put up a warning finger. "It mightn't be tobacco."

"What on earth do you mean?" I found a small tobacco tin and seized it with a triumphant smile. "Here it is!" I opened it to find a collection of small blackish pebbles. "You're right. This isn't tobacco." Realisation dawned and I held out the tin breathlessly. "Is this opium?"

Sebastian peered into the tin and took out a pebble, rolling it closely between his fingers. He gave it a quick sniff and replaced it. "Yes, and rather good quality, too. They mix it with tobacco here to smoke in the *nargileh*. Quite a different process than the opium pipes of the East. Now be a good girl and put it back."

"I will not," I told him squarely. "I'm smoking it."

He grabbed the box away from me and put it back into the cupboard, slamming the door firmly and blocking it with his own body. "You are not," he told me sternly. "What on earth has got into you? I thought you were a respectable girl, and here you are trying to steal opium and smoke it!"

I gave him a dark look. "I told you I wanted adventure. When in the whole of my life am I going to get the chance to smoke opium again?"

"Anytime you like if you stay out here," he returned. "But stealing the captain's choice cache won't win us any favour when he finds out. And he will find out. It smells, you know."

"No, I don't." I narrowed my eyes at him. "Do you?"

He had the grace to look a little uncomfortable.

"You do! You've smoked it," I said.

"You needn't sound so admiring. Yes, most people do when they spend enough time in this part of the world. It isn't so frowned upon as it is at home. It's a Turkish custom, you know. And it's spread rather widely."

"What was it like?" I demanded.

He opened his mouth then snapped it shut again. "You are a maddening child," he managed through gritted teeth.

"Either you tell me, or I will just light up that pipe when you're asleep," I warned him.

He crossed his arms over his chest, and the gesture pulled his shirt open a little to show a tantalising peek of firm muscle. *Fine for him to talk about me torturing him*, I thought darkly. He certainly had no idea the effect he was capable of creating.

If my eyes lingered on the strip of bare chest he was showing, he didn't notice. He was thinking. He rubbed at the beard along his jaw. "The smoke smells like ripe fruit, ripe to

"You are," I argued. "I should know. I took a course in psychology. The Freudian sort," I added loftily. "Tell me about your dreams."

"I am not going to tell you my dreams," he said flatly. "But I can assure you I am entirely and wholly without repression, at least as much as any proper English gentleman can be," he added wryly.

"Then what is it?" I asked. I wouldn't have had the nerve to ask if I could have seen his face. But the dark is comforting that way. It lends courage when you haven't got enough of your own. "Some people think I'm rather pretty," I said slowly. "And we're alone. In the dark. On a bed. And you haven't so much as tried to kiss me. Why?"

He gave a heavy sigh. "Poppy—" he began.

I cut him off. "Never mind. If you have to explain, it's not going to change anything." I cleared my throat. "I still say there's something wrong with you, though."

He gave a short, mirthless laugh. "I daresay."

I went on in a slow, dreamy voice. "I suppose there's someone back in England. I ought to have considered that before. There is, isn't there? You're trying to be faithful to her. What's she like? Accomplished, no doubt. I imagine she rides well and has perfect hair and arranges flowers and does nice things for the poor. She probably calls herself Pamela."

"Why Pamela?" His voice sounded amused.

"All accomplished girls with perfect hair are called Pamela. Everyone knows that. I suppose you were just waiting to find Gabriel and put that business behind you before you married her. You'll be very happy, I'm sure. Now the war's over, you can find a nice living somewhere and marry her and breed Bedlingtons."

He gave a low, rumbling laugh. "Why Bedlingtons?"

"They were the stupidest looking dogs I could think of," I said savagely. I turned on my side and punched the pillow.

"I've always thought Bedlingtons were perfectly nice," he said.

"You would." My throat was tight and hot, but I swallowed hard until the feeling went away. I made my breathing deep and even, and after a long while I think I convinced him I was asleep.

And in the dark silence, he spoke, in a still, quiet voice so soft I almost didn't hear him and I realised it was a scrap of poetry.

"'I sing the Poppy! The frail snowy weed! The flower of Mercy! that within its heart Doth keep "a drop serene" for human need, A drowsy balm for every bitter smart. For happy hours the Rose will idly blow— The Poppy hath a charm for pain and woe.'"

He said nothing else, and after a while I heard his breaths come in a slow, even pattern, and I knew he slept. But I lay awake, thinking of the charm of the poppy.

When I woke, the light was streaming in the porthole. Sebastian had risen and washed, and courteously stepped out of the cabin while I did the same. When he returned, I stood with my back to him in my chemise and trousers as he laced me back into the corset. He jerked hard on the laces, never saying a word, and when he had tied them smartly he stepped out again until I had finished dressing. For all its glamour, I was beginning to loathe my beautiful Circassian gown, and I wished fervently Demetrius had given me one of the loose, enveloping black robes to wear instead. I would have suffocated, but at least I could have moved freely.

When Sebastian returned the second time, he brought a tray of food from the cabin boy and we fell on it like savages.

"It's amazing how this sort of thing whets the appetite," I told him as I reached for another bit of flatbread slathered in cherry jam.

He nodded. "You'll learn to eat as much as you can when you find food. You never know when you'll eat again. Although in our case, this only need hold us until luncheon."

I brushed the crumbs carefully from my fingertips. "I've been thinking about that," I began.

He held up a hand. "I told you last night. It is out of the question."

"Oh, please," I pleaded. "Ashkelon is right on the way— you said so yourself. We can disembark and have a look at the monastery where you found the map. I know Gabriel said he searched, but what if he missed something? It need only delay us a day. And it would add considerably to the confusion if anyone were following us," I added slyly.

Sebastian did not rise to the bait. "The sooner I get you to Cairo, the better," he told me in a tone that brooked no argument.

I tried a different tack. "You have a remarkably stunted sense of adventure," I replied. "Surprising, given your occupation, but I suppose that's why they kept you in the office."

He gave me a bland look. "Yes, I'm sure that's it."

I tipped my head. "I hate that."

"What?"

"When you give me that agreeable tone when I know perfectly well you don't agree with me at all."

He shrugged. "A wise man doesn't fight every battle that comes his way, my dear. I save my strength for the fights that matter. And your assessment of my character does not matter to me in the slightest."

"Well, that's wounding. We're co-adventurers together," I pointed out. "We've put our lives in each other's hands. You ought to care what I think of you." He said nothing but continued to eat placidly while I found myself getting more and more enraged. "What do you think of me?"

He put down his bread and sat back, folding his arms over his chest. "Do you really want to know?"

I rolled my eyes in exasperation. "Of course. I wouldn't have asked otherwise."

"Fine. You're impulsive. Now, I rely on intuition, but I have the experience to back it up. You, my innocent flower, do not. And one day that might get you killed. If you want to play at being a detective, you would do reasonably well at finding lost dogs and the odd stray sock, but anything more dangerous would be like handing fire to a baby."

I gaped at him. "That is the most outrageous, unfair—"

"But you more than make up for it by your ability to accept criticism so reasonably," he said with a sunny smile.

"Rat," I said succinctly, but I was smiling a little in spite of myself. "You don't really mean that, do you?"

He considered a moment, choosing his words carefully. "You do have a good brain, and you don't rely on it nearly as much as you should. Poppy, I'm the first one who will defend the hunch. God knows I've seen them save a life more times than I care to count and in ways I cannot understand. But you also have to have a plan. Situations like the one we currently find ourselves in are like chess games. You must not only plan your own strategy, but anticipate your opponent's."

I thought that over, then ventured a question. "What if your opponent does something you couldn't anticipate, not with all the planning in the world?"

He grinned. "Then you have to conjure solutions out of thin air with nothing more than your wits and a bit of luck.

And everything I just said about strategy won't matter a bit because that's when that intuition of yours will come in handy." He paused. "And you have to be ready for the luck to run out because one day it will."

He spoke quietly, his words weighted with conviction, his eyes holding mine. I tried to take a deep breath and realised I couldn't.

"Have you ever run out of luck?"

He hesitated then gave me a thin smile. "How could I? I'm just the office boy, remember?"

He seemed shuttered then, like a house that a moment before had been welcoming and warm but had suddenly closed its doors. I pressed further.

"Tell me about working here. During the war, I mean."

His lips parted, and his eyes took on a faraway gleam. Just then there was a knock at the door.

The cabin boy called out something in Arabic, but I understood one word and I jumped to my feet as Sebastian gave me a grudging nod.

"Very well. We can go above deck and look at the port."

I didn't stop to give him a chance to change his mind. We had reached Ashkelon.

SEVENTEEN

We hurried up to the deck just as the steamer docked, and Sebastian guided me to an out-of-the-way spot where we wouldn't interfere with the business at hand. Sailors shouted and laughed at one another as they manoeuvered themselves about, unloading goods and the few passengers who wished to go ashore. The port was much smaller than I had expected and not in excellent repair. It was difficult to imagine that it had once been the gateway to the southern lands of the Outremer, the Crusader kingdoms wrestled from the Muslims and lost again in countless battles and untold lives. As we stood on the deck, Sebastian quietly pointed out where the fortified towers had once stood, fifty-three of them built by the Fatimids to repel the Crusader armies. He was careful to keep his voice to a whisper to conceal the fact that we were speaking English, and to anyone watching, we would have looked like a devoted bridegroom and his shy bride, taking the air on our sea voyage. We attracted no attention.

At least, not at first. But as the last of the new passengers came aboard and the cargo hatches were neatly closed, I became aware of a prickling between my shoulder blades. I did not turn, not then. I waited a long moment, keeping my expression calm so my eyes shouldn't betray anything. After I had counted to thirty, I reached down to tighten the lace of my boot. As I did, I darted a glance between my arm and the side of my body. Behind us and a deck above, I saw him.

I rose slowly, pointing to a spot on shore as if asking Sebastian a question. He leaned near and I murmured softly, "On the deck behind us. A man named Faruq. He is the driver of the Comtesse de Courtempierre."

Sebastian merely smiled at me fondly and pointed elsewhere. *"Habibti,"* he began loudly. I knew the endearment meant something like *sweetheart*, and he was playing his part to perfection. He lowered his head close to mine, and when he did, his voice was deadly serious even as he smiled into my face.

"Are you sure?"

I gave a single quick nod.

"Very well." He turned back to look at the tired remnants of Ashkelon.

"What are we going to do?" I hissed.

He gave me another of his fond looks and dropped his head to whisper into my ear. "Remember when I told you that you must always have a contingency plan?"

I nodded and he turned so that only I could see his face. Then he winked.

Instantly, I felt the initial cold rush of terror ebb, and something warm and certain filled me. We would be fine.

Of course, in the next moment, the fear was back and treble what it had been. I felt a bolt of sheer panic, and my palms went icy cold. Sebastian took one in his. He had not looked at me again, but kept his eyes fixed on the silhouette of the town. How he knew what I was feeling, I could not imagine, but he held my hand firmly in his own.

"You have to trust me, or this won't work," he said tightly.

"I trust you." The words were faltering, and he heard my hesitation.

"Mean it."

"I trust you," I said, this time with more conviction.

"Halting, but it will have to do," he said. Still he stood, waiting for something. I didn't know what, and I dared not look behind me. I couldn't tell if Faruq had left his perch on the deck above us or if he had even spotted us. There was a chance he hadn't, but would Sebastian take the risk of fleeing to our cabin knowing the villain was on board? It made perfect sense now. Faruq had been in league with Hugh and had followed us out of the villa, intent upon killing him and taking the gold for himself. *A quarrel amongst thieves*, I thought coldly. And now he was following us in order to get us to lead him to the gold. Then what? Would he kill us as brutally as he had killed Hugh?

I tortured myself a few moments with thoughts like those while Sebastian still stood, looking for all the world like a bored tourist. I was screaming inside for him to do something, anything, and it wasn't until the sailors moved to the gangplank that he finally made his move.

Just as they began to heave it back onto the steamer, Sebastian grabbed my hand and lunged for it. Caught by surprise, the sailors had only winched it back a few feet, but the gap seemed like a yawning abyss as we pounded down the gangplank towards it. The further we got, the more the gangplank bounced, tossing us this way and that as we teetered near the edges.

I saw the end of the gangplank bouncing higher and faster and knew there was no way in my tight gown and thick corset I could ever make the leap. But Sebastian had anticipated that, too. At the last moment, he grabbed me by the waist and tossed me onto the dock. I landed in a pile of rope, and looked up just in time to see him take an almighty leap and clear the gap by mere inches. The crew laughed and waved and finished winching back the gangplank as Sebastian gave them a quick salute.

He put out a hand and lifted me from the coil of rope, setting me on my feet. I glared at him, wishing I could unleash a stream of choice words on him. But that would have to wait. Sailors and fishermen and merchants were crowding the docks, most laughing and pointing. Sebastian gave them a good-natured smile and sketched a gesture of *salaam*, saying something pithy in Arabic. He put an arm around my waist and squeezed and they all laughed as they parted and let us pass. I darted one glance behind to see the steamer easing away from the dock. And on the top deck, Faruq stood, watching us with hate burning hot in his eyes.

"That was close," Sebastian hissed in my ear. He took me by the hand and pushed me forward, away from the docks and the laughing spectators until at last we reached an alley where no one had seen our dramatic exit from the steamer and we stopped to catch our breath.

"What did you say on the dock?" I asked him.

"Something to the effect that I was too eager to sample the charms of my bride to spend another night of my honeymoon on a narrow ship's berth," he told me absently as he studied our surroundings. "Only not in quite such gentlemanly terms."

"I was right to call you a rat," I replied. "What now?"

He pursed his lips in annoyance. "Now we find horses and provisions and get out of town as quickly as we can. The next port isn't far and our friend will certainly disembark there and make his way back. And if he has co-conspirators, he'll no doubt warn them where we were last seen."

I turned to him with shining eyes. "That means—"

"Yes," he said irritably. "That means you get your way after all. We're going to the monastery."

I tried not to gloat, particularly as hiring a horse was impossible. Sebastian could only manage a donkey, and it was so old and decrepit it made the donkey from Damascus look like a Derby winner. Sebastian had only his purse of money and our papers with him. The rest of our provisions—food and goatskins and saddlebag—had been left in the cabin of the ship. He moaned loudest about the loss of his razor, and we dared not take the time to look for one in Ashkelon.

"You have a beard in any event," I pointed out reasonably. "I can't think why you need it."

"Because a neatly trimmed beard marks the difference between a gentleman and an ape," he told me coldly. "We are also out of soap."

I sulked a little at this, but he secured food and water and had the little donkey packed and ready to go within half an hour of jumping off the steamer. I moved to mount and held up my foot for him to help me up. But he was already on its back, gathering up the rotting rein.

"Where do I ride?" I asked.

"You don't." He clucked gently to the donkey and it perked up its enormous ears. They walked off, the little donkey waving his ears happily while Sebastian sat upright as a lord on his swaying back. I trotted after them.

"You're not serious."

Sebastian flicked me a glance. "In a Muslim country, a wife does not ride while her husband walks."

I gave him a withering look.

"I know it is the custom but surely—"

"Hush. Mind your place and don't look so sullen. It's only until we get outside the city. And watch your feet. You trod in something a goat left behind."

I swore savagely, lifting my beautiful dress out of the goat dung and hurrying after him. I continued to swear with every step, absolutely certain Sebastian was enjoying this more than he should. I stumbled and slipped on the disgusting stones of the streets and dragged my embroidered hem in the muck, tripping over it occasionally. I fell behind a little, and Sebastian did not wait for me. He continued on at the same stately pace with no regard for my irritation. Once he even looked back and winked at me. "An adventurer should expect physical hardship," he called softly.

He stopped at one point to take water from his new goatskin, and after a long, noisy drink, held out the skin to me, waving it a little. *"Habibti?"*

I caught up to them, baring my teeth in a vicious smile I hoped he could see through my thin veil. "Stop calling me that."

"It's a term of endearment," he said, sounding a trifle hurt. "It means—"

"I know what it means. And it's becoming increasingly inapt. I think I like you less and less as this trip goes on," I told him.

He blinked rapidly. "You wound me, dearest. Here I am doing everything I can to give you the Levant at its finest. I've set up camp for you within sight of Lady Hester's home at Djoun. I've secured the finest shipboard accommodations for you—"

"Stop speaking," I told him, securing the goatskin and flinging it back. "Stop speaking now and continue not to speak until we get where we are going."

"I am yours to command."

I raised my hand, but he had already touched the little donkey's flanks and they were moving on.

Sebastian was as good as his word. Once we reached the

outskirts of Ashkelon, he dismounted and led the donkey, leaving me to trudge along behind. We walked in silence, but he knew where he was bound. He did not hesitate or look around, and I wondered how long it had been since he had travelled this way. We walked for hours, taking small dusty roads that grew narrower and narrower until they were little more than goat tracks leading upwards into low hills. We skirted a few of these into ever more barren country, and finally, when I thought I couldn't walk another step, he raised his hand. "There."

I looked to where he pointed and saw absolutely nothing—just a bare brown stretch of hillside leading up to two taller peaks.

I shook my head and Sebastian pointed, more emphatically this time. "In the saddle between those two peaks."

I squinted and still couldn't see anything.

He persisted, pointing with more emphasis. "Beyond the little river. Can you see the white line in the rock? That's the path."

I shrugged. "You've eyesight like a hare," I told him.

He gave a short laugh and walked on, encouraging the little donkey, who twitched her ears at him and batted her long lashes.

"I think that animal is flirting with you," I told him as I struggled to keep up.

"I have a way with females," he said blandly.

"Not all of them," I countered with a tartness I hadn't quite intended. "Shall we call the donkey Pamela?"

He laughed again and murmured an endearment to the donkey, stroking one of her long, floppy ears. She gave a happy little bray, and they carried on, toiling upwards into the hillside. I panted after, scrambling over rocks and pits in the path while they seemed as leisurely as if they were out for a Sunday promenade. They crossed the narrow river together, picking a careful path between the stones while I hesitated on the bank.

On the other side, Sebastian turned. "Don't tell me you're afraid of a little fresh water."

"It looks cold," I called.

"It's bloody freezing," he returned cheerfully. "But neither Pamela nor I are coming to carry you over, so you might as well get along."

With yet another muttered curse, I took up my skirts in my hands and walked into the river. Sebastian lied. It wasn't freezing—it was the most horribly frigid water I had ever felt in my life. I yelped as it ran over the tops of my boots, and Sebastian shrugged and pointed to the snowy mountain peaks in the distance.

"Melted snow," he explained.

"Yes, thank you," I said, struggling out on the other side. "That's terribly helpful."

I pushed past him to lead the way up the hill path, thinking only of a warm fire and sleep. Sebastian lagged behind, no doubt looking for pursuers, and I was content to be alone for a bit. From time to time he disappeared completely, but he always found me again. At last, as the last rays of the westering sun disappeared behind the hillside, we reached the saddle between the peaks, and I saw the monastery for the first time. It was a ruin, roofless and missing a few walls, but here and there I could see traces of vast fortifications. The stones that remained were crumbling, some scorched by fire, and I was amazed to see how seamlessly it blended into the landscape. We had been nearly on top of it before I had even seen it was there, and I felt marginally more relaxed about our chances of eluding our pursuers.

"It looks like one of the Crusader castles," I observed.

"Because it was built with the same purpose in mind," he

told me. "Christians weren't always the most popular fellows out here. Many of the monasteries were built to withstand a siege."

"From whom?"

He shrugged. "Muslims who didn't much care for being lectured to by foreigners. Warlords, brigands, thieves. Take your pick."

Sebastian attended to the donkey and fetched water while I poked into the various rooms that were still standing. He found me in the largest room and the only one with a fireplace.

"The old chapter house," he told me. It was missing half its roof, but it was in the best repair of any I had found.

"I suppose it will have to do," I said cheerfully. We set about making it habitable, and I made up a makeshift pair of beds while Sebastian conjured a fire.

I gave the blankets he'd handed me an inquisitive sniff and reared back.

"They reek of donkey," I protested.

He quirked up an eyebrow at me, and I put on a determined smile. "But that's to be expected, I suppose. I guess we're lucky to have anything at all to lie on."

He gave me a nod of satisfaction before turning back to the fire. He was kindling it with a handful of small twigs and I looked over his shoulder.

"There isn't much firewood, is there?"

"Just the burning bush," he said evenly.

I shrugged. "I don't know why they call it that. It doesn't seem to be burning all that well."

"They call it that because it's the actual burning bush, you heretic. You know, Moses?"

He was still occupied with the tricky aspects of starting a fire from pithy green wood, and it smoked like hell as it caught.

"You're having me on," I said finally, waving aside some of the smoke.

"I am not. The original burning bush is said to be at Saint Catherine's monastery, but the monks who settled here claimed to have brought a bit of it with them while they searched for a place to build their community. They wandered this whole countryside, stopping each night. One morning, when they woke, the bush had put down roots, planting itself into the ground. They decided to build there, since the bush had chosen."

I snorted. "Sounds more like one of the brothers got tired of wandering and decided this was as good a place as any to stay."

He gave me a lopsided grin. "Such cynicism in one so young."

I shrugged. "I prefer to think of it as a healthy practicality. I do have some, you know. I'm not entirely useless."

He was quiet a long moment as he fed larger bits of wood to the hungry fire. "I would call you many things, Poppy. Useless isn't one of them."

He rose swiftly and disappeared, returning in few minutes with a goatskin of water and the food he had bought in Ashkelon. The last of the purple twilight had faded, leaving us in darkness, with only the fire for light and the dim stars just beginning to shimmer to life.

He heated flatbreads until they were charred and delicious and so hot they burned my fingers. He passed me one and some sort of salty cheese. "Eat up. There's dried fruit and some nuts as well, but I don't want to dip too far into the supplies. We don't know how long we'll be out here."

He handed over a jar of apricots soaked in honey and when I dipped the bread into the delectable stuff, the result was so sublime I rolled my eyes in ecstasy.

"This is the best meal I have ever eaten in my entire life," I said through a mouthful of the concoction.

He smiled. "I do have my uses."

"I'm sure you do," I told him solemnly. I chewed for a moment then ventured something of an apology. "You know, it's been weighing on my mind, involving you in all of this."

He cocked his head. "Involving me?"

I waved a hand. "In this sort of escapade. I mean, I know you worked with Gabriel Starke and that must have been very thrilling indeed being his underling, but this must be quite beyond the scope of your usual activities."

He put down his bread. "Underling?"

"Yes. Working under Gabriel Starke. It must have been absolutely ripping to be his foot soldier. Oh, don't worry. You're doing very well at leading this little expedition," I assured him. "But I am sorry to have dragged you into it all."

He seemed to choke a little and he cleared his throat before he managed to speak. "How precisely do you think you dragged me into it?"

I flapped a hand. "This whole mess with Hugh. The way I see it, you were simply coming back to find Gabriel and make certain he was alive and well. That's very loyal of you, and certainly something one would expect of a trusted lieutenant," I said hastily. "But I know you didn't expect to track down the gold for yourself. And they'd never have found you if it weren't for me. It's very kind of you to humour me by taking this route to Cairo, and I know it must be taxing your abilities."

He looked thunderstruck, as if someone had just hit him with a hammer, and I hurried to reassure him. "But you really are doing a smashing job of it. This food really is delicious," I told him again.

"Yes, Gabriel always did praise my abilities in the kitchen," he said tightly.

I sighed. Somehow I seemed to have offended him again, and I observed, not for the first time, that Sebastian could be a trifle prickly. He fell into a reverie then and said nothing for a long time. The silence fell like the night, deep and purple and heavy between us.

I looked up at the stars again. "They're so close, you could almost believe you could touch one," I mused.

"So long as it isn't the naughty star that goaded Peter Pan into flying off with Wendy," he said absently.

I blinked at him. "What did you say?"

He stirred from whatever had been preoccupying him. "The star. That was the reason Peter Pan fled the nursery with the Darling children. A naughty little star told him the adults were coming back. It was now or never."

"I know," I said, feeling an odd warmth creeping up my chest. "I mentioned it once to Hugh, but he didn't know what I was talking about."

He shrugged. "I blame Nanny. She was always reading to me. Some of it stuck."

"You've mentioned her before. What about your parents?"

He took a deep draught of water from the goatskin. "God, that's foul. I would sell my own sister for a bit of good Irish whisky right now."

He sat back, resting one wrist on his upraised knee. He had taken off his outer robes and his headdress, and again I thought he had the look of a buccaneer, albeit a rather distinguished one. I told him so and he laughed.

"Well, Hook did go to Eton," he pointed out.

"You didn't answer my question. About your parents."

"What do you want to know? They were parents. They had me and promptly forgot."

"That's terrible," I protested.

"But quite natural when one is the youngest of seven."

I gaped at him. "And I thought Mother was overly enthusiastic with five."

"Yes, well. My parents had seven sons. The eldest is twenty years older than I am, and our parents have been dead for quite a long time. It was rather a relief to them to be able to hand me off to Nanny. I wasn't like the rest."

"Why not?" I nibbled at another flatbread, not even minding that this batch tasted strongly of smoke.

"They're all academics. Scholars and clergymen with extremely esoteric interests. I'm politely regarded by them as little better than backwards. They don't think I'm actually mentally defective, but if you asked them, they'd say I was slightly imbecilic."

"That's outrageous! You're one of the cleverest men I've ever met. I'm quite sure Gabriel Starke couldn't have managed half of what he accomplished out here without your help. You're very skilled with maps and languages and—what's so funny?"

He was smiling broadly at me, and the effect was fairly devastating.

He shrugged again. "I just find it amusing to hear what you think of me. A man is never quite certain how the gentler sex perceives him. It's nice to know I'm not entirely stupid in your estimation or only good for my prodigious skills in the kitchen."

"I think you know better than that."

"But you still don't think much of me as a field agent," he said, tipping his head thoughtfully.

I evaded the implied question. "Tell me about this organisation you work for. The one that recruited you and Gabriel Starke in London."

He looked as if he were about to change the subject, but after a moment he sighed. "It's called the Vespiary."

"Like a wasp's nest?"

"Clever girl. Yes. It was formed as a sort of experiment in the 1890s. There were many in the Government who believed Germany was a threat—a rising and credible one. They stepped up their efforts at espionage in all the usual areas, ferreting out all sorts of military secrets, spying on members of political cabinets. But there seemed to be a clear need for another group, one that could handle anything that fell outside the usual channels. The times were changing and espionage had to change with it. Not everyone agreed, so the Vespiary was formed to see if it could hold its own against the more conventional sorts of information-gathering. It specialised in recruiting people with unusual talents, misfits if you like."

"Lost Boys," I said softly.

"And girls. You ought to have met Jocasta," he said, his expression dreamy. "But yes, the ones who were a bit adrift were the best recruits. They took young people mostly, those who had gifts and didn't know what to do with them, people who would have been crushed by the system if they'd been recruited by the more formal organisations. This one was nothing like those. It was a noble experiment, held together by the force of the personalities that ran it. They took people from their own circle when they could, relying on loyalty to bind them together as much as their devotion to duty."

"It sounds magnificent," I breathed.

"It's a job," he corrected gently. "But yes, it has its moments."

"And that's how you met Gabriel and the rest of the Lost Boys?"

He nodded. "We weren't the whole of the Vespiary, not by a long shot. But we were the most unconventional of an unconventional group, and most of us were frightfully young and wet behind the ears. So, they put us together. Some of us had gone to school together. Some were bound by ties of blood or friendship. Some of us were strangers. But the seven of us were like family. Only now it seems one of us has turned."

His voice had hardened and the line of his shadowed jaw went rigid.

"The missing map?"

He nodded. "One of us must have come back here and retrieved it before Gabriel could get back."

I hesitated. "Do you think it's possible that Gabriel took it and lied?"

He spread his hands. "Anything is possible. I've learnt that lesson more than once and in painful ways. But no. I don't think he did. Gabriel has always been quite forthright about his sins. If he'd taken it, he would have said and dared me to make an issue of it."

"Would you have?"

He fixed me with a solemn stare. "I would have thrashed him all the way to Mesopotamia and used what was left to saddle my horse."

I felt a tiny shiver at his words. He didn't seem as if he were jesting, but I knew perfectly well that Sebastian was the last sort of man to engage in a physical fight. He'd proven that often enough by fleeing at the first sign of trouble during our little adventure.

"What do you think will happen with his wife, Evangeline? Do you think they'll reconcile?"

His eyes were oddly bright in the firelight. "Yes. She's the only woman he's ever loved, and Gabriel is the most loyal man I know. He never even touched another woman all those years when he was pretending to be dead."

"How do you know?"

His look was inscrutable. "Men talk."

"About that?" I gaped at him.

He shrugged. "Desert nights get long. Sometimes you're too cold to sleep. Sometimes you're too bloody tired. And sometimes you know the odds against you are so long, the next morning might never come. So you talk. And Gabriel only talked about Evie."

"Who did you talk about?" I asked, feeling oddly breathless. "The estimable Pamela?"

"No one, Poppy. There is no Pamela. There never has been. I've never even met anyone called Pamela."

I started to smile, then faltered. "Wait, you don't mean... you've never? Oh, my. I suspected as much. Being a clergyman would be vastly inhibiting. And besides, I suspect you're quite shy."

He stared back at me, his expression puzzled. "Poppy, what the hell are you talking about?"

"The fact that you're a virgin," I said boldly.

"I bloody well am not!"

"There's no shame in it," I assured him. "In fact, I think it's rather sweet. I'm sure you'll meet the right girl and feel perfectly inclined to amend matters when you marry her. And really, you should. Shall I send you *Married Love*? You know, you ought to read up on the intricacies of marital love."

"Oh, yes," he said, his voice tight. "The bloody sex-tides."

I brightened. "Exactly. Of course, if I'd known you were inexperienced I never would have told you all about that. I must have shocked you terribly," I said reasonably.

He shook his head.

"What's wrong?" I asked, moving closer. "Do you have something in your ear?"

"My head is buzzing," he said, sounding a little dazed.

"Maybe something flew in. Let me look," I told him. Before he could refuse, I sat next to him, peering into his ear. "I don't see anything." I rose on my knees and put one hand under his jaw, brushing the softness of his beard as I tipped his head. I lowered my face to his to peer into his ear. "I still can't see anything."

"There's nothing in my ear," he said tightly. "Now go sit over there."

His tone was cold and clipped and I gave him a pitying look. "I understand. Really, it's quite normal for a virginal male to be nervous in such proximity to the opposite sex. But you must overcome frigidity if you ever want to have a normal relationship with a woman."

His voice was strangled now. "For the last time," he said, grinding out the words through clenched jaws, "I am not a virgin. And I am not frigid. In fact, I am the very opposite of frigid."

I shook my head. "I read about this in my psychology course. It's called 'overcompensation.' It's when a male attempts to overcome his natural reticence around women by—"

I never finished the sentence. With a roar of pure outrage, Sebastian flung himself to his feet, his hands tight on my wrists as he pulled me up close. His eyes blazed, but when he spoke, his voice was surprisingly calm.

"I see that I have your attention. Good. Listen well. I am not a virgin. I am not frigid. I have utterly no difficulties whatsoever with communicating my desire to a woman when I choose to. And this conversation is at an end."

In spite of his last sentence, he hesitated, his mouth hovering near mine. I arched my back and parted my lips, waiting for the kiss that never came.

He stepped back, releasing my hands as quickly as he had seized them.

"Sebastian," I began.

He held up a hand. "Not a word."

He moved away, clenching and unclenching his hands. He turned slightly, his face half in shadow and half lit in the hellish light of the fire.

"I'm going to check on the donkey. I will be a very long time. Kindly be asleep when I return."

And with that he swung on his heel and left.

EIGHTEEN

I did not sleep, not for a long time, but still he did not return and the fire burned itself to ash under the cold and distant stars. Sometime later, far into the night, Sebastian came back, noiseless as a cat, just before the rain began. A soft pattering at first, it soon fell in sheets through the broken roof. Exhausted and peevish, we hauled our bedding under the nearest bit of roof and tried to retrieve what we could of the broken night's rest. I dozed fitfully, damp and cold, and when the rain finally stopped, I fell into a peculiarly shallow sleep where I dreamt of crisp sausages and hot cups of tea.

When I woke, I was alone and freezing. Sebastian had already risen, and I was wrapped in his outer robe as well as my own. He had started a fire with what looked like broken bits of chairs and had apparently just completed some basic ablutions. He was stripped to the waist, wearing only his trousers and riding boots. I blinked furiously, not entirely certain if he were a particularly delicious mirage. His body was utterly gorgeous, and as I stared open-mouthed, he shrugged into his shirt and reached for the inner robe that he left open like a dressing gown as he worked. He warmed more flatbreads and shoved a handful at me.

"Good morning," I told him.

He rolled his eyes. "I would sell you to a Turk's *harim* if it would get me a cup of coffee," he replied.

I realised he wasn't much of a morning person and applied myself to my flatbreads. Afterwards, I was thrilled to find he had warmed a little water and I took a vessel of it into one of the ruined inner rooms to wash as best I could in spite of the corset. I consoled myself by mentally composing a strongly worded note to Demetrius to send coffee when we reached Cairo.

I emerged to find Sebastian tamping down the coals carefully with a booted toe. "When do we have to leave?" I asked.

He shook his head. "We don't. Remember that little river we crossed yesterday? It's in spate now after the rain."

I blinked. "Do you mean we can't cross it?"

"Not unless you've an aeroplane tucked away in that," he said, nodding towards my full skirts.

"Regrettably, no. Still, there must be something we can do. What about climbing up higher and going around?"

He looked amused. "Not possible. The source is a few thousand feet up and miles away. We've not got the equipment, the clothes, or the experience for such an undertaking."

I sat down with a sigh. "Fine. We're stranded. For how long?"

He shrugged. "The wind has turned and the day looks fine. No more rain is coming, so it might go down enough by tomorrow."

"Have we enough food?"

"Travelling with you is like trying to provision Napoleon's army," he told me. "I've never seen a girl who could eat so much and have nothing to show for it," he added, eyeing my slim waist.

"You didn't answer my question," I pointed out.

"Yes. There are more flatbreads and dried fruit and things, and if you're really desperate, I saw a few burrows on the way up. I could go and snare a rabbit."

I stared at him in mingled horror and fascination. "Could you really?"

"Yes. Why?"

"I don't know. It seems such a frightfully bloodthirsty thing to do."

He rolled his eyes. "Perhaps you'd like to have a look around the place. I'm going to tend to the donkey."

He left me then and I amused myself by poking about, climbing over broken stones and remnants of walls, peering into storage rooms and wrecked cupboards. Almost nothing remained of the years the monks had spent there, only a few bits of furniture, riddled with worm and rot, and the faint outlines of a proper herb garden in one of the courtyards.

I found Sebastian long after midday, sitting in the main courtyard, deep in thought.

He looked up when I approached and gave me a quick glance from head to toe. "I've seen fewer cobwebs in haunted houses. You're practically a cocoon," he told me.

I plucked at the sticky silks. "And it wasn't at all worth it," I protested. "Nothing but rubbish left."

"What were you expecting? Templar gold?"

"Maybe," I admitted. "Or a cursed opal necklace. A Chinese jade horse would have been nice. A cache of French porcelain. Even a box full of love letters would have done. Anything other than spiders and broken statues. It's as bad as General Tilney's laundry list," I said.

He gave a shout of laughter. "Oh, God. That's it! You're

Catherine Morland, aren't you? Always prowling about, looking for adventure where it doesn't exist. You think you're living in Northanger Abbey."

He kept laughing, amusing himself at my expense while I stood, hands on hips. "Laugh all you like, Slightly," I said with a smile.

He sobered instantly and gave me a quelling look. "No one but Gabriel calls me that."

He turned away to stir the fire, whistling a soft tune. It was familiar, a waltz of some sort, one of the innocuous little melodies that was so popular that year. It reminded me of the song Hugh and I had danced to on the deck of the Mediterranean steamer. It seemed a lifetime ago, and in the cold grey light of morning, the whole business seemed sordid and distasteful. A man was dead and Sebastian was whistling a tune.

I told him as much and he shook his head.

"You can't think like that, Poppy. You have to look at the broader horizon."

"And what is the broader horizon here?" I demanded.

He began to enumerate on his fingers. "First, we're still at large. Whatever plot is swirling around us, we've kept our heads and we haven't been taken. Second, we're alive, which is more than Mr. Talbot can say."

"Don't," I begged.

"It's the truth," he told me, his voice gentle. "This isn't a game for soft hearts, Poppy. If you can't think about a man being shot to death and be glad it was him instead of you, then you need to go back to England right now and beg Gerald to have you back. Perhaps you could start practising your knitting and flower-arranging on the trip home?"

I squared my shoulders. "You know nothing at all of what I want if you think there's any way I could be induced to marry Gerald. I won't marry him—or any man, for that matter."

"Really?" He cocked his head. "Has proximity to me put you off my sex altogether?"

"No," I told him. "You'd probably do better than most. But the longer I'm out here and the more I see of the world, the smaller and smaller marriage looks. Nothing but sitting by the fire in matching slippers and talking over the price of tea," I said with a shudder.

"I don't think that's always the case. The Starkes, for instance."

I shrugged. "They're not even together. She's on her way back to England and he's here."

"Not for long," he assured me. "Gabriel will win her back."

"How can you be so certain?"

"Because I've never known him to fail at something he wants. And he's never wanted anything like he wants Evie."

He fell to stirring the fire with the toe of his boot, his expression inscrutable.

"Are you in love with her?"

He jerked his foot, kicking up a shower of sparks. "I beg your pardon? In love with whom?"

"Evangeline Starke," I said. "It makes perfect sense. She's beautiful in her own way—and adventuresome. As soon as you realised where she was, you dropped everything and rushed here to find her. But she is your best friend's wife, which I suppose gives you a great deal of conflict over your feelings. Perhaps that's why you're so awkward with women," I mused.

"Oh, for Christ's sake, not this again," he said with a scowl. "Poppy, will you please stop psychoanalysing me? If I wanted to lie on Dr. Freud's sofa I'd go to Vienna myself. I'm not in love with Evangeline. I've met her precisely once, and that was for ten minutes when she was at the train station leaving Damascus and my only concern was in finding Gabriel. And for your information, she's not even my type," he said, getting to his feet. "She's got black hair."

I tugged on my now-black curls as he left to check on the donkey. "Probably prefers blondes," I muttered. "Or redheads," I added with a shudder.

He had left the map that had been tucked in his belt, and I pulled it out, tracing our journey with my finger. We were in the hills outside of Ashkelon, the city of silk. Cairo was to the south and west, roughly two hundred miles, it looked like. And none of the terrain looked easy. There were hills and river marshes and rocky fingers of desert between. Little wonder he had agreed with me we should go by sea to Alexandria. I knew he wasn't pleased by the detour, but I was thrilled at the chance to explore the monastery where the documents had been found.

I washed quickly and went to look at the map again. This time I noticed the page folded under it, a single piece of writing paper scribbled with my handwriting. I was still holding it when he returned.

"You stupid, stupid man," I said, holding up the page.

He didn't even have the grace to look embarrassed. "Surely you didn't think I was really going to send that note."

"But the poor old fellow will be so worried about me!"

Sebastian shrugged. "That was not my primary concern."

"No, your primary concern is making sure that if we are apprehended, you can claim you were acting alone and abducted me. This note makes it perfectly clear we're in this together, but without it, you can take the blame for all of it."

He folded his arms over his chest and waited patiently for me to finish. I ranted a few minutes more, raging at him for various acts of stupidity and stubbornness, which he accepted with a politely attentive expression.

"Finished yet? Because if you're done abusing me, I thought you'd like to see the space where we found the documents."

I snapped my mouth shut. I had a good quarter of an hour of scolding left in me, but I was far too eager to explore. "Show me," I ordered.

He led me to what must have once been the chapel. It was laid out in the usual cruciform shape, and there was a rectangular hollow in the stone where an altar had once stood.

He sketched out the details of what the chapel must have once looked like, warming to his theme and tossing around words like *transept* and *apsidiole* while I seethed with impatience.

"Sebastian," I said finally, a note of threat in my tone.

He grinned. "I just wanted to see how long you could hold out. Come along. It's along this way, down the crypt stairs."

I shuddered. "It's in the crypt?"

"It's the safest place to hide things. Don't come over all swoonish on me now. I won't let the dead get you," he promised. "And you can even see remains of the temple of Venus that stood here before the monastery. Did I tell you the name of the little river? It's called the River of the Lady's Milk because of how white the froth is when it foams up in full spate. They say it's from the milk of Venus when she nursed Cupid, although the holy brethren who once lived here changed the story a bit to make it Mother Mary's."

I followed him, as enchanted with his stories as with the possibility of finding something interesting. Down, down, down we went, down the twisting stone staircase into the crypt. He'd fashioned a torch out of some twigs and a bit of rotting fabric, which burned too quickly and smoked like hell. "We won't have long down here without good light and the air isn't any too nice," he warned me. It was an understatement of criminal proportions. The air was utterly fetid, rank with the odour of rot and decay. It was the stink of ages, of bodies wrapped in linen and left to lie in alcoves cut from the stone.

I covered my nose with my hand. "Ugh. How could they just leave them to lie like that?"

"Would you want to dig a grave through all this stone?" he asked reasonably. "Besides the desert air is dry enough it usually desiccates the bodies. At least that's what they expected. Don't imagine they took into account how close they were to the sea as the crow flies. The moisture in the air must have rotted these lads," he added with a nod to the skeletons with their ragged shreds of flesh. They were like something out of a nightmare, fleshless faces with noses missing and eyes long gone. Lips that some mother had once kissed had fallen away, hands that had once folded together in prayer had withered to narrow bones that rattled as we passed, and I clutched Sebastian's hand, grateful to find it warm and firm and very much alive.

He led me to the far end of the crypt where the first abbot's body lay, looking only a little worse than the others. His wrappings were also of sheer linen, but he had been disturbed, and recently from the look of it.

"Gabriel said he'd been here," Sebastian said thoughtfully. He reached under the abbot and I stifled a shriek. He quirked me a look. "Easy, princess. He can't feel anything."

He reached further under the old fellow, and to my horror, began to pull him out. I swallowed hard as Sebastian set the corpse reverently on the stone floor of the crypt and turned back to the alcove. The back of the alcove was not solid. It had been fashioned of hewed stones set atop one another, where all the others were clearly carved straight out of the rock. I watched in fascination as Sebastian took the knife from his boot and worked it deftly into a crevice between the stones.

He murmured to the blade, coaxing it sweetly as he moved it back and forth.

Suddenly, the stone fell free, landing with a resounding thud on the shelf below, and I understood why he had been so careful to remove the dead abbot's bones. They would have been crushed under the weight. Sebastian leaned forward, bracing one thigh on the shelf to peer into the hidden space behind the grave.

"Let me," I said, shocked to hear my own voice.

He turned back, and I saw he was a little pale. "Are you sure?"

"Quite," I said with a great deal more bravado than I felt. He stepped back quickly, too quickly, I thought, and I understood something about him I had not known before.

"You're afraid of close spaces," I said. "A claustrophobe."

"I told you to stop analysing me," he growled. "But as it happens, you're nearly right in this case. I don't much care for tight spaces. Now get up there if you're going."

I thought of what Gabriel had told me of Sebastian's time in a Turkish prison and wondered if this had anything to do with his dislike of closed spaces. But one glance at his tight features and I didn't have the heart to ask. He gave me a boost up and I found myself crouched on the abbot's former resting place. I manoeuvered behind the stone and put out my hand into the space behind. It took all my courage to reach into that gaping black maw of a hole, and when I put out my hand, I wasn't certain I would ever draw it back again. Who knew what lurked inside? Spiders, scorpions, snakes? And those were only the horrors I knew about. God only knew what else might lurk inside a thousand-year-old tomb in the desert rock.

I stretched out my arm until my fingers brushed the back of the hiding place. There was nothing inside but dust and bare stone. I swept it from side to side with my fingertips, moving methodically from one end to the other, raising the dust from the floor. I coughed, but kept going, up the left wall and then the back, tracing the mortar in every stone for a broken place.

"Poppy, it's empty," Sebastian said, his voice tense. No doubt the extended time in the crypt was playing havoc with his claustrophobia, but I was determined to do a thorough job of it. I felt, no, I *knew* there must be something left behind. And when I touched the right wall of the hiding place, I found it. A scrap of paper wedged tightly into a gap where the mortar had broken away.

I gave a little shout of triumph and pulled it out. I backed out of the space, right into Sebastian's arms. He dropped me to my feet instantly, and I felt a little giddy from the lack of air.

I brandished the little wad of paper at him, but he held up a hand. "The torch is almost out. We're getting some fresh air and some light before we look at that," he ordered. He returned the stone with fluent profanity and then popped the abbot back into his resting place with a good deal more haste and less reverence than he had removed him. He hurried me up to the chapel and out into the well court, both of us heaving in great breaths. The air was sweet and heavy and we drank it in. Sebastian's colour improved, but he was draped with cobwebs and there were a few festooning my hair, as well.

He reached for the paper. "Not so fast," I told him, holding it just out of reach. "It's my discovery. I should get to open it."

He sighed. "Fair enough."

The paper was dry and it crackled in my hands, but it was not ancient. It was the edge of a newspaper, torn off in haste it seemed. The date of the newspaper was 8 July, 1917 and Sebastian raised his brows.

"Is the date significant?" I asked.

"Two days after Lawrence and the Bedouin routed the Turks at Aqaba," he reminded me. "Things were chaotic in

Syria just then, with Turks redoubling their efforts to keep all the Bedouin in line. There were raids against tribes, atrocities you can't even imagine. Whole families thrown into pits and set alight, entire clans killed by thirst," he told me, his expression grim. "It was a bleak time to be here."

He peered over my shoulder at the rest of the scrap. There was nothing more in print, just a few scribbled words.

TAKEN IT. SB.

"Taken what? And what is SB?" I asked.

He was white-lipped and when he spoke, his words were stiff. "The 'what' is obviously the map to the Ashkelon hoard. And SB is Stephen Baleister."

"Who is that?"

"A ghost," he told me, and in spite of the warmth of the sun pouring through the broken walls, I felt a shiver.

"Ghosts don't write, at least not the ones I've read about," I said with an effort. "Now, let's be practical about this. Who *was* Stephen Baleister?"

Sebastian had busied himself with activity, stoking up the fire and setting out the flatbreads to soften. He fed the donkey and drew fresh water, and when he finished, he paced the court, moving methodically from one end to the other, striding slowly as he worked it out. "Stephen was one of us."

"A member of the Vespiary?"

"Specifically, one of the Lost Boys."

"How many of you were there altogether?"

"Seven including Gabriel and me. And I'd have given my life for any of them. Funny thing, I would have sworn they'd have done the same."

"But it doesn't make sense," I protested. "Why would this

Stephen Baleister take the map to the gold and then leave a note saying he'd done it?"

"I don't know," he said simply. "Stephen was—" He broke off, a small smile playing about his lips. "Stephen was a prankster. He was always thinking up a scheme or two to pass the time when we were holed up somewhere. It would have been just like him to take the map and think it was a great joke."

"So he might not have betrayed the rest of you and stolen the gold for himself," I said reasonably. "For that matter he might not have even found it at all. Perhaps he merely removed the map for safekeeping."

"He might have done," Sebastian conceded.

"Then all that remains is to find him," I stated.

Sebastian's smile was thin. "A neat trick if you can manage it. I've already told you, Stephen's a ghost. Worse than that, in fact."

"What's worse than being dead?" I demanded.

"Stephen Baleister walked into the *Badiyat ash-Sham* one day and never came out again. The desert swallowed him up. And once the desert decides to keep you, you belong to her."

I shivered again. "I've never heard you talk like that, Sebastian."

He shrugged. "It's this place. When you're back in England with its snug little ways and tidy hedgerows it's hard to believe a place like this even exists. But I've seen things here I cannot explain, and even if I could I'm not certain I'd want to. This land is old, Poppy, older than you can imagine. Men have been fighting and bleeding into this earth for thousands of years, long before there was an England. Look at this monastery. It started as a temple of Venus, hewn out of the living rock. Men worshipped here for centuries before Christ was even a child. This whole land is sacred space, marked by death itself. It's almost as if the constant wars have left scars upon it that can never be healed. Men come face-to-face with their own mortality here, and no one leaves the same as they were when they came."

He fell silent, and I let him brood a long moment before I spoke. "What if we could find what happened to Stephen? He must have family somewhere. What were they told?'

He recalled himself as if he had been far away, and his eyes settled on mine. He looked a thousand years older suddenly. Facing the ghosts of his past was a cruel thing to ask of him, and for an instant I regretted insisting we come to Ashkelon.

"Stephen was from Africa, British East Africa, to be precise. He left a wife named Jude."

I shook my head. "That poor woman. Never knowing what happened to her husband."

"I know. The Vespiary made inquiries after his disappearance, but no trace of him was ever discovered. Of course, they couldn't spare much in the way of manpower. He was a casualty of war, they decided. No doubt come across by some Turks and thrown into a hole somewhere in the desert. Not a very nice end for him."

"But you don't know that," I argued.

A small, humourless smile touched his lips. "You sound like his wife. The Vespiary never told her what assignment he'd been given—not even that he was in Syria. She thinks he was doing reconnaissance for British pilots in North Africa, for the bureau in Cairo. That was the cover the Vespiary had concocted for him, and they never corrected it, not even when they told her he was missing."

"That's horrifying," I said, my voice catching. "What if she went looking for him?"

"Then she'd be looking in the wrong place by a few hundred miles," he said savagely. "She wrote back to the Vespiary, begging them for details, but they couldn't give her any, could they? So they kept lying to her and she kept writing back. It seemed to be driving her mad, never knowing what became of him."

"Where is she now?" I asked gently.

He shrugged. "Still in Africa. They had a farm there, breeding horses. She married again this year, but from what I gather, she's not entirely happy."

"I'm not surprised she's unhappy. She still doesn't know," I said. "Do you think it would help her to move on, if she knew for certain what happened to him?"

"It could help all of us," he replied. "Or it could give us nightmares to last the rest of our lives."

"You don't know that," I repeated.

"And you don't know what happens to prisoners of the Turks," he said flatly. I thought again of what Gabriel had told me about Sebastian's experiences during the war, the quick reference to imprisonment and worse, and I opened my mouth.

"Don't," he said simply, and I said nothing.

He stopped pacing and went to stand at one of the ruined window embrasures, bracing his hands on either side. The sun was high over the valley below, and far in the distance I could just see the thin blue glittering line of the sea.

"I'm sorry," I told him. "For what it's worth, I'm truly sorry."

"Thank you," he said simply. He gave a great sigh and something seemed to go out of him as he watched the sun dip below the nearest peak. "That's close enough," he murmured.

"Close enough to what?"

"Cocktail hour," he said with a sudden grin. "While you were poking around amongst the cobwebs today looking for buried treasure, I found something far more valuable."

I caught my breath. "Sebastian!"

He strode to the edge of the court and wrenched open a

wooden packing case. He reached in and lifted out a dusty, cobwebbed bottle. "Vintage champagne," he announced with a smile. "Let's get roaring drunk."

I had my fears that the stuff might have turned to vinegar, but as soon as I took my first deep swig from the bottle, I smiled. The bubbles tickled my nose, sharp and beguiling, and when I looked at the label, I gave a squawk.

"Gerald ordered this for our engagement party, but even he wouldn't spring for this vintage," I told Sebastian. "My God, it must be worth a fortune."

"A thousand pounds a bottle," he said cheerfully, taking a hefty swig from his own bottle. "Fitting that we're drinking it in a monastery, really, given poor old Dom Pérignon. Do you know what he said the first time he tasted the stuff?"

"'I am drinking the stars!'" I quoted, affecting a thick French accent.

Sebastian laughed, a rich, baritone laugh that echoed against the night sky. We'd been drinking for the better part of two hours as the twilight lengthened across the valley, wrapping the peak in violet shadows that deepened to black velvet.

He nodded towards the ruined garden. "There used to be myrtle there. And roses—flowers sacred to the Great Mother, Astarte, Venus, Mother Mary. Whatever they choose to call her."

I lifted my bottle and peered at him through the thick green glass. "You know, you're quite irreligious for a clergyman."

"I am a citizen of the world," he announced. "I believe in all religions and none."

I hooted with laughter. "Don't let the Archbishop of Canterbury hear you say that," I said severely. "You'll be derobed, disrobed, what's the word?"

"Defrocked," he supplied.

"Yes, *that*. I'd like to be defrocked. This dress is murderous," I said, tugging at the sharply carved horn sewn to the bodice.

"I'd like to defrock you," he said seriously. "But it would be against the rules."

I laughed again, looking up to see the sky reeling in response. The very stars seemed to be laughing back and I pointed them out to Sebastian. He was just draining his second bottle, and as I showed him the stars, he threw his head back and began to speak.

Do what thy manhood bids thee do,
from none but self expect applause;
He noblest lives and noblest died
who makes and keeps his self-made laws.
All other life is living Death,
a world where none by Phantoms dwell,
A breath, a wind, a sound, a voice,
a tinkling of a camel-bell.

I gasped. "Oh, Sebastian, that's lovely! Did you write it?"

He gave me an indulgent look. "No, it's *The Kahsida*, Richard Burton's translation. Surely you've heard of Sir Richard Burton?"

"Of course," I said repressively. "The famous explorer and orientalist. He lived in this part of the world for a time with his wife, Isabel. I read her letters on the voyage out. She was devoted to him. She followed him in his travels, sometimes dressing as a boy. You ought to have let me dress as a boy," I protested, tugging at my gown again.

"It would never have done," he told me. "You're far too, well, you're just awfully—"

"Yes?" I asked eagerly. "I'm too what?"

"Too much a *female*," he said finally.

"That's a bit of a letdown," I said. I peered again through the bottom of my bottle. "I'd like some poetry about me."

"You shan't have any. I'm not wooing you," he said severely. "So stop trying."

"I'm not trying," I told him with considerable indignation. "If I were trying, I should just kiss you to shut you up. You're a very taxing individual, you know, although I must say you do have a rather handsome mouth when it isn't all covered in whiskers."

"I shall think of them as my chastity belt," he advised me solemnly.

"Oh, you are maddening," I said. "But I will forgive you because I think I am going to need your help very soon."

"What sort of help?" he demanded.

"I think," I said slowly and with as much dignity as I could muster, "I am going to be very sick indeed."

And I was.

The next morning I apologised profusely about the state of his boots, but he merely waved me aside. "Unless you can conjure a cup of coffee and a bacon sandwich, I don't want to hear it," he told me. There were purple shadows under his eyes, and I suspected I looked no better. I remembered nothing after being lavishly sick on his boots except a fleeting sensation of being tucked tenderly into a robe.

But Sebastian had taken it back, wrapping himself against the morning chill as he went to the window embrasure to survey the landscape below.

"How does the river look? Will we be able to cross today?"

He narrowed his eyes, looking sharply down the hillside.

I went to stand beside him. "Really, Sebastian, you're more difficult to travel with than Mother and her thirty trunks. At least Mother *speaks* in the morning. You hardly say two words and even then—"

He swung around, his eyes cold. "Be quiet, Poppy. You can abuse me later. For now, we're not alone."

I looked past him to the goat track below, and for the first time I spotted him, a solitary figure on a white horse, winding his way upwards, ever upwards to where we waited.

I gave an involuntary gasp and Sebastian's jaw hardened.

"Don't fret, child. Death rides a camel in this part of the world. He doesn't come on a pale horse."

But, of course, Sebastian was wrong.

NINETEEN

I argued for fleeing immediately, but Sebastian pointed out there was nowhere to go but straight down the same track as our visitor. The monastery was cradled in the saddle between the two peaks, with sheer walls on two sides and a deep drop on the back. Only the narrow track by which we had come provided any means of escape, and if we attempted it there was nowhere in the barren, scrubby landscape to hide from our visitor.

"Besides, he's clearly after us," Sebastian pointed out. "Why not let him find us?"

I stared at him in horror. "Because he might be armed. Because he could be dangerous. Because we have nothing for our defense but a pile of rocks and a donkey," I said, somewhat hysterically.

Sebastian merely shrugged. "Who said anything about defense? We ought to just give ourselves up if he is armed."

I felt a rush of cold rage unlike anything I had ever felt before. "I had my doubts about you, Sebastian Fox. And now you don't even have the nerve to stand up for us? You are the most contemptible, loathsome, cowardly," I kept on in that vein, pouring out scorn as he watched the visitor's approach, seeming not to hear me.

"Aren't you finished yet?" he asked at one point.

"I am not," I assured him, launching into a fresh attack on his character.

He bore it remarkably well—largely by not listening at all. He simply marked the visitor's progress up the hill, timing it perfectly so that as soon as the caller rode within the monastery walls, Sebastian emerged from the chapel to greet him politely.

"*Assalam aleikum,*" he said, sketching a courteous gesture.

Faruq grinned and leaned forward in his saddle. "You are a courteous fellow," he said, eyeing Sebastian with assessment. "I did not expect so gracious a greeting."

Sebastian shrugged. "I see no reason for violence. Far better to be reasonable with each other, don't you think?"

Faruq dismounted, holding the reins of his horse lightly in his fingers. Sebastian jerked his head towards the stable where the donkey was tethered. "You'll find bedding in there for your horse as well as fodder and water."

Faruq inclined his head. "You are all that is hospitable, sir, but, alas, I cannot stay. I have come for the map."

Sebastian's expression was rueful. "In that case, I'm sorry, old man. I haven't got it."

Faruq bared his teeth in a parody of a smile. "You will forgive me if I do not believe you."

"It's really immaterial whether you believe me or not," Sebastian pointed out. "I haven't got it."

Faruq's gaze fell on me. "Perhaps you do not, sir, but—"

"Touch her and there will be violence," Sebastian said in the same friendly tone. The calm, pleasant voice was at such odds with the words that it took Faruq a moment to realise he had just been threatened. He grinned, with marginally more warmth than before.

"So it is like that? This is good to know. It helps if one's enemy has a weakness," he said in the same polite tone Sebastian had used.

Sebastian did not stir a step, but somehow he seemed larger than a moment before, more solidly imposing as he stood between Faruq and me.

"Would it help at all if I swore an oath that the map was removed before I arrived and that I don't know where it is now?"

Faruq merely made a guffawing sound and Sebastian nodded. "I expected as much. Pity. It happens to be the truth."

"Sometimes the truth is painful," Faruq answered.

"Tell me," Sebastian said in his maddeningly conversational tone, "how did you find out about the map? Were you working with Talbot?"

Faruq's complexion darkened with rage. He cleared his throat and spat heavily onto the stones. "He was a son of a devil, that one." He nodded to me. "He said very disrespectful things about you, miss. But he thought you could lead him to the map. And as it happens," he added with a smile, "he was correct."

"If you weren't working with Talbot, how did you know he was looking for the map?" I ventured.

His expression was opaque. "My sources are my own, miss. And the gold you seek is Syrian gold. It belongs to my people."

"It bloody well does not," I answered roundly. "It's French. If anything, it ought to go back to France."

His face reddened again. "The French have no claim to anything that is ours. The gold will go to support our efforts to establish our own kingdom."

"One sympathises," Sebastian said, sounding for all the

world like he meant it, "but I'm afraid the point is entirely moot. I told you truth, old boy. I haven't got the map."

"But you have seen the map," Faruq said, his gaze sharp.

"Well, yes, but only once and long ago," Sebastian admitted.

"Must you tell him everything?" I demanded.

Sebastian shrugged. "Occasionally one can head off unpleasantness by being forthright."

"Not this time," Faruq assured him. "You have seen the map. You must remember it."

"Not a bit," Sebastian said cheerfully. "You see, I only had a quick squint by candlelight. I know the hoard was stashed somewhere in the vicinity of Ashkelon, but these hills are full of hidey holes. Couldn't tell you anything more if my life depended upon it."

Faruq laughed. "It does not," he assured Sebastian. From the folds of his robes, he produced a pistol and pointed it straight at my heart. "Hers does."

My entire world seemed to narrow to a single point—the black hole at the end of Faruq's pistol. I was aware of Sebastian near me, unmoving and his voice still maddeningly calm.

"Oh, do stop waving that thing around," he told Faruq.

"Sebastian," I croaked.

His expression was one of acute boredom. "Well, honestly. It's just bad manners, and damned silly to boot. To begin with, if you kill her, do you really think I'd tell you anything? I'd turn the bloody gun on myself just to spite you."

Faruq considered this. "Very well." Without another word, he levelled the gun at Sebastian. "I must persuade you."

Without another word, he pulled the trigger. The explosion was deafening in the still air, and for an instant I thought he had merely meant to frighten us. Then I saw the spreading crimson stain on Sebastian's robes as he slid to the ground.

I shrieked his name and flung myself on top of him, but his

eyes were closed, and I whirled to Faruq. I cursed him then, hurling every insult I could think of, most of them highly profane, thanks to my younger brothers' vocabulary. I rose, my hands curled into fists and he waved the gun.

"But I did not kill him," he protested. He brandished the pistol at me, warning me to keep back. "Look," he urged. "I only grazed his arm."

I turned back to where Sebastian was lying flat on his back. I saw then that the stain was confined to his sleeve, and I fell on him again, my face close to his.

"Sebastian, can you hear me?"

A sound seemed to roll up from his chest, a deep rattling groan, and I gave a choked sob. "Oh, Sebastian, you mustn't die. Can you hear me?"

"A dead man could hear you," he muttered. His eyes fluttered open, and he gave a sigh.

I gripped his face in my hands. "Are you really all right?"

"Not at the moment," he told me in a strangled voice. "You are sitting on my stomach."

I climbed off and he sat up, brushing the dust off his clean sleeve. The other one was torn and he was still bleeding, but slowly now. I peeled back the cloth to see a slender mark, the barest furrow in his flesh.

"The bullet barely touched you," I told him coldly.

He gave me a sulky look. "It still hurt."

I stood up and faced Faruq. "He's fine."

Faruq nodded. "Just as I told you. I am a very good shot. I meant only to persuade him to give me the information he remembers from the map."

"Why not ask her?" Sebastian demanded with a jerk of his head towards me. "She saw it longer than I did."

"I did not—" I turned to gape at him, and he looked at me, his face in profile to Faruq. Carefully, he winked with the eye closest to me, and I covered my surprise. "That is, I did not see it for long, but I daresay I remember more of it than you do," I said.

Faruq looked pleased. "Excellent. Between the two of you, I will have the directions to the gold." He drew a piece of paper from inside his robes and a stub of pencil. "You will draw what you remember."

Sebastian touched his bleeding arm. "I'm afraid you shot me in my writing arm, old man. And the lady might remember the landmarks, but she's got utterly no sense of scale," he said quickly. "We'll have to lead you there."

Faruq didn't like it but he had no choice. Sebastian waited calmly for him to reason it out, and apparently Faruq didn't like the option of firing his weapon again. He nodded finally, and I felt rather than saw the tension in Sebastian's arm ease.

Faruq tossed us ropes from his saddlebag. "You will bind each other. There will be no trickery, for I will look at the knots when you are finished."

We did as he told us, and I tried hard not to jar Sebastian's arm too badly when I tied him up. He merely gave me a casual look and clucked his tongue at the stain on his sleeve.

"Pity. I quite liked this robe. It was very expensive," he told Faruq with a touch of asperity.

Faruq ignored him and, after inspecting the knots, lashed the two of us loosely together by a long rope. He gave a nod. "And now we will go. You will direct us," he told me.

I closed my eyes as if trying to remember, or at least I pretended to. I peeped through the fringe of my lashes to see Sebastian give a quick flick of one finger. West. I made a show of opening my eyes widely and said with a decisive nod, "West."

Faruq stepped back and let me go ahead. Sebastian trotted immediately after, and Faruq brought up the rear, keeping enough of a distance he could easily shoot us before we managed to unhorse him, but not so much we could lose him in the scrubby hills.

After we had walked a long way, dodging low bushes and winding our way through the hills and out onto a desert plain, I ventured to ask Sebastian a question that had been nagging at me. "Why did you tell him I had seen the map?"

I kept my voice very low and Sebastian's reply was almost inaudible. "Because information is what will keep you alive. If he thinks you know, he won't kill you. If you don't know, he has no reason to spare you."

I thought this over. "But if we both know, there's no point in letting us both live. And you indicated to him that I remember more of the map than you do."

"Exactly," he said, his jaw rigid.

I tripped over a bush as I understood what he intended. "You want him to kill you instead of me if it comes to it," I said, hardly managing to keep my voice down.

He shrugged. "It won't come to that. I won't let it," he promised.

"But if it does," I persisted, "you made the choice for him. He'll kill you and spare me."

"Only until he discovers you don't have the faintest idea of where you're going," he warned. "So mind you make it look convincing. Now, hush before he decides we're plotting against him and kills me for sport."

I bit off my reply and stumbled ahead, hardly aware of putting one foot in front of the other. I wouldn't have believed him capable of it, but not only had Sebastian thought with lightning speed on his feet, he had ensured with the lie that if one of us were killed, it wouldn't be me. It was the most heroic act of sacrifice I had ever seen, and my eyes burned with unshed tears.

"God, don't get sentimental," he hissed.

"I can't help it," I whispered back. "It's so brave, so—"

He swore at me then, and I lapsed back into silence, the tears drying up as fast as they had come. He was the most maddening creature I had ever met, I decided. He made what might prove to be the ultimate sacrifice for me with one breath and cursed at me with the next. I squared my shoulders and stomped on, leading the way with absolute conviction. It was only when I'd covered another half mile that I realised pricking my temper had been another of his clever tricks. If I was angry, I hadn't the time to be frightened or overly emotional, either of which could be fatal in our current predicament. I thought of my Aunt Julia then, and her penchant for confronting murderers without adequately thinking things through, and I cursed my impetuous March blood.

We walked another few hours, stopping occasionally for water, and it was on one of these stops, while Faruq worked a stone out of his horse's shoe that Sebastian caught my gaze and flicked a quick glance to the horizon. I looked to see that Faruq was still occupied, then peered into the distance. There was a slight smudging of the horizon, a blurring of the line between earth and sky that could mean only one thing. We were being followed.

I felt a rush of confidence then, and as soon as we had drunk our water, I set off again, but this time I held the pace as slow as I dared. Faruq fussed a little, but his horse seemed perfectly content to amble along, and Sebastian said nothing. I understood he didn't dare add to the delay to give our pursuers time to catch up, but he was careful not to move faster than I did. He didn't look back, but once he tripped over a bush and I saw him dart a quick glance under his arm as he righted himself. Faruq did not notice, but merely clucked his tongue in irritation, urging us forward.

"I say, it's getting a bit warmish," Sebastian said finally. "How about another drink?"

Faruq sighed, checking his horse. "You are worse than the woman," he told Sebastian, but he was unwilling to let either of us collapse on the walk. That would have meant either shooting us on the spot or sharing his horse, and he didn't seem keen to do either for the moment. Sebastian drank deeply from the goatskin then ignored Faruq's outstretched hand and passed it to me. I drank my share, darting a quick glance to the horizon. At the last second, Faruq noticed the direction of my gaze, and Sebastian lifted his bound hands.

"There!" he proclaimed.

Faruq turned to look where he pointed, in the opposite direction of our pursuers.

"That is where the map leads," Sebastian told him firmly. Ahead of us there was a ridge, and atop the ridge stood a square Crusader castle, crumbling to ruin.

"Isn't there a single building in this bloody country still standing?" I muttered.

"Syrians don't take care of their things," Sebastian told me solemnly.

That earned him a quick slap across the face from Faruq, and when it was done, Sebastian was smiling with a bloody lip.

"You oughtn't provoke him," I told him softly.

He shrugged. "I was bored."

I rolled my eyes and we moved on, out of the shadow of a spindly tree and up the ridge. The going was slow with our hands bound before us, and more than once Faruq cursed us, his tone so vicious I was glad I didn't speak Arabic. But Sebastian kept up a steady translation, commenting with admiration on the ruder bits.

"I say, old man, you're quite wrong. I would never do that

to a donkey," he called back at one point. "They kick, you know."

"His temper is worsening," I told Sebastian quietly as we scrambled over stones.

"He's getting nervous," he replied, using the sound of the shifting rocks to cover our voices. "It's going to make him unpredictable."

"Then should you really be baiting him?" I demanded.

"I know what I'm doing," was all he would say in reply. We toiled upwards, climbing over ever-larger rocks until at last Faruq was forced to dismount and leave his horse. He carried his saddlebag and kept his pistol trained upon us, but he needn't have bothered. With the tortuous ground and our hands firmly bound, we were lucky to keep upright, and we didn't always manage that. More than once we stumbled, sometimes because I got too far ahead and sometimes because Sebastian lagged too far behind. We grew too tired and too hot to talk, and finally we reached the top of the plateau, the ruined tower of the castle keep looming above us in the afternoon sun.

"The Chastel Noir, built by the Templars during the Crusades and ugly as sin," Sebastian pronounced. "Part of a series of citadels they erected to establish Western rule in the Outremer."

"Invaders," Faruq spat. "Coming here to take away our faith and replace it with your own."

"Steady on," Sebastian said lightly. "I seem to recall your lot did the same thing to Spain. It's a bloody bad idea when anyone does it, I think we can agree."

Faruq did not respond. He merely jerked his chin towards the castle keep. "Inside."

I moved to obey, walking under the arched stones that had stood nearly a thousand years, impervious to the desert sands and sea-borne winds. It might stand a thousand more, bearing no trace of the lives that had been lost within its walls, I thought grimly. And two of those lives might well be ours.

TWENTY

Faruq still gave no sign of noticing our pursuers and Sebastian was careful not to draw any attention to them. I was fairly giddy with the notion that help was so close at hand, but Faruq had already proven he was at ease with violence and not particularly sensible when it came to employing it. I made every effort to keep myself calm and focus on the essentials. The sun was lowering itself beyond the western horizon. Somewhere behind the hills the Mediterranean Sea was glittering in the waning rays, and I wondered if I would ever see it again.

Sebastian read my thoughts as handily as a carnival trickster. He caught my eye and gave me a firm nod, lifting his chin with an expression of resolve so complete, I felt my chest tighten and sudden tears prick my eyes. He wanted to save us, and he would try until his last breath to do it.

I made up my mind then that I would do everything in my power to save us both. I could not have his death on my conscience, and although the current situation was beyond anything I had experienced, there had to be something I could do.

Faruq fed and watered his horse, and after it was comfortably settled turned his attentions to us. "I will leave you tied together for now," he told us. "You can eat easily enough."

He proved his point by giving us nothing but cold flat-breads, which we shared between us. Sebastian scrupulously tried to divide the portion in half, but I refused to finish all of mine, and he shrugged and took the rest, bolting it down with scarcely a chance to chew it. He must have been utterly starved, I thought with a pang. When we had eaten, Faruq untethered us from one another long enough to let us take a moment's privacy behind a bush that had forced its way out of the citadel walls, twisting itself into a parody of a shrub. It wasn't much privacy, but it was something, and I was grateful to have a moment to myself even if my hands were still bound. I must have taken too long because Faruq raised his voice, calling out cheerfully, "If you are not out by the time I count to twenty, I will shoot him in the other arm."

I was back before he reached five. Sebastian gave me a ghastly smile, and I thought it must be playing havoc with his nerves to be threatened so often with physical violence. I tried to give him a reassuring smile in return, but I suspected it came off a bit sickly. I was wondering what was keeping our saviours from staging a rescue, and it was not until Faruq left to take his own moment behind the bush that Sebastian muttered an answer to the question.

"Waiting for daylight," he said softly. "Suicide to try this track in the dark. Better to come on at first light and try to surprise him while he's still asleep."

I nodded and Sebastian leaned into me, giving me a cordial shove with his good shoulder. "Try to get some sleep tonight. The real fun will start tomorrow."

His sudden bravado moved me as much as the sight of him, battered and bloodied, and I promised myself I would

stay awake as late as I could, plotting some sort of strategy to
free us both.

But the long walk and the hot sun had taken their toll,
and by the time the purple twilight had faded to blackness, I
slipped into sleep. Faruq did not kindle a fire, and Sebastian
and I slept back to back, taking warmth from one another as
the cool velvet shadow of night fell over the citadel. Faruq
talked in his sleep, muttering something in Arabic, while Sebastian slept heavily, rolling over onto my arm more than once
and pinning me under his substantial weight. I tried to shift
him without waking him, but it proved impossible, and so I
slid into sleep again, dreaming I was weighted down by stones,
crushed to death by Faruq's slow torture as he demanded the
location of the treasure—a location I could not give.

I woke with a start, my face damp with sweat, to find Faruq
grinning at me.

"Pleasant dreams?" he asked.

"Yes," I said loftily. "I was handing you over to the authorities for arrest. It was quite gratifying."

He laughed then, but there was an edge to his mirth that
told me I had struck a nerve. He reached out a booted foot
and kicked Sebastian, who groaned deeply.

"Don't do that!" I ordered.

Faruq shrugged and I roused Sebastian as gently as I could.
He slept like the dead, and in the end I was forced to pinch
him soundly on his bare cheek just above his beard.

"Ow!" he complained, sitting upright and rubbing at his
cheek. "That was uncalled for."

"Not entirely," I told him. "It's morning."

He looked around, a small smile touching his lips. "So it
is." He took a deep breath, filling his lungs with the sweet
sea-borne air of the hills, and I marvelled at his good mood.

"You haven't any coffee. I would have thought you'd be a misery this morning," I told him.

Faruq rose to check on his horse, and Sebastian turned to smile at me, his expression deeply malicious. "A misery? Not a chance, dear child. There's going to be a fight today. And a good one."

I stared at him in dismay. "Sebastian, I hardly think you're in any shape to take on Faruq," I began.

He kept his grin. "It won't be with Faruq."

Before I could ask what he meant, he rose and stretched, testing his wounded arm. He looked through the slit in the robe.

"How is it?" I asked.

"Passable. It could do with a thorough cleaning and perhaps a stitch or two, but I've had worse."

"I can't imagine how," I said repressively. "Honestly, if you insist on treating this all as a game," I began, but he had stopped listening. He had edged us closer to the wall of the citadel, a broken course of stones that only came to our waists. He peered over, sweeping his eyes over the plain below. His gaze fixed on a small tree some hundred yards off the base of the hill. There was movement underneath it, and his smile deepened. "Come on, then," he muttered.

"Where are they? Who are they?" I asked softly.

He shrugged. "No idea. But pretend you're admiring the sunrise. It's beautiful, isn't it?" he asked, jerking his chin towards the rays that spread over the length of the desert landscape. The dusty rocks were every colour of gold—bronze and apricot, copper and peach—

I gasped and Sebastian shot me a quick look. "What is it?"

"Peaches," I told him slowly. "I know who Faruq's partner is." I thought back to the day I had lunched with Armand, his elaborate pursuit of me—too elaborate it had seemed at the

time. I thought of the apparent genteel poverty of the Cour-
tempierres, the missing art and furnishings, the *comtesse*'s lack
of jewels. They needed money, lots of it if Armand was going
to sustain the lifestyle he enjoyed. He and Hugh must have
concocted the scheme together, each of them playing for me
until the *comtesse* proved troublesome by setting Faruq on me
and following me herself. That must have been her idea—
to put a little distance between her beloved son and me. She
forced the matter, letting Hugh work on charming me into
divulging something. No dirty work for her precious Armand.

Sebastian was still looking at me intently and I roughed out
the idea for him as swiftly as I could. "And you don't like coincidences," I finished. "In my theory, there are none. Hugh
needs a local contact to help him out, Armand needs money.
They conspire together and either take Faruq into their confidence to help and he double-crosses them or he overhears
enough to make his own play for the gold."

Sebastian nodded slowly. "Well done, Poppy. I think you've
sussed it. Pity it's probably too late."

"What do you mean too late?" I demanded.

But he merely nodded to where Faruq was standing at the
edge of the precipice, staring, his mouth open in rage.

He turned slightly, but before he could say a word he gave
a little shudder and only then did I hear the shot. It was a
strange trick of the distance that I could see the bullet strike
his head before I heard it, but the sound of it still echoed over
the desert floor even as Faruq fell to the ground.

"Oh, my God," I managed, turning my face to Sebastian's
shoulder.

"Don't look again," he ordered me. He pulled off his outer
robe, laying it over the remains of Faruq's head.

It was better now that I could not see him. It seemed hours
but in fact it was only a minute or two before they reached

us—Armand and the *comtesse* and the colonel, very red in the face and still holding his rifle.

He glanced down at the motionless form of Faruq. "Always was rather handy at a distance," he said mildly. "The villain had it coming, although I'm sorry you had to see it, child," he said to me.

My knees nearly buckled with relief. "Colonel!" I cried. "I'm so happy to see you."

"And I you, my dear," he said with a regretful tone. "But I do wish it had been under more pleasant circumstances."

"So do I," I told him fervently.

But even as I said the words, something hovered in the air, crushing my euphoria. "Oh, Colonel," I murmured. "Not you."

He shrugged, lifting the rifle. "I'm afraid so, my dear. But you've been mighty useful, and I thank you for that."

He nodded towards my bound wrists. "I say, there's no call for a white woman to be trussed up like that. Cut her loose now," he ordered Armand.

Armand complied with a curl to his handsome lip. "I don't know," he said softly into my ear. "I rather like you this way. Perhaps I'll keep you when this is all over."

Armand had no personal interest in me, of that I was absolutely certain. He simply wanted to unnerve me by threatening me with the most intimate sort of violence, and it was a coward's trick.

I gave him a cold smile. "You'd have to use force, Armand. I'm afraid that's the only way I'd have you."

His smile thinned and he gave my ropes a quick twist, tightening them like a garrote around my poor wrists. I wouldn't give him the satisfaction of screaming, but something in my face must have shown because Sebastian chose that moment to speak up.

"Is this the famous Continental wooing up close?" he drawled. "Not terribly impressive, Count. Come here and hold hands with me and see if you like it better."

Armand—understanding it for the threat it was—laughed, but I noticed he was careful to stay far out of Sebastian's reach even though his hands were still bound.

The *comtesse* moved forward to Sebastian, her robes fluttering in the breeze. "Here is a copy of the document you and your colleagues found at the monastery near Ashkelon, the same document given to Lady Hester Stanhope. It is written in mediaeval Italian, and it details the locations of several treasure troves hidden by Christians along the coast when this was the kingdom of the Outremer. We do not care about the smaller treasures. You know the one we want," she told Sebastian in a chillingly conversational tone. "The Templar gold, all three million coins of it. It is here, somewhere along this coast. And you will find it for us."

Sebastian said nothing for a long moment then stirred lazily. "Oh, sorry, is this where I ask what dire thing will happen to us if we don't?"

Her smile was thin. "I think you know the answer to that. For every hour you delay, I will remove one of Miss March's fingers," she said, grabbing my hand. She pulled up the index finger of my right hand. "I think I will begin with this one to give you an incentive to work hard."

She put out her free hand and her son handed over his dagger. She put it to the base of my finger, pricking out a ruby droplet of blood.

"Oh, don't let's descend to melodrama," Sebastian said, rolling his eyes. "I can tell you right now without even studying the document that you're in the wrong part of the country for that. In fact, you're in the wrong country altogether."

"What do you mean?" the *comtesse* demanded, her eyes narrowed.

Sebastian looked bored. "We're in Palestine, dear lady. The treasure you want is in the Lebanon."

"And how do you know this?"

He waved a hand towards the document. "Because the three locations detailed in the map are Ashkelon, a site north of Jaffa, and a third site just out of Sidon, near Lady Hester's home at Djoun. Now, why else do you suppose the lady chose to make her home on that remote hillside save for the fact that it was an abandoned monastery? Shall I give you a moment to work it all out?" A note of condescension crept into his voice. "Very well, I'll just hand it to you on a platter. She chose that location precisely because it was where the treasure was originally buried. She didn't have to dig it up. *It was there all the while.*"

I had no idea what Sebastian's strategy was. He told me he had already searched the place thoroughly himself, and he had insisted there was no way the treasure could have been buried there. He had sworn that too much time had passed and too many owners and squatters had come and gone. But the instant I grasped what he was up to, so did the *comtesse.*

Her smile was predatory. "Very clever, Mr. Fox. It is no coincidence, I think, that you have given us the location farthest from where we now stand. You hope that we will take you with us all the way back to Sidon. It is a substantial trip. You are thinking you could well make your escape while we are en route."

He shrugged. "I'm merely giving you the facts as I see them. If you choose to ignore them, so be it. Don't find the gold. I don't much care."

"But you will, I think," she said, picking up my finger where she had left off.

Just then the colonel, who had been remarkably restrained during the exchange, spoke up. "I say, Sabine, that's just not cricket. You can't maim an Englishwoman for sport. I won't have it."

She turned to him, her eyes glittering. But she gave him a gracious nod and dropped my hand. She held out the dagger to her son, and as she passed it to him, their eyes met. Something was decided between them, wordlessly, and I felt a chill pass through me.

Before I could understand what was happening, Armand stepped behind the colonel and embraced him. Reaching in front of the old man, he slipped his blade from one ear to the other. A spray of crimson showered the sandy ground, and it was done. The colonel slipped to his knees, an expression of surprise on his ruddy features, and then he fell to his face.

I could not speak. The sound was stuck in my throat. But there was another sound, a high keening moan of despair, and it was not until the *comtesse* lifted her hand and slapped me sharply that I realized it was mine. I fell silent, grateful for the burst of pain in my cheek.

She turned to Sebastian, and I was relieved to see she looked unnaturally pale. If she was not entirely comfortable with her son's violence, there was a chance for us yet.

"That was…regrettable," she said in a broken voice. She paused and gathered up her composure, unlike her son, who was cleaning off his knife with a twist of scrubby grass and whistling a dull tune. "The colonel expected us to share the wealth evenly, and that would not do. I have taken all the risk, and all the reward shall be mine," she said, her voice a little more resolute.

Sebastian shook his head slowly. "You're not very good at this, are you? It's quite apparent that as soon as we help you find the gold, you're going to let that little brute have his nasty way with us. What possible incentive do we have to help you? And stop with the threats of mutilation, will you? It's unseemly and not very elegant," he told her severely.

She smiled a little in spite of herself. "I do not like it this way, you are right. But Armand is correct. We have suffered enough at the hands of others. The war, your war, took everything from us—my husband, our money. This treasure is our one chance to regain what we lost. Nothing will bring my husband back again, nothing will give Armand his father again, but with it I can buy back his patrimony. I can secure his inheritance in France, the inheritance his family have held for four hundred years. I can give him that."

"But at what cost?" Sebastian asked gently.

"At whatever cost necessary," she said. I saw regret in her eyes, and I think if it were not for her son, she might have shown us a little mercy then. But Armand was not merciful, and so the *comtesse* could not afford to be.

She drew in a deep breath. "You will help us because for every minute we are moving closer to the treasure, you have another minute of life. And you are a creature of hope, I think, Mr. Fox. You will plot and plan and wait for your chance, the chance that will not come. But you will spend your last hours hoping, and that will be enough for you."

Sebastian's mouth lifted in a ghost of a smile. "In that case, I am yours to command, *comtesse*. Take us to Sidon and we'll find your gold for you."

And so we turned our backs on the western horizon and Cairo and safety and set our faces to the north, to Sidon and Djoun and the broken-down home where Lady Hester had lived out her days in decaying wealth. That was the lowest point for me, the moment when my spirits began to falter, and I wondered if we would come out of this adventure alive.

Until then, even through Hugh's death, it hadn't seemed entirely real. Perhaps because I hadn't been there to see it. But I had seen the others, and I would never forget them. There was an element of game to it all, like a chess match with an unseen opponent, pitting one's wits against another's. But there would be no civilized handshake at the end of this, no cordial goodbyes. There would be winners and losers, and the stakes were death.

My hands began to shake, and I looked at Sebastian. His unshaven jaw, dark and unkempt, was lifted high, and his expression was one of thorough boredom. Did he fully understand the depths of our predicament? I wondered. There was a touch of insouciance about him still, a casual coolness that meant he was either blithely hoping for the best, or simply refused to dwell on the unpleasantness awaiting us. I turned away, hotly impatient with his optimism. I would have to find a way out of this. For both of us.

The *comtesse* and her son took us to a little cove just south of Ashkelon where we boarded a private boat under cover of darkness. They had skirted the town, waiting until the local folk were tucked up in their beds before cloaking us in dark, muffling robes and leading us through the stony streets. Armand had made a point of brandishing his knife at us while his mother draped us in our robes.

"I would be only too happy to use this. Do not give me a reason to do so," he warned.

Sebastian yawned widely, earning him a quick slap from Armand, but I was careful to keep my eyes downcast and give him every appearance of obedience. We approached the little cove with a series of whistles and signals from the *comtesse* to the crew of the small boat. They did not appear to know each other well. The *comtesse* kept her face closely veiled and the captain addressed her only as *sitt* or lady. He and his crew were remarkably lacking in curiosity, scarcely looking at us as we boarded, and I theorised they were no doubt smugglers, such as roam the coast of every sea, trading in any sort of endeavour if it brings them coin. He had probably been born to the trade and owed no allegiance to anything save his own pocket. That meant there was no hope for Sebastian or me to persuade them to our side. The *comtesse* had undoubtedly paid them well for their services, and more importantly, for their silence. After they landed us at Sidon, they would promptly forget about us, and in the meantime, nothing but trumping the *comtesse*'s fee would win us their loyalty. Between us, Sebastian and I had our papers and a few miserable bank notes, but nothing near enough to pay for a crew to turn on the *comtesse*.

In any event, we had no opportunity. We were taken below and promptly locked into a bare cabin without light or food and left there for the duration of the journey.

"Sebastian," I began.

"Don't," he said softly. "Just go to sleep. One of the first rules of this game, love. Rest when you can. You don't ever know when you'll get another chance."

I did as he told me, curling myself into as comfortable a position as I could manage. But sleep was elusive, and I could hear the occasional movement that told me Sebastian was wakeful, too.

"I know you don't want to talk, but I can't sleep. And all I can think about is that knife of Armand's," I told him miserably.

He gave a sigh. "Come here."

I felt along the floor until my fingers brushed against his boot. Using that as a guide, I pulled myself along until I was beside him. He lifted his arms and lowered them over me, tucking me under his shoulder, resting his chin atop my head.

"What do you suppose happened to Peeky?" I asked.

I felt his chest rumble under my cheek. "We're for it, and you're worried about the bloody dog?"

"I hope they left him with the *comtesse*'s maid. She seemed a nice enough girl. I think she would take good care of him," I said, more to convince myself than anything else.

"I'm sure the dog is fine," he told me.

I raised my bound hands to poke his chest. "Do you really think we're for it?"

"It's not so grim," he said.

I gave a short, bitter laugh. "It is. We've got twelve hours to sail to Sidon and a few hours after that to reach Djoun. And when we do and you can't find the gold, they'll kill us."

"They'll try," he said lightly.

I turned, muffling a sob on his chest. "I don't want to die," I told him. "There are too many things I haven't done. Plus, I quite like living."

"Well, so do I," he replied. "There, now, stop snivelling. You're getting my shirt wet and it's already foul enough as it is."

I raised my wet face, and somehow—I never understood quite how he managed it—he was kissing me.

After a long, intoxicating moment, he drew back, smacking his lips. "Salty, but delectable," he murmured.

"Sebastian, be serious," I told him sharply.

His tone was wounded. "I am serious. Your tears are stinging the cut he left on my lip. But as kisses go, it wasn't half-bad. I imagine it could be quite good indeed if you applied yourself."

I opened my mouth to blast him, but he had other ideas, and I discovered Sebastian could be very persuasive when he put his mind to it. I found myself kissing him back, far more enthusiastically than I had ever kissed Gerald, and the results

were staggering. I was hot and then cold, shivering and breathless one minute and panting the next.

"Move just a little to the left," he instructed at one point.

"Do you like that?" I asked huskily.

"No," he said in a rasping voice. "You were grabbing my
bullet wound."

I started to apologise, but he smothered it with another kiss
and I gave myself up to it. There was every chance this was
going to be our last night on earth, and if it was, I argued with
myself, why not make the most of it?

The fact that our hands were still bound slowed us down,
but only a little. Sebastian proved to have boundless ingenu-
ity, and although the corset was immovable, he managed quite
nicely in spite of it.

When we had finished, in a tangle of robes and ropes and
garments still half-fastened, he collapsed, his head pillowed on
my chest. I touched his hair lightly. "Are you quite all right?"

"Mmmm." He groaned. "Rather. Do apologise for the
sleepiness. I expect my sex-tides are just low," he said with a
snicker.

His weight was slack and from the movement of his chest,
I could tell he'd fallen asleep. I gave him a good shove, but
he didn't move, and I did not entirely mind. His silky beard
brushed my neck, and his warm breath flowed in and out
over my skin as he slept. I cradled him and I felt a new ten-
derness for Sebastian. He had been my partner in this adventure, and while he had been grim and boorish at times when
things were going well, our present predicament seemed to
bring out the best in him. He was cheerful in the worst possible circumstances, buoying my spirits with his optimism
and sunny disposition. And just when I had felt at my lowest
ebb, defeated and worn, he had distracted me with warmth
and companionship.

And a culmination that would have impressed Marie Stopes herself, if I were honest. If Sebastian were capable of that sort of result with his hands tied together, I shivered to think of what he might accomplish with a proper bed and a bottle of champagne for encouragement. I sighed and stretched a little, feeling a warm surge of well-being and sleepiness. And lulled by the rocking motion of the ship and Sebastian's steady, even breathing, I felt myself slipping into sleep.

At the last moment, without quite intending to, I poked Sebastian lightly in the shoulder.

"Hmm?"

"Why does Gabriel call you Slightly Soiled?" I whispered.

His voice was thick with sleep. "Because I once hid in a cart of donkey manure to avoid capture," he told me. "And if you ever repeat that, I'll deny it. Now go to sleep," he ordered.

And I did.

I woke to the rasp of a key in the lock, and I bolted up, horrified to realise Sebastian and I were still in a state of disarray. I barely managed to shove him awake before they came, but not before Armand noticed our clothing and made several crude remarks for his own amusement. The *comtesse* pretended not to hear, but she gave me a sour look that showed precisely what she thought of young ladies who consorted unbecomingly. I didn't care. No doubt a better woman would have spent the night in prayer and contemplation, but I didn't have the makings of a martyr. I struggled to my feet and Sebastian did the same, hurriedly straightening our clothes as they shoved us up onto the deck. It was morning, perhaps the last morning of my life, I thought, and I stopped a moment to watch the sun glittering on the sea.

"Are you composing a sonnet?" Armand demanded. "Get off the boat."

I looked around. "There's no dock," I protested. The crew had brought the boat in as near to the shore as they dared, in a small cove like the one they had used near Ashkelon. In the distance I could just make out the profile of the citadel of Sidon, shimmering under the rising sun.

Armand smothered a retort and reached out, sweeping me into his arms and dumping me into the sea. It was frigid and I sank for a moment, flailing wildly as my heavy robes dragged me down. The salt water was like a slap to the face, shocking and numbing, and as I sank, lower and lower, my hands grew heavy with the cold. And then I felt it, the bottom of the sea, as I sat down hard. I shoved my feet under me and stood up to find the water at my waist and Armand laughing uproariously.

He moved to Sebastian who lifted a hand in an obscene gesture and leapt from the boat under his own power. Armand slid carefully over the side, and followed us, leaving his mother to make her own way, carried by one of the crew as delicately as a baby. I struggled along, soaked to the skin and weighed down by my sodden robes, until we reached the sandy shore. The sailor who carried the *comtesse* collected his purse and she stood staring at me in distaste. She hadn't even got her shoes wet, and I gave her a nasty look as she swept past.

"Come along. I want to reach Lady Hester's house by midday," she called.

Sebastian and I walked behind with Armand following us. I watched closely for any opportunity to make a move, but for the first few hours, I was too hampered by my wet clothes to do much of anything. I tried to hold the robes away from my legs, but they wrapped around, clinging with each step, tripping me up so often that the *comtesse* finally gave a sharp sigh and told her son to cut them off.

He leered a little as he hacked at the wet cloth, but it seemed more for form's sake than anything else. He kept looking to see if Sebastian noticed his hands lingering on my calves, and when he saw Sebastian was studying his fingernails instead, Armand applied himself to the job at hand. He made a mess of it. The beautiful Circassian gown was shredded just below the knee and the undergown cut off a little below that. I wasn't sad to see it go. The gown had been the most beautiful thing I'd ever worn, but I'd had it on for the better part of a week and I would have cheerfully burnt it myself at that point.

He hacked the extra length of the hanging sleeves as well, and freed from them, I walked more quickly, keeping pace with the *comtesse* as she led the way up into the hills. She skirted the village of Djoun, keeping well away from inquisitive villagers, and winding us around the deserted goat tracks dotted with scrubby bushes. The comtesse knew the area well. We were walking near the edge of the steep path, a sheer wall to one side and a long drop on the other.

"You've been here before," I said conversationally.

She curled a lip. "I have been everywhere."

"Have you ever been over a cliff?" I asked.

She turned to me with wide eyes, but before she could manage to speak, I reached out with both hands and shoved as hard as I could, pushing her over the cliff.

She shrieked as she fell, until I heard the ominous thud of a body landing upon rock, and then the only sound was Armand's howl of pure animal rage. I hadn't thought beyond the moment I would shove her over the side, but I had prayed for a chance, anything, no matter how slender. And in the end, it was Sebastian's size that saved him.

He and Armand had been walking side by side as the *comtesse* and I had, and when I shoved her over, Armand threw himself at Sebastian, intending him to suffer his mother's fate.

But Sebastian lowered himself, using his weight to anchor himself to the narrow ledge. If he'd been luckier, Armand would have gone straight over, just as his mother had. But he caught himself by the roots of a bush, and hauled himself back to his feet just as Sebastian rose.

The moment it had taken Armand to recover was all the time Sebastian needed. While Armand had been scrabbling at the bush, Sebastian had extracted a dagger from his boot and with a surgeon's precision, sliced cleanly through the ropes at his wrists. They dangled free as he whirled to face Armand, and to my utter astonishment, I saw that he was smiling.

It was the most gruesome thing I had ever seen, and I wasn't sure which was worse—the smile itself or the bloodbath that followed. Sebastian was methodical and precise, inflicting just enough injury each time Armand came at him to stop the charge but no more. He was letting Armand tire himself out, blood pouring from each wound Sebastian had incised. Armand came at him, again and again, slashing wildly, but Sebastian was mathematical in his approach, never allowing Armand to stay near enough for long enough to inflict any real damage of his own. Each time, Sebastian countered his wild lunges with a chillingly adept slash of his own, so quick I could not quite follow the movement until the blood rose and bubbled out of Armand's flesh.

Armand was bleeding freely from a dozen wounds and still he came, fueled by rage and grief and a drive to destroy. But Sebastian was calm and emotionless, cutting into him as neatly as he might slice a steak, choosing where he would inflict his next blow with the most damage and the least risk to himself. And finally, when Armand threw himself forward one final time, Sebastian sidestepped and came around, one hand at Armand's jaw, the other drawing a slender scarlet line from ear to ear. And then it was done.

I was on my knees. I couldn't stand, not after what I had just seen, and I was profoundly sick behind one of the bushes before I could manage to speak.

"Sebastian," I said.

He turned then. He had not moved since Armand had fallen into a wet crimson pool at his feet. And as I watched, he cleaned the blade calmly on the edge of his robe and came to me. He lifted it to the ropes at my wrists and severed them in one quick flick.

"Sebastian," I said again, dumbly. I did not know what to say or how to think. I only knew that we were safe now, safe because Sebastian had methodically and skillfully taken a man apart with nothing more than his will and a dagger he'd apparently had hidden in his boot the entire time.

There were too many questions to answer, too many even to ask, and I felt dizzy as he put the blade back into his boot.

"It's over now, Poppy," he said gently.

Just then a rock moved on the path above us, and I gave a shudder. "The *comtesse*," I said through chattering teeth. "She must have had accomplices."

A shadow fell over the path as a familiar figure came around the side of the hill.

"Masterman!" I cried.

She smiled. "Good Lord, whatever have you done with your hair?"

"What on earth are you doing here?" I demanded, never happier in my life to see anyone.

But she was not looking at me. She was smiling coolly at Sebastian. "It seems I am too late to effect a rescue."

He glowered in return. "What the bloody hell are you doing here? I thought you were in London."

Her smile didn't falter. "Is that any way to greet your superior?"

And that is when everything went quiet and the world began to turn and I slipped into the darkening rabbit hole.

TWENTY-ONE

I came to a little while later. We were in a makeshift camp of sorts at the foot of a rocky ridge. A fire had been lit and food was cooking, something hot and savoury from the smell of it, and Masterman was looking at me anxiously as she forced brandy down my throat.

I choked and waved her off.

"Try whisky," Sebastian said helpfully. "She seems to prefer that."

I sat up, my head swimming. "Would either of you care to explain what this is all about?"

They exchanged glances. "Well, it's rather a long story," Masterman began.

"Then the sooner you start, the quicker you'll finish," I told her coldly.

"It isn't entirely her fault, Poppy," Sebastian said.

"How do you even know each other?" I demanded. "You've only met the one time, at Father's cottage. And what did you mean, Masterman, when you said you were his superior?"

They exchanged glances again as if to decide which of them

would begin. Sebastian must have lost because he started, somewhat reluctantly. "Do you remember when I told you the Lost Boys were under the direction of the Vespiary? Well, Masterman is part of the organisation, as well."

I goggled at her. "You're a *spy*?"

She gave me a pained look. "We really don't like that word. It has such unpleasant connotations."

"But that's what you are," I countered. "Both of you."

Sebastian's expression was guarded. "Yes, Poppy. In fact, Masterman was directly responsible for supervising the Lost Boys."

"You mean, she really is your superior?"

Masterman's lips thinned. "Yes, and a bloody awful job it's been. You've never seen such a group of diabolical misfits in your entire life. I spent the entire war trying to keep tabs on them. They were never where they were supposed to be. And when the war was finished, only half of them were accounted for. I've spent the time since then trying to track the rest down."

I turned to Sebastian. "And that's what you were both doing here? Looking for Lost Boys?"

Sebastian gave me an oblique look and I understood there were some things even Masterman did not know—the existence of the Templar hoard for one. "Of course," he said blandly. "What else?"

Masterman broke in. "Gabriel Starke was our greatest loss. We wanted to be able to close his file. Sebastian insisted he didn't know what had become of him, but when he disappeared suddenly in London, I theorised he was chasing down a lead on his whereabouts. They were close. I knew if anyone could find him, Sebastian could. So I arranged to follow him to Damascus and ascertain how much he'd learned."

I shook my head, regretting it instantly as the dizziness

swam up again. "No, you didn't. *I* arranged to come to Damascus to find out what had happened to Sebastian."

Masterman's look was coolly assessing. "Did you?"

I thought back, more carefully. "You utter monster. You arranged it all, didn't you? The cryptic clues, the whole adventure. You set me a trail, knowing I'd follow it and lead you right to him."

"Not entirely," she said modestly. "I didn't arrange for the job with the colonel. That, as it turns out, was a complication from another side. I still don't know exactly what he was after with you, but I'm sure Sebastian could fill in the blanks," she said, giving him a cool, level stare.

He shrugged, his expression inscrutable. I was not about to tell her about the gold. I had almost died because of it, and as far as I was concerned, it could stay lost forever.

Masterman went on. "But I did slip Sebastian's childhood book into his room at Mrs. Webb's. I thought you'd respond to it. You're rather soft-hearted, you know."

"That is the most breathtakingly cynical thing I've ever heard," I told her, my voice bitter. "But it isn't the whole story, not by a long shot. You were working for the viscountess before the wedding, and I didn't meet Sebastian until that day. How could you possibly have known he'd help me run away?"

"Yes, Masterman," Sebastian said nastily. "How could you possibly have known?"

She stubbed out her cigarette carefully. "Easy, Fox. We've got to tell her the truth, whether you like it or not."

Sebastian crossed his arms over his chest. "Shall we draw for it?"

"No," she said with a sigh. "I'm the senior. It was my mission in the first place." She turned to me, choosing her words carefully. "Poppy, it was felt that you might possibly have a place in the Vespiary. It was my responsibility to assess your abilities, to determine if an offer should be made to bring you on board with us. Sebastian was between assignments just then, so when I decided you might possibly not go through with your wedding, I put him in place and told him to act if he thought you needed assistance."

I stared from one to the other. "You're mad. Both of you. You can't seriously expect me to believe that some mysterious spy group found me out of the blue and wanted to recruit me for espionage, so they just happened to hang around my wedding in case I decided to bolt."

Masterman's voice was gentle. "I had seen enough of you to believe you were not entirely happy about your marriage to Gerald. I had orders to extract you using whatever means necessary to ensure your safe departure. Sebastian was the most capable man I had at my disposal, and I would like to point out, he did an heroic job of getting you out of there. I had my hands full keeping your mother out long enough for him to get you away."

"You kept my mother out?"

She gave me a thin smile. "I pretended to lose the key to the dressing room. It bought Sebastian just enough time to get you to his motorcar."

I shook my head. "But that still doesn't explain why this agency, this Vespiary, would pick me out of millions of people to recruit. I'm nobody to them."

She exchanged another glance with Sebastian, then seemed to steel herself. "Poppy, you're already one of us. Who do you think founded the Vespiary?"

I opened my mouth, then snapped it shut as my head began to spin again. "Oh, God. Father," I muttered.

"He assisted your uncle, Nicholas Brisbane, in founding the organisation in 1890 with the help of a distant cousin, Sir Mor-

gan Fielding. Since then, several members of the March family
and their circle of friends have been engaged in espionage."

"You're mad," I repeated. "Not even Father would ask a
pack of spies to haul me out of my own wedding."

"Of course not," Masterman said indignantly. "We were
only to assist if you bolted. Until then we were under strict
orders simply to watch over you. If you were content to marry
Gerald, we were to do and say absolutely nothing to betray
our assignment."

"I can't believe Father would abuse his position by making
a perfect stranger pretend to be my lady's maid," I said flatly.

I sat in stunned silence while Sebastian gave Masterman
a cool look. "Tell her the rest. Do it now," he insisted. "She
won't thank you if she finds out later."

"Tell me what?" I demanded.

Masterman's expression didn't change, but something about
the chill in her gaze reminded me that Sebastian was her sub-
ordinate. "Very well. We're actually not strangers, Poppy. We
haven't met before, but we are family. My name isn't Masterman, it's March. Perdita March. My father, Benedick, is
brother to your father. I'm your first cousin."

I bolted to my feet. "That's enough. I don't want to hear
anymore. Not now."

She nodded. "Very well. I'll go and see if my men have
finished preparing the food." She grinned. "Very useful that
I managed to make contact with your young friend Rashid,"
she told Sebastian. He started in surprise and she smiled. "Yes,
I know more of your field contacts than you imagine. I made
Rashid's acquaintance, and informed him if there was trouble
to find me. After he left you on the road from Damascus, he
noted that you were being followed, and it concerned him.
He reported to me, and I asked him to rally his tribesmen.
He was only too happy to raise a contingent of Bedouin to

come to your rescue. I think they're rather disappointed there isn't a fight on after all. I expect I'll have to pay them double for the disappointment." She turned back to me. "You need feeding. I expect that's the reason you fainted. You're young and strong, and you've done very well for your first field assignment." She glanced to Sebastian. "But I think some of that must be credited to your handler."

She left then, and I whirled on Sebastian.

"My what?"

He had the grace to look abashed. "Your handler. It's the term for the agent assigned to look after you when you're in the field."

"I wasn't in the field," I told him.

He said nothing, waiting for me to work it out. "Oh, my God," I said faintly, groping for the seat again. "You've been assessing me this entire time, too. Was it all a charade? Just a game? Is there even any gold?"

He darted a look to the doorway where Masterman—or Perdita—had disappeared. "For God's sake, lower your voice. Yes, there is gold, and no, I don't know where it is. The London office doesn't know everything," he said grimly. "Perdita thinks I was here solely on the trail of Gabriel Starke. She believes the colonel and his crew were involved in something nefarious and that you got mixed up in it accidentally by overhearing something you oughtn't at the villa. She thinks that put you in danger and that's why we were framed for Talbot's murder and chased around the Levant."

I put my head in my hands. "You lied to her."

I peeped through my fingers to see him tip his head to one side. "I do so hate that word. I prefer to think of it as being economical with the truth. Besides, I don't think you have any cause to throw that particular stone. If you'd told me about Perdita being out here in the first place, I could have gone directly to her when Talbot was murdered and avoided this entire desert chase." I felt a little abashed, and he went on, his voice marginally warmer. "Look, I told Perdita as much as she needed to know. My first loyalty is to the other Lost Boys," he told me flatly. "They were my family when I had none. Do not mistake me—I would never betray the Vespiary, but they do not need to know everything."

"I understand," I said slowly. And to my surprise, I found I did. I gave him a long look, taking him in from dusty boots to blood-spattered shirt. I shuddered. "I don't even think I know you at all. All this time, I thought you were some poor wretch who scribbled figures in ledgers and pushed maps around." His smile was warm.

"I've done that, too."

"But Gabriel told me about you. I should have listened. He said you were a devil. He told me he'd never seen anything like you in a knife fight," I told him.

He shrugged. "Everyone has a skill."

"And yours is cutting people into small bits."

"Poppy, I do what I have to in order to protect myself and whoever is under my protection. In this case, you were my responsibility."

I shook my head, trying to clear away the cobwebs. "I actually thought I was going to have to save you. You were always so damnably cheerful, so optimistic. I thought you were too dim to understand real danger, but now I understand. You were never in danger, were you? You knew what you were capable of, so you didn't worry at all."

"Poppy," he said softly, "I've found that playing the fool disarms people. I've avoided more fights than I care to count because someone thought I was a cheerful imbecile and let me go about my business. But that stupid insistence on hoping for the best isn't just a façade. It's the only thing that saved my life when in that prison. Every day I woke up and I looked at the sun, and all I could think was at least this was one more day they hadn't broken me, one more day I could say I had seen. And every night, I had one more day notched on that wall that I had seen through to the end. I believed I was going to survive, and I did. And nothing I will ever again face in my life will be so bad as what I suffered there. Unless you can't forgive me," he finished.

I stared at him, and saw his burnished skin had gone pale.

"I began this because I was given an assignment, and when I left to find Gabriel I thought I'd never see you again. But when you showed up in Damascus, all I could think was I'd been given a second chance. I knew Perdita would have my guts for garters for haring off without permission, and I thought if I could give her something useful, it might appease her a bit. I knew how much it meant to her to assess your abilities. And there is no one better at that than I am. It was the best excuse I had to keep close to you, to protect you, with my life if I had to. And I would have, Poppy. You know that—I know you do."

His face went blurry and tears fell on my hands. "I don't know what I know," I said simply. "It's all too confusing now."

"It won't be," he promised. "You've had a day that would have broken most people. You've seen a man killed in front of you."

"And I've killed someone." I buried my face in my hands again. "Oh, God. I killed someone. The *comtesse*."

"The *comtesse* isn't dead," he said, taking my hands from my face.

I peered at him suspiciously. "Are you sure?

"Quite. Rashid's kinsmen found her at the base of the little rise you knocked her off of. She's injured, but not fatally. They're taking her back to Damascus now."

I felt a rush of relief so profound it was like being reborn. "Thank God." A sudden thought occurred to me. "You had the knife in your boot all along. Why didn't you tell me? Why didn't you use it?"

"If I'd told you, you might have betrayed knowing it somehow. So much as a single glance at my boot would have given us away. And I used it when I needed it. Not before. I had to do it when we stood a chance of getting clear."

"But we outnumbered Faruq," I protested.

"Faruq wasn't the head of the conspiracy," he reminded me. "I could have dispatched him and we still would have been at risk from the others. It was far better to let him take us along like useful little goats until we could turn the tables."

I shuddered as I thought of how close we had come to losing our lives. I looked up at him, needing him to understand. "I didn't want to kill her. I just wanted—"

"I know," he said simply.

"But when you went after Armand," I said slowly. "You did want to kill him."

"I didn't just want to. I needed to," he explained, unflinching.

I nodded, almost but not quite touching his hand. "I know."

After we had been fed, we departed for Beirut. We might have gone to Sidon, but Masterman—or Perdita, as I had to think of her—thought a larger city would be better. Rashid's Bedouin kinsmen had brought camels and horses to spare, and they ran us up the coast in a sort of caravan. The bells of the animals' headstalls jingled as we rode, swift as the gathering wind, and behind us their banners streamed out just as they had in the days of the Crusader knights. Perdita had organised hot water and fresh clothes for us before we left the camp, and she eyed Sebastian's wounds.

"Best get those cleaned up and bandaged, Fox. I don't think the hotel will appreciate you bleeding on the floors."

He shrugged. "Scratches."

She gave him a severe look. "You need stitches and that arm is well on its way to infection. Either clean it up now or we can wait a week and take it off at the shoulder."

He smothered a curse and strode off, clean clothes in hand. She turned to me with a thin smile.

"Don't mind him. It takes some that way."

I felt heavy and sleepy, as if waking from the past few days to find they were only a dream, as insubstantial as a mirage in the *Badiyat ash-Sham*. I roused myself to respond.

"What does?"

"The end of an assignment. Some agents feel euphoric, thrilled at a job well done. Others tend towards anger. Sebastian is one of the latter."

"Why should he be angry?"

The look she gave me was pitying. "Because the thing he's best at in the world is what he just did. And it's over."

"You mean he's good at killing people."

"It was his primary job here. Didn't he tell you? He was Gabriel's protection officer. Whenever he was in a tight spot, Sebastian is the one who waded in and took care of things."

"Gabriel tried to tell me," I said woodenly. "I thought he was joking. I thought Sebastian was a sort of clerk."

"That's what people were meant to think. He's made a good job of cultivating that sweetly cheerful, scholarly façade. People underestimate him. It's his greatest advantage."

"I underestimated him," I admitted. "I've spent the past weeks believing he was something entirely different than he was, thinking I was saving him. And all this time—"

I faltered, feeling more of a fool than I had in the whole of my life.

Perdita took pity on me. "Don't crucify yourself over it, Poppy. He's fooled people with far better reason than you to suspect what he is. It's his job and he does it well."

By midnight we were in Beirut, where Perdita had arranged a suite of hotel rooms for us. I fell into bed and slept the whole night and most of the next day, rousing late in the afternoon. Perdita sent up an attendant—armed with various potions—from the hotel's salon to turn my hair back to brown. I almost didn't know myself when she was finished. The flat black glamour of the henna was gone, and in its place was the girl I had once known, only different. Irreparably and incomparably different.

When the attendant left I washed again, filling the bathtub with scalding hot water and handfuls of scented salts. As the water cooled, I drained and filled it again, and a third time, scrubbing my skin until every particle of dust and dirt had been removed. My trunk had been brought from Damascus and was waiting for me, every garment neatly folded in tissue, just as Masterman always insisted. I wondered if Perdita had packed it herself and decided I didn't care. There was a note instructing me to join her for dinner and I slipped into my peacock evening gown, watching the silver beads flash in the light. It wasn't half so glamorous as my Circassian robes, but it was distinctly more comfortable. I had thought it would be just the two of us, but when I appeared at Perdita's door, Sebastian answered. He was dressed in formal evening wear, his beard neatly barbered. He handed me a cocktail before I'd even crossed the threshold.

"Dutch courage?" I asked thinly.

"The only sort I've got left," he replied, lifting his glass. I followed him to the main room of her suite. A table had been set for dinner, and the waiters were busy lifting domed lids off an assortment of dishes. Perdita sat at the head of the table with Sebastian and me on either side. She was wearing a scarlet wool dress, very simply cut but striking, and I wondered again if she deliberately played down her good looks. She might have been stunning with a little effort, but she seemed unaware of it or unwilling to do anything about it. I wondered if I would ever understand her, but her smile to me was one of genuine pleasure.

"Glad to hear you slept the day through," she said, waving us to our chairs. "It's the best remedy for an experience such as you had."

She showed the waiters out, leaving us to dine tête-à-tête, helping ourselves from the heaped platters of food. Sebastian poured the wine, generous servings, and as the evening wore on, the food and wine began to work their magic. We had started out stiffly, with Sebastian nearly silent and Perdita steering the conversation. But by the time we had dipped into the finger bowls and helped ourselves to the piles of honey-drenched rose toffees and nut-studded baklava, we had all begun to thaw.

"So," Perdita said, sitting back and surveying Sebastian, "it's time for your report. I shall want a formal one for the record, but you can write that up on the voyage back. Give me the high points."

"Report on what?" I asked, hiccupping only slightly as I finished my third glass of wine.

"You," Sebastian replied. He tipped his head, studying me in the candlelight, and for once I didn't look away. I don't know if it was the wine or the evening, but I felt reckless, stronger than I had ever been before. I lifted my chin and studied him right back. He looked different, but then a razor and a bit of hair trimming can do that for a man. It was more than that. He was dressed impeccably. His evening clothes, unlike his curate's garb, were beautifully tailored, and I wondered if he didn't have more in common with the dashing desert warrior than the shambling English clergyman after all.

"She's rough yet," he said slowly, his eyes roving from my lips to my eyes and back again. "She has enormous potential, but she needs just the right handler to keep herself from getting killed. She needs to be trained in unarmed combat as well as light weapons. I suspect she might prove an excellent shot, and she has good reflexes. I'd recommend a small pistol rather than knife work for her. She's competent in navigation, but a thorough training in maps is essential. You might take a look at her linguistic skills. I taught her a word or two of Arabic and her gift for mimicry is substantial."

I stared at him, mouth agape, as he enumerated his findings. He stopped, a slow smile curving his lips.

"Go on," I prodded. "What are my flaws?"

"Nothing that can't be remedied with training," he said smoothly.

Perdita looked from one of us to the other. "Excellent. How long until she's field ready?"

He shrugged. "Six months. But only if she works extremely hard. And only if she's able to trust her instincts. Without that, there's no point. She'll fail."

I felt a rush of blood flood my face. "My instincts, in case you failed to notice, were appalling. I trusted the wrong people, suspected the wrong people."

His thoughtfully assessing look never faltered. "Did you? I seem to recall you never fully trusted Hugh Talbot, not even when he was kissing you in the moonlight."

"Well, of course not, he was a cad. Any girl could have told you that."

"I also know that you told Perdita you didn't like the atmosphere at the *comtesse*'s villa. Another point in your favour."

"The house was creepy," I said sullenly. "Anyone would have disliked it."

"Furthermore, you were intent upon following me half-way across the world because you were convinced something had brought us together for a reason. You weren't wrong," he said, his voice low and caressing.

"Perdita—" I began.

"Perdita could never have got you on that ship if you hadn't insisted upon going," he said flatly. "You drove this adventure, Poppy. From the beginning. We were only in place to offer you assistance if you needed it. You unearthed every lead, followed up every clue. You did it yourself."

"He is right," Perdita broke in, her voice gentle. "I offered you no more than a nudge. It was up to you to pursue it. Which you did—with a vengeance."

Her eyes were almost feral in the candlelight, and I saw how much satisfaction she took in her job. "You enjoy this, don't you?" I said, almost accusingly. "You like moving us all about as if we were chess pieces on a board."

She gave me a calm smile. "We all have our strengths, dear. Mine is knowing people. That's how I knew Sebastian could lead me to Gabriel."

Sebastian didn't move, but I sensed him stiffen. Perdita flicked him a glance. "Don't worry, Sebastian. I won't press you. I know you saw him and that's enough for me. You might find it hard to believe at times, but I do have a soft spot for my Lost Boys. I simply wanted to know he was alive. He's finished with us and I have to accept that. It's enough to know he survived." She paused, and looked as if she were struggling with emotion. But she mastered it immediately and rose, taking a deep breath. "I'm going to bed. You two are free to stay as long as you like. The view from the balcony is particularly nice," she said.

She left us then, and Sebastian lifted a brow. I nodded and he guided me onto the balcony. It overlooked the Mediterranean, the sea shifting and glittering under a blanket of stars. A low moon hung in a curve just above the horizon and I shook my head.

"It's too much. Do you think she arranged for that, too?"

"Probably," he said lightly. "And the flowers," he said with a nod towards the perfumed vine blossoming on the column beside us. The scent of jasmine was heavy in the air.

"Poppy," he said finally, "you said you wanted adventure. You said you wanted to finish something. You did both. And it doesn't have to end here. You do have the makings of an agent if you want the job. Perdita will take you and train you well."

I gave him a long look. "What makes you think I can do this?"

"Because it's been my job to watch you," he told me. "I've followed you even when you didn't know you were being followed. I've tested you and pushed you and warned you—"

"You were the shadow who warned me off in the *souk*," I said in a small, hollow voice.

"And the beggar who read your palm," he said with a grin. "But no matter how much I warned you, you wouldn't give up." He stroked his beard thoughtfully. "Although you might have done a better job of penetrating my disguises. I'll tell Perdita to make sure she includes basic physiognomy in her training program. A little knowledge in that field and you'd have been able to tell it was me from the bone structure." He gave me another small grin then sobered. "Poppy, I've seen you under the most demanding circumstances. You were frightened, hunted, cold, hungry. And through it all, you didn't lose your head. You were mentally fit, optimistic, rational. But most of all, I saw what you did on that ridge when you seized the moment and didn't hesitate to shove the *comtesse* off."

I shrugged. "I did what anyone would have done under the circumstances," I said.

His eyes held mine steadily as he shook his head. "No, you didn't, Poppy. Perhaps one woman in a thousand could have done that. You seized the opportunity and you acted, without hesitation and without fear."

Something within my chest tightened then, some feeling of pride that I had risen to a challenge and given him a reason to think me worthy, and—more importantly—given myself a reason to feel worthy.

Still his eyes never left my face. "And I know you have what it takes to be one of us for another reason, perhaps the simplest of all."

"What's that?"

"I saw what else you did when you shoved the *comtesse* off the cliff."

I shook my head. "I don't know how you saw anything. I hardly remember, it's all such a blur. Tell me," I said, venturing a small grin. "What did I do that was so surprising?"

"You smiled."

TWENTY-TWO

We parted at Southampton. Sebastian had work in London, Perdita told him firmly, and she was taking me straight to Father's for a long-overdue chat. Through Perdita's efforts, the story had been squashed in the international newspapers, and the only thing the London papers reported was the sad death abroad of a war hero. There was a lovely obituary for the colonel, and Perdita sent a handsome wreath to his memorial service. Cubby was listed as chief mourner, and I heard later he was the heir to his uncle's modest fortune as well as Peeky. And as I read the obituary, my eyes lingered on Cubby's name and I thought back to our conversation that fateful day at lunch. He had introduced us, giving me the opening I needed to follow Sebastian to Damascus. I had assumed it was Hugh who managed the affair, but I asked Perdita if the colonel could have arranged it and she thought it likely.

"We suspect he may have been tracking Sebastian and waiting for him to make a move to find Gabriel. Although, what the old fellow would want with Gabriel, I can't imagine. He might have had his own contacts in French or Syrian intelligence working counter to our interests," she finished with a shrug. She did not pursue the matter, and I wondered how much she suspected. The explanation of competing intelligence agencies running afoul of one another was too easy. She ought to have dug deeper, but perhaps she knew if she did, she would uncover things about her beloved Lost Boys she'd rather not know. She had collected them, misfits and renegades, and shaped them into a family. Turning a blind eye to their unsanctioned exploits might be the only way to avoid catching herself between opposing loyalties.

She went on, knitting up the loose ends as neatly as if she were making a jumper. "The donkey cart was Faruq's doing at Armand's behest. The idea was to make you nervous of the city so you would be likelier to put your trust in either Armand or Hugh. They were prepared for the wind to blow either direction," she added. "Not a bad plan, all things considered. But they reckoned without your eccentric sense of duty to find out what happened to Sebastian Fox."

I said nothing. Even after all that had happened, I could not explain what had compelled me to travel halfway around the world in the hope of saving a man I had only met once.

A sudden thought struck me. "How were you able to hush it all up? There hasn't been a breath of it in the newspapers, and none of the French authorities in the Lebanon seemed bothered in the slightest by what we were up to. It's almost as if we weren't there at all."

"Officially we weren't," she said with a cool look.

"But how? Does the Vespiary have an understanding with the French government?"

"With the government? No. But the government is made up of individuals, you know. And I have made a friend or two along the way."

I stared at her, comprehension dawning. "A friend. You mean a man!"

"Poppy, you may be adept at winkling out other people's secrets, but I think I'll keep my own, if you don't mind."

She said nothing more about the subject, but my imagination filled in the gaps. It was delicious to think about the possibilities. Was he her opposite number in French intelligence? An army general? Ambassador? Junior minister? He must be highly placed if he could do her such favours. And he must be very fond of her to bother.

But Perdita was as good as her word, and she refused to speak another word on the subject. She left me at the village of Abbots Burton. "Aren't you coming?" I asked as I alighted at the station.

"Alas, no," she said with a bright smile. "Work. I've spent too much time away from my desk as it is."

"Coward," I said, returning the smile.

She smoothed her skirt. "Well, I don't relish the idea of explaining to Uncle Plum *precisely* what you've been up to. I think you'll find it best if it's just the pair of you." She paused and put out her hand. "I hope to see you next week in London, Poppy."

She had offered me a post with the agency, and training was due to start in just a few days. A handful of days to make my choice.

I shook her hand slowly. "I don't know, Perdita."

"Yes, you do," she said with that familiar mocking look.

I walked slowly to Father's cottage, letting myself through the wicket gate as I approached. "So you're back," George said sourly when he let me in. "He's in the studio. I suppose you'll want to spend the night."

I told him I would and went to find Father. He was perched

on a stool, putting the finishing touches to a portrait. He turned when I entered, lifting his brows in a rueful smile.

"Ah, the prodigal returns."

"Hardly prodigal when your own father is responsible for your running away," I returned evenly.

"Hoist with my own petard," he answered, turning back to the portrait. I stood beside him. The subject was beautiful, that much was apparent from the structure of her bones. But something was off in the face, some vitality that seemed lacking.

"All these years and I've never managed to capture her," he mused. He dipped his head towards the stack of canvases against the wall. They were all the same subject, a dark-haired woman, and it was easy to see he had painted her through the years. The hair had silvered and the cheeks had wrinkled, but the bones were always the same.

"It's Aunt Violante, isn't it? Uncle Lysander's widow. I read about her in Aunt Julia's memoirs. You're in love with her."

He did not deny it. "She is the reason I was never able to make a go of things with your mother. Poor Araminta. She knew I was in love with another woman when we married. She thought I'd grow out of it. She gambled poorly."

I smoothed my jacket. "Well, congratulations. You've actually made me pity Mother. I never thought that would happen."

He put down his brush and fixed me with a bright gaze. "Poppy, your mother knew precisely what she was getting herself into. I never made a secret of my love for Violante. Araminta thought she could change me. She was wrong. Let that be a lesson to you."

"What? Don't try to change a man?"

"Leopards and spots, child," he said sagely. "We all have them, and they're indelible. And I'm not just talking about a man. I mean you. It's time for you to take hold of who you are with both hands and stop pretending to be something you aren't."

"I walked out on my wedding to Gerald," I reminded him.

"Because I offered you the means," he countered. "I provided you with people to help you get away. But walking away from something is only living your life as a repudiation. How will you live it as an affirmation?"

I blinked at him. "Have you been studying psychology?"

He shrugged. "One must keep up with the times. I mean it, Poppy. To walk away from something is only half the picture. What are you walking towards?" I said nothing and he gave me a pitying look. "You still don't believe in yourself quite enough, do you?"

"I don't know. I don't know myself," I said slowly. "I've sort of stumbled into this opportunity, and I want to take it. I want to train and learn and go back into the field. I think I'm suited to it. I just wish I knew."

His smile was proud and devilish. "You have everything required to make a success of it, Poppy. Why else do you think I chose you?"

I blinked. "Chose me?"

The smile deepened. "You still haven't put all the pieces together, have you? I told you I had reports of you growing up. You thought I meant only your schoolmistresses and dancing masters, but there were others. People who knew what I was looking for in you. And they found it. It takes a unique combination of characteristics to do this work, child. I'd never have considered you for the job if you hadn't shown them—and in spades. Every time you broke the mould and did something audacious, every time you thwarted expectations, I knew you had it in you. It was my job at the Vespiary to assess potential in the young ones, and I got quite good at it," he said with an air of satisfaction. "But you're the only one I ever had to assess at a distance, from second-hand information and my own instincts. But you are one of us, Poppy. I know it in my bones and in my blood, and I am not wrong. I chose you because we will ask much of you, but you have everything you need to answer that call." He paused, and when he spoke again, his voice was softer. "I've read the reports from Perdita and young Fox. You have quite a promising future at the Vespiary if you want it."

I brushed away the sudden tears and squared my shoulders. "I do."

"And what about Fox?" he asked shrewdly.

"Oh, I expect I'll marry him," I told him. "But not now. Perdita and I have work to do first."

Perdita, with a stroke of inspiration, paired me with another of the Lost Boys to complete my training. Affectionately called Nibs by the other Boys, he had known Sebastian, and he understood—perhaps more than anyone else would have—what it was like to be in the field with him.

"Did you happen to see his knife work?" he asked me the first day.

"There might have been an occasion," I said, thinking of the bits of Armand scattered on the hilltop ridge.

He shook his head admiringly. "Finest skill with a blade I've ever seen. Of course, he only uses it as a last resort. Gets far more enjoyment out of running about in bits of disguise. Rather like me." A sudden grin lit his slim, handsome face. "You don't recognise Selim the beggar from outside the restaurant in Damascus, do you?"

I thought of the grimy beggar with the outstretched hand and pleading eyes. "But—but you've got both legs! I distinctly remember stepping over your stump to get into the restaurant."

The grin deepened. "A particularly effective trick, don't

you think? Hell on the knees, of course, but worth it. I made rather a packet doing that and learned quite a lot to boot."

"But what were you doing there? I thought all the Lost Boys were scattered after the war."

He gave a nod to Perdita's closed door. "I'm the only one of the Lost Boys who stayed in the field in Damascus after the war. I was supposed to be looking for Gabriel," he finished coolly.

"And not trying terribly hard to find him, I'll wager," I said. "I won't ask if you ever found him. I suspect you wouldn't have told anyone if you had."

The grin was back. "Smart girl. Now, time to practise your unarmed combat. Come at me and I'll flip you."

For the first time in my life, I worked hard, day and night, and within five months—not the six she had anticipated— Perdita had deemed me ready. In spite of the fact that Perdita was in command of the Vespiary, she liked to preserve the fiction that she merely carried out her brother Tarquin's orders. She claimed it was because she could keep an ear closer to the ground with regard to what the operatives were thinking, but I suspected it was because she enjoyed getting her hands dirty.

The day I went to see her she was in Tarquin's office, and I was told to wait a few minutes. I picked up a newspaper to pass the time, skimming the society columns with interest. One item in particular caught my attention: Gerald Madderley, heir to Viscount Madderley, announced his engagement to a certain South American nitrate heiress. I smiled to myself remembering what Cubby said about her squint. Good for Gerald—I only hoped the girl had low sex-tides to go with her pots of money.

I turned the page to glance over the world news. It was at the bottom—a small piece with no details, just the barest facts:

a grisly discovery had been made in the Syrian desert near Palmyra. It was the remains of a party of English archaeologists that had gone missing between Damascus and Baghdad in an arid stretch of the *Badiyat ash-Sham*. Curiously, only two bodies had been found, both of them male. Of the lady who had been travelling with them, there was no trace, and it was apparent that the bodies had lain in the desert for some time. As it had been so many months, no attempts were being made to find the lady and she was presumed dead, as well.

I put the newspaper aside, thinking of the cool beauty with the raven hair who had prepared our dinner on the plateau in the shadow of Mount Lebanon. Had she seized the opportunity to do away with her travelling companions? Or had they been victims of tribal warfare? Desert brigands? The possibilities were endless, but so was the desert, and it occurred to me that the *Badiyat ash-Sham* was a very good place to make a new beginning.

I was still thinking of Rosamund Johnson when a buzzer sounded indicating Perdita was ready for me. I let myself in and closed the door behind me. She was standing at the desk with a companion—a raven, an enormous bird with feathers so black they had a blue sheen to them in the light, precisely the same colour as Rosamund Johnson's hair, I thought idly. Perdita smiled without looking up as I entered.

"Handsome fellow, isn't he?"

The bird quirked its head in my direction and gave me a long sideways stare. Its eye looked like a polished jet bead, cool and impervious.

"Very," I said. He might have been unnerving at close range, but he was still a beautiful creature.

"Our Aunt Julia had one, as you will remember from reading her memoirs," she said, holding a bit of meat between her fingertips, just out of range of the bird. "Grim was an actual

Tower raven. I'm afraid this lad's provenance is much less impressive. Still, he's clever."

She dropped the meat into a small box and snapped it closed. She tapped the box once and the raven bobbed his head. "That's for me," he said in a peculiar little voice.

"Yes, it is. Go to it," she commanded. The bird eyed the box greedily and applied himself. Within a moment, he had it open and was tearing into the meat. I looked away as Perdita wiped her hands.

"Much faster this time. They really do learn. Fascinating, isn't it?"

"Is he a pet?" I asked.

"No. A wager, actually. Tarquin thinks they can't be trained to do fieldwork, but I think they can."

"Fieldwork? A bird?"

She shrugged. "They're teachable and intelligent, more so than most creatures. I have no doubt I can put him to good use."

The raven was still enjoying his titbit when Perdita handed me a piece of paper. "Your first assignment. You'll be in the field but not entirely on your own. It's a bit of information gathering, nothing too taxing. And I've arranged for you to partner with an experienced agent to keep an eye on you." She paused, a ghost of a smile touching her lips. "Just a precaution. You've done well, Poppy. And I think you'll be an asset to the Vespiary."

She handed me a sealed envelope with my orders inside. I did not open it, and when I hesitated, she looked up. "Yes?"

"Would you have given me this chance if it weren't for who Father is?"

"No," she said simply. "But that doesn't mean you don't deserve it. From its inception the Vespiary has been unique. Every member has been known to one of the seniors and re-

cruited based upon a sound knowledge of the recruit's character and abilities. It's how we've managed a rather impressive
rate of success when other offices have failed," she finished
with a note of satisfaction. "No one knows you better than
your family, your friends. So long as sentimentalism doesn't
blind you to a person's faults, that familiarity makes you the
best possible judge of where to put your loyalty."

"You're sentimental about the Lost Boys," I said quietly.

She considered this. "I suppose," she answered slowly. "The
Vespiary has been everything to me, Poppy. When it came
time for Uncle Brisbane and your father to pass over control,
I was chosen, even above my brother Tarquin, because I had
the passion to make it my whole life. I never wanted a husband
or children. I wanted the Vespiary. It has been everything to
me, spouse, partner, child, and I have given it the best of me.
I *will* give it the best of me until I have nothing left to give.
And that's why I deserved it. I've built it into an elite group,
and I am proud of the work we have done. But don't mistake
my affection for the Lost Boys as weakness. I turn a blind eye
sometimes because it suits the interests of the Vespiary not to
go deeper." Her gaze held mine with a cool detachment, and I
suspected then that she knew everything about the gold, about
the tangle of relationships between the Lost Boys, every secret
they had tried to keep from her. She was Mother, folding up
the shadows and smoothing away the things that could trouble them while they slept off the fatigues of their adventures.

I wondered for a moment if she would appreciate the comparison, but as I turned to leave, I noticed the bookshelf behind her desk. In pride of place, next to her copies of our
Aunt Julia's memoirs was a well-worn edition of *Peter Pan and
Wendy*. She saw my eyes resting on the book and gave me a
bittersweet smile.

"Someone has to stay home and keep things tidy," she said
simply.

★ ★ ★

I left Tarquin's office, clutching my orders in my hand. Outside, a clergyman was waiting. He rose when I approached, lifting his hat. His hair was tousled but his chin was clean-shaven since the last time I had seen him.

"I prefer the beard," I told him.

There was a tiny smile, almost against his will, it seemed. He flicked a glance to my orders.

"Have you opened them?"

"Not yet."

"Egypt," he said succinctly. "Mine, as well."

"So you're my senior?"

He gave a small shrug. "Perdita thought it advisable. We have already shown we work well together, and I hear you've learned a thing or two from Nibs."

His tone was emotionless when he mentioned his friend. "He's a surviving Lost Boy. Do you think he knows where the…" I hesitated and glanced around even though we were alone in the office. "Where the you-know-what is?"

He shook his head slowly. "I don't know and I don't care. I've had a chance to think it out, and I don't want to know. It's torn too many of my friends apart. Best to let it lie."

I considered a moment. "I read the newspapers in July. I know Damascus fell to the French and they're in power again. Do you know what's become of Gabriel?"

He grinned. "He's in the South Pacific working on his suntan. With Evie."

"So they found their way back to one another? After all that time?" I breathed. "How marvellous."

He looked inexpressibly sad for a moment. "Yes, they got their happy ending after all, it seems."

I took a deep breath and made a decision. It was as much an impulse of the moment as shoving the *comtesse* off a cliff, but it felt every bit as right. "How long do you think the Egypt business will last?"

He shrugged. "Once we arrive, a week or so at most. Just a bit of information gathering and a report to write, but Perdita's given us two months."

"Excellent. That should give us plenty of time."

His eyes were wary. "For what?"

"A honeymoon. I should like to go back to Syria and see if we can sniff out what happened to Stephen Baleister. Even if we can't find the…erm, what you were looking for, at least there will be an answer once and for all about what happened to him. You'll get your trust back in your friends. I think that's the best wedding present I can give you."

He shook his head. "I must be hallucinating. You just said honeymoon. And wedding present. In the same breath."

I put a hand to his cheek. "Poor Sebastian. I did rather spring it on you. I'm proposing. I don't want a lot of fuss about the wedding. Heaven knows I've been through all that before. What do you think of a nice quiet ceremony on the ship over? The captain can marry us. It will add a nice bit of romantic flavour to our cover story, don't you think?"

"You want to marry me?" he said slowly.

I blinked. "You really didn't know? Even after what happened on the voyage to Sidon? Really, Sebastian, I wouldn't have done that with just *anyone*."

A muscle in his jaw tightened. "Poppy, you watched me dismember a man. I thought that put you off me. And as far as what happened on the ship, you thought you were about to die. It does rather make one do things out of character."

"Not me," I said, putting both arms about his neck and stretching up on tiptoe. "You haven't answered. Will you marry me? Or would you rather I get down on my knees to ask you properly?"

His voice was strangled. "The position does have a certain primitive appeal, I admit. But, Poppy," he said, reaching up to take my hands in his, "I don't think—"

I looked at him in disbelief. "Don't tell me you don't love me. I refuse to believe it. I've had months to go over it all in my mind, and I finally understand why you were so peculiar with me, so prickly. You were trying to do a job and your feelings for me were interfering. And they were interfering because you adore me," I said triumphantly.

"Adore you? I would kiss the ground where your shadow fell just to be near you. I've been half out of my mind these past five months staying away from you," he said, and my heart twisted to see him lay bare his own. "But my feelings don't change the fact that I've nothing to offer you. Darling, I don't know if Perdita mentioned it, but the Vespiary pays about as well as a button factory. They've always had agents with private means, and my means are slim to nonexistent. You have to know going forward that we'd have nothing except each other." Pain and hope and joy and despair warred on his face, and I put my hands up again to cup his neck.

"Nothing except each other. And my trust fund."

He blinked. "Say that again?"

"My trust fund. Reginald settled a trust on each of us children. He didn't like me to feel left out, so he set aside a sum for me as well, to be paid out on the occasion of my twenty-first birthday or my marriage, whichever comes first."

He shook his head again, as if trying to clear it. "I can't believe this."

"It's perfectly true, my love. You had the sense to fall in love with an heiress, even though you didn't know it. I think your instincts must be just as sound as mine."

His arms went around me then, and what followed was a

demonstration of affection so impassioned, I doubt the Vespiary had ever seen the like.

"Perdita is still in the office," I murmured into his ear.

He grabbed my hand and gave me a stern look. "Then it's a bloody good thing we're leaving for Egypt tomorrow."

"It is," I agreed. "It seems your sex-tides are running rather high."

"You have no idea," he told me.

And so we left England for Egypt. Our assignment did not go precisely as anticipated, and there was an exchange of unpleasantries we hadn't expected. But we met with friendship too and resolved a few of the little mysteries we had brought with us from Damascus. We did not find the gold, nor did we find Stephen Baleister or discover what had become of Rosamund Johnson. Those murky waters were left for others to plumb. But Sebastian found his trust again, and as I had told him, that was the greatest wedding present I could give him. That and my copy of *Married Love*. He laughed when he unwrapped it, but I caught him reading it that evening, and not long after, my Aunt Portia mentioned the cordial letter of thanks he had sent her. Because, as Mrs. Stopes says, "EVERY heart desires a mate." I don't know if that's true—Perdita seemed perfectly content without one—and if I hadn't met Sebastian, I might have done the same. But I did meet Sebastian, my very own Lost Boy, and that made all the difference.

★ ★ ★ ★ ★

ACKNOWLEDGEMENTS

As ever, tremendous thanks to my readers! Every day you reach out to share with me the ways you are supporting my work, and I am humbled and grateful. I am so happy to share my stories with you. And heartfelt thanks to the booksellers and librarians who share my stories with others.

I am incredibly grateful to the MIRA team for their enthusiasm and the exquisite care they have lavished on my novels. Many, many thanks to the unseen hands whose efforts are often unremarked upon but so very essential—and much appreciated. I am particularly indebted to my dynamic and inspiring editor, Tara Parsons, and her assistant Leonore Waldrip whose hard work and dedication have made this book an absolute pleasure to write.

Huge thanks to my agent, Pam Hopkins, who has given me everything a writer could ever hope for in an agent and so much more.

And thanks most of all to my family—thanks to my parents for support and endless kindnesses, and to my beloved husband, for everything and for always.

NIGHT OF A THOUSAND STARS

DEANNA RAYBOURN

Reader's Guide

1. At the start of *Night of a Thousand Stars*, Poppy has cold feet about a brilliant marriage to an English aristocrat. She chooses to run away. What would you do?

2. Sebastian is a stranger to Poppy—and a man with many secrets. Why does she trust him? Would you?

3. Poppy feels indebted to Sebastian and travels halfway around the world to track him down. How far would you go to settle a debt?

4. One of Poppy's greatest strengths is her people skills. How does she demonstrate this?

5. Poppy and Sebastian meet an interesting crew of characters. Who do you find most interesting? Who would you like to see more of?

6. Poppy has had very little interaction with her father's large, eccentric family, yet she exhibits many of their most notable characteristics. Do you believe blood will tell?

7. Gabriel Starke from *City of Jasmine* makes a brief appearance in *Night of a Thousand Stars*. How would you characterize his relationship with Sebastian?

8. When Poppy is forced to make an instantaneous choice between Sebastian and Hugh, she does not hesitate. Would you?

9. Masterman is concealing a great secret. What do you make of the revelation of her true identity?

10. In the confrontation on the cliff, Poppy reveals herself to have certain characteristics she never suspected. What are they?

11. What do you think lies ahead for Poppy and Sebastian? What are their prospects for happiness in the future?

What was your inspiration for *Night of a Thousand Stars*?

This book is a follow-up to *City of Jasmine*, with different main characters but the same setting and a few supporting characters that will be familiar faces. It gave me a chance to visit that world again and pick up the threads of a story that reaches beyond the events of *City of Jasmine*. It was also my chance to fully bridge the divide between the Julia Grey books and my current 1920s project—something that was teased in the novella *Whisper of Jasmine* and hinted at in *City of Jasmine*.

You've created such a dynamic cast of characters— specifically Poppy and Sebastian. When you started writing, did you have their journeys planned out, or did they reveal themselves as you wrote? Did any of the other characters surprise you or change along the way?

Sebastian's arc is a much smaller one than Poppy's, and that was deliberate. I wanted to focus on her story, her changes, her understanding of her destiny and how she wants to shape it. Sebastian ended up coming out a bit tougher than I imagined at first, but as I wrote Poppy—and she kept getting stronger—I needed Sebastian to be a strong partner for her. There are some light moments between them; the opening is certainly a '30s screwball comedy! But there are some deadly serious times as well, and I wanted them both to be able to handle those with aplomb. That meant stiffening both their spines. They encounter some truly nasty people during their adventure, and they had to rise to the challenge.

In *Night of a Thousand Stars*, 1920s Damascus is almost a character in and of itself. What drew you to this setting, and what kind of research did you do to bring this fascinating moment in history to life?

Damascus has sat at the crossroads of history for thousands of years. Conquerors and crusaders, pilgrims and kings have walked its streets, and it is one of the most evocative, magical settings you could possibly ask for. After using it for *City of Jasmine*, I wasn't quite ready to turn loose of it, and since I had a storyline I wanted to pick up again, it seemed like a gift to be able to continue to use Damascus. I've read memoirs and biographies, especially those of early Western travellers such as Lady Hester Stanhope and Lady Jane Digby. Since my main character was an Anglo-American coming to the East for the first time, I needed the perspective of a somewhat sheltered and Eurocentric viewpoint being expanded and challenged.

We discover that Poppy is a member of the March family, revealing the connection between your recent historical novels and your immensely popular Lady Julia Grey series. How did it feel to finally come clean about what readers have long suspected? Can you elaborate on the ties between these two series?

It's such a relief to finally be able to talk about it! I've been keeping it secret for over a year, and it's been killing me not to share it with readers. I have dropped hints in a few of the 1920s projects, but *Night of a Thousand Stars* is the first book to use a grown-up March from the generation of characters who were children in the Julia Grey series. I have woven the two worlds together pretty thoroughly—readers still don't know all the connections! And that's been tremendously enjoyable for me. Some readers picked up on hints early on and began to email, asking if they were on the right track, and I've had a wonderful time watching them put the pieces together.

What was your greatest challenge while writing? Your greatest pleasure?

The greatest challenge is always getting into the chair. It's very easy to get excited by a new story; it takes discipline to sit down and actually write it. At the start of a new book, I have a page minimum that I have to hit every day before I let myself get up. By the last third of a book, I have to have a page maximum so I don't rush the ending because I'm so excited to be wrapping it up. The greatest pleasure is getting to spend so much time with characters I love. I have enjoyed every world I've built, and being able to immerse myself for months on end is pure joy.

Can you describe your writing process? Are you an outliner or a "pantser"?

I'm an organized pantser. I know point A, point Z, and probably G, M and R along the way, but how I get from each of those points to the others is a mystery to me when I start. Luckily, my books all tend to have a particular structure and in order for them to make sense, they have to have a logical progression. If I'm feeling particularly creepy, I tell people I know what the skeleton looks like, but not the hair color or shape of the nose...

Those things come about organically when I'm writing, weaving in details I've picked up from research or collected along the way.

What can you tell us about the project you're working on next?

My next release is another Lady Julia novella out in November—*Bonfire Night*—just in time for Guy Fawkes Day!